A TRAIL OF EVIL

James M. Flynn

ACKNOWLEDGEMENTS

I OWE A DEBT OF GRATITUDE TO THE FOLLOWING PEOPLE WHO REVIEWED AND ADDED THEIR COMMENTS AND CRITIQUES OF THE FIRST DRAFT OF THIS WORK. THE INCLUSION OF MANY OF THOSE COMMENTS AND CRITIQUES WERE INSTRUMENTAL IN THE SHAPING OF THE COMPLETE BOOK. THANK YOU FOR YOUR ENCOURAGEMENT.

BARBARA BOYETT
JOANN BRITT
JERRY BRITT
PAUL BERNIER
CAROL CAROLE
KELLY DURANT
DORRIS ELIZER
GLENDA FLYNN
KATHY GIOIA
MARGARET GOULD
LEANN HAWKINS
TOM MOWERY
CHRISTIE MUNDY
DIANE REINA

THANK YOU ALL FOR YOUR TIME AND EFFORT.

A SPECIAL THANK YOU GOES TO MY WIFE GLENDA. WITHOUT HER REVIEWING AND READING, RE-READING AGAIN AND SOMETIMES LISTENING WHILE I READ, AND MAKING SUGGESTIONS TO HELP ME WITH DIFFERENT PARTS OF THE FINAL VERSION OF THIS WORK, IT WOULD STILL BE FAR FROM COMPLETE.

FOREWORD

The author wishes to convey to the readers that this story is exactly that, a story - a complete work of fiction. Although totalitarian regimes have been known to persecute minorities and persons that dissent from the regime, it must be noted that the author did not determine if, or to what extent, this may have occurred in Italy during the Mussolini regime.

Again, whether or not such persecutions occurred in Italy, the references to that behavior by some of the characters in this story is fictional.

In the U.S. portion of this story many of the characters in Chapter 21 were patterned after people known and loved by the author in Denny Camp over sixty years ago. The author was the paper boy Micky (true) and his stepbrother (Jack) was Whisky Red. Except for a few persons, the names were changed and certainly their behavior was modified for this story.

He sat beside her. His face was crimson, and he did not speak.

She touched one hand to his cheek then leaned over and kissed him on the mouth.

"Is that what you want?" she asked.

Barely able to speak, he whispered "Yes."

She kissed him again then took her hand and rubbed his upper leg.

He ejaculated, then moaned "Oh, no," and jumped up to leave.

"It's okay I understand," she said.

"I have to go," he said and ran out the door.

Two days later Gina left an order at the shop to be delivered. Leonardo delivered the order and stayed to make love with her.

When he returned to help close the shop, he was more helpful and more talkative than usual. So much so, that while he was emptying the meat cooler wastewater without being told, Angelo commented to Carmine, "Is this the same miserable helper we have every other day?"

"Perhaps he is changing. Maybe he's growing up," she said.

"I doubt it. Something happened today,".

"If something happened, he will tell us."

But he never did.

CHAPTER TWO

Leonardo made deliveries to Gina every Monday and Thursday. The deliveries always started the same way. She would answer the door in a robe and negligee. They would have cake and coffee and then make love.

"Doing this is so wonderful I would like to come every day," he said one Thursday.

"Let's keep it on delivery days," she said smiling.

"Why?" he asked.

"Because that makes it so special for both of us, my love."

"Okay, but I don't understand," he said while dressing to leave.

"You will someday," she said and kissed him goodbye.

Angelo and Carmine were not the only ones to notice the change in Leonardo, so did his sister. Angelina noticed that Leonardo was more helpful, more talkative, and noticeably more excited during the week and less so on weekends.

One Monday afternoon she told her mother she needed to go to the library. Carmine let her go. Angelina put on a scarf and one of her mother's aprons and followed Leonardo on his deliveries. Nothing unusual happened until his last delivery at Gina's. He went inside and stayed.

Gina's apartment was in a building on a narrow side street less than a block from the main avenue. Angelina crossed the avenue to a city park that bordered a creek. She sat on a bench and watched the apartment. It was an hour before Leonardo came out. He walked quickly to the corner where several customers sat at tables outside a restaurant on the main avenue. Leonardo paid no attention, instead he crossed the narrow side street to a newsstand on the opposite corner where he purchased an evening newspaper for his father.

Angelina followed him home confident she knew his secret. Over the next two weeks she managed to follow him enough to learn that Leonardo stayed after deliveries to Gina's on Mondays and Thursdays, when he seemed to be most happy. Her first thought was to tell her parents what she found out, but that would mean she would have to tell *how* she found out. Besides, Leonardo was now much bigger and stronger than her and she did not want to risk his anger. She decided to keep his secret and divulge it only if it was to her advantage.

CHAPTER THREE

One Tuesday Leonardo finished his deliveries early and decided to stop at Gina's. He knocked on the door. She opened it and at first flashed a big smile. A moment later she frowned and said, "Leonardo why are you here today?"

"I finished my deliveries early; you look very nice. Can I come in?" he asked smiling and reached out to touch her.

"No," she said and pulled back from his hand. "I must put my make-up on. You must leave now. Come back Thursday."

"Where are you going?"

"I'm not going anywhere. Someone is coming here to see me." she said impatiently.

"Who?" he asked no longer smiling.

"A benefactor."

"A benefactor?" he repeated. A confused look came over his face.

"Yes, do you think my pension is enough to pay for everything?" she said clearly irritated.

"I did not know," he said quietly.

"Now you do. I must entertain a benefactor this afternoon. Don't worry you are still my young lover. But you must leave today," she said and closed the door before he could respond.

He stood outside for a moment then walked slowly to the avenue where he slumped into a chair at the restaurant's corner table. A moment later a waiter with a menu and napkin containing silverware approached.

"May I help you sir?" he said as he set the table.

"Sir. May I help you?" he repeated.

Finally, he shook Leonardo's wrist. "May I help you?" he asked again.

Leonardo appeared to look past him. "No," he said.

"Then you will have to move. The tables are for customers only."

"Oh," said Leonardo as he stood. He started to cross the street in front of a fast-moving horse-drawn cab. The driver hollered "Stop." The waiter grabbed him by the arm and pulled him back to the curb.

Leonardo turned and said, "Thanks, I'm okay now."

"Be careful," warned the waiter shaking his head. "You can get run over very easily."

Leonardo turned back to the avenue. In a minute he crossed and sat on a bench in the park. He watched Gina's building. A little while later a man carrying a small bouquet of flowers turned from the avenue onto the narrow street and quickly walked to Gina's door. He knocked and she opened the door and let him in.

Leonardo bent forward at the waist and put his head in his hands. He sat like that for several minutes, then he leaned back on the park bench and ran his fingers straight back through his hair. His eyes were wet but there were no tears on his cheeks.

He resumed watching her apartment. In a little while the door opened, and Gina stepped out followed by the man. They walked to the corner restaurant. A waiter approached and appeared to ask a question. The man turned to Gina who motioned to go inside. The man spoke and they disappeared inside.

Leonardo watched a little longer, then walked back across the avenue to the newsstand where he purchased a newspaper for his father.

On Wednesday, after his deliveries, Leonardo again watched Gina's apartment. In late afternoon another man knocked on her door. A moment later she opened the door and let him in. Leonardo watched for over an hour before the man left. Then he purchased a newspaper for his father and went home.

On Thursday Leonardo made his regular delivery and Gina was waiting for him as usual.

Neither mentioned Gina's benefactors and they followed their normal routine of coffee and cakes then love making.

Trying to keep the mood light she asked, "Would you like a glass of wine?"

"Yes."

She opened a bottle of red wine and poured them each a glass. They drank in bed propped up by pillows.

"Thank you, this is very good wine," he said.

"Better than coffee, eh," she joked.

"Yes, much better."

"I thought so. Sitting here in bed with you it relaxes me, how about you?"

"Oh, yes," he said and leaned over and kissed her.

"Oh, ho. Are you getting ready, again?"

"Maybe," he said.

Gina drank her wine quickly then poured herself another. Leonardo sipped his wine much slower. After her third glass she went to the toilet. While she was gone Leonardo searched her purse and found her apartment key. He put it in his trousers and slipped back in bed.

She poured a fourth but fell asleep with it in her hand. Leonardo removed it and put it on the dresser beside his empty glass, then he dressed and left.

On Friday afternoon Angelo insisted Leonardo stay after the shop closed and help scrub all their equipment as well as the shop floor and the toilet. Angelina made all the deliveries and brought home her father's newspaper.

At suppertime Carmine called the men upstairs to eat. After supper Angelo and Leonardo worked a while longer. It was dark when they finished, and Leonardo did not leave to spy on Gina. Instead, he went to bed and slept soundly.

On Saturdays the shop closed early, and the last delivery was made by Leonardo before noon. When he returned his mother had lunch ready and the family ate together. Since it was a week of good sales and long hours of extra hard work, Angelo paid Angelina and Leonardo more money than usual. Both accepted it quickly, barely pausing to say thanks.

Angelina stayed to help Carmine clear the table and wash the dishes. Angelo announced he had a meeting to attend at three PM and Leonardo went to the park to see if Gina received any benefactors.

While he watched, Leonardo sipped a beer he purchased at the newsstand. A little before three PM Leonardo noticed a man coming down the narrow street from beyond Gina's building. When he reached the building, he stopped and knocked on her door. Leonardo recognized the man. It was his father. Gina opened the door and Angelo entered.

Leonardo sat very still for a few minutes, then he turned his back to the street and watched the stream bordering the park flow slowly toward the sea. After a short while he turned around and crossed the avenue to the newsstand. He bought another beer and drank as he walked.

CHAPTER FOUR

Sunday night Leonardo went to bed early. He laid there, feigning sleep, listening. First, he heard Angelina's deep regular breathing from the other side of the privacy curtain strung down the middle of their tiny room. Next, he heard his father's deep loud snoring and his mother's softer snoring. He continued to feign sleep until after midnight when he dressed and slipped out of the apartment. When he reached the street, he paused for a few seconds to pull his cap low, almost to his eyebrows, then turned and started walking toward Gina's. If he had looked up, he would have seen Angelina watching him from the window above.

He walked quickly staying in the shadows when he could. As he approached the newsstand a policeman checked its' door to make sure it was locked. He peered inside then crossed the narrow street to the restaurant where he continued his ritual. Leonardo remained in the shadows until the policeman was well up the avenue, then he quickly walked past the newsstand

and approached Gina's apartment. He took the stolen key from his pocket and put it in the lock. He tried to turn it first one way then the other, but it would not release the lock. He knocked on the door quietly at first then louder and louder until she called out from the other side.

"Who is there?"

He said softly, "Young lover."

"It's very late, can't you wait until tomorrow?"

"I need to see you now, tonight."

She opened the door then went back to bed. He took off his clothes and put them under the bed. He slid in next to her. Her back was next to him. He massaged her and managed to arouse her. They made love.

Afterwards she said, "No coffee and no cakes. This is a first."

"You think this is funny?"

"No, my dear it's just a first with you," she said.

"Do you have coffee and cakes with your benefactors?"

"That is different. I entertain them."

"You entertain them, but you took advantage of me, I'm not even eighteen and you seduced me."

She laughed. "You seem to enjoy being seduced. How many times have I taken advantage of you? Don't forget to count tonight."

"You whore," he ranted. "My father is one of your benefactors."

"I suppose I take advantage of him, too. But he freely admits he enjoys being taken advantage of. Now leave I am tired of your boyish behavior."

He got on his knees in the center of the bed and struck her hard in the face. She put her arms up to cover her head. "Please," she said, "I was joking, please stop."

"No," he said and punched her hard in the chest and stomach. She started to scream but he gripped her throat with both hands and pushed hard with his thumbs, crushing her larynx, and silencing her scream. She turned toward him kicking, causing him to loosen his grip, but he crawled onto her waist and continued choking. She tried prying his hands loose, but his grip was too strong. She looked at him wide-eyed and mouthed "Please" before losing consciousness.

He went to the kitchen and returned with a large knife. She regained consciousness and swung her legs over the opposite side of the bed. She tried to stand, but he grabbed her arm and forced her back to the middle of the bed. He released her arm, and they sat close, facing each other. She sobbed and began a near-silent crying. Blood bubbled at the corners of her mouth. He put his arms around her and held her for a long moment. She did not respond, and he sat back facing her again. Suddenly he stabbed her viciously in the chest. She looked down at the blood pouring from her body. Her head wobbled to one side. She slowly raised her head, looked at him and mouthed "Why?".

His upper lip curled above his gums, and he snarled like a dog paused in the middle of a fight. He grabbed her by the hair and dragged her to the foot of the bed. With one hand he held her head high in front of the dresser mirror. “Watch Bitch,” he commanded. Then he took the knife and touched it to her neck. She shut her eyes tight. He slowly pulled it across her throat. She made a faint struggle, then slowly slipped lifelessly to the floor.

He took his clothes to the kitchen and washed himself completely before dressing.

He strew the contents of the dresser and closet on the floor then took her jewels and money and returned the key to her purse.

He paused for a moment and stared at her body. He cut off her ring finger and said aloud, “A trophy to remember you.”

He began to sweat. It was cold and appeared first on his upper lip and forehead then engulfed his chest and upper arms. He began pacing between the rooms, stopping often to listen. At the door he stood motionless for several minutes. His hand shaking, he slowly opened it and peered out. The street was deserted. He walked to the avenue and looked in both directions. Satisfied, he walked away quickly.

A few moments later he slowed his pace and a strange euphoria swept over him. It was more powerful than anything he ever felt. He went home and slept the sleep of the exhausted.

"What? You are crazy!" he said incredulously, shaking his head and smiling as he looked at Angelina.

"I don't think so," she said staunchly.

"Why do you think such a thing about your brother?" he asked, looking at her seriously but not angrily.

"Because I'm sure he did it. He was her lover. I saw him go there."

"So what. I heard she had many so-called lovers," he said dismissively.

"Maybe so, but he snuck out the night she was murdered, and went in that direction," she said in earnest.

"That does not make him a murderer. He is still a boy." Again dismissively.

Determined to make him take her seriously she said, "I believe he is capable. Remember when we caught him in the basement beginning to skin the puppy while it was still alive?

He was silent for a moment.

"If you go to the basement, you will see a bucket with a cover. There is a slit in it with water below. Mice and rats would fall through, and Leonardo would torture them using a wooden spoon."

"How do you know?"

"I saw the trap set up with cheese for bait and later I saw dead mice floating in the water."

"That does not mean he tortured them," he said quietly and stared at the floor.

"Think of the puppy," she repeated in a tone trying to implore him to see the possible truth to what she said.

"I will question him about this. Do not say anything to anyone else."

———————

That evening Angelo called Leonardo back down to the shop.

"What do you want me to do?" he asked, leaning against a counter in the back of the shop.

"I want you to answer some questions truthfully," said Angelo watching his son carefully.

"What about?" asked Leonardo, nervously shifting his weight from a slouch to upright.

"The woman who was murdered about a month ago. I checked your bed that night, you were not in it," he said, carefully watching his son's expression.

"I woke up and went for a walk," said Leonardo defiantly.

"Where?" he asked, with an accusing tone in his voice.

"Along the river," he again answered defiantly.

"I have been told you and she were lovers." Angelo again probing, hoping his son was innocent.

"I made deliveries, nothing more. But sometimes I go to the park close to where the woman lived. I saw men visit her apartment. Different men on different days of the week, even

Saturday" he said even more defiantly with a sneer and looked Angelo straight in the eye.

Shaken, and beaten, Angelo said, "It's time you thought about a trade."

"I want to attend the University." Leonardo said quickly, pressing his advantage.

"Why. What do you want there? That is for the rich." Angelo said lamely.

"I can continue to work here in the shop. With your help and living at home I can manage the fees. I have already passed the entrance examination," he said boastfully.

"What do you want to study?" asked Angelo, looking for a way to regain the upper hand.

No longer defiant, he said, "I want to be a doctor, a psychiatrist. I am already studying."

Feeling he had an opening to recoup his stature Angelo pondered his reply and then said, "We will see. I will think about this University business."

———————

Angelo spoke dismissively to Angelina the next day, "Leonardo went for a walk. He says he never was the woman's lover. He only made deliveries."

"What about the animal tortures?" she said, trying to reason with her father.

"Killing mice and rats is a service not a crime. Your brother is innocent. I don't want to hear any more about this," he said and walked away.

Five years later in 1932 at the age of 22 Leonardo entered the University of Naples with his father's blessing. He was now a young man of considerable size at six foot two and one hundred and eighty pounds. His hair was brown. His eyes were dark brown, almost black. His nose was slightly oversize in a non-distinguishable face. His most noticeable feature he inherited from his mother, his ears. They were large, protruded out from his head and bent slightly forward. He was neither handsome or ugly and therefore was not noticed in a crowd and he liked it that way.

CHAPTER SIX

(Leonardo) Fontana's dream was to be a doctor. He also liked and was attracted to power. On campus at the university, he attended political speeches and demonstrations supporting the forces of Democracy, Communism and Fascism.

Fontana's imagination was captured by the leader of the Fascist party, Benito Mussolini. He went to hear him speak at a football stadium in Naples. He was a powerful speaker, and his speech went on for more than two hours. He talked about bread and jobs in a society where work was rewarded. He talked about the 'descendants of Rome' and how things were much better with him leading Italy. Fontana came away favorably impressed.

In 1937 Fontana finished his undergraduate work and was accepted in medical school. He still lived at home but was increasingly at odds with his father. Angelo was a Catholic and believed in a democratic Italy. Leonardo leaned more toward concentrated power, more autocratic, less democratic.

After attending several Mussolini speeches in Naples and other cities Fontana started attending open Fascist meetings and often made comments extolling the Fascist movement and Benito Mussolini.

His attendance was noticed by Bernardo Muscanti a Fascist party district organizer that started out as a small-time Naples hoodlum. He was short, about five feet four inches tall and thin about one hundred twenty pounds. His face was thin with dark brown eyes close to a large nose and cheekbones sharp against the skin. He rarely smiled through large lips that covered protruding front teeth. His features were exaggerated by sallow skin and black hair. His looks and his demeanor gave off an aura of toughness that served him well in the underworld. He ran a string of prostitutes. The youngest and prettiest he put in a private house run by a tough old madam. When the girls got too old or fat or troublesome, he put them to work on the street. When they could no longer work the streets, they disappeared either by agreement or by force.

When anyone important, especially politicians, came for a visit the madam sent a runner to track him down. He would make an appearance to chat with the guest. These conversations, often accompanied by a free visit, made it easier for him to conduct illegal business dealings with little impunity.

When Mussolini made his bid for ultimate power Muscanti was recruited along with many others to help persuade people to 'do the right thing' and not oppose him. After Mussolini gained ultimate power, Muscanti donned a mantle of respectability. He helped at Mussolini rallies renting stadiums or theaters, setting up security and of course selling tickets and even arranging for waiters and friendly 'hostesses' at smaller more intimate gatherings after the speeches.

Muscanti had Fontana checked out to determine if he was what he purported himself to be. Satisfied with the report, Muscanti invited Fontana to his apartment for a preliminary meeting. They talked politics and philosophies in general and found themselves to be virtual soulmates. Both desired to be rich, liked women, fine clothes, automobiles, were enamored by Mussolini and were willing to use whatever power they had to achieve their goals.

Muscanti liked Fontana. He was smart and refreshing to be around, a step up from the small-time hustlers and politicians he regularly associated with and since he was studying at the University, he felt Fontana could eventually be useful. After a few more meetings, Muscanti agreed to sponsor Fontana and he joined the Fascist party in October 1938.

In power Mussolini sought to limit resistance to his authoritarian rule.

The propaganda of the party was strong, and though not officially deemed to be enemies of the state, people in many groups including gypsies, homosexuals, communists, and members of the outspoken fascist opposition were harassed and falsely accused of crimes with the intent to silence their opposition and strip them of their wealth. Some were sent to prison holding cells where they waited trial on trumped up charges.

Fontana quickly gravitated to the party's darker side. In 1940, after he assisted Muscanti on several anti-fascist raids, Muscanti arranged an interview for a prison Doctor position in Rome.

CHAPTER SEVEN

Fontana arrived at the address and was surprised by the appearance of the building. It looked like a warehouse of some sort. Steps led up to a door at one end of a loading dock. Halfway down the dock a hand cart was positioned near a set of double doors. Above the doors a large sign read BARUZZINI BROTHERS, IMPORTERS. There was no obvious external security. He checked the address again and decided to try the single door. He quickly climbed the steps and used the large brass knocker. There was no response. He knocked again harder and longer.

A guard opened the door, took a long look at Fontana, and asked in a surly tone, "What do you want?"

The guard uniform reassured Fontana. "I'm here to meet with Warden Garibaldi."

"Do you have any identification papers?" Asked the guard as he looked up and down the street.

"Yes," said Fontana and handed him a letter.

The guard opened the letter and compared it to a list on a clip board hanging from a nail beside the door. He smiled and waved Fontana inside. “Follow me. The Warden is not here right now. He is expected later.”

He led Fontana to an office. “You can wait in here. Would you like some coffee while you wait?”

“I would like some espresso if you have it,” said Fontana.

“We don’t have espresso. It’s impossible to find.”

“Then you can bring me some coffee. Black coffee,” he said and sat down.

After more than an hour a man entered and limply shook Fontana’s hand. He was a nervous little man in his late fifties or early sixties with gray hair, dark brown eyes, bushy eyebrows, and a thin hooked nose in a pock marked face with a sallow complexion. He walked with a cane and stooped slightly even when seated.

He said, “Thank you for waiting. I’m Ferdinand Garibaldi warden of the main prison just outside Rome, not far from the Vatican.” He extended his arms, palms up, and slowly moved his head from side to side before continuing, “Unfortunately this pitiful facility is part of that prison, but officially it does not exist. I assume you are Leonardo Fontana?”

“Yes.”

“Please,” he said gesturing to be seated. He read Muscanti’s letter of introduction.

“I see we have a mutual friend.”

“Yes,” said Fontana smiling, “he is a good friend.”

"Good. You are here because of your medical expertise and your work as a member of the party. If you accept the position offered, you will be responsible for counseling selected inmates to obtain confessions. Let me be perfectly clear. You must always try reasoning sessions first. But if reasoning fails you are to try other options, ones that do not scar or maim inmates because they must appear in court to read their confessions aloud in front of a judge or a tribunal. You will report to me weekly. Officially neither I nor the court know of any other options you use to counsel inmates. Is that clear?"

"Yes," said Fontana.

"Good. Do you have any questions?"

"Is there any particular option that is specifically forbidden?"

"As long as the results are obtained without the physical problems I mentioned you will be within the scope of the job. Any other questions?"

"Who would I report to here?"

"No-one. You will oversee the facility and report directly to me. Officially you will be working as a physician at the prison. How long do you need to decide if you accept or decline the position?"

"I will accept right now if you want me."

"I know Muscanti from the old days. We were like brothers in Naples." He stared hard at Fontana with unblinking eyes. "We discussed the situation here and he highly recommended you. I need no other references. You are hired."

"Thank you, I will do my best."

"One thing," he said rising. "Keep in mind what has been said here today. At all cost you must not violate the trust put in you. I repeat, at all cost. Is that clear?"

"Absolutely."

Garibaldi called in a man from outside the office.

"Fontana, this is Vincent Montinaro my right hand. He is Assistant Warden at the main prison."

"Nice to meet you," said Fontana smiling. He extended his hand which Montinaro shook.

"Me too," he said then continued, "Warden, do you want me to call in anyone else?"

"Yes, the clerks and chief of Security. Close the door on your way out. When you have them ready, just knock and bring them in."

"This won't take but a few minutes then you can tour the building."

"Sounds good," said Fontana.

"The last few men that tried to do your job didn't have the stomach for it and resigned. I hope you will do better."

After a knock on the door, Garibaldi said "Come in."

Fontana and he stood. "This man is Dr. Leonardo Fontana," he said smiling. "He is my new Deputy Warden and will oversee this facility. Any questions? None? Good? Then spread the word that you have a new Warden. Doctor, do you want to say anything?"

"Yes, only this. I will be making a tour shortly. You can introduce yourselves then. Thank you. You may return to your posts."

After they left Garibaldi spoke, "I must return to the prison. You two make a good tour of the facility. I will send a car back in an hour or so. Goodbye."

"Goodbye," they both echoed.

———

Montinaro, a man of medium height and large girth, led a slow tour of the facility, a three-story affair. The first floor consisted of three offices, another room with tables and chairs for staff eating and a large kitchen to prepare meals for the inmates.

The second floor had three offices, the largest one for Fontana, one for his two assistants and one shared by the guards and a nurse to complete paperwork.

There was a locked and barred confinement area with four cells, two on each side of a wide center walkway. Just inside the area was a desk and chair and another chair sat at the far end of the walkway. From these two positions guards could see inside all four cells. Each cell held one inmate and had a bed a sink and a commode. There were three guards per shift. One guard stayed outside the confinement area and two routinely worked inside. They received meals from the kitchen and delivered them to the inmates, moved inmates to and from interview rooms or the Infirmary, assisted with obtaining confessions and any other duty demanded by the facility Deputy Warden.

Outside the confinement area at the far end of the second floor there were three interview rooms. This is where Fontana along with two assistants, former guards that were members of the Fascist party, would later hold inmate counseling sessions.

The third floor had one office used by the guards and the facility nurse, an infirmary of four beds, and six cells in the confinement area that housed two inmates each. There were three guards on day shift and two on the other two shifts.

———

Fontana's first inmate to counsel was a man from Sardinia, Enrico Vinateer. Diego, one of Fontana's assistants said he had been counseled before but would not confess. He was accused of selling goods on the black market, a completely bogus charge. His actual crime was he repeatedly cursed Mussolini as a murderer while selling fish from his stall at an open-air market. His charge was serious, but he could confess to a lesser charge of profiteering and receive a short prison sentence.

Fontana tried the mandatory reasoning with him for several sessions. He explained that his fish market business could be confiscated but if he confessed it could not be taken from his family. That was a lie. Even after confessing, a business could be confiscated and sold. He also told Vinateer members of his family could be brought in for questioning or even be put through sessions and made to testify against him. Why bother to resist he reasoned when eventually you will have to sign anyway? Vinateer had been through reasoning sessions before and refused to sign. He repeated that the reason for his arrest was he cursed Mussolini as a murderer. Finally, Fontana asked him why. He responded because the Army took his two sons to fight in North Africa where they were both killed. Fontana laughed and called him a fool.

Next Fontana tried repeated questions under bright lights. He took turns with an assistant every two hours for ten hours. No confession. Next, without a break he started Vinateer on sleep deprivation with questions and threats. This went on for another two days before Vinateer lost his bowels and completely collapsed.

After a few hours sleep Vinateer was wakened and taken into a room with a large tub of water.

"I will offer you one more chance to confess before we continue," said. Fontana.

"I will not confess to a crime I did not do," said Vinateer defiantly.

"We shall see," said Fontana. Then to his assistants, "Tie his hands behind his back then put him in the tub and hobble his feet."

"Make him kneel with his left side closest to the edge of the tub."

"Vinateer how do you like the water now that it is chest deep on you? Can you swim?" Asked Fontana laughing.

"I don't mind the water, though I prefer it warmer. I can swim," said Vinateer sneering.

"Good," said Fontana and pushed his head underwater and held it for fifteen seconds.

"Are you ready to confess?" Asked Fontana feigning anger.

"No, never," said Vinateer loudly.

"We shall see how you do with another opportunity to be a fish." Fontana pushed his head underwater for thirty seconds.

"Are you ready?"

"No, never."

"Are you sure? We have all day to do this," said Fontana shrugging.

"I am sure," he said, still loud.

"I am a patient man Vinateer," said Fontana and held his head underwater for a full minute. This time Vinateer came up gasping for breath.

"Are you ready to confess?" Asked Fontana quickly.

"I would rather drown than confess to a crime I didn't commit," said Vinateer still defiant.

"I will be happy to oblige you," said Fontana and held his head underwater for a minute and thirty seconds. Vinateer struggled with all his remaining strength but could not raise his head above the surface for air. Finally, Fontana let him up.

"Are you ready, Vinateer?"

"No," he said, but when Fontana reached to push his head under again, he said, "Enough".

"Does that mean you are ready to confess?"

"Yes."

"Remove him from the tub," said Fontana smiling.

He was pulled from the tub and dried off before being taken to a room where he signed a confession admitting profiteering. Fontana called the torture his drowning rat treatment.

George, one of his assistants said, "No-one tried going beyond the bright lights before."

Fontana laughed and said, "I have much more in store for those who refuse to sign."

The next man had also been through the reasoning and bright light questioning routines. His name was Gregorio Martino. Fontana rushed him through the mandatory reasoning sessions and the bright light sessions were also shortened. During the drowning rat treatment Martino refused to give in and passed out under water before he was pulled up by Fontana. His assistants pulled him from the water and used lifeguard techniques to revive him. Martino refused to sign. Fontana seemed delighted and after a few hours rest he took him back to the tub. This time ice was added to the water. After thirty minutes he was asked if he was ready to confess. He refused. Fontana had him put back in the tub. Some of the water was removed and more ice added. Martino was kept in the freezing water for another thirty minutes. He was again asked if he would like to confess. His head hung down to his chest and he slurred his answer, but again refused. Fontana told him he was glad and placed a cap on his head similar to one used in electrocutions. Then he splashed water on Martino and had one of his assistants turn on the power. Fontana had the voltage gradually increased until Martino started screaming. Fontana stopped the power and again asked Martino if he wished to confess. He sat silent in the water until he heard Fontana give the order to resume then said he was ready to confess. As usual he was taken to sign his already written confession. But he had burns on the top of his head and could not be sent to court until they healed.

Fontana sent a weekly progress report to Garibaldi in which he listed the inmates being counseled. On a bi-weekly basis Garibaldi met with Fontana and his upper-level staff to review progress.

"I see in this report Martino confessed three weeks ago. Is this correct?"

"Yes," said Fontana.

"Then why has he not been sent to read his confession in court?"

"We were exercising a new option where an electrical charge ran through a cap placed on an inmate's head in a tub full of water. Unfortunately, Martino refused to confess before his head was blistered by the cap. We are waiting for it to heal before sending him to court."

Garibaldi said, "I gave you explicit instructions that any option beyond reasoning sessions could not create any scars or permanent injuries and yet you placed a man in a tub of water and put such a cap on him? What part of the instructions did you not understand?"

Visibly embarrassed Fontana said, "I understood the instructions. The voltage was turned up too high. It will not happen again."

"Doctor, it better not happen again or there will be some permanent changes made around here. Do we understand each other?"

"Yes, sir."

"That option is scrapped. Do you understand that instruction?"

"Yes, sir."

Fontana showed no visible anger at the time, but when Garibaldi left, he seethed.

Sometimes Fontana had as many as five inmates in different stages of torture at the same time. Women inmates were rare and after a few sessions he invariably offered to let them alone for sex. Most obliged to stop the torture. He let them be for days and sometimes weeks, but when he tired of them, he continued with the sessions until they confessed.

Sometimes he continued torture even after an inmate confessed. No-one questioned him. The guards were afraid of him and to a man considered him mad.

He became so adept at torture that only the death of an inmate prevented him from extracting a confession. Warden Garibaldi received so much praise about obtaining confessions that even he accepted the occasional death of an inmate. Fontana simply signed a death certificate certifying the cause of death to be heart attack. Since there were no marks on the body this explanation was readily accepted.

After confessing, inmates were required to read their confessions aloud in court prior to sentencing. Most sentences involved signing statements saying they were now and would remain loyal supporters of the Fascist party and included prison terms from a few months to several years of hard labor.

One of the benefits of working in the prison system was the systematic theft of inmate personal effects. Watches, rings, bracelets, gold chains, broaches and earrings were routinely confiscated. These items were placed in a property bag and a receipt given to the inmate. When an inmate was sent for counseling these items were also sent. If the inmate was found innocent, which did rarely happen when word came down that an inmate was not to be counseled beyond reasoning sessions, then the items were returned.

The second way an inmate was supposed to get his possessions back was when he completed his sentence. That did not happen. When an inmate left to serve his sentence in a regular prison, the valuable items in his property bag were removed by Fontana. Later he shared the loot with Muscanti. The system worked well until June 1942 when Fontana again extended a torture session too long and the inmate died. He signed a death certificate that indicated the inmate died of a heart attack and the prison authorities did not question the cause of death. However, one of the guards knew the inmate and wrote anonymous letters to a judge and the inmate's family stating that the inmate may have died of a heart attack, but it was caused by powerful electric shocks routinely used to obtain confessions. Suddenly the outside world was looking in and Fontana and his tactics became a liability. All counseling to obtain confessions was stopped. The facility was closed, and Fontana reassigned to the main prison.

The day Fontana reported to the main prison Garibaldi called him to his office where he introduced his staff and those that would report to Fontana. In front of them all he said, "Dr. Fontana is here because his major lapses of judgement at another facility resulted in its' closure." He looked directly at Fontana and continued, "Dr. Fontana I sincerely hope we can count on you to carry out your duties here in a more professional manner."

Fontana replied, "Yes sir, I will truly do my best for you and the facility."

"You better," said Garibaldi.

Fontana resented the rebuke but managed to remain calm in his dealings with Garibaldi. Instead, he began following Garibaldi when he left the prison after work. He learned, 'for future reference', Garibaldi and his wife lived on a barge on a quiet slew near the main river channel.

CHAPTER EIGHT

When Fontana was reassigned to the main prison Muscanti came to divide up the last of the jewelry taken from prisoner property bags and they went to a local restaurant.

"Why did they decide to close down the holding cells?" Asked Muscanti.

"Because one of the prisoners died from a heart attack while being interrogated."

"But that wasn't the first time. Why the fuss this time."

"Because one of the staff knew the prisoner and wrote anonymous letters to his family and the court claiming the heart attack was caused by electrical shocks used to get confessions."

"Was it?"

"Probably."

"Do you know who wrote the letters?"

"I think so but I'm not sure."

"Any chance the facility will be reopened?"

"I don't think so. Everybody's worried about a possible Allied invasion."

"That reminds me if the Allies invade and Italy falls, Anti-Fascists will be in power. That will be bad for us. Court documents will be examined, and new trials held. Prisoners could become accusers. I'm working on a plan to change my identity and get to Spain. From there I'll go to South America, probably Argentina. I can help you leave, too, if you decide to go."

"I'm working on a plan to cover my tracks. But I could use your help."

"What do you want?"

"I would like a commission in the Army."

"Remember this, the longer you wait to leave the more difficult and expensive it will be."

Muscanti wrote down a name, address, and telephone number. Beside it he wrote the word antelope.

"This is the name of a man you can use to leave the country. Antelope is my code name, use it to be trusted. Memorize the information today and burn the paper. Do not carry it with you or try to hide it."

"I will do as you say."

"If all else fails you can come to thirty-three Cavour my safe house. Do not write the address down and only come if absolutely necessary. The old code I gave you will work there. I will do what I can to help with the Army. Wait to apply until I tell you one way or the other."

"I will, and thanks."

"I must go now my old friend. Be careful. I hope all goes well for you. Goodbye."

"I hope things go well for you, too. And as always, I appreciate all you have done for me. Goodbye."

They shook hands and hugged before they parted.

——————

In December 1942 Muscanti told Fontana to apply. He did and received a commission as an Army Major. He was not immediately assigned. His Army personnel file indicated he was 'political'. He was given minor duties in Rome. He purchased expensive tailored uniforms, like those worn by Mussolini. He even purchased similar boots. He carried a riding crop, actually a steel rod covered by woven leather, even though he had never ridden a horse in his life. Some of the soldiers jokingly referred to him as 'Benito Junior' or 'Little Benito.

Since he had no combat experience, in March,1943 Major Fontana was assigned as a liaison officer to the Germans. The hope of the Italians was to use liaisons to help restrain the Germans, but Major Fontana saw his role differently. He saw his role as another opportunity for unrestrained power over nearly helpless victims.

He quickly became involved in schemes to force Anti-Fascists or other ‘undesirables’ to turn over property. Many ruses were used but the main ones were unpaid taxes and enemies of the state. Once the property was seized it was sold illegally, often to the very people that caused the seizure. Small landowners, especially Jews, were often the victims.

CHAPTER NINE

Guido

Slightly North and West of Rome the land responded well to efforts to grow all sorts of crops including staples of wheat and corn and was particularly well suited for vineyards and olive groves. Due to the importance of their food crops many of the local farm families had been declared exempt from the military draft like workers in defense plants. Even the local Jewish farmers worked in relative safety, secure in the knowledge of their exemption due to the nation's tremendous need for the food they produced.

The Sabatini family owned a farm on a series of low hills near the village of Veranza. Morning mists and sometimes fog that rose up from the Tyrrhenean Sea onto the land helped to take some of the sting out of hot summer weather.

Vincenzo Sabatini, though now over seventy, still labored on the farm alongside his two sons Guido and Alberto and four grandsons. Vittorino and Marcus were sons of Guido and Maria and Diego and Gabriella were the sons of Alberto and Sofia. During harvest time it was not unusual to see the Sabatini women working side by side with the men. The family had no tractors or threshers, their biggest working assets were two horses and the equipment they were used to power.

The oldest grandson was twenty-year-old Vittorino. He had completed school at the age of seventeen and now worked full time on the farm. The nation was at war and taxes were very high to pay for it. There were constant campaigns for people to show their patriotism. Posters and radio broadcasts urged everyone to save scarce resources, to volunteer for the armed services and to help in every way possible. People responded, but not enough men volunteered for the beleaguered armed services. The government increased the involuntary conscription to include some farm men. The notices were posted in all village post offices and printed in newspapers.

On a warm August morning in 1943 Vittorino and his younger brother Marcus were working with their father Guido in an olive grove. A military truck with a red cross painted on its' side came up the hill and stopped just outside the vineyard. Two soldiers emerged from the truck. One wore Officer insignia, red epaulets, and a red beret. The second soldier wore no such insignia. When they approached Guido met them.

"What do you want?" he asked.

The officer spoke, "Mr. Sabatini I am Lieutenant Giuseppe Arturo from the Medical Services arm of our Armed Services.

"I ask you again, what do you want?" Said Guido, impatient that the work had been interrupted.

"We are here to give you and your son Vittorino a choice," said Lt. Arturo.

"What type of choice?"

"All young men over eighteen that are physically fit and do not work in an exempt defense plant are required to serve in the Armed Services. I am here to offer your son an opportunity to serve in a non-combatant role," said Lt. Arturo.

"What kind of role?"

"If he joins right away, signs the paper today and leaves tomorrow, he can serve in the Medical Corps."

"Today! Tomorrow! Why so soon?" Asked Guido shaking his head and holding his hands out while shrugging his shoulders.

"Because the need is now, that's why we're here. If he does not volunteer the next step will be conscription into the regular Army. Soon."

"We must have time to discuss this matter," said Guido angrily.

"We will walk a little way down the hill and smoke a cigarette or two. We'll return for your answer."

"You better make it more than two. This is a family matter," said Guido.

He turned and said, "Marcus go home and bring your mother here." He spoke reassuringly to Vittorino. "I will go to see the mayor."

"What can he do?" Asked Vittorino.

"He might be able to get this stopped."

"I don't think so. I believe it's now the law. It was in the papers recently. I read all about it," said Vittorino.

In a few minutes Marcus returned in a horse drawn cart with Rosa. Sitting in the cart, obviously worried and upset, she asked Guido, "Marcus spoke of a choice. What is this choice?"

He put his hand on the seat next to her and explained it all, then added "I think maybe we should seek the mayor's help."

"I don't believe he can help, he's powerless against the national government," she said quickly while watching the soldiers, then asked, "Do you think they are bluffing?"

"We have no way of knowing. We must stall for time but not give up this option in case they are telling the truth." Vittorino and Rosa nodded.

In a few more minutes the Medical Corps men returned.

"What is your decision?" Asked Lt. Arturo brusquely.

"We haven't reached one. This is my wife, Rosa. We need more time to make this important decision," said Guido in a more friendly tone.

"I am honored to meet you Mrs. Sabatini," said Arturo and made a slight bow.

"Thank you," said Rosa.

Turning to Guido, Arturo said impatiently, "I gave you all the time I have to give. You must decide."

"We want a few days to discuss it with the rest of the family," said Guido.

"You wait that long to sign, and the Medical Corps option could be gone. He will end up in the Regular Army," said Lt. Arturo, this time in a more even tone.

"Look," said Guido. "If you need good young men like you say, you ought to be willing to come back tomorrow for a decision. He would have a few days anyhow. What's the difference?"

Lt. Arturo put his hand to his chin while he pondered the situation. "Alright," he said. "We will be back in the morning."

The soldiers returned to the truck and left.

When the truck was out of sight the whole family got in the cart and hurried back to their home. Guido and his sons replaced their skull caps with traditional Italian worker caps and Rosa changed her head scarf. Then Guido headed the old horse and cart down the steep road to their home village of Veranza. On the way he instructed the family, "I will do the talking with the mayor." Once there, they didn't stop until they reached the front of the mayor's cafe. The family went inside, and Guido carefully selected a table on the right-side wall near the kitchen and as far away from the occupied tables as possible. The cafe had a mixture of mostly small two and four seat tables and a few larger ones like the one Guido chose. The cafe was a popular place for villagers to meet and even now at mid-morning about half of the dozen or so tables had customers. Some were relaxing with a final cup of coffee after a late breakfast while others, mostly retired workers, met with friends for a coffee or espresso. Smoke, mostly from cigarettes and the semi-sweet smell of pipe tobacco, hung like a soft cloud in the air.

The Sabatinis knew most of the customers and exchanged greetings, some with just a nod or tip of the cap, some spoke, a few shook hands.

The mayor's wife came to take their order with menus and a damp rag to wipe the table. Though quiet and mirthless she was never-the-less respected for her hard work. Many villagers speculated those qualities, rather than beauty, were the reason the mayor married her, since in his youth he was known to appreciate the company of much more attractive women.

"What can I get for you? We have a very limited menu."

"Give us all coffees" and in a low voice meant only for her to hear "and tell the Mayor Guido Sabatini and his family are here on a matter of some importance."

"He may be busy," said the wife also in a low voice.

"If he wants to keep the vote of ten Sabatinis he better get un-busy. This is important," said Guido again quietly.

The wife went into the kitchen and a few minutes later served the coffees. "The Mayor will be out to see you in a few minutes," she said then continued "there is no milk or cream. The government has taken it all for the Army. The only food we can offer is bread with jam or gravy for breakfast. For lunch we have vegetables only."

"The coffees are enough, thank you," said Guido.

A few minutes later Mayor Davinti emerged. His sleeves were rolled up and he wore a tan apron that covered his clothes from chest to knees. The strings were looped together in the back and tied in front at his waist. It had stains from wiping his hands when he cooked. He stopped to speak to his wife at the coffee stand just outside the kitchen's swinging doors. From there waving and nodding, he observed the cafe customers. Satisfied all seemed normal he proceeded to the waiting Sabatinis. Guido rose and shook the mayor's hand. Though not particularly tall himself, Guido was at least a half a head taller than the mayor. Though short the mayor was not small. He was thick at the neck and through the chest. His ample belly protruded under the apron. Both arms and hands were large. He smiled broadly from a generous mouth in a round friendly looking face with large heavy jowls and dark brown eyes.

"Good morning, Guido, and to you too Rosa, and your boys. My, how big they have grown. Good Italian cooking, eh boys."

"Good morning, Mayor," said Guido.

"Good morning, Mayor. I hope the cooking is good. I try," said Rosa smiling back.

"It is all good," said Vittorino.

"Yes," said Marcus.

"Please join us," said Guido.

"Thank you," said the Mayor. He sat on the front edge of a chair at the head of the table. "Now what is this urgent business you want to discuss."

"You can help our son Vittorino," said Guido.

"How?" Asked the Mayor and looked at Vittorino.

"By stopping the Army from conscripting him. This morning two soldiers in an Army truck with a red cross on it came to our farm. The officer, Lieutenant Arturo, said my son would soon be drafted. But if he signed the papers right away, he could go in the Medical Corps in a noncombat role. Otherwise, he would be drafted into the regular Army. We need your help to stop the draft."

The Mayor nodded intently at the concern in Guido's voice. When he finished the Mayor ran his left hand through his dark black hair. Leaning forward to speak he quickly tapped his hand to his broad forehead and brought it close to his other hand, palm up, over the table. Moving them slightly apart he raised them a few inches higher and brought his arms tight to his sides, all the time shaking his head slowly from side to side.

Speaking slowly in a caring tone he said, "I am sorry to tell you there is nothing I can do to help. The Army has been conscripting everyone, including farmers, ever since the law went into effect. I have personally and officially tried to stop them but have had no success. My own nephew was taken only last week. I did everything I could. Nothing helped. My advice to you, if you decide to stay here, is to take the offer the officer has made."

"So, you think the officer was telling the truth about a non-combatant role?"

"I don't know. If you decide, make sure he writes it on the papers before, remember before, you sign." And in a whisper, he added "Try to bargain for time. The Americans and the English are marching in Sicily. Italy will surely give up soon."

"What did you mean by your remark 'If you decide to stay here'?" Asked Guido also in a whisper.

Looking around again at the cafe customers, the Mayor continued in a whisper, "I mean you are Jews. Be careful this offer may be a ruse. I see you are not wearing skull caps. That is good. If I were you, I would look for a way out of here. The Germans are pretty much in charge here now. They are insisting on the arrests of Jews. Italy is trying to resist but it is getting more difficult. If you decide to leave Italy, you will need hard currency. American dollars are preferred. English pounds, also. Either staying or going I will do what I can to help."

"Thank you, your honor. What do we owe you for the coffees?" Asked Guido as he pulled out his purse.

"Nothing, those grounds have been used at least twice." He turned to his wife standing nearby "Refresh their coffees and there will be no charge."

Turning around to face the table he said, "I'm sorry I can't stop the conscription." Then again, in a whisper "Be careful. People are being deported. Some that resist are shot. It is not a good time to be Jewish."

"It has been this way for thousands of years," said Guido.

"Goodbye, and good luck," said the Mayor as he rose and started back to the kitchen.

"Goodbye," said Guido.

On the way back the family discussed the situation.

"I wonder how much information the mayor has that we don't," said Rosa.

"I don't know but I don't think he would repeat rumors. He may hear it in his cafe or from the underground. I'm concerned about deportations and people being shot. We must stall for time. If things are as bad for Jews as the Mayor says we must consider leaving. We must meet with the family. My father and brother may have some information or a solution we haven't thought about," said Guido.

When they arrived at the farm Guido went to his parents' home. When he told them about the soldiers and what the mayor said, Vincenzo insisted the entire family meet for supper.

Everyone came. Each family brought as much food as they could for the occasion. While the women finished preparing the food the men sat outside on the large patio. Grape vines woven over a wooden framework provided shade.

Vincenzo opened some of his best wine and said a blessing. "We praise you, Eternal God, Sovereign of the universe, Creator of the fruit of the vine."

"The mayor said we should stall for time to keep Vittorino out of the Army as long as possible if we decide to stay. He also said people, Jews mainly, were being deported and some that resisted were even shot. He said if it was him, he would consider leaving Italy," said Guido.

"I have been here for seventy years and haven't had any problem. The Mayor may be over stating the situation," said Vincenzo.

"I agree. Politicians can be a little dramatic sometimes," said Alberto.

"I think we should at least consider leaving Italy," said Guido.

"I agree. I believe the Mayor was sincere and believes Jews are in danger," said Vittorino.

"I agree with my father and Vitorino," said Marcus.

"How? How can we leave? It will take a lot of money," said Vincenzo.

"The underground may help," said Guido.

"You mean that derelict that comes every week begging for money or even food?" Said Vincenzo.

"I have given when I could. No questions asked. He comes again tomorrow morning early. I'll ask what he knows, then we may want to meet again tomorrow evening," said Guido.

"Make sure you find out what he knows not just what he has heard," said Alberto.

"Yes, that's important, what he knows," said Vincenzo.

"I agree," said Guido.

The men sipped the homemade wine Vincenzo provided for the occasion. There was some small talk about weather and crops but eventually a quiet settled over the group. Each man was left to his own thoughts. Guido's remarks echoed in their minds, some purposefully others involuntarily.

"The draft into the Army can be serious," said Arturo. "The Medial Corps is the best service for your son. I have the papers with me."

"Yes, yes" said Guido "but how do we know he will be put in the Medical corps?"

"I will write the assignment on the papers. No one can change that when it is done in such a manner. I will show you."

The Lieutenant pulled some papers from his briefcase. "See here", he said. "I can write it here," indicating a blank on a paper.

"Let me have all the papers," said Guido.

"Well," said Lt. Arturo "you needn't look at them all."

"Yes, I must."

"OK," said Arturo, then to the other soldier "Get my other briefcase."

When the solder returned with the other briefcase, a different set of papers was produced.

"I had the wrong set of papers," said Arturo. "You may read these."

Guido read them all then had Arturo fill in the papers designating "Medical Services only" on the assignment blank. He also insisted on a duplicate set to keep.

"You are suspicious" said Lt. Arturo.

"Careful, only careful. I know the world," replied Guido.

Then Vittorino signed.

"You are ready to go now?" Asked Lt. Arturo.

Before Vittorino could answer, Guido said "No. We need four to five days to ready him for war. It is our custom."

"This is silly" said Lt. Arturo. His tone changed since the signing.

"Not to us," said Guido.

"Come now, you must come now. If you don't there may be consequences."

"What kind of consequences?" Asked Guido.

"I am not at liberty to say," said Lt. Arturo.

"We must prepare him for war," said Guido.

Arturo pulled Guido aside to speak to him out of earshot. "Look" he said. "You know the war has taken a bad turn. Nazis and fascists are running things like this now. You are Jews, it could be bad for your whole family."

"Are you threatening me?" asked Guido.

"No, no. What I am telling you is the truth. If he comes now, it could delay actions against your family."

"You say could delay actions," said Guido.

"Yes," said Lt. Arturo.

"So, what you are telling me is that my whole family could be in danger because we are Jews."

"I am forbidden to say such a thing. But yes, it is true, sadly."

"How much extra time will we gain if he goes now?" Asked Guido.

"I don't know maybe a few days."

"What could happen?" Asked Guido.

"It depends on who comes. Maybe just a fine. Maybe worse. I have heard of deportations."

"How much time do we have if he doesn't go now?"

"I cannot say, I have been sent out by the draft. I am not part of the others. I can tell you this, if we must come back, I may not be in charge."

"So, either way we could be deported or worse?"

"That is true. The advantage of him going now is that he will be in the Army, and it could possibly delay action against your family."

"For a few days," said Guido.

"Yes, maybe more. People that show loyalty are treated better. It all depends how busy the Nazis and Fascists are."

"Let me ask one more question. Do you know if any action is planned against my family now?"

"No. I don't have access to that type of information. But there could be a problem, some members of the draft are Fascists. They would know your family is Jewish and pass that information to the others."

"Oh, now I see the connection. I still think we need the time to prepare him for war."

"All right, I will add four days to the date of beginning service," said Lt. Arturo.

"This is crazy. Surely, they must realize the war is lost?" said Guido clearly frustrated.

"The fascists will never admit that" said Lt. Arturo.

"We must have the time," said Guido.

"Make the most of it," said Lt. Arturo. He turned and walked back to the truck. When he got there, he turned and saluted Guido and Vittorino.

———

When Lt. Arturo returned to headquarters, he turned in his report about the meeting with the Sabatini family. All such reports routinely circulated through headquarters staff before going to the draft board. When Major Fontana read Lt. Arturo's report, he became very interested. He called him to his office and questioned him about the Sabatini family. When he learned they had a small farm and were Jewish he became incensed.

"Who do these people think they are?" He asked Arturo.

"I don't know," said Arturo.

"They must be taught a lesson, so this does not happen again," said Major Fontana.

"So what does not happen again?" Asked Arturo.

"The fact that they refuse to serve in our Armed Services."

"Up until now they have been exempted due to the importance of the farm work. But now the oldest son is going to serve," said Arturo.

"When do you plan to go back?"

"In four days."

"That's too late we go for these Jews tomorrow."

"But I agreed to four more days so the oldest son could prepare."

"No need to wait. We will deal with them tomorrow. Have a truck and soldiers ready."

CHAPTER TEN

Guido waved back to Arturo then turned to Vittorino. "Come," he said. "I didn't realize it was this bad. We must warn the family and do what the mayor said. We must leave Italy if we still can."

"But if I go now, it will delay things," said Vittorino.

"No, the Fascists and maybe Nazis will still come. They hate our people. We must try to leave before they come."

"How? It will take much money."

"The Traveler that comes by here may be able to help us. Now go prepare the cart. I have business to take care of in the village this morning."

Guido changed from his work clothes and dressed for the meetings he planned. He was ready when Vittorino pulled up in the cart but decided to wait on the Traveler.

It wasn't long before he came. He looked like a beggar, worn out clothes and unwashed with an unkempt beard. But his eyes were clear, and his stride was strong.

"Good morning, Guido," he said.

"Good morning, friend."

"I hope you have something for me to eat," said the Traveler.

"Yes of course," then to Vittorino "Get this man the food package we have prepared and give us a few minutes of privacy."

"What is the occasion?" asked the Traveler warily.

"I need information," said Guido looking directly at the Traveler's eyes.

The Traveler looked at Guido sizing him up, "I will help if I can."

"We have heard stories about Jews being deported and worse. What do you know about this?"

"I believe it is true," said the Traveler quietly.

"Do you know, or have you only heard? I need to know," said Guido forcefully.

"I know so. I have seen it happen during my rounds."

"You have seen people deported?"

"I cannot say deported. I have seen people evicted from their property. If they objected, they were beaten and taken away in trucks."

"And murdered?"

"I have not witnessed murders, but I have been told of bodies being discovered."

"Then why haven't you told us?" demanded Guido.

"I have tried to warn you. I have told you the Fascists are getting desperate and doing illegal acts. Today I have been instructed to warn you of a situation you and your family may find yourself in very soon."

"What is the situation," asked Guido clearly disturbed.

"An Army Major named Fontana has recently been transferred to this area. He's a political appointee and a Fascist. We have been told that he came from a political prison where he was vicious. He has already confiscated property south of Veranza. He will surely find out about your farm."

"I need your help," said Guido.

"How?"

"I need a contact. Someone that can help us leave Italy before it is too late."

The Traveler sat still and did not say anything.

Taking deep breaths to calm himself Guido repeated, "I need help now. From you."

"I don't know, one slip of the tongue can mean many will die," said the Traveler looking down at the ground and slowly shaking his head and pursing his lips.

"I have always helped your cause with money and food. Do you think I didn't know where it was going?"

"Yes, yes," said the Traveler. "I must think."

"Let me give you a name I think is a possibility. If I am wrong, correct me. Remember I need help."

"It will be very expensive," said the Traveler.

"I know. Now the name I am thinking of is Mayor Davinti," said Guido staring at the Traveler.

"I cannot comment. Remember one slip about anyone, right or wrong, could mean death," said the Traveler trying to avoid Guido's eyes.

"I understand. Thank you."

"There is nothing to thank me for," said the Traveler a little too forcefully as he picked up his package and left.

When the Traveler left Guido climbed in the cart to leave. Vittorino came outside.

"Father, I would like to go with you."

"No," said Guido, then changed his mind. "First tell Marcus to go to his grandfather and tell him to have the family meet at their house in the evening after supper. Hurry. Then you can come with me."

The old horse seemed to sense the urgency. He moved faster than usual, trotting most of the way to the village square where Guido tied him to a post across the street from the Mayor's cafe.

They did not go directly to the cafe. Instead, they went across the square to a store owned by a friend.

"Can I slip out the back door to the alley?" he asked.

"Yes, but be careful," said the friend.

Vittorino stayed behind in the store. Guido walked down the alley to another friend's house. He knocked and was invited to enter. Once inside he asked this friend for some help.

"Will you go to the bank and ask the banker to let me in through his private entrance at the back of the bank?"

"Yes."

"I need to see him because…

"Stop, I probably know why but if I don't hear it from you then I can truthfully say I knew nothing," said the friend.

The friend left and a little while later returned. "The banker agreed to see you as requested," he said.

Guido continued his route through the back streets and alleys until he reached the bank's back door. He knocked softly and the door opened. The banker let him in to his private office. Guido had been there before and had always admired it. It was well furnished with leather chairs and a large sofa. The desk alone was worth more than a peasant could earn in a year.

"Thank you for seeing me this way," said Guido.

"What can I do for you?"

"I need to see inside my safe drawer but I'm afraid I'm being watched."

He gave the banker his key. In a few minutes the banker returned with the drawer.

Guido opened the drawer. He took out an envelope and checked its' contents. Satisfied, he smiled and removed a prize family possession, an unusual broach of a peacock. The bird was made of gold and decorated with emeralds, rubies, and sapphires. It was very large and very beautiful. He gave the drawer back to the banker.

"That is a beautiful broach," said the banker.

"Yes, I think so, too. It was my grandmother's. Thank you for allowing me to come this way. I appreciate it very much."

"Be careful. These are very bad times," said the banker. "I agree you being Jewish, it is very possible you are being watched."

"I will and thank you again," said Guido as he rose to leave.

He left through the private entrance and retraced his steps to his friend's store. He purchased some small items and they returned to the cart. He observed the street and noticed the same man that sat on a bench near the bank when they arrived was still sitting there and seemed to be watching them. Good, thought Guido, at least I know where our spy is. He spoke to Vittorino and they started towards the Mayor's cafe.

As they approached the cafe Guido deliberately slowed his pace to give the impression that nothing of importance was happening. Once inside the cafe he quickly looked around to see who was there. Only two old men sat drinking their coffee. He led Vittorino to a table and told him to wait. He walked quickly past the mayor's wife directly into the kitchen. The startled Mayor looked up from his cooking.

"What do you mean barging in here like this?" Asked the Mayor, more careful than angry.

Guido nervously blurted out, "I need your help, Mayor."

"I told you yesterday I cannot stop the conscription."

"I come for something different. My family must leave Italy."

The Mayor stirred a large pot of sauce stalling for time, "What does that have to do with me? I am the mayor not a travel agent." He managed to sound annoyed.

"I believe you can help with the arrangements," said Guido suddenly much calmer.

"You are crazy. I know nothing of this," said the Mayor feigning anger.

Bluffing and determined he stood close to the Mayor, "I am certain you can help if you will. I have contributed to your cause through a Traveler that comes at least once a week to our farm. Do you think I didn't know where the money and food were going? Please give me more credit than that."

The Mayor took a deep breath and exhaled loudly into a sigh while staring at Guido. He wiped his hands on his apron more from absent minded habit than necessity. He walked to the door and opened it a crack to see who was seated inside the cafe. Satisfied he gestured to a small table at the back of the kitchen. Guido followed and the Mayor offered him a seat. Then he said with an audible sigh, "You are probably being watched. Why do you bring this trouble to me?" He put his hand on his forehead and rubbed it.

"I have no choice we are desperate." Relief from the struggle of wills was in his voice.

"Desperate people do stupid things," said the Mayor again sighing audibly. He took a cigarette paper and a pouch of tobacco from the center of the table and began to roll a cigarette. "I bought this a long time ago for times like these."

"I don't have time for word games. I need help now," said Guido again pressing.

"It will take money. How many people?"

"Ten".

"Out of the question," said the mayor shaking his head.

"Ten. I have the money."

"It will take much money. People have to take risks and to get them to do that we have to pay, dearly," said the Mayor relaxing and sitting back in his chair. He struck a match and lit the cigarette.

"I understand. How much is dearly?"

"The money will have to be American dollars or English pounds, not liras. For ten people at least fifty dollars a person, maybe even more," said the Mayor puffing on the cigarette.

"I have American dollars."

"I will try to make contact today. But I will need some money in advance."

"How much?"

"About half. Can you get it to me today?"

"I have it with me."

He pulled the envelope from inside his shirt and with trembling hands counted out two hundred and fifty dollars.

The mayor took the money, then said "Come back tomorrow morning with a load of vegetables and eggs. Maybe a goat or two for slaughter. That will give us cover for watching eyes. I will let you know then if it is possible. Bring the rest of the money, also. Remember it may take more. I don't know".

"Thank you. I will be back in the morning."

The Mayor went to the door and cracked it.

"A spy is in the cafe. We must discuss about the food there, so he knows of the transaction," he whispered.

The Mayor opened the door. Guido walked to where Vittorino sat. The Mayor followed and said in a voice loud enough for the spy to hear. "Remember, besides the vegetables and eggs, I need at least one goat to slaughter, two goats if you can. I am out of meat. I need this tomorrow."

"I will speak with my father and brother about the goats. One goat I feel sure about, but I doubt if my father will part with two."

"Do what you can to convince him."

"We will return in the morning. That's all I can promise."

He offered his hand but the Mayor did not shake it, instead he walked back to the kitchen.

When they returned to the farm, Guido decided to meet with his father and brother rather than wait. He told them about the meeting with the partisan Traveler and securing his money from the bank. Neither Vincenzo nor Alberto had any foreign currency. Guido explained selling food was the excuse he needed to return to Veranza for the next step in the arrangements to leave. Both agreed to gather what vegetables they could spare to sell to the Mayor. Vincenzo also agreed to provide two goats. Guido did not tell them who his contact was.

The next morning, they loaded the cart and Guido and Vittorino drove to the village. They went to the rear of the Mayor's cafe to unload. The Mayor made a big deal out of accepting the food. While Vitorino did the unloading Guido and the Mayor met at the little table in the kitchen.

“What arrangements have you made?” Asked Guido, his eyes shining and fixed on the Mayor’s.

“It is in process,” said the Mayor casually, while rolling a cigarette.

Leaning forward over the table’s edge Guido asked, “Where, what process?”

“I need all of your names and ages for the documents”.

Frustrated, Guido’s voice seemed to catch in his throat and became a little higher.

“Why? What documents? I don’t understand.”

“Do you think you can leave here in a rowboat? Think man. Papers are necessary,” said the Mayor striking a match and carefully lighting his cigarette, his eyes on Guido.

“Yes, yes, I know. I’m just nervous,” said Guido dabbing sweat from his forehead with a handkerchief.

In a commanding tone the Mayor said, “Write down the information. Now.”

Guido made out the list and gave it to the Mayor.

“It will be another fifty dollars each.”

Guido paused, then said quietly in a beseeching, questioning tone, “You said fifty dollars total. Why so much more?”

“Things change. You have ten people. Expenses add up. People take chances and must be paid or bribed,” said the Mayor nonchalantly.

“Which is it paid or bribed?” Asked Guido clearly disheartened.

"Both. Paid to forge the necessary papers and bribed to let you on board ship."

"What ship?"

"There is a ship with a red cross on it in the harbor at Nalatia. It left Tunisia full of immigrants, the Allies agreed to let it go to Spain, but a bad storm forced it to Italy. It will be leaving the day after tomorrow. You must be smuggled aboard. The Traveler will bring your papers to you. He will also tell you how to proceed to Nalatia. Now do you have the money?"

"Yes. But it will be almost all I have."

He counted out the money. The Mayor put it in his pocket.

Guido looked at the Mayor who looked away. He wanted to ask how much the Mayor would keep but didn't. It was misery money, and he didn't want to know.

The Mayor left the kitchen and spoke to his wife. When he returned, he was excited and said "It is good, a spy is in the cafe. Have a coffee or two and maybe some cakes. I will make a big deal out of paying you for the food, for his sake."

Guido went out the back door and spoke to Vittorino. "Do you need my help?"

"No. I'm almost finished," he said. "How did things go with the Mayor.?"

"Good. I'm going around to the front entrance. Move the cart and join me inside when you finish."

Guido entered and sat at a table near the kitchen. In a few minutes Vittorino joined him.

The mayor's wife brought them coffees. Guido ordered small cakes for each of them.

They waited for the Mayor, conscious of the spy while pretending not to notice him.

It was a long wait. The mayor's wife brought more coffee. The Mayor finally appeared wearing his apron and bubbling over with good cheer. He bowed to his wife. Then reached out and held her in a dance embrace and hummed loudly as they danced around and through the tables back to her coffee stand. The customers laughed and cheered. He bowed deeply holding his wife's hand. She bowed also and received a round of cheers. Then, laughing, he walked over to Guido and Vittorino's table. He held his arms at shoulder height, dipped and raised them, again and again, imitating an orchestra conductor.

Bowing again, he said, "You are a life saver. The food you brought is excellent. Thank you. I will butcher one goat tonight. How did you ever talk your father out of two?"

"I assure you it was not easy. But we are glad to help during these times."

"There will be no charge for the coffees or the cakes," he told his wife and turned so the spy could not see him wink while talking to Guido, "Speaking of these times I hope we are soon victorious over the Allies."

"I agree whole heartedly," said Guido smiling.

The Mayor pulled out his purse and paid Guido in liras.

"Thank you. We will be going to our farm when we finish."

"Goodbye," said the Mayor.

"Goodbye," they echoed.

CHAPTER ELEVEN

While Guido and his sons Vittorino and Marcus were loading the cart to take to Veranza, Lieutenant Arturo reported to Major Fontana. He entered Fontana's office, came to attention, and saluted. "Sir, my men are ready to go to the Sabatini farm."

"How many men besides yourself?" Asked Fontana, not bothering to return the salute or look up from a large map on his desk.

"Seven sir. One sergeant and six privates. All good soldiers," said Arturo still standing at attention.

"That's too many. Reduce your force to the sergeant and two privates." Fontana gave a salute that was more of a wave.

"Major, I would like to keep all seven. You never know what can happen. A good show of force can sometimes prevent problems before they arise," said Arturo still at attention.

Leaning forward, his elbows on the desk and chin resting on his hands, Fontana asked, "Are you expecting a problem?"

"No sir. But you never know."

"Lieutenant, reduce your force. We will have more than enough men."

"Will we be taking a staff car, sir?"

"Yes, now get going," said Fontana clearly losing patience.

Arturo went outside. Sergeant Grimaldi and the men stood beside a truck.

"Sergeant, dismiss four of your men. The Major feels six is too many. I will ride with Major Fontana. You lead the way."

"Yes sir," said Grimaldi and dismissed four of the six.

A few minutes later a staff car pulled around to the building's front, followed by a truck with German markings.

Major Fontana came out of the building. He stopped halfway down the building's steps to put on a pair of gloves. Then he strutted towards the staff car with his riding crop in hand. He was accompanied by a German officer. They were talking and laughing as they approached the car.

"Let's go. You and your men lead the way," said Fontana. "We will follow close behind."

Sensing something was very wrong Arturo said, "Sir, surely one truck with soldiers is enough," gesturing toward the Italian Army truck.

"Lieutenant I am ordering you to go. Now," said Fontana loudly.

Arturo returned to his truck. "Sergeant drive slowly. I must think."

The sergeant asked, "Why do you think the German Lieutenant is coming and why the truck? Who do you think is in the back?"

"I don't know, but I don't like it."

"If it's some of the Germans I see around headquarters it's bad news."

"I agree when we dismount tell your soldiers they are to take orders only from me. Understand?"

"Yes sir. Thank you, sir."

"Tell them to be ready."

"Yes sir."

The trip that took forty-five minutes the day before took over an hour before they even reached Veranza.

"It's only about five kilometers farther," said the sergeant glancing at Arturo.

"Yes, I know."

Eventually they turned onto the farm road. The sergeant pulled the truck up onto the grass of a little hill slightly to the side of Guido's old farmhouse. Major Fontana's car stopped a little farther away. Lt. Arturo and his soldiers exited their truck and the Major, and his driver and the German Lieutenant exited the staff car.

The German Lieutenant ordered the driver of the second truck to pull it opposite the Italians. The rear of the second truck faced the area in front of the house.

"Get everyone out of the house and have them sit there in the yard," said Major Fontana pointing to the area between the German truck and the house.

"I will greet them and ask for Vittorino," said Lt. Arturo turning toward the house.

Clearly agitated, Fontana said, "You will follow my orders. Now send your men to empty the house!"

The sergeant looked at Lt. Arturo.

"Do as the Major says."

The sergeant and his men went to the house and entered. They ordered everyone outside and had them sit in the yard. The whole family was present except Guido and Vittorino.

The sergeant completed the search and reported to the lieutenant. "All clear," he said.

He was about to say more but Arturo cut him off saying "I see that everyone is here." He looked hard at the Sergeant hoping he would act it out.

"Yes sir."

Fontana walked quickly towards the family. He began circling them counterclockwise, strutting with his riding crop in his left hand. He slapped it nervously against his leg as he walked. His face was deep red and drawn tight, the veins on his neck stood out and his eyes darted to each family member as he walked.

"I see you wear skull caps in the presence of officers serving in the Army," he said loudly, still circling.

"We wear our caps for religious reasons not as an affront to anyone," said Vincenzo calmly. His eyes followed Fontana as he spoke.

Fontana stopped circling and walked directly to Vincenzo. He tapped him lightly several times on the chest with the end of his riding crop. Then he shouted, "Who owns this farm?"

"It is the family's farm," said Vincenzo again calmly.

Fontana moved a few steps away, then quickly turned and asked, "In whose name is the property registered?"

"My name and my wife's name," said Vincenzo again calmly.

"That will change today. Where are the land title papers?"

"At our house over there," said Vincenzo indicating his home across the field.

"Lt. Arturo have your sergeant and one other soldier accompany this man to his house for his title papers."

"May I ask the Major why?"

"No, you may not."

Arturo spoke to his sergeant, "Do as he says but take your time."

They took Vincenzo for the papers. It was a while before they returned.

Fontana took the papers from Vincenzo and inspected them. Satisfied, he went to the staff car and returned with a pen and ink.

He spoke to Vincenzo and Maria. "You must sign this farm over to the state for back taxes you have not paid".

"We owe no back taxes," said Vincenzo calmly standing in front of Fontana.

Fontana set down the pen and ink and title papers. He looked around, smiled, then removed the glove from his right hand, walked to Maria and slapped her face with it.

Vincenzo and Alberto lunged at him, but Fontana struck Vincenzo hard across the forehead with the riding crop and the German Lieutenant pulled his pistol and struck Alberto on the side of his head. As both men went down Gabriella and Marcus rose and came forward to help. Both officers aimed their pistols and Maria stood up with her arms outstretched to stop her grandsons. Alberto was knocked nearly unconscious by the blow. Blood streamed from Vincenzo's forehead. "You bastards," he said.

Stepping forward, Lt. Arturo said in a loud voice, "Major Fontana I protest the way these people are being treated."

"Shut up Lieutenant," said Fontana. Then to Vincenzo, "Now you will sign."

"Never," said Vincenzo.

Fontana swung the riding crop hard. The blow landed on the left side of Vincenzo's face between the cheekbone and the ear. Vincenzo went down to his knees. He propped himself up with his hands. Maria screamed and went to her husband.

Standing with her left arm around him, she wiped blood from his face with the hem of her dress. "Let it go. Sign it before he kills us all," she said.

Vincenzo took the pen and signed, then Maria signed, also.

Fontana took the paper then said to Lt. Arturo, "We are ready to finish this mission."

Moving closer to Fontana, Lt. Arturo said angrily, "I protest your treatment of these innocent people."

"They are vermin," shouted the German Lt. "They must be stamped out".

Fontana turned to Arturo. "Which one refused to join the Army?"

"I told you yesterday he did not refuse. He still has three more days to report."

"It doesn't matter. They must all be treated as the vermin they are," shouted the German Lt.

"Yes, yes. Lieutenant Arturo, point him out," said Fontana.

"May I ask why?

"Because we are going to shoot him first."

"I refuse to point anyone out."

"I tell you now. Call your men to attention," said Fontana.

"Attention," Lt. Arturo said. His men snapped to attention.

"Now I give you the order to have your men shoot these Jews."

"And I tell you no. I refuse this illegal order."

"Then I will have you court-martialed."

"Do what you will. I will not order my men to shoot these people."

Fontana spoke directly to the sergeant. "Give the order to fire."

The sergeant looked at Arturo.

"Lower your weapons," said Arturo. Then to Fontana, "We are soldiers not murderers."

Fontana turned to the German Lt., "Bellheimer get your men ready."

The German barked some quick orders. The canvas across the back of the German truck opened and a dozen soldiers emerged. They quickly contained the family on two sides. Three took up positions directly behind the Italian soldiers. A machine gun was mounted in the middle of the truck's rear opening and aimed at the Sabatini family. The women began to cry. The men moved to shield the women.

"Now" said Fontana glaring at Arturo, "you will see how real soldiers do their duty." He walked behind Vincenzo and shot him in the back of the head, killing him instantly. The force of the bullet forced him to fall face down in the grass.

Maria, Vincenzo's wife of over fifty years, looked up at the sky and screamed, "No God, please," then collapsed beside him. She pulled his body onto her lap. With her left arm around him she cradled him against her chest. Her right hand held his head next to hers. She kissed him on the forehead and stroked the side of his head and began to slowly rock back and forth.

Before the stunned Italians could do anything, Major Fontana moved out of the way and motioned to the German Lieutenant. The Lieutenant gave the order "Fire." The machine gun bullets ripped into the Sabatini family and in less than thirty seconds they were all dead or dying. The Lieutenant motioned with his arm and the machine gun stopped its' deadly chatter.

Fontana and the German Lieutenant walked among the family shooting anyone still moving. When they finished Fontana pulled a knife. He bent over Maria's body and pulled her wedding band from her finger. Then he cut the finger off. He repeated this with Rosa and Sofia. "Souvenirs," he said.

Fontana and Bellheimer went into the house. Fontana went straight to the back bedroom. On the dresser he found an envelope with three hundred American dollars and a very beautiful peacock broach. "Good, very good. But there should be much more money. Look carefully." They continued to search the house, but no more money was found. The German Lieutenant then ordered his men to search the bodies for valuables which were divided between Fontana and himself. Finally, they searched the other two farmhouses but found no more American money.

Fontana and Bellheimer joked about the morning and how they caught the whole family at home at one time.

The Italian soldiers refused to take part in the looting. Afraid the machine gun would be turned on them, Lt. Arturo ordered his men into their truck, and they left.

Shocked by the brutality, the two young privates cried as they rode. The sergeant and Lieutenant had difficulty seeing the road through tear filled eyes.

Lt. Arturo swore, "I'll see that bastard faces a firing squad." To the sergeant he said, "Make a detailed written statement on what you saw and did today. Have each private do the same. I will bring charges against the Major."

"What about the Germans?"

"I will report their role to my superiors. They will have the Germans charged with this atrocity."

CHAPTER TWELVE

Outside the cafe Vittorino turned to his father, "When I was moving the cart to the front of the cafe, I saw an Army truck with a red cross on it leave the village."

"Was it headed to our farm?"

"No, it left the village in the opposite direction. I couldn't tell which direction it came from. I believe it stopped at the fountain for some water."

"Did you notice anything else? Anything unusual?"

"No, I tied up the horse and came in the cafe."

"I didn't see anything unusual either," said Guido.

On the way back to the farm Guido told Vittorino about the plan laid out by the mayor.

"Where did you get the American money?" Asked Vittorino.

"We saved it for many years before the war. When your mother and I sold flowers and cakes to American tourists we often took dollars for payment as a hedge against inflation and in case of an emergency. Now we have both."

"I see. Very smart. Did Alberto and grandfather do the same?"

"They preferred liras. If they accepted dollars, they traded with us for liras."

They rode the rest of the way in silence. When they approached their home neighbors were blocking the view of the yard.

"Something is wrong," said Vittorino.

Guido urged the horse into a trot. As they got closer the group separated and they could see what the neighbors were looking at. Guido stopped the old horse. Both men climbed down from the cart. Neither spoke nor moved, only stared. Bodies were strewn over the ground. Guido slowly looked around. Then he screamed in a high-pitched voice, "No, God! No! Why this?" He stumbled forward and collapsed next to his mother. He held her hand in his and kissed it. He put his arms around her and held her in a gentle embrace. He whispered, "I love you. I will keep you in my heart. I will never forget you." He held her a few minutes longer, then kissed her on both cheeks and laid her back on the ground. He went to Vincenzo and hugged him in a tight embrace. He whispered, "Papa, every manly thing I know about life I learned from you. I love you dearly." He kissed his forehead and laid him next to Maria. He went to Rosa and held her for a long time, then kissed her on the forehead and both cheeks. He put his nose in her hair and smelled it as he did in their most intimate moments, and whispered, "You are my life, the reason I live. I love you with all my heart." He kissed her lips and laid her on the soft grass.

He went to Sofia. She was lying face down. He turned her over and said, "You have been a sister to me, and I will miss you." Finally, he went to his brother and nephews. He straightened them and placed them side by side and said, "My brother I dearly love you and your family. Without you and our parents and my Rosa, life is gone from me," and he wept.

Vittorino watched his father then went to his mother. He cradled her in his arms and kissed her cheeks. He said, "Mama, I love you so much, I can't bear for you not to be with us. I will pray for your soul though I know you will be in Heaven." He held her for a few more minutes, then laid her back on the grass. Next, he went to his grandparents and hugged them both and said he loved them. Finally, he picked up Sofia and placed her beside her husband and sons. "I love you all" he said and sat with his father, and they wept.

Slowly Vittorino observed the bodies. It was obvious that some had been shot more than once. When he looked at his mother, he realized her ring finger had been cut off. He looked at his grandmother and aunt. Their ring fingers were gone, too.

After some time Vittorino realized that his brother wasn't among the dead. He said to his father, "Marcus."

A neighbor stepped forward and said, "He is in the house, badly wounded. We have sent for the doctor and the police."

He rose and touched his father's shoulder and said, "I must see him."

Guido remained among the dead. Vittorino went into the house. His brother laid on a couch in the main room. Two neighbors held compresses to help stem the flow of blood, one to an arm and one to the side of his throat.

"He wakes up, then passes out again. I pray the doctor comes quickly," said one neighbor. Vitorino knelt beside him. He noticed his hair was matted with blood but the wound to his head was no longer bleeding. Marcus opened his eyes. He tried to say something but grimaced in pain.

"Who did this?" asked Vittorino.

"Soldiers," said Marcus.

"The ones I was to go with, Lt. Arturo?"

"They were here."

"I will make him pay."

"No. They wouldn't do it. Arturo refused the order to shoot us."

"Then who?"

"A Major named Fontana shot grandfather. The Germans used a machine gun. I was hit and knocked out. Later I played dead when they searched us."

"Arturo should have stopped it," said Vittorino.

"He tried. I don't think he could. There were too many others."

Marcus lost consciousness again. Vittorino thanked the neighbors for their help then went outside to sit with his father.

Some men were returning with shovels and picks to dig the graves in the family cemetery.

One man was making pictures with a large, old camera. When Guido saw what he was doing he had to be restrained. He screamed at him "You think this is a pretty picture? All Jews lying dead?"

"No," said the man. "I do it for evidence against the ones who did this. With your permission I will continue."

"Go ahead," said Vittorino. "Papa, we want the evidence and the world to know." His voice trailed off. He sat down with his head in his hands.

The doctor arrived with the police. He was led to Marcus and immediately began treating him. A neighbor pulled a stool close for the doctor. He took his stethoscope from his bag and listened to Marcus' heart. He returned it to his bag and pulled out some alcohol and heavy bandages with gauze.

He spoke to the neighbor holding the compress on Marcus' arm. "Hold the compress higher on the arm." The neighbor did and the doctor poured alcohol on the wound, turning the arm as he did. He wrapped it in gauze, and a heavy bandage then taped it. "You can let go now," he said.

Marcus woke and mumbled something.

"Sit still. You are going to be alright. Now, slowly remove the neck compress," he said to the second neighbor. He did, and the wound oozed blood. The doctor examined the wound, poured on alcohol, and proceeded to bandage Marcus' throat. Next, he examined and cleaned the head wound with alcohol.

He shaved the immediate area, then reapplied alcohol and bandaged the wound.

The police chief spoke to the doctor, “Can I question him about what happened?”

“Yes, when he regains consciousness. But only for a moment. I need to get him to our infirmary.”

A Rabbi arrived and spoke as he sat on the grass between Guido and Vittorino, “I am so very sorry for the loss of your loved ones today. Let me offer a simple prayer. Oh God, merciful God creator of the universe I ask for your blessing on the souls of this family.” He sat for a long time on the grass next to Vittorino. Then he went inside to see and pray for Marcus. Then he began preparations for the funerals.

The Mayor arrived and sat staring from his wagon. The Rabbi approached him and said, “We need help.”

“What happened here? Who did this?” asked the Mayor.

“I don’t know for sure. I have heard soldiers did it. I need your help to get coffins to bury the dead.”

“Of course. How many?”

“Seven are dead. One son inside is badly wounded. The coffins must be simple wooden ones.”

The Mayor got down from his wagon and walked over to Guido where he sat down. “My friend, I am so sorry for your loss. We will do everything we can to find out who did this.”

At first Guido said nothing. Then he said “Marcus is inside. He might know, I must go to him.” He got up and walked slowly to his home.

The Mayor followed. Inside the chief of police was just finishing talking to Marcus. "An Italian Major named Fontana and a German officer named Bellheimer. Is that right?"

"Yes, they were in charge. Our soldiers refused to shoot. So, they got the Germans to do it. They had a machine gun."

The doctor spoke to the Mayor, "He needs to be transported to the town infirmary. We could still lose him."

"I'll take care of it," said the Mayor. To the police chief he said. "Have one of your men get a stretcher and put Marcus in my wagon. I'll have one of the men outside take him, the doctor, and your officer to the infirmary. Make arrangements for a twenty-four-hour guard until further notice."

"Yes sir," said the chief.

"Now, what have you learned about what happened here?"

"I questioned Marcus, and he told me the same thing he told Vittorino. The family was inside Guido's house waiting for him and Vittorino to return from Veranza. A car with two officers in it and two Army trucks, one Italian with a red cross on it and one German, pulled into the yard. They ordered everyone out of the house. An Italian Major named Fontana made the grandfather and grandmother sign the farm title papers, by beating them. Lieutenant Arturo tried to stop it. Fontana ordered Arturo and his men to shoot the family, but Arturo refused. Then the Germans got out of the other truck. Fontana shot the grandfather, and they machine gunned everyone. I'm sure there's more, but he keeps passing out."

"Okay," said the Mayor. Make a complete report. Find out who discovered the bodies, and what anybody saw. We must pursue justice for the Sabatini family."

"Yes sir," said the chief.

The Mayor walked outside and spoke to two men. "One son is inside with the doctor. The police are going to put him in my wagon. I need one of you to take him, a police officer, and the doctor to the infirmary then go by the undertaker's for coffins. I need the other one to take Guido's cart for coffins, also. Tell the undertaker I said we need seven coffins. They must be simple wooden ones. If he doesn't have seven, he must make them. We must have them back here for burial today."

The Mayor got the police chief and two other men along with the Rabbi and the man with the camera to help move the bodies to the veranda for shade. The Rabbi, with help from neighbor ladies, began preparing the bodies for burial. The mayor got the rest of the group to accompany him to the cemetery. A handful of men were working on graves. They had already completed two and looked tired. The Mayor and the others relieved them. Then the men returned to relieve the second group. The work went faster with the relief and by midafternoon the graves were completed.

The first load of coffins arrived in Guido's cart. There were four of them. The driver said the undertaker needed to make one more but that the pieces were already cut, and it would soon be done. Within an hour the Mayor's wagon arrived with the last three coffins.

The Rabbi directed the placement of the bodies in the coffins, then the lids were placed on the coffins, and they were carried to the cemetery. Guido and Vittorino, their shirts torn as outward displays of grief, stood at the side of the first grave.

The Rabbi delivered a heartfelt eulogy. "Each member of this family was a true believer in God. They had a strong love of one another. All were good children of God. They contributed to the community through work and financially. This loss is felt by friends and loved ones alike and will be for years even decades. I ask you God for your blessing on these deceased loved ones."

Then the Rabbi led the reciting of the blessing. "Blessed are You, O Lord our God, Ruler of the universe, the True Judge." He then read the twenty third psalm and the mourners recited the Kaddish, the mourner's prayer.

One by one each casket was placed into the ground and as people passed by, some tossed a small amount of earth into the opening others tapped the earth near the graves.

When the final casket was lowered the same men that dug the graves filled them.

With the dead buried and the living in shock or unconscious the neighbors began to arrive with food, far too much for Guido and Vittorino. They sat along with others at a hastily set up outdoor area with the food on a tablecloth on the ground. Tired from digging or numb from what they saw or did they prepared to eat. But first the Rabbi addressed the group. "It is our custom to wash our hands and give a blessing before eating the mourner's meal." He then washed his hands and recited the blessing, "We praise You, Eternal God, Sovereign of the universe, for You cause bread to come forth from the Earth."

While they were eating the Mayor spoke. "I swear the people responsible for what happened here today will be brought to justice." But everyone knew that was highly unlikely.

Before he left the Mayor spoke quietly to Guido and Vittorino. "Be careful. These are ruthless people. They may come back when they find out Marcus survived, and other family members were not present during the attack. This is not a good time to ask, but I must know if you will still be leaving?"

Vittorino said, "No, we will not be leaving. With Marcus hurt and the rest of our family murdered there is no longer any reason to leave. We will stay here and try to bring these murderers to justice."

The Mayor handed him an envelope. It contained five hundred dollars. "It is the bribe money. We won't need it now. I will keep your papers in case you change your mind."

Vittorino accepted the money. They shook hands and the Mayor left.

The police chief came and spoke to Vittorino. "I have verified what you said with Marcus when he was conscious. I also have the statements of neighbors. One of my officers saw the two trucks come through the village this morning. That ties it together."

"What will you do?" asked Vittorino.

"I will try to get arrest warrants."

"Do you think you can?"

"I don't know. It will be very difficult now. When the allies come it should be easier. That's all I can say."

Vittorino walked to where his father sat. When he sat down, he realized it was the same place they sat earlier in the morning before they went to the village.

Guido was still in a state of shock. Tears ran down his cheeks continuously. The outward sobs subsided, replaced by a jerking and spasms of the chest that he couldn't control.

Vittorino cried, too. He hugged his father, but nothing helped. When the sun finally set, he walked out into the empty yard thrust his fist in the air and said, "I swear by the heavens I will not stop until I find the men responsible for these murders."

Neither man could eat the food brought by the neighbors. After dark Vittorino convinced his father to go to bed. For a long time, he could hear Guido mumbling and crying. Exhaustion overtook both men and they slept fitfully.

CHAPTER THIRTEEN

In the morning Vitorino fixed a breakfast of eggs and bread and they finally ate.

"I'm going to the village to swear out warrants for the ones that harmed our family," said Guido.

Vittorino said, "Remember what the Mayor said about them. They are ruthless. When they find out Marcus lived and we weren't home, they may return. Let's wait to see if the Traveler comes by today or tomorrow. If he does, he may have some news."

Guido started to speak, then looking at Vittorino he paused. "All right we'll wait. But not beyond tomorrow."

The Traveler came in the late morning. He approached the patio and took off his hat and held it in both hands against his heart. "I am very sorry for the loss of so many of your family," he said.

"Thank you," said Vittorino. He paused, then spoke emotionally barely above a whisper, "We are still in shock."

"I understand."

Guido was pacing anxiously on the patio. "What is happening in the village? We are worried about Marcus, and I want to get warrants sworn out."

"Right now, the whole village is in shock. People didn't believe this could happen here. Your situation is very fluid. You should stay away from the village. There are known spies there. They may not be connected to Major Fontana and the Germans, but they could still be a source of information. You may have to go into hiding until the allies come."

"They will get away," said Guido. He stopped pacing in front of the Traveler. He held his hands in tight fists waist high.

The Traveler paused, then said in a quiet reassuring tone. "The village police are trying for warrants and Lieutenant Arturo will present his case for court-martial proceedings. You cannot do more than that."

Then dropping his hat to his left leg, he continued in his normal tone. "Besides, Major Fontana is claiming your family was armed and resisted and they had no choice but to respond."

"That's a dirty lie," said Vittorino angrily.

"Of course. Everyone knows that. At this point Major Fontana thinks you are all dead. But when he finds out otherwise, he may try to have you killed. Hide in the barn tonight. I will be back with more news tomorrow. I'll try to find out more about Marcus. I know he's still alive, but I don't know how well he is."

Vittorino and Guido spent the night in the barn. The next day the Traveler returned.

This time he sat on the patio but still held his hat in both hands close to his heart.

"Marcus is doing better. The Mayor and Chief of police have him under a twenty-four-hour guard. He's moved every day to keep his location secret."

"Do you know where they have him hidden?" asked Guido.

"No, I don't, and for his sake I don't want to know. The less that know the safer he is."

"Yes, that's right," said Guido nodding.

"I'll see the local leaders of the Underground today and ask them if they will hide you until it is safe for you to return. In the meantime, I think you should stay in the barn or even better in the chicken house. Especially during the day and the early evening hours."

Gesturing with open arms and his head tilted slightly to one side to give a questioning look, Guido asked "When will you return? We can't live with chickens and horses forever."

"I can't promise I'll be back tomorrow, but I will return as soon as I have news for you."

———

The Traveler returned in two days. Guido and Vittorino sat smoking on the patio.

He said, "You have a choice to make. You can stay on the farm and risk being killed because word has spread you are still alive, or you can join the Underground under certain conditions."

Guido said, “We refuse to live with the chickens any longer. What are the conditions?”

The Traveler sat on the edge of a chair. He twirled his hat slightly and looked down at his feet. “You must not wear skullcaps or say Jewish prayers in public. Your possessions including farm animals and anything sellable will be confiscated by the Underground. You must also agree to fight with the Underground against the Fascists or Nazis if needed.”

Astonished, Guido looked at Vittorino then the Traveler and said in a voice that rose as he spoke, “Those are pretty hard conditions. Is there anything else? Do they want one of my kidneys?”

“I know the conditions are tough. I’ll leave you alone to discuss. Call me when you’re ready.” He walked toward the barn to smoke a cigarette.

Guido sat down on the edge of his chair. He extended his hands palms up and shrugged. “I don’t know about this. First the Fascists and Nazis murder our family and now the Underground wants everything we have worked for our whole life. When does it end?”

“When does what end?”

“Misfortune,” said Guido solemnly.

Vittorino shrugged and shook his head, “I don’t know. Maybe never.”

“Son, what are your thoughts about this? I’m not thinking so well,” said Guido as he rolled another cigarette. “I’m very tired.”

"I'm not sure. I am tired of living with the chickens. I know we, especially you, would be giving up a lot if we agree, but if we survive, we will still have the farm and the five hundred dollars we got back from the Mayor. That would be a start."

"Yes, and if we don't agree to the terms, we will have the farm as it is plus the five hundred dollars and a little more money I had with me when we went to see the Mayor. But we will risk being killed. Not very much of a choice either way."

"One other thing," said Vittorino, staring hard at his father. "If we join the Underground, we might have a chance to fight against the Fascists and Nazis. Maybe a chance at revenge in a way."

"Yes, that's true," said Guido nodding his head in agreement. "We can also do our prayers in private. So, I guess that settles it. I think we agree to accept the terms. Is that right?"

"Yes," said Vittorino also nodding his head slightly.

"I'll call him back and tell him." Guido whistled to get the Traveler's attention, then waved at him to come back.

When he got back, Guido frowned and shook his head while looking at the ground.

"We don't like the terms, but we can't keep living with the chickens, so we accept them."

The Traveler said, "I will be back soon to take you to a safe place to live."

"One thing, we are worried about Marcus' condition. Can you find something out, please?" Asked Guido with a long emphasis on the 'please'.

"I will be in Veranza tomorrow morning. I'll check then," said the Traveler picking up his bundle to leave.

——————

The next day the Traveler returned. He told them Marcus had been moved again and was much better. He also told them to be ready to move into hiding the next day.

That night Guido slit the seams of his coat. He hid as much American money as he could between the lining and the garment's outer cloth. The rest he divided up with Vittorino and they each hid some in their cap.

Early the next morning the Traveler returned and led them to a farm 30 kilometers away. The farmer and his wife were both friendly. They were sent to sleep in a room in the barn.

CHAPTER FOURTEEN

When Fontana returned to headquarters from the Sabatini farm, he immediately filed a request for court-martial charges against Lieutenant Arturo. He claimed, Insubordination and failure to follow a direct order. He further claimed Lt. Arturo's inaction gave comfort to armed insurrectionists and caused a serious situation to escalate into armed conflict.

His narrative of the incident at the farm said: 'The joint command arrived with the sole purpose of escorting a non-co-operative conscript, Vittorino Sabatini, to headquarters so he could serve in the Medical Corps. When we arrived the Sabatinis refused to co-operate. They were armed and belligerent. They would not let us escort Vittorino off the farm. I ordered Lt. Arturo to act forcefully to prevent the escalation of the situation. He refused and forbade his men from following my direct order. This brazen disregard for a direct order gave comfort to the insurrectionists, creating significant risk to the mission. And therefor it became necessary to take defensive action to prevent loss of life to the joint force I commanded. It is my belief if Lt. Arturo had acted forcefully and responsibly this incident may have been avoided.'

He requested immediate proceedings. The charges were filed with the military police.

They also received a serious complaint filed by Lt. Arturo describing in detail Fontana and Bellheimer's actions. With the change in the political and military situation it was decided both charges would need to be thoroughly investigated.

For a few days nothing happened. When Fontana inquired, he was told about an investigation being conducted by Colonel Antonio Myrano. Through an officer friend close to the investigation Fontana learned that two members of the Sabatini family were not present during the attack including the one Fontana said refused to join the Army. Worse yet, one young man had survived and was being hidden in Veranza. Even more damning said the friend, pictures of the death scene appeared to confirm Lt. Arturo's charges.

Word came back to headquarters that the local authorities were requesting arrest warrants for 'Those responsible for the deaths of seven members of the Sabatini family'.

The German soldiers that accompanied Fontana and Bellheimer were transferred and not available for questioning.

The disappearance of the German soldiers did not slow Colonel Myrano's investigation, politics did. The German liaison office made it clear the Germans regarded the incident as 'an unavoidable act of war'. The pressure on Fontana and Bellheimer was temporarily eased.

On September 3, the Allies invaded the toe of Italy from Sicily. On September 8,1943, Italy surrendered. On the 9th the Allies landed at Salerno and their advance put pressure on the German lines.

Even though Italy surrendered, and many Italian forces were disarmed by the Germans, others were forced to help the Germans, and Fascists, and still others including Fontana, continued to voluntarily help them.

Other Italian soldiers surrendered to the Allies so they could join in the fighting against the Nazis.

Fontana was able to keep his position of authority because of his arrangement with the German district commander who shared in the loot he and Bellheimer confiscated, including land they resold for gold and jewels or hard currencies.

By mid-May 1944 it was obvious that Rome would soon be in allied hands. Fontana's authority was quickly evaporating. He and Bellheimer decided to execute their escape plans, first a ship to Spain then to either South America or the United States. The contact they made their original escape plan with disappeared and they were forced to replan their departure.

Bellheimer was very worried. "You said the plan was foolproof, now here we are without a contact. I don't want to stay in Italy much longer. I could end up with a rifle company on the front lines," he said as he paced around Fontana's office.

"Don't worry I will call my old mentor, Muscanti," said Fontana smiling broadly.

"Then do it." said Bellheimer loudly.

Fontana called the emergency number Muscanti gave him. The operator said the number was no longer in service.

"The number's no longer in service, I'll try one of his Captains." He gave an operator the number. The operator said that number was no longer in service, also. Fontana resorted to giving names to operators, but nothing worked. Finally, he put the phone down.

Nervously tapping the ashes off his cigarette, he sat staring at the far wall. "It looks like the contact will have to be made in person,"

"When can you do it?" Asked Bellheimer, still pacing.

"I can't, you'll have to go before it's too late," said Fontana rising from his chair.

Bellheimer stopped pacing and turned to face Fontana. "Why me?" He asked, exasperated. "He's your contact."

"He's our contact now," said Fontana loudly. "And because you're a German officer. You can get a pass to Rome, and no one will question you." Then sharply, "Now stop stalling. Get a pass or orders."

"Okay, okay. I'll try to leave tonight. Now give me the information I'll need," said Bellheimer, his voice rising, also.

"Get the pass. I'll have the information when you get back here," said Fontana again tapping a cigarette nervously over an ashtray.

Bellheimer put in a request for a pass to Rome.

"No passes are being authorized due to the fighting," said the Colonel in charge of his section.

Bellheimer returned to Fontana with the bad news. "You will have to go. No passes are being allowed." he said smiling.

"Damn," said Fontana. "I guess this means I'll have to forge one for myself. I'll leave this afternoon."

———

Fontana left for Rome in a staff car. He was stopped several times by Germans, who demanded routine information, but he made it to Rome. Since he wasn't very familiar with Rome, he stopped and bought a cheap map. Muscanti had told him the safe address was near the colosseum on Cavour. He found Cavour and followed it to the address, number thirty-three. He parked the car and knocked on the door.

A man about twenty-five or so answered the knock. He didn't say anything.

"I'm here to see Gus," said Fontana nervously watching the street.

The man flipped a lit cigarette into the gutter and asked, "Do you have a message?"

"Tell him this. The paper mill is gone, and I need some glue."

After a few minutes one of Muscant's captains came to the door.

"Oh, Doctor," he said "Come on in." He shook Fontana's hand and led him to a room on the second floor. Muscanti was waiting for him.

"Fontana, my old friend, welcome." Said Muscanti smiling from a couch. A glass of red wine sat on the table next to him. He rose and crossed the room to Fontana. Both men clasped the other's right hand and reached out with their left hand to the other's shoulder to come together for a friendly hug.

Before Fontana could answer Muscanti pointed to a nearby chair and said, "My old friend please have a seat." And to a man standing near the door, "Bring another glass and a fresh bottle of wine." Then, "How have you been Leonardo?"

"I have been fine. And you?"

"Outside of a few aches and pains, I have been fine also."

"Is there anything serious?"

"No, nothing serious. Now tell me how has the Army been treating you? I heard you were under investigation for murder."

"Yes, but that has been quashed by the Germans. They declared the incident a legitimate act of war."

"Well, that's good, now why have you come to see me? I know it's not just to talk about my health."

The man returned and poured Fontana a glass of wine and freshened Muscanti's.

"I need help to leave the country."

Muscanti held out his glass and Fontana touched his against it. "Salute" said Muscanti obviously in no hurry.

"Salute," said Fontana. And they both took a large swallow of wine.

"I thought you had a plan," said Muscanti, leaning back and crossing his legs at the ankles.

"I did, but my contact has disappeared."

"That is sad, it's getting hard to find people you can trust." Then to the man by the door. "Leave us and close the door. I will ring when I need you." Then to Fontana, "What was your plan?"

"To get to Spain then to the U.S. or South America, maybe Argentina."

"If I remember, you speak English without an accent. Correct?" Said Muscanti as he took another drink of wine.

"Yes, that's right." Said Fontana, pulling out a pack of cigarettes and looking for an ash tray.

"I no longer smoke and don't allow it in my quarters."

"Oh," said Fontana and put the pack back in his pocket.

"I recommend the U.S. Without an accent you should have no problem. A lot of Germans are going to Argentina."

Realizing he was the only one in a hurry, Fontana leaned back and took another drink of wine. Then he asked, "Do you have any connections that can help."

"Yes, I can help you with that."

"There are two of us. One is a German officer I have been working with," said Fontana leaning forward.

Muscanti got up and refreshed both of their glasses of wine then sat back down and said, "I'm like most Italians, I don't like Germans."

"You would probably make an exception for this one, he's pretty ruthless."

"Maybe, but I doubt it."

Muscanti recrossed his legs and took another sip of wine. He stared at Fontana for a long moment then said, "Old friend, for old times' sake I will not charge you anything, but it will cost him one thousand American dollars."

"Thank you, I appreciate what you are doing for me. I have three hundred for him with me now. I'll have the other seven hundred whenever you say."

"How soon do you want to leave?"

"As soon as possible,"

Muscanti pushed a button on the table next to him. "Give me the names you want on the papers. There is a ship in Nalatia. It sails to Spain in three days. Meet me there at Cafe Roma the day after tomorrow at this time. Have the rest of the money with you. Okay?"

"Yes, I will, and we'll be there," said Fontana. "And thanks." He quickly wrote out the names and handed them to Muscanti.

The door opened and the man stood waiting.

Muscanti stood and they again shook hands and hugged.

"Goodbye. I must make the arrangements."

"Goodbye," said Fontana and followed the man back out to the street.

Outside it was nearly dark. Fontana glanced at his map then drove to Garibaldi's home, the barge on a slew just off the main river channel. He parked nearby on a side street. He waited until dark then put a large knife and sheath in his pocket and walked to the barge.

The black-out curtains were closed but light coming from inside could be seen around the edges. The barge was tied tight against large round mooring posts that lined the riverbank next to the street. A short ramp led to the barge. Fontana quickly crossed it and the narrow deck and knocked on the door. No one answered his knock. He knocked louder several times before the door opened as wide as a safety chain would allow.

A woman he could not see asked, "Who's there?"

"Leonardo Fontana. I'm in Rome for the evening and stopped by to pay my respects to Ferdinand. He was my old boss at the prison. Is he by any chance home?"

"Yes, he's on the deck on the other side. I'll tell him you're here."

"Thank you."

Mrs. Garibaldi closed and locked the door then went to the other deck where Garibaldi was having a glass of wine with his former deputy warden, Montinaro.

"One of your employees from the prison is here to see you," she said.

"Who?"

"A man named Fontana. He said he wanted to pay his respects to you."

"Fontana? Don't let him in. Just wait inside, I'll be in to see him in a few minutes." Then to Montinaro, "I can't imagine why he came here to see me. He can be trouble. There's no telling how many of those deaths he signed off as heart attacks at the other facility were caused by him torturing people"

"I agree he was too aggressive."

"I'm leery of him. I heard he got in some trouble in the Army."

"What was it about?"

"I don't know for sure. All I heard was he had some scheme going on about seizing property for back taxes."

"That sounds like him."

"You stay here out of sight. I'll see what he wants."

"Okay. Leave this door open so I can hear. If he tries to cause trouble, I'll be ready."

"Good. Use that paddle leaning against the wall behind you."

A few minutes later Garibaldi answered the door. "Hello, Fontana what are you doing here?" he asked warily. A cane in his right hand helped support his weight.

"I was in Rome for the evening and thought I would like to see you. To pay my respects to my old boss. Are you still working at the Prison?"

"No, I gave that up."

"Dear, why don't you invite him in for a little while? Asked Mrs. Garibaldi.

Garibaldi hesitated, he stood at the door with the chain still on it.

"Look," said Fontana "I'm sorry I disturbed you. Maybe another time would be better. I just wanted to say hello and thank you for giving me a start at the prison. I'll go now," he said and turned to leave.

He lit the kerosene, closed the door, walked up the ramp and gave the barge a push into the stream. He walked a little way toward his car then turned and said aloud, "Who would have thought you, Garibaldi, would deserve such a fine Viking Funeral."

He laughed as the barge engulfed in flames drifted slowly in the stream.

Fontana went back to his headquarters, elated. Two days later Fontana and Bellheimer met Muscanti and the man that smuggled them aboard the ship. It sailed for Spain on May 19, 1944. Fontana and Belllheimer were listed as crew members but did no work.

CHAPTER FIFTEEN

All through the late summer and fall Guido and Vittorino worked on the farm to earn their keep. They helped in the fields and worked with the livestock They picked late apples and pears and loaded the farm wagon but did not go to the town market. They cleaned stalls and pens. In the winter they cut and stacked firewood. They worked on the farm buildings and the equipment. Anything to keep busy. Always looking for the time to return home.

The Traveler came by at least once a week with news. On April 19,1944 he stopped by the barn. Guido and Vittorino were smoking their pipes outside.

"Good afternoon, Traveler," said Guido.

"Good afternoon. Are you two ready to leave this place?" He asked smiling.

"Of course," said Guido. "Is it safe to go home now?"

"No not yet. But do you remember what one of the conditions to receive help from the Underground was?"

"Yes, we agreed to fight if the Underground needed us," said Guido.

"Well, get ready. They are making plans that will probably affect you."

"When?" Asked Vittorino.

"I'm not sure but the allies are pushing the Germans north and they are reducing their strength in this area and around villages including Veranza."

"What should we do to get ready?" Asked Vittorino.

"When the time comes be packed and ready to go. That's about it."

———

After dark on April 30th the Traveler returned.

"The time has come. Be ready to leave in the morning."

"We will," said Guido.

"I'll be here before noon to take you to the meeting place. Men are gathering today and tomorrow. We expect at least one major engagement soon."

———

In the morning about 10:00 the Traveler returned.

"Good morning. Are you ready to go?" He asked.

"Yes," said Guido. "We have said Good-bye to the Barundis and thanked them for letting us stay here."

"Good. I thanked them last night."

"Where will we be going?" Asked Vittorino anxiously slinging his pack over his shoulder.

"About halfway to Veranza. Let's go."

———

They walked until a little afternoon before stopping to eat the bread, boiled eggs and boiled potatoes Mrs. Barundi packed for the trip. An hour later they arrived at an encampment in deep woods. The Traveler took them to meet a man named Vincent.

"Vincent these are the men I told you about last fall, Guido and Vittorino," said the Traveler motioning toward them with his hand.

"Good. I believe you are father and son, eh?" Said Vincent smiling broadly as he rose to shake their hands.

"Yes," said Guido.

"Have a seat." Said Vincent pointing to a bench while he looked them over. Then continuing, "This afternoon I'll find out more details about our mission. Others should be arriving soon. How familiar are you with guns?"

"I would say a little bit. At the place we stayed the Traveler brought by some guns and we fired them." Said Guido.

"What kind of guns were they?"

"One day he brought a pistol," said Guido.

"And another day a shotgun," said Vittorino.

"That's right," said Guido.

"Okay," said Vincent. He turned and entered a nearby tent. A moment later he came out with a pistol and a shotgun.

"Guido, I believe you should have the shotgun. It's a twelve gauge. It holds two shots one for each barrel. It's old but it's good. You must wait until someone gets fairly close to shoot. I will give you some shells later."

"Good. The one we shot only had one barrel."

"Vittorino, if I remember the Traveler said you were fairly good with a pistol. This one is a five shot thirty-eight caliber revolver," he said handing Vittorino the gun. "Here is your ration of shells, fifteen. When you use most of them, come to me for more. But don't worry I will make sure you have enough before each mission. Come with me, now. I'll show you where you'll sleep tonight."

They followed Vincent across a grassy area to a tent about fifty feet away. The tent's opening faced the area they just left.

"This tent is for four men. Two others will be joining us today. Today I need one of you to go with me and four others to do some work." He stopped talking and looked at them.

Vittorino said, "I will go."

"Good, come with me. Guido, we will be back this evening."

Vincent went back to the area they just came from. He went inside and pulled out two large packs. "Here Vittorino you carry one of these. Keep your pistol in one of your pockets."

A few minutes later four men joined them. One man was introduced as Gregorio, one as Diego, one as Felipe and one as the Captain.

The Captain quickly took charge. He looked carefully at the assembled group.

"You men will help set explosives for tomorrow's mission. It is extremely important that we be as quiet as possible. Vincent, do you have everything we need?"

"Yes, everybody brought the packs I gave them this morning. So, we should be ready to go."

"Alright, let's go. Vincent, you lead. Remember keep as quiet as you can."

They walked for a little more than an hour before they stopped. Vincent motioned for the Captain and he came forward.

"Sir, this is the road they have been using," he said standing in the middle of a single lane dirt road.

The Captain moved to the far side of the road where he looked first in one direction then the other. "Do you have a particular spot picked out?" he asked.

"Yes." He turned to his left facing up the hill. "I recommend we go a couple hundred meters farther over the rise ahead. We will have good cover for the attack and after the mission we can retreat to this path."

"Okay, sounds reasonable," said the Captain nodding. Then looking directly at Vincent, he continued, "Before the attack tomorrow I want the entrance to this path camouflaged with fresh cut brush."

"Yes sir, I'll take care of it."

"Good, let's go."

"They walked to the top of the rise and down the other side to a more level area where Vincent stopped and faced the Captain. "They come twice a day bringing supplies to the front. The trees along this route give them cover from allied planes. Where we are now is one of the most open places on the road, but it will still give us enough cover for an attack. They try to hurry through here so they shouldn't notice any small cuts in the road."

"How many charges do you plan to set?" Asked the Captain.

"Six." He pointed to each spot as he talked. "The first one to be detonated will be right here. Its' timing is crucial to stop the column. Then one about a hundred meters in the rear to box them in. Then one on the far side, two in the middle and finally one on the same side as the path we will retreat to."

"Okay. What kind of cover will the men have?"

"If we get here about nine tomorrow morning the men should have about three hours to dig some holes for protection."

"Okay. Let's get started. I want a man to go about three hundred meters in each direction to watch for anyone coming. Vittorino, you go in the direction we just came from. Diego, you go farther on down the road You must watch from where you can see fairly far. If anyone comes, run back to where we can see you and wave. I will be watching from here. Then get off the road. Any questions. None, that's good. Now go." Said the Captain.

Vittorino walked back over the rise and down the other side until he came to a bend in the road where he stopped to watch. Diego did the same thing in the other direction.

At the ambush site Vincent had the men make thin cuts in the road for the wires and dig holes for the charges. After the charges were laid, the men worked to make the ground look as natural as possible. Then the wires were extended another one hundred meters from the road to a central location picked to activate the charges. When the work was completed, the men walked back to the camp site.

When he got back Vittorino told Guido about his day. Guido said they had a meeting in camp about the ambush and that no-one was allowed to leave until the mission was complete. Felipe and Diego were assigned to share the tent with them. Less than an hour after they returned, they ate supper. After supper Vincent held a squad meeting. He named Vittorino assistant squad leader. He passed around a piece of paper that showed how the four squads would be placed along the road. Their squad would be on the right flank. Each squad had eight men. He also handed out more ammunition. Guido received twelve shotgun shells and Vittorino received another fifteen bullets for his pistol.

The next morning everyone was wakened at four thirty. Each man received rations of two biscuits for breakfast and two for lunch.

A Colonel named Altera briefed the men on the mission stating that the objective was to make the Germans realize there was organized resistance behind their lines and therefore more troops would be needed to guard supply routes. He said that after the initial detonation of the explosive charges, one man from each squad would toss hand grenades at the Germans from a forward position. Altera emphasized the importance of everyone listening to their squad leader. He said there was a total of thirty-four men going. He also gave everyone the opportunity to back out. No-one did.

They left for the ambush site at five thirty and arrived at eight thirty. The squad leaders spaced their men out and they began to dig foxholes for protection. Two men to a hole.

Vincent asked for a volunteer to throw the grenades. Vittorino and Felipe volunteered. Vincent chose Felipe. He gave Felipe three hand grenades and placed him about twenty-five meters from the road where he helped him dig a shallow foxhole. He told him to start throwing the grenades as soon as the first charge went off. And when he threw the last grenade to run parallel to the road as far as the path and go down it at least one kilometer and wait for the others to join him.

At noon everyone ate their last two biscuits. At one thirty a column of Germans approached. There were three trucks, each one towed a canvas covered trailer. When the lead truck got directly over the first explosive it detonated blowing the truck upward and sideways on the road where it sat burning. Immediately the rear charge went off. The other two trucks stopped. The men placed forward threw their grenades at the two remaining trucks then ran to their assigned positions.

One was a direct hit. The underground fighters began their small arms fire at the column. The third truck in line was full of soldiers and they emptied out and took up positions on each side of the road. The third charge on the far side of the road was detonated and two of the soldiers were blown into the air. Some of the soldiers moved back toward the truck where they set up a machine gun and began firing in the direction of the small arms fire from the underground. Then the two middle charges were detonated. One of them damaged the third truck. The final charge on the side of the road nearest the underground fighters blew more dust and dirt and momentarily silenced the machine gun. Vittorino fired his revolver and reloaded and fired it again twice more. Guido fired his shotgun but knew he was too far away to do much good. At that point the underground fighters left the scene having destroyed at least two of the trucks and damaged a third. Nine enemy soldiers were killed or wounded.

The four squads met up on the path where Felipe waited. Everyone was accounted for. Nobody was wounded. The ambush was considered a huge success. Colonel Altera believed that the Germans would return with more men and try to hunt them down. When they got back to camp, he disbursed the men. Each man received three days' worth of rations and was told to expect to be contacted soon for another mission.

Vittorino and Guido left with the Traveler. They walked for a day and a half before they arrived at a small farm farther east. They stayed there hidden by the farm family getting out in the daylight only after another two days.

After three days the Traveler left to see others that had fought. He was gone for another five days before he returned, again in the evening.

Vittorino saw him coming and waved. Guido was inside the barn.

"Good evening, Traveler it's great to see you," he said smiling.

"You, too."

They shook hands and Vittorino moved a crude stool close to his. "Be my guest," he said indicating the stool. "I'll get father." A minute later Vittorino and Guido emerged from the barn.

Guido shook Traveler's hand heartily and, while shaking his head, said "We were beginning to worry about you. Did everything go Okay?" Then he sat and began to roll a cigarette. Vittorino moved another stool close.

"Would you like the makings?" Guido asked pulling the tobacco pouch strings to close it while he continued to carefully roll the cigarette.

"Yes, thanks," said the Traveler as he reached for the pouch and papers from Guido. He took a few minutes to roll a cigarette, then they lit their cigarettes from the same match struck by Guido who carefully blew it out.

Each man drew deeply on his cigarette and blew the smoke out into the stagnant evening air.

"What have you learned?" Asked Vittorino leaning forward.

"I was able to contact Colonel Altera and his staff at their homes. The Planner, too. The colonel was right. Two scouts watched the campsite. The Germans did find it and left some booby traps. They followed a deliberate trail we left through the roughest countryside and after two days gave up. We are to meet again in three days."

"Where?" Asked Vittorino anxiously.

"For security reasons I can't tell you yet," said the Traveler again drawing deep on his cigarette. He dragged his stool closer to the barn and balanced himself on the rear legs with his back against the barn. "I am dog tired; do you have any water?"

"Yes," said Vittorino and went to get him a glass. A moment later he returned.

"Thanks. I'll stay here tonight. We'll leave in the morning. I can tell you this, we have located an encampment of Fascists. If they don't leave, they will be our target."

"Why would they leave?" Asked Guido.

"Because the Allies are pressuring, and the Germans are withdrawing north. The Fascists will probably stay close to the Germans for protection."

"Good that means we can return home." Said Guido.

"Probably soon."

Vittorino stood. He looked in earnest at the Traveler. "Who is this Planner and what exactly does he do?"

"The Planner oversees the local Underground. He is very good at organizing. Colonel Altera and one other Colonel take their orders from the Planner."

"I hope this is our last mission. We need to find out what's happening in Veranza. We don't want Fontana and Bellheimer to get away." Said Vittorino.

"I agree," said the Traveler. He finished his cigarette and leaned forward setting his chair on all four legs. He stood up and yawned while he stretched. "I'm going to bed," he said and went into the barn. Vittorino and Guido followed a short while later.

The next next two days they walked westward. The third day they walked in a northwest direction.

"We're getting close to our home." Said Guido.

"Yes. When we meet today, we will be almost directly north of Veranza."

A little after noon they arrived in camp. About half the former group was there. Vittorino was sent a kilometer to the east to prevent a surprise attack from that direction. He was relieved two hours later.

In the evening Colonel Altera received a coded message by courier. The Fascists were seen packing to leave camp. He called an emergency staff meeting to discuss the situation. They knew the Fascists had over forty men and were camped about eight kilometers away. The staff was divided on what to do. Two wanted to attack right away and the other two advised to wait. He called in Vincent to check on the ammunition supply. Vincent said they had enough ammunition but no grenades. Including himself and the staff they had fourteen men in camp. Colonel Altera decided to make a night march to surprise the Fascists early the next morning. He sent out word to eat cold rations, olives, beans, and biscuits and prepare the men to leave in one hour.

Before leaving Colonel Altera called a camp meeting and told the men the situation. He concluded by telling them that it was a dangerous plan and offered anyone the chance to leave with honor. None did. They immediately set out for the Fascist camp. It was the first quarter of a new moon and very dark which slowed the march. When they got within two kilometers they halted and sent out two scouts, Vittorino and Vincent. Vincent led. It took almost two more hours before they were able to get close to the camp. The camp had several small fires when they arrived, but they soon burned down except for one in front of a large tent. The traffic to and from the tent led them to believe the commander was inside. It was another hour or so before they located two guards. One was within a good stone's throw of their position and the other one was on the other side of the camp. Vincent made a simple map of the camp, and they withdrew.

They reported their observations to the Colonel and his staff. They decided to march the whole column to within a few hundred meters of the camp. At that point Vincent and Vittorino were again to get close enough to observe the camp until the guards were changed. When that happened Vittorino was to "silence" the nearest guard and Vincent the one on the far side of the camp.

After the meeting Vittorino met with Guido.

"They want me to kill a guard. I don't know if I can do that" he said with his head in his hands and staring at the ground.

"Think of our family, murdered by Fascists," said Guido putting his arm around his son.

"I have."

"What exactly did they say?"

"They said I was to silence the nearest guard and Vincent the one on the other side of the camp," he replied shaking his head. "I don't know if I can do it."

"You were told to silence the guard, right?"

"Yes," said Vittorino shaking and rocking back and forth.

"Then that's your answer," said Guido his arms outstretched, palms up. "Silence him! Here take some rope and some rags to make a gag. Hit him hard enough to knock him out then tie him up and gag him."

"That's not what they meant."

"Would you rather kill him?"

"I don't know."

"Then take the rags and rope. You can decide when you get close but decide before you attack him. Okay?"

"Yes, yes, I will. Thank you, father."

The Colonel made the two squad leaders check out the group's equipment for noise. Chains and crosses, watches and rings and anything metal was put in pockets and men were made to walk around to make sure nothing rattled or made any noise. Then they marched closer to the camp and Vincent and Vittorino were sent to silence the guards.

It was a long wait before the guards were relieved. When they were, Vincent and Vittorino waited until the guards walked around observing the area before settling down. The one Vittorino was assigned to silence eventually set his weapon on the ground and sat on a stool. Obviously bored, he lit a cigarette and began whittling on a stick. Vittorino made his decision. He crept soundlessly closer, he held his pistol in his right hand and a bayonet in his left. His muscles were taut. The blood running through his temple pounded so loud he felt sure the guard could hear it. He took the last stride quickly and struck the guard hard on the back of the head. He turned slightly then reached out for his weapon and Vittorino struck him on the side of the forehead near the temple. He crumpled from the stool to the ground. Vittorino quickly tied his hands and feet and stuck a large gag of rags in his mouth and tied them at the back of his head. He walked back to the column where he was able to say he had done his duty.

Colonel Altera positioned the men on two sides of the camp then they calmly walked to within a few meters and on signal shot the few men still up. The Fascists began emerging from the tents. The commander ran out of his tent brandishing a pistol and was promptly shot by Vittorino. Guido was close enough that he shot a man who ran from a tent firing wildly in the dark. Vittorino fired again but missed his target. Two ran in the direction of Vittorino and Guido. Vittorino shot one and Guido, his shotgun empty, used it as a club to knock the other man down. While Guido reloaded his shotgun Vittorino ran to the spot and pointed his pistol at him. He did not shoot. The man reached for his rifle, but Vittorino kicked it away and again pointed his pistol at him. “Shoot him.” Said Guido. The man held his hands between the barrel of Vittorino’s pistol and his head which he turned to one side and begged. "Please, don't kill me. They made me do this. Please don't kill me." Vincent came running and said "Shoot him now. We must go." Vittorino looked from his father to Vincent then back to the man. He re-aimed his pistol and shot him in his foot. He picked up the rifle.

Vincent walked calmly over and raised his rifle to shoot the wounded man. Vittorino stepped in between them.

"Move," said Vincent. Motioning to one side with the rifle.

"No," said Vittorino.

"I said move or I will shoot you both," said Vincent his face reddening with anger.

Guido stepped forward. He had a scowl on his face and aimed his shotgun squarely at Vincent, and said menacingly, "You shoot my son, and it will be the last thing you ever do. It's over. Let him be. He will be more trouble to them wounded."

Vincent looked at father and son, both with weapons pointed at him. He smiled then shrugged and lowered his rifle. "Okay. You're probably right."

The whistle blew for retreat. They ran the few hundred yards to their meeting place. Six of their men had been wounded and one was killed outright. The body of the dead man was carried by two of his friends. Colonel Altera ordered Vincent to lead the way south and west in the direction of Veranza . They marched the rest of the night, carrying the dead man and two others on stretchers. By morning one more man died. Close to Veranza Colonel Altera sent for the town doctor. He came and attended to the wounds. Three were not serious but did need cleaned and fresh bandages. Two more were taken in the Doctor's cart to the Infirmary in Veranza where he operated.

Colonel Altera grieved openly over the loss of two of their men. Tears ran down his cheeks as he spoke about them. He called them heroes and said he would put them in for a medal with the new government as soon as he could.

He deemed the operation an overall success. At least eleven Fascists were killed, two by Vittorino and Vincent before the attack, two by Vittorino during the attack and one each by seven other men including Guido, Vincent, and Felipe and the rest by members of the other squad.

After the meeting Vincent asked Vittorino why he did not shoot the man Guido hit with his shotgun. Vittorino said he couldn't. The 'man' he said was only a boy no more than sixteen years old and begged for his life. Vincent did not say anything, he just put his hand on Vittorino's shoulder and nodded his head.

——————

Shortly after the ambushes the Germans moved farther North and people in the villages celebrated. American and English troops were welcomed by all except the Fascists and their sympathizers.

Guido and Vittorino returned to their farm to find people living in Vincenzo and Maria's house. When questioned they said it was abandoned and they had nowhere to go. Guido told them why it was abandoned and said they could remain in the house for a short while.

Then they worked to put their home in a livable state. Most of the furniture was gone or ruined. Vittorino called on the nearest neighbors to borrow a bucket and some soap. They took him to their barn. Inside was much of the furniture and other missing items, including their wagon and even the old horse. They hitched the horse to the wagon and helped with the loading.

"How did you know to come and get this?" Asked Vittorino.

"The traveling partisan told us to come and save what we could for your return," said the husband.

"We thought the underground or looters would get it all."

"We got what we could, but they got more and sold it to fund their cause, so they say."

"My father and I are very grateful to you. I can't describe with words how grateful." He turned and hugged the man and his wife.

He took the first load home. Guido helped unload the wagon onto the veranda. He too was emotional. They worked hard to clean the house then made two more trips for furniture and supplies. At days end their house was clean and furnished though some of the items had originally been Alberto and Sofia's or Vincenzo and Maria's.

The next day Marcus returned home. He had recovered as much as possible in Veranza and was hidden by the police until it was safe to return. It was a happy reunion. Hugs were given freely between father and sons and brothers.

When things settled down and they had eaten Vittorino told them what he had sworn to do about the men responsible for the dreadful day when their family was murdered.

"I agree we must try," said Guido. "But how and where do we start?"

"I have given much thought to how and where we start. I have also thought of the possibility that we were betrayed."

"Betrayed. By whom?" Asked Guido. "Only one person, the Mayor, knew anything about our plans."

"Perhaps more knew. Secrets are hard to keep. People were asked to forge documents and perhaps others knew or guessed what we were trying to do," said Vittorino.

"Who do you mean, may have guessed?"

"Your two friends you used to get to the bank. Especially the one that went to the bank so you could enter without being seen. Also, the banker. He could have checked your safe box before he gave it to you. If he did, he would have known about the cash and the broach," said Vittorino.

"You're right," said Guido letting his open left hand slowly rub from his cheekbone to his chin while nodding slowly. "I never thought about betrayal. What about the mayor?"

"I doubt it. He returned five hundred dollars. He could have kept it and we would never have known. We could eliminate him by asking for our papers."

Guido stood up "Good idea. Let's start in the morning. Right now I'm tired. Let's go to bed." He yawned and stretched, and they went to bed.

CHAPTER SIXTEEN

The next morning Marcus prepared the cart, and they went to the village. When they arrived a large gathering of people were in the square near the bank. The bank was closed. The banker stood in the middle of the crowd. He had been stripped of his clothing down to his underwear. Two large rough ropes extended from his neck, each one controlled by a villager.

Shouts of "Traitor, Fascist dog, and hang him," among others, grew louder and louder.

The chief of police and one of his men managed to make their way to the center of the crowd. The chief raised his arms above his head and brought them slowly downward, bouncing them slightly up and down to quiet the crowd. As he did, he spoke to the banker loud enough for the crowd to hear.

"I have a warrant for your arrest. You are charged with fraud, theft and aiding in false arrests, imprisonments, and murders."

After the announcement the crowd began chanting "Hang him, hang the murderer."

Mayor Davinti was at the edge of the crowd facing the banker and the police. He climbed on a chair from the cafe. “Please,” he said. “Listen to the Chief.”

The Chief told the crowd “The banker will be put in jail and a trial will be held as soon as possible and everyone with evidence can participate.”

Several villagers rushed the police and dragged the banker to the fountain near the edge of the square. They threw one of the ropes over a limb of a nearby large tree. The mayor’s chair was wrested from him and placed under the branch.

“Hang him, hang him,” shouted several in the crowd.

Guido maneuvered the cart close to the fountain. He held the old horse steady. Vittorino stood in the cart and began to speak loudly above the noise of the crowd.

“My father, my brother and I know exactly how you feel. This man may have betrayed us. Seven members of our family were murdered by Nazis and Fascists.”

A man shouted, “Your family along with others will be avenged with his hanging.”

“Yes, that is true. But what about the others?”

“What others?” The man shouted back. “Let’s hang him now.”

“No.” Shouted Vittorino. “I want him punished as much as any of you, but realize he is part of a group that sold out to the Fascists and the Nazis. Kill him now and we will lose his knowledge. Put him in jail and we can use him to find more traitors.”

At this the mayor regained his chair and spoke, "Vittorino is right. We must proceed with the arrest so we can learn more. I assure you he will be punished but it must be according to the law."

A slow murmur went through the crowd. The mayor sensing the worst was over, continued, "Listen, please, let's not do something we will forever be ashamed of. Let's do the right thing here today. Let today be the day we start to root out other criminals. Some may be people we don't even suspect. Please go home. Let the police do their job and the court do its' job. If you don't want to go home, then come to my cafe. I will provide free coffee and cake as long as it lasts." At this the mayor got down from his chair and began walking to his cafe. He motioned for Guido and his sons to join him. They tied the horse and followed the mayor and so did many others from the crowd.

The Chief of police and his officer untied the ropes and led the banker to the village jail.

Inside the cafe the Mayor motioned for Guido and his sons to sit at a table near the kitchen door. The cafe soon filled with people from the square. Many stopped at the Sabatini table. Some to offer condolences for their losses and others to welcome them back home. Most seemed relieved that the villagers did not hang the banker. The Mayor and his wife and two daughters busied themselves serving coffee and cakes. The Sabatinis were the last to be served because the Mayor wanted to join them. He spoke directly to Vittorino, "You did a fine job helping to calm the crowd."

"We feel we were betrayed and want all that are connected to be caught and punished," said Vittorino.

"The papers you had prepared for us. Do you still have them?" Asked Guido.

"Yes. I have the ones for you three and two others," said the Mayor.

"What happened to the other five sets?"

"They were given to others to help in their escape."

"We want our papers and the other two sets," said Guido.

"As you wish. When this crowd thins out, I will get them for you."

"Did you suspect the banker?" Asked Vittorino.

"Yes. We suspected him but we couldn't do anything about it."

"Couldn't or wouldn't?"

"A little of both, probably. If he had been dealt with earlier others would have been alerted. By letting him operate until today we gained more information about them."

"Are you at liberty to talk about others?" Asked Guido.

"Not yet. More arrests are coming," said the mayor. He thought for a moment then said "I will give you an example. One of those that wanted the banker hung will be arrested. He is afraid the banker will talk, that's why he wanted him hung today. He probably believed if it was quick, he might escape prosecution."

Vittorino spoke softly. "Marcus can identify the Major and the German officer that murdered our family."

"I don't know very much about that except that the police have filed charges and warrants have been issued," said the Mayor.

"The Italian officer that tried to stop it is Lieutenant Giuseppe Arturo. We want…

Before Vittorino could finish the mayor interrupted saying "Lt. Arturo is setting up an office here tomorrow. Since Italy surrendered the Americans wanted to keep order. The Italian army in the liberated zones is doing that now."

"Where is he going to set up the office?" Asked Guido.

"In a vacant store on the opposite side of the square."

The Sabatinis and the Mayor conversed for an hour or more, until the crowd in the cafe thinned out considerably. Then the Mayor left to get the papers that Guido requested. It wasn't long before he returned. He handed Guido two passports for each person, one Italian to be used to get to Spain and one Spanish passport to be used to leave Spain.

"We thank you for trying to help us leave Italy and for what you did to help us at our farm that terrible day. You have been more than a mayor you have been a good friend to our family," said Guido.

"You are very welcome and if there is anything else I can do, let me know."

Outside the cafe, Vittorino spoke "Let's walk to the other side of the square. I would like to see where Lieutenant Arturo will be making his office."

"I agree," said Guido.

Once there they located the vacant shop. While standing in front of it an army truck pulled up next to them. Three soldiers got out, two privates and Lieutenant Arturo. The Sabatinis immediately recognized him and hailed him as he went to open the shop. Lt. Arturo turned and walked to them. He recognized them and began to apologize for the atrocities committed against their family.

"I am sorry, so very sorry for the loss of your family. I thought I could stop it by refusing Major Fontana's orders, but I was wrong. He had German soldiers hidden in the other truck, about a dozen. They mounted a machine gun and opened fire. I thought they would kill us, too but they didn't. I filed charges against Fontana and the Germans, but the Nazis wouldn't allow them to proceed. They called it a 'Legitimate act of war'. Can you believe it? Fontana even filed charges against me. As ridiculous as it seems they are still open. The three men with me that day have given sworn statements about what happened. Please believe me we did not harm your family."

"We know you refused the Major's orders. My son Marcus survived the attack. Neighbors found him and called a doctor and the police. He received treatment late that morning, otherwise he would not have lived. This is him." Guido put his hand on Marcus' shoulder.

"We want to know everything we can find out about Major Fontana and the German officer that ordered the murders," said Vittorino.

"Of course, I will tell you what I know about Major Fontana. He went to the University in Naples where he studied to be a doctor, I don't know if he finished school or not. He spouted off often about his role as a doctor in the prison system. He was a real Fascist and he hated Jews, that's for sure. Since he fled, I've talked to some of the men that knew him in the prison system. They said he was vicious with prisoners, torturing for confessions and sometimes just for the pleasure of doing it. He preyed on the women, sometimes keeping them for sex, before sending them for trial. One thing, he cut off the ring fingers of two women he killed. They said he would laugh about it saying he kept them for souvenirs."

"That's what he did with my mother and grandmother and aunt," said Vittorino.

"Where is he now?" Asked Guido.

"No one knows for sure. A few of the Germans at the local staff level decided to surrender to the Americans. They gave detailed statements including information about Major Fontana and Lieutenant Bellheimer. According to them Bellheimer was bad but not nearly as bad as Fontana. One of the Germans said he was part of a plan to escape to either South America or the United States, but he backed out because he was afraid of Fontana."

"These Americans. Do you think we could talk to them or are they hard to get along with?" Asked Vittorino.

"I have an unofficial relationship with the American Captain that did most of the questioning. His name is Johnson,

Captain Albert Johnson. He doesn't speak German and very little Italian. I sometimes interpret for him. He will be here tomorrow to inspect the office."

"An American inspecting an Italian office. How did that come about?" Asked Vittorino.

"It's simple they're in charge."

"Is that good or bad?"

"It's a lot better than Germans in charge. They don't go around looking for trouble, but they aren't afraid of it either. Sort of a lot like Italians. As a matter of fact, there are a lot of Italian Americans in their army."

"We will be here tomorrow morning. Do you think we can talk to this Captain Johnson?" Asked Guido.

"Come by and we'll see."

On the way home Marcus asked Guido, "Papa what do you know of these Americans?"

"In general, I liked most of them. They were pretty easy going and not as demanding as some of the tourists we sold to."

CHAPTER SEVENTEEN

The next morning Guido and Vittorino arrived at Arturo's office at ten A.M.

"Good morning. I spoke to Captain Johnson by radio yesterday after you left. He said he would bring whatever information he had about Major Fontana and the German Lieutenant," said Arturo.

At eleven thirty the Americans arrived. There were four of them. Captain Johnson, sergeant Mueller, private Ranier and an interpreter, corporal Harding. Lieutenant Arturo introduced everyone. The American sergeant and private went about inspecting the office while the others talked.

Guido sat on the edge of his chair and blurted out, "I demand to know all the information you have about Major Fontana and the German Lieutenant."

The American interpreter relayed the message to Captain Johnson. Captain Johnson's friendly demeanor vanished. At first, he looked astonished. He paused for a moment. Then he scowled at Guido and was very blunt. "I don't like your attitude, you have no standing here whatsoever, and for that matter neither does Italy. Now you better leave," he said looking directly at Guido.

Lieutenant Arturo angrily turned to Guido. He raised his voice to a near shout and interpreted word for word Captain Johnson's reply then added, "What in the name of God do you think you are doing? I have asked, I repeat asked, this man for his help. Understand this if he will let you stay there will be no more demanding anything. Is that clear?"

Guido put his hands on his face before he spoke. "Yes, yes. Please explain I am, we are, just so anxious to find these men. I apologize. I know better, I assure you it won't happen again."

The interpreter relayed the full conversation between Arturo and Guido. Captain Johnson got up to leave. Arturo put his hand on his sleeve, "Please stay Captain and let these good people stay, also."

"Why?" Asked Johnson obviously angry.

"Because you are our only source for information about these murderers and we need you," said Arturo still seated and with his hand still on Johnson's sleeve.

Vittorino dismayed at the turn of events and anxious to save the meeting said, "I'm sorry for my father's rude outburst but he is consumed with grief. These men led by Fontana murdered his wife, his mother and father, his brother and sister-in-law and two nephews."

Captain Johnson sat back down. "I know. You have my total sympathy. I am here to help you if I can. But I will not listen to demands."

"Thank you," said Vittorino. Guido repeated his son's 'thank you'.

"Now, what is it I may be able to tell you that I haven't already told Lt. Arturo?" Said Captain Johnson opening his briefcase.

"First, can you confirm the name of the German officer?" Asked Vittorino reading from a prepared list.

"We believe he is lieutenant Bellheimer."

"May I ask where you obtained your information? I'm sorry I should have asked that first."

"The German headquarters group in Naftalia left shortly before our troops arrived. Some of their soldiers deserted to our side. We also overran Lt. Arturo's headquarters group. Since the King had kicked Mussolini out of power some of the Italian armed forces came over to our side. Many Italians knew about Fontana and Bellheimer's exploits. Lt. Arturo was able to identify several of the headquarters deserters. They were very willing to talk."

"Can you tell us where Bellheimer or Fontana are now?"

"No, I don't think anyone can. But I will tell you what I have found out. Apparently, they were very close. When our troops broke out from Anzio and approached Rome Fontana and Bellheimer saw the handwriting on the wall, so to speak. They began to make escape plans. One of the men that was supposed to go with them decided at the last moment not to go through with the plan. He was afraid Fontana would kill him."

"Do you know their plans for sure?"

"So far, the information you are asking for I already gave to Lt. Arturo. I'm sure he resents you asking the same questions he may have already given you the information about," said Johnson, looking from Vittorino to Arturo.

"I'm sorry but these are questions we have had for a long time," said Vittorino.

"It does not bother me that some of this information I may have already mentioned," said Arturo.

"O.K. said Johnson. The anti-fascists aren't the only ones with an underground network. There are also fascists. Their resources are very similar. The three of them contacted the fascist underground. They had papers made up. Italian passports to get to Spain and Spanish passports to leave Spain to travel to Argentina or the U.S. Fontana preferred the U.S. but Bellheimer preferred Argentina. Money was no problem, they had both robbed for years."

"Where is the third one. The one that surrendered?"

"He is in a prisoner of war camp, near Naples."

"Was he involved in the murders?"

"No, we don't believe so. He worked directly for the local commandant. He stayed at headquarters."

"How do you know?" Asked Guido.

"The soldiers with Arturo on that day all say he wasn't there, Arturo, also."

"Where do you think they are now?" Asked Vittorino.

"We believe they are in Spain or maybe Portugal. Nobody knows for sure."

"How would they get there?" Asked Guido.

"We believe by cargo ship well south of the American lines. Perhaps from Naples or Salerno or further south."

"How can this be, we are at war?" Asked Vittorino.

"Italy needs food. Cargo vessels bring in food from other parts of the Mediterranean Sea area. Spain and Portugal are allowed to send food, only. When they leave Italy to return, people could be smuggled aboard," said Johnson.

"So, they have slipped away," said Guido.

"So far. We have issued warrants. We know the names on their Italian passports. Fontana's is Davani and Bellheimer's is Bellamy."

"What are the chances of catching them?" Asked Vittorino.

"Not good. They are not a high priority with the allies and apparently they have plenty of hard currency, dollars and pounds. All we can do is try and hope they will make a mistake that they can't talk their way out of."

"Do you know their names on the Spanish passports?" Asked Guido.

"No. We can only hope the names are the same," said Captain Johnson.

"How did you find out the names on the Italian passports?" Asked Vittorino.

"From a fascist prisoner. He knew the names on the Italian passports but not the Spanish ones."

Sergeant Mueller finished his inspection and spoke to Captain Johnson, "I believe there is plenty of space for us to have a small office in the rear if we can get a partition built. That would leave space for the Italians in the front. The only thing is records security. Good solid locks are needed."

Captain Johnson turned to Arturo, "We need you to take care of getting the partition built. We will provide the locks. When records are stored here involving the names and information concerning Fascists or Nazis or any other classified information, the office must be guarded until the records are transferred to our main office."

"I understand. But I only have four people including myself," said Arturo.

"That's enough people," said Captain Johnson.

Guido turned to Vittorino "Do we have any more questions for Captain Johnson?"

"Only one. Can you help us get on a ship going to Spain?"

"No. I don't have any authority and I doubt if the U.S. army would be sympathetic. It's like I said before it isn't a high priority and the red tape would be a mile long, sorry."

"I understand," said Vittorino.

"I wish I could be more help," said Captain Johnson. Then he asked the question on everyone's mind. "Will you try to pursue Fontana and Bellheimer without any official government help or blessing?"

"We will have to think about that," said Guido.

"If you do, I can possibly help get you through to the south where you may find a ship willing to take you to Spain," said Captain Johnson.

"Thank you. We will discuss all of this. Thank you again for your help."

"You are welcome." Then to Mueller, "Show me your planned office layout."

Guido and his sons left the meeting with mixed feelings. On the way home they discussed Captain Johnson's offer, but no plans were made.

CHAPTER EIGHTEEN

Vittorino

During the next few days plans to pursue Fontana and Bellheimer were discussed. Finally, Vittorino said he planned to go to Spain. Guido said he should go, not Vittorino. But Vittorino argued that Guido was needed to work with the Mayor and Arturo to make sure the government voided the paperwork filed by Major Fontana transferring the title for the farm to the government. Guido finally relented and gave almost all the hard currency he had to Vittorino. He only kept one hundred dollars he felt might be necessary for bribes to make the title restoration go smoother.

Guido suggested that they should again contact the mayor for help to arrange passage to Spain, but Vittorino argued against doing that saying the mayor knew they had at least five hundred dollars and as middleman might want to make a profit. Instead, he suggested they should first talk to the Traveler who still came by but less frequently. Guido agreed.

When the Traveler did come, they gave him food and asked for his help.

Vittorino told him their overall plans and asked for contacts in Naples to help him get passage to Spain on a ship. He also asked for help in Spain.

The Traveler said he would get with the underground the next day.

Before he left Guido reminded him to thank the underground for all their help and to please mention that they had participated in two engagements against the Germans and Fascists.

Early the next morning Vittorino and Guido went to Veranza to see Lt. Arturo. They asked him to contact Capt. Johnson to see if the help he mentioned was still possible. Arturo assured them the next Friday, a mere three days away, Captain Johnson would return to Veranza and they were free to come and meet with him again. They pressed Arturo to contact Capt. Johnson by telephone since the lines had been repaired. Arturo called Capt. Johnson. He said he would do what he could to arrange the help they needed but he would need a few days' notice to make arrangements.

Guido and Vittorino thanked Lt. Arturo then walked across the square to the mayor's cafe. Guido, ever suspicious, wanted to see what the mayor knew, if anything.

Inside the cafe the patrons were more animated with their conversations. Cakes were on tables. The coffee smelled stronger, and the smell of food cooking rolled from the kitchen.

The mayor's wife greeted them with a hearty "Good morning."

"Good morning to you," said Guido.

"What can I get you?" She asked.

"Two coffees and small cakes, please," said Guido.

She went to the counter where cakes and a pot of coffee waited. She deftly handled the cakes with one hand and the coffee and cups with the other.

"Did you want to see the Mayor?" She asked while pouring the coffee.

"Not if he's busy. We're just here to drink coffee," said Guido as nonchalantly as he could.

"I'll tell him you're here," she said and disappeared into the kitchen.

Quickly the Mayor came out to greet them, wiping his hands on his apron before shaking hands with them.

"Gentlemen, what can I do for you?" Said the Mayor sitting down at the table.

"Nothing that I can think of," said Guido looking wryly at Vittorino.

"Are you sure?" Asked the Mayor. The expression on his face seemed to be questioning the answer from Guido.

"Yes, at the moment we just want coffee and some of your wife's delicious cakes," said Guido. "The only other thing I can think of is your continuing support to help with voiding the illegal transfer of our farm to the former national government."

"Of course. I don't think that will be a major problem," said the Mayor.

"I have applied to the Magistrate but have not heard anything," said Guido.

"Sometimes these things take a little more time than we think they should," said the Mayor.

"Do you think we could shorten the timeline? I would like to rent the houses of my father and brother, and I may even have to evict some squatters living there now."

"I believe you would be safe to go ahead and rent the houses. In the meantime, I will continue to work in your behalf on the property transfer matter. Again, I ask you is there anything else I can do for you?" A knowing look was on his face.

Guido and Vittorino pretended not to notice, and Guido replied, "Nothing at the present, your honor."

"Very well. I must get back to my cooking, goodbye."

"Goodbye," said Guido.

"He knows," said Vittorino.

"Yes, someone told him of our plans. The question is did he tell the others about our dollars or did he keep that information to himself," said Guido.

"What do you think?" Asked Vittorino.

"I think there was no real advantage to the Mayor for him to tell. Surely, he wants to make a deal himself, for a price," said Guido.

"For the five hundred dollars he knows about?"

"Probably, but now he knows there may be more players. He cannot go back to the Underground and tell them about the five hundred dollars now. It's too late. He would lose credibility. He's in a tight situation and he knows it. If he thinks about it, he may offer us a better deal. We'll see. In the meantime, let's see what the others have to say."

"This seems to me like it could be a dangerous game to be playing," said Vitorino.

"It could be, but we hold pretty good cards. If you remember the underground helped us before without asking for money. That means the Mayor didn't tell them about us having American money then. That makes twice he didn't tell. They don't like that. Now what he has to hope is that if we deal directly with someone else in the underground, we don't let it slip about him knowing about the dollars. Let's see what happens."

On Sunday morning the Traveler returned but this time he had another member of the underground with him known to them only as the Planner. The Traveler started to introduce the Planner, but he stopped him saying, "I remember Guido and Vittorino they were both active in our cause. It's good to see you both."

"It is very good to see you Planner," said Guido. "I hope this means our request has been approved."

"It is my wish that we may lay the plan outline today. Your contact said you need help with passage on a ship to Spain and help in Spain. Is this correct?" The Planner looked from father to son.

"Yes," said Vittorino. "I will be leaving to find the men that murdered our family."

"What is your final destination?" Asked the Planner.

"America. We believe they are going to America."

"How do you know they are going to America? Many leaving to escape prosecution are going to South America, especially Argentina," said the Planner.

"Fontana, the Italian was known to favor America," said Guido.

"How do you know this?"

"From an American army captain, Captain Johnson. He interrogated some German headquarters staff that worked with Lieutenant Bellheimer and Major Fontana. He also interrogated some prison staff where Fontana used to work. They told him the same thing, that Fontana wanted to get to America. He even volunteered to go as a spy. He speaks very good English, with little or no Italian accent," said Vittorino.

"This Captain Johnson, can he be any help?" Asked the Planner.

"Yes. He will get me through the allied lines to Naples or Salerno, but I need help with the passage," said Vittorino.

"I will tell you this now. We have tried to locate both, Fontana and Bellheimer, but they have slipped away. The fascists have helped them and will continue to help them get passage out of Spain. As you may know General Franco is officially neutral in this war, but he helps Fascists when he can. One other thing you should know, since you won't be helped by the Fascists you may be a suspected anti-fascist and could run into trouble there. We don't have a strong network in Spain. You could be killed."

"I am determined to find these men," said Vittorino.

"I understand. But let me offer you a reasonable alternative, one that I believe will work better for you."

Vittorino sighed and looked skeptical at the Planner. He was about to speak when Guido spoke "What is this reasonable alternative that you say will work better?"

"Your contact, here with us now, said you believe Fontana and Bellheimer may have left Italy as much as four weeks ago, or maybe more," said the Planner.

"That's correct. We don't know for sure," said Guido.

The Planner looked directly at Vittorino and spoke. "The chances of you catching these men in Spain is almost zero. They will have contacts, you don't. They have at least a four-week head start on you and by the time you could sail to Spain they will probably be five or even six weeks ahead of you."

"I know. But I don't know what else to do."

"I do," said the Planner. "If you really believe they will go from Spain to America then you can possibly make up much of that time by going directly from Italy to America. Of course, it depends on checking ship schedules from both Spain and Italy to America, when and where they go, but it just might work out for you."

"That does sound like a possible alternative," said Vittorino.

"Now when can this Captain Johnson help you?"

"He needs a few days' notice."

"To make the arrangements you must be the local messenger. I will give you a note to give to a local helper. It will get you a passport. It will also contain instructions to get information about ships sailing from Spain and Italy to America. All the recent ones and the next few weeks schedules," said the Planner.

"I already have a passport," said Vittorino.

"Is it real or counterfeit?"

"I don't know."

"Get it, I'll check," said the Planner.

Vittorino went to his bedroom and returned with his passport.

The planner looked it over then said, "Did the mayor get this for you?"

"Yes."

"I thought so. This was prepared by a member of the Underground working in the passport office. It is real. I suspect it cost you quite a bit, too?"

"Yes," said Guido. "To us it was a lot. We don't have much."

"Don't worry. The mayor will be the one you will give my note to. He will be instructed to make the arrangements. For you to get on an American-Bound ship, you will be listed as a Sicilian needing work. He will get you another passport.

When you get it, destroy this one. I assure you the mayor will be very helpful and this time there will be no charge. After all, you fought with the partisans and you will be helping us by finding these two in America," said the Planner.

"Why Sicilian?" Asked Guido.

"Because Sicily has been under Allied control much longer. The Americans seem to feel much better about dealing with Sicilians. They don't know much about 'The Brotherhood.'"

At this they all laughed.

The Planner began to work in earnest on the note to the mayor. When he finished, he rose from his chair and handed it to Guido.

"Put this in an envelope and seal it. Give this to the mayor today. When he finishes reading it, he will ask you who gave you the note. You are to say you don't know the name of the person that gave it to you."

He waited until Guido did as instructed then said, "I will be back on Wednesday afternoon, goodbye."

"Goodbye," they repeated.

Guido and Vittorino hitched up the old horse and started for Veranza. It was close to noon when they arrived at the square. Feeling no fear of discovery, they proceeded directly to the cafe. It was closed until noon because it was Sunday.

They waited in the shade of the old Maple tree that had held the hangman's noose a few days earlier. Soon church bells rang out announcing the noon hour. Still, they waited a while longer. At last, the cafe opened, and they crossed the street.

They were among the first to enter and immediately went to a table near the kitchen.

The mayor's wife spotted them and came to take their order ahead of others. Guido ordered coffees and asked her to tell the mayor of their presence. While sipping their coffees the mayor joined them at their table. "Good morning gentlemen," said the Mayor.

"Good morning, Mayor. I have some business I need to discuss with you," said Guido.

"I thought you might want some help. Come in the kitchen where we can plan in private." They followed the Mayor to the small table at the rear of the kitchen.

"It is my understanding you or maybe Vittorino will be going after the ones who murdered your family. Is that correct?"

"Yes. Vittorino will be the one to go," said Guido, looking from the Mayor to his son.

"Very well. You must realize that it will be very expensive to make the necessary arrangements for transport to a port and get Vittorino on a ship to Spain. I assume that's where you want to go."

Guido gave a knowing look at Vittorino. They both smiled slightly.

The Mayor continued, "You already have the passport. It will take time, and as I said quite a bit of money. I hope you still have the dollars from before."

"Yes. We still have some dollars," said Guido.

"Good. I will start to make contacts tomorrow."

"I think you may want to read this before we make any more plans," said Guido as he handed the envelope to the Mayor.

The letter was quite succinct: "We have met with the bearers of this note. They were soldiers in the fight in the region. They need assistance. You are instructed to help them accordingly. They have transport arranged to get Vittorino to Naples when needed. You are to do the following:

1. Determine what ships, if any, are leaving Italy for America.
2. Use our contacts to find out if we can get Vittorino on board as a Sicilian seaman. If so, make the arrangements and get a passport made for Vittorino as a Sicilian.
4. Get the schedules of all ships that have left Spain for America in the last month and those that will be leaving in the next few weeks.
5. You are to meet with our representative at the Sabatinis on Wednesday at 5pm.
6. There will be no charge for this service.
7. You are to ask the Sabatinis 'who gave you this note'. They should say they don't know the name of the person. Burn the note after you memorize it." T.P.

Guido and Vittorino studied the Mayor's face as he read. A veil came down across it. His shoulders sagged. He did not smile when he finished.

"It looks like things have been decided for us. I am to ask you 'Who gave you this note. What is his name?"

"We don't know his name," said Guido.

"I will do my best to complete the requests in this letter. I will see you on Wednesday at 5 o'clock."

"Here?"

"No, at your place. There will be a meeting to finalize plans. Now go have some lunch. No charge. No charge for anything. Forget what I said about expenses to get you on board ship."

"Thank you," said Guido.

"Very well. I must start this now."

He was rereading the note when they left the kitchen. He burned it and scattered the ashes outside.

The Sabatinis accepted the mayor's offer of a free lunch. Afterward they walked across the square to see if Lt. Arturo was working. He was not, only one soldier was in the office, and he did not know when Arturo would return.

Back at the cart Vittorino removed a bucket and filled it at the fountain for the old horse. It was hot and the horse drank deeply. Then they returned to the farm.

The next two days passed without incident. On Wednesday morning Guido went to Alberto's house to make arrangements with the squatters living there.

"You are welcome to stay in this house, but you must pay rent or work on the farm," said Guido.

The father and son laughed at Guido. The father said, "We will not work without pay and we will not pay rent."

"Then you better get ready to leave."

They laughed and sneered at him. The father waved a sickle and said, "You come back to my house again and I will make you eat this sickle for rent."

Guido did not reply but walked across the large field to his barn. He climbed the ladder to the loft where he picked up the old shotgun given to him by the underground when he and Vittorino returned home. It was the old double barrel 12 gauge. He took shells from a shelf and loaded it, then walked slowly back to Alberto's house. This time he did not knock. He shot one of the chickens in the yard. The squatters came to the door, but none ventured out.

"You don't scare us. You can't shoot us. You have no title to this land now," said the father.

"This is your last warning. I asked you to work on the farm or pay rent, now I'm telling you to leave while you still can." Guido raised the shotgun. The squatter closed the door. Guido walked closer and fired from the patio. He blew a hole in the door. Immediately a scream was heard from inside.

"Please stop," said a woman's voice.

"All of you out here now," said Guido.

They filed out. The father and mother, two boys and a girl.

"Now," said Guido. "Get your stuff out of this house, all of it. I will be back in an hour. Be ready to go and have the house cleaned."

"I was hit when you fired, I need a doctor," said the father.

"Send one of your boys to Veranza to get the doctor. The rest of you get busy. Remember I mean business." He returned home. An hour later he returned to inspect the house. It was fairly clean but did not suit him.

"Clean it again," he told the wife and daughter. The father sat on the patio.

"Get off my patio." Guido told the father.

"We will do as you requested. We will work," said the father as he moved off the patio.

"I gave you a chance. You refused to work or pay rent. Now you must go. You have a hand cart, load it and get going. Take only your possessions. If I ever see any of you on this farm again or if anything happens to one of these buildings, or to my livestock, or to anything on this farm, I will come for you. I will find you and I will kill all of you. Is that clear?"

"Yes," said the father staring at the ground.

Guido looked at the others. They quickly nodded.

"Remember this. You are known and I will find you. There will be no mercy. Now finish cleaning this house and leave."

Vittorino came to the house to check on his father.

"Let's go they have been warned," said Guido.

When they got out of earshot Vittorino asked his father "Would you shoot them?"

"I don't know, I only know I am very tired of people. I need a rest from people."

"Will you be able to deal with the government about the farm?" Asked Vittorino.

"Yes. The mayor, chief of police, Lt. Arturo and his soldiers have given sworn statements. The mayor says he will push it himself."

"For a price," said Vittorino.

"Originally yes. But I don't think so now. You saw the look on his face when he read the note from the Planner. I believe he will be afraid to ask for money. I will bring it up when we meet this afternoon."

The mayor arrived a little early for the 5 o'clock meeting. He rode in a cart driven by one of his sons. They were greeted by Guido.

"Please have a seat in the shade of the patio," said Guido smiling.

"Thank you."

"Would you like some wine, or would you prefer water?" Asked Guido.

"Water, please. I need a clear head for the meeting."

A little after 5 o'clock The Planner arrived.

"Hello, my friend," said Guido smiling.

"Hello to you Guido and to you Mayor Davinti,"

"Good afternoon, Planner," said the Mayor.

"Please everybody come inside," said Guido.

He put some bread and cheese on the old table from Vincenzo's kitchen. He also offered wine. The Planner and the

Traveler accepted. The Mayor said he preferred only the water he already had. Marcus and the Mayor's son accepted water. When everyone had settled down the Planner asked Marcus and the Mayor's son to go back outside to the patio.

"Mayor what have you been able to find out?" Asked the Planner.

"Three ships have left Spain for America in the last four weeks. 'The Emerald Sea' should have docked in New York on May 20th, 'The Caspian' should have docked in New York on May 23rd and the last one, the 'El Dorado', should dock in New Orleans, Louisiana on June 9. I was not able to confirm if either of the wanted men was on board any of the ships. I was able to confirm that all the sailors had Spanish passports. I have no information about passengers. There is one more ship, 'The Liberty' set to sail on the 30th of June. All the crew is said to have Spanish passports and it is said to have no passengers. Its' destination is also New Orleans and it's due to dock on July 24th."

"What information do you have regarding Italian ships leaving for America?" Asked the Planner, taking notes.

"The only ship leaving Italy for America is 'The Palermo'. It's due to sail from Naples on July 3rd and due to dock in New Orleans on July 29. I have a Sicilian passport for Vittorino, he could be registered as a sailor on 'The Palermo' if he can be in Naples and working by June 20th to establish himself as a crew member," said the Mayor scanning the room as he talked.

"After working on this and talking to people what are your thoughts to proceed?" Asked the Planner.

"I believe they would not have gone to New York. What I hear is harbor security is very high there. I think New Orleans is the best bet for Vittorino to catch them or to find out where they went. It is a slim chance, but it is the best chance," said the Mayor. He shrugged and tilted his head slightly and raised his hands from the table as if to say 'who knows'.

"I agree," said the Planner. Then he busied himself making notes before he spoke.

"This is the plan. Vittorino, you will leave Veranza with Captain Johnson's help on the 15th. When you arrive in Naples go to the dock area on La Plaza Columbus. There you contact a fish and seafood vendor named Rossalini at the open-air market. We will contact him ahead of time, so he will be expecting you. Rossalini's stall is gray and trimmed in green. You say to him, 'Do you have any unusual fish?' He will ask, 'What kind of fish do you want?' You say 'Whale'. He will say 'Whale is not a fish'. Then he will give you instructions when and where to meet a man with your seaman's papers on the 16th or 17th. Mayor Davinti I want you to make the final arrangements with Rossalini. You have done this before, so you have the necessary contacts. Agreed?" He gave the Mayor a steady look.

"Agreed," said the Mayor nodding his head quickly.

"Now, Vittorino you must go to Veranza tomorrow to make the arrangements with Captain Johnson for transportation to Naples," said the Planner.

"Yes sir, first thing tomorrow morning."

"Mayor Davinti is there any progress on negating the false sale of our farm?" Asked Guido.

"Yes. I'm glad you asked, it is going very well, and we are able to move it without any cost since it was clearly an illegal transfer to the government," said the Mayor quickly.

"My sons and I wish to thank you Planner and you Mayor Davinti for all your help, and you too, Traveler for your help, also."

"You are certainly welcome," said the Planner.

"Yes, very welcome," said the Traveler.

"Yes, certainly," said the Mayor.

The next morning Vittorino and Guido met with Lt. Arturo who called Captain Johnson. He said he would work on the arrangements to transport Vittorino to Naples on the 15th.

On the 15th Guido and Marcus took Vittorino to the Mayor's Cafe early. He gave them nothing in writing and only said the instructions had not changed since the Wednesday meeting. He shook Vittorino's hand and wished him luck. They then went to Lt. Arturo's office where he had an American Army Jeep waiting. Lt. Arturo shook Vittorino's hand and wished him luck. The sergeant driving the jeep was ready to leave.

"I love you both and I shall miss you very much," said Vittorino.

The three hugged each other in a hard embrace. Each promised to write once Vittorino was established in America.

Vittorino climbed in the Jeep and left on his long journey. All Vittorino had to identify Fontana and Bellheimer was a picture taken of them in Fontana's office. It was a fairly good close-up. He was determined to put the picture to good use in his search for the men that carried out the murders of his family.

CHAPTER NINETEEN

Deception

Fontana and Bellheimer worked hard to erase any accents from their speech. Fontana had been working on it for years and had no problem. Bellheimer tried hard but the going was slow, so Fontana did most of the talking.

In New Orleans they bought tickets for New York City. But when they reached Baltimore they changed to Ithaca, New York. Ithaca was a small city, but Olivier and Barnwell University's main campus was there.

Through correspondence before the U.S. involvement in the war Fontana, posing as Dr. Giuseppe Montanari, developed an informal relationship with Miss Jeanette Strube a clerk in the University's records office. He requested and received a photo from her. As he hoped, she did not appear very pretty. He avoided sending one of himself claiming he did not have a good one. He wrote that he intended to visit the U.S. and would like to see her when he did. She wrote back immediately encouraging him to come as soon as his military obligations were over. After the U.S. declared war, all communication between the U. S. and Italy was discontinued.

Now, he planned to exploit the knowledge gained in the prior relationship to help him secure the necessary credentials as a psychiatrist.

When they arrived in Ithaca Fontana insisted the first thing to do was locate the college. The next thing they located was Miss Strube's apartment. It was on Elm Street about a mile from the college. They rented an apartment a few blocks from hers. Then they began to observe her actions and habits. After work she usually went straight home and stayed there. Occasionally a man would come by in a car and pick her up, usually on a Friday or Saturday about 7 P.M. Where he took her, they did not know. They usually returned about 9 or 9:30. He was allowed in but did not stay more than an hour or so and never overnight. Saturdays she sometimes walked to a nearby park and read. If there was an exhibit at the college she usually went, mostly with another woman from the college and sometimes with her male companion. They discovered he also worked at the college.

Fontana bought an old car but needed a ration card to get gasoline. Not able to get a card, he bought gasoline on the black market.

Finally, after a few weeks he decided to make his move. Flyers posted on the campus and around town advertised an art exhibit at the university. Fontana bought a ticket for the 2 PM Saturday showing.

He arrived at precisely 2 PM. He wanted her to notice he was already there when she arrived if she came. Jeanette arrived shortly after 2 PM. There weren't many people already in attendance. She noticed Fontana, he seemed to be moving through the gallery very slowly. Others went around him. Soon she caught up to him. When she did, he said casually how much he appreciated the show especially the sculpture, something he knew she did as a hobby. She said yes, she agreed. They moved along together, slowly, chatting and making comments as they went. He introduced himself as Leonard Franklin, new in Ithaca, looking for a job. She told him her name and asked what he was looking to do. He explained he was doing some writing but without success. He said any job would be welcome. She told him to apply at the college. He thanked her and reverted to his slow pace. A friend of hers appeared and the two of them moved on at a quicker pace.

The next week he met her again. This time at the park. Again, he was already there, reading, when she arrived. She noticed him and came over to him and they exchanged greetings. They both read for an hour or so. Then as he prepared to leave, he asked her if she would like to join him for a cup of coffee. She thought for a moment then said, "Why not." They walked to a nearby cafe where their conversation continued. Fontana knew quite a bit about the European masters and skillfully let her drag it out of him, while feigning interest in their conversation. She mentioned about an impending show the next week at a ballroom at the Shaefer Hotel, one of Ithaca's most prestigious. He asked her if she planned to go. She said yes with her fiancé, professor Worth from the University. He told her he might attend, also. They parted. She returned to the park, and he went home. He was elated, her response to him was very positive. He told Bellheimer to watch her house that evening and follow Worth home if he had a date with Jeanette.

Bellheimer watched the house from their car. Worth appeared about 6:30. Bellheimer left and returned about 9 PM. At 10 PM they appeared in Worth's car. He walked her to the door but did not go inside. Bellheimer followed Worth across town to his home in an upscale neighborhood. Bellheimer circled the block and returned to watch. When Worth did not leave after 30 minutes, Bellheimer left.

The next Saturday the show at the Shaefer started at 2 PM. Professor Worth and Jeanette were already there when Fontana arrived. He moved slowly through the gallery but eventually caught up to them when they were talking to another couple. He managed to catch Jeanette's eye and she introduced him to her fiancé Professor John Worth head of the Department of Psychiatry at the University and the other couple. The man was an administrator at the University, the woman was his wife and a secretary in the same office as Jeanette. The five discussed the paintings and sculptures. The show was both for local artists and contained a select few works from European masters. Professor Worth was obviously an art novice and in attendance to please Jeanette. Fontana sensed his chance to influence Jeanette even more. He slowly, but deftly, began to talk about the virtues and shortcomings of the paintings of the master's on display. As the group moved on, he began to make comments on most of the new artists compositions, also. Jeanette and the other couple were very interested in his comments and just as he thought would happen, Professor Worth began to show an irritated manner. The Professor's comments were mostly made in asides to Jeanette but were apparent to all. Fontana caught Jeanette's eye, apologized for his intrusion, and excused himself.

Alone, he noticed Worth and Jeanette having a slightly heated discussion that he felt was about him. He smiled wryly as he continued slowly through the exhibit.

The other couple soon finished and waved at him as they left. Fontana waited for a little while then approached Jeanette and Worth and said good-bye assuring Worth he was glad to meet him. Jeanette was gracious and Worth was merely perfunctory.

These 'chance' meetings went on for several weeks. Sometimes Jeanette was alone, other times Worth was with her. With all of this, Worth grew more and more irritated and saw Fontana as a rival, something Jeanette did not agree with. They argued more and more about it until the Professor proposed calling off their engagement. At first Jeanette was dismayed and conciliatory, but when he demanded she give up her friendship with Fontana and rebuff him completely she refused his attempt at control. The die was cast. She knew Worth was bluffing but told him she agreed to calling off the engagement. He was shocked and tried to back pedal, but she was hurt and firm. He finally suggested a 'cooling off' period of a week or two to think things over. She agreed.

A few days later Fontana arranged another 'chance' meeting at a cafe she frequented for lunch. She was with the co-worker Fontana had met. Jeanette saw him and waved. He approached their table and the three made some small talk and they invited him to join them for lunch. The friend had to return but Jeanette still had time and stayed. Fontana knew Worth hadn't come to see her in several days. He asked about him. She told him of their break-up. He did not press her for a date. They parted after lunch.

The next Saturday he saw her at the park. They exchanged greetings and after an hour or so of reading he asked her to join him for lunch. She accepted. Over lunch he asked her to join him for dinner and a movie the next Friday. She hesitated, saying she would have to check her calendar. He asked if he may call her to find out her answer. She gave him her phone number. He called later in the week and asked her again. She agreed to go. He was elated, the first step of his plan was finished. Now, at last, he could go forward.

The dinner date was a success. He continued his slow and careful pursuit. She gradually shifted her focus from the Professor to Fontana. By the time Worth contacted her again she decided he was not for her. She told him it was best they parted as friends. He asked her if she was seeing anyone else. When she said yes, he asked her if it was Fontana. She confirmed it was. He then proceeded to lecture her, bringing up his prior comments and trying to win her back by reason, but she was through, and he finally realized it and said a bitter good-bye.

As for Fontana, he kept her busy. He skirted all personal questions by saying he chose Ithaca as a place to pursue his writing because of the cultural influence of Olivier and Barnwell University and the peaceful atmosphere of the community.

After three weeks of courting her, he invited her over to his apartment for dinner. She asked what to bring and he told her "Just yourself." Up until this date he had always walked her to the door and kissed her good night. He never asked to come inside even though he felt she would let him.

He prepared a fresh salad and fixed a spaghetti dinner with sauce he learned to make from his mother. It was good and she raved about it, especially the sauce. They had a bottle of good Italian wine and made love for the first time.

Lying next to him, she said "I don't know when I've enjoyed an evening so completely."

"I feel the same," he dead panned.

"I mean it. I love you totally. I've never felt this way about anyone before in my life."

"I love you, too. Maybe too much," he said.

She stayed until midnight and then went home.

Things progressed until they were seeing each other almost every night. He was gentle with her, always considerate, always complimentary.

She soon found herself wanting to see him in the middle of the day or waking up with desire in the middle of the night. Her heart was light when she was with him, and she felt a loneliness she had never felt before when she was unable to see him for a day or two.

By the spring of 1945 they were a couple that appeared to be on the verge of marriage. She was spending most nights at his apartment forcing Bellheimer to rent another. He was careful to lavish attention on her.

She began to be impatient with their lives and asked often about their future together. This was exactly what he wanted to hear. He told her he wanted to marry her, but he had to solve a problem first. He repeated this on several occasions. She pushed him to tell her the problem.

One evening after they made love, she was lying next to him and began rubbing his chest then she kissed him hard on the mouth and started talking.

"You must know I am deeply in love with you. I want to spend the rest of my life with you, but every time we talk about it you say you have a problem. I want to hear about this problem. Maybe we can solve it together. You're not married, are you? That would be about the worst thing I can think of."

"No, it's not anything like that."

"Then tell me what it is."

He moved to the edge of the bed and sat with his head in his hands and said, “I don’t see the possibility of a solution.”

“For God’s sake, Leonard what is the problem? Maybe, just maybe, I can help you find a solution?”

He shrugged and went to a bureau drawer. He removed a file from it and handed it to her. She went slowly through the file. It contained all his faked “original paperwork” from Naples showing he was an M.D., and that he completed the requirements to be a psychiatrist. She was stunned. She went through it again.

“This says you are a psychiatrist,” she said.

“Yes. In Italy, I can’t practice here.”

“Then you are really Italian?”

“Yes, I was raised in Italy. I served as a physician in the Army. When Italy surrendered, I came to America. I have tried to become licensed here but have not been able to do so.”

“This says your name is Baresi.”

“Yes, that is my name. I had to use another name to leave Italy, the Fascists were very violent at the end. I took the name Leonard Franklin from a telephone book in New Orleans. It has a nice American sound to it.”

“So, what will you do now.?”

“I don’t know, I want to marry you but can’t without my American license. It is very hard.

“Can you go back to school.”

“It would take many years. If only I could obtain my license. We could get married, perhaps even move away.”

Her head was swimming. She got up and dressed to go to her apartment.

He just sat there and said, "I'm sorry."

She left. He didn't call her the next few days.

Bellheimer, always impatient, asked, "You have told her you need a license, why not ask her to get you one now?"

"Because if I pressure her too much at first, she may refuse altogether. She must make a move or suggest one. Then I can move on it," he said.

CHAPTER TWENTY

Vittorino had never been to sea before the long trip to America, made even longer by the necessity to zigzag as part of a convoy to avoid submarines. The crossing took an extra day due to the stormy weather in the Atlantic. He was seasick the first few days but had to work anyhow. The weather in the Gulf of Mexico was very calm and welcomed by the crew.

Vittorino officially left the Palermo August 1, 1944, three days after it docked in New Orleans. He rented a room in a boarding house and settled in. He had a worker's visa and spent the next few days showing the picture he had of Fontana and Bellheimer in bars and restaurants and other shops near the docks. It took two days to visit them all. No one he talked to remembered seeing either one of them. On the evening of the fourth day he got a break. He was eating at a local restaurant and showed the picture to his waitress. She asked why he wanted to know about them. Vittorino knew immediately after her question that she had seen one or both of them. Vittorino said Fontana was family and he wanted to know if he was still in the area. The waitress said she didn't know the answer to that, but she did wait on them about a week earlier. Sensing he was close, Vittorino asked several more questions, but she didn't have or wouldn't give any more information.

As he was leaving, she called out to him and told him something she heard them talking about. She said they had a map of the U.S. and talked about going 'up North', but where 'up North' she did not know. She said that was all she could remember. He thanked her and left her a generous tip.

On the one hand Vittorino was elated they came through New Orleans. At least he knew they were in the U.S. But now the question was whether they were still there, or had they moved on? He decided to invest a few more days in New Orleans trying to pick up a better trail. He made his search area larger and spent several days showing the picture but had no luck. Finally on the eighth day he showed the picture to a bus driver at the Trailways bus depot. The driver looked at the picture in Vittorino's hand then took it in his own left hand and flicked it with his right middle finger. He looked at Vittorino then asked, "Why do you ask about these two?"

"It's important I find them."

"Why are you looking for them. You're not a cop you have an accent, a Guinny accent."

"What's a Guinny accent?"

"Italian."

"Yes, I am Italian. These two murdered seven of my family in Italy. I have trailed them to the U.S."

"You should go to the police."

"I will when I have a real lead."

"Then you have one now. They rode my bus to Nashville, Tennessee. That's as far as I go. They had tickets to New York city. They had to change buses in Nashville and then again in Baltimore on the way to New York."

"When will they arrive in New York?"

"Yesterday."

"Yesterday?"

"Yes. You may as well go to the police now. I'll tell them what I know."

Vittorino went to the police, but they had no paperwork or official information about Fontana and Bellheimer so they could not act, but they said they would contact Italy to see if there was a warrant for them. They gave Vittorino the station telephone number and told him to keep checking back. They said they would forward what information they got from Italy to the F.B.I. and New York city police.

Vittorino got on the same driver's bus the next morning. He arrived in New York the next day and began to search again. No one at or near the bus station recognized Fontana or Bellhimer's picture.

After several days searching and visits to police stations Vittorino realized he had to make a change in plans. He applied for U.S. citizenship at a courthouse in White Plains, N.Y. He was not screened very well and realized that many people were applying. His name was added to a list, and he was given the necessary paperwork. He was told to return when he completed the application, which he did.

He wrote a letter to his father and brother Marcus.

17 August 1944

Dear Papa and Marcus,

I landed in New Orleans and found out Fontana and Bellheimer landed a few days before me. They took a bus to New York City, and I followed. New York is very big, and people are very busy. I have shown the picture of Fontana and Bellheimer at Police stations and businesses near the bus station. No-one has seen them. I have decided to get a job and keep searching when I can. I tried to rent an apartment in the town of White Plains, but I need a job before they will rent me one, so I am staying at a Y.M.C.A. It's not bad but it's a little crowded. I applied for several jobs nearby. One at a gas station looks promising. I also applied for American citizenship. I believe it will help in the long run. The local police department has an auxiliary and I plan to apply to help out in my spare time.

How are things going at home? Have you been able to get the farm back in our name?

Your son and brother,

Vittorino

Vittorino left the number of the hall phone at the Y.M.C.A. when he applied for jobs, but it was always busy and no one was there to take messages, so he checked every day at every place he left an application. His speech wasn't too bad, but writing in English was a challenge.

"There's something else I want to talk to you about," said Nelson.

"What?"

"You live at the Y.M.C.A., right?"

"Yes, that's right."

"Besides teaching the class on American History I volunteer at the Y.M.C.A. myself."

"What do you do?"

"Referee basketball and boxing. I thought since you were already here you might volunteer, too. Do you know anything about basketball or boxing?"

"No."

"Maybe you could keep time for boxing and keep score for basketball."

"I'm willing to try."

"Come to the gym about six tomorrow."

"Okay."

At 6 PM Vittorino came to the gym. Mr. Nelson called him over to a table alongside the basketball court and introduced him to a man named Ed Charney.

"I'm refereeing and Ed here is going to keep score. He'll show you how to operate the scoreboard so you can do it when he can't make it."

"Come sit next to me," said Ed and he proceeded to show Vittorino how to operate the scoreboard.

Before the game started Vittorino had several questions about points and different types of shots, etc. Ed answered them all and let Vittorino keep score for the last half of the third game.

"Well how did it go?" Asked Mr. Nelson.

"He did fine. I think one more night with me and he can solo."

"That's great can you come in Friday, Vittorino?"

"Yes."

On Friday Ed turned the score keeping over to Vittorino after the first game. Vittorino had more trouble keeping track of the fouls than the score, but Ed's patience paid off and by the end of the third game Vittorino was in complete charge.

The next week there was an amateur boxing tournament at the Y.M.C.A. Vittorino had never seen a boxing match and watched Ed closely. Ed was not only in charge of timing the rounds, but also of the referee and judges' scorecards. It took several matches before Vittorino felt comfortable enough to time one. He did well and by the second night was able to solo.

Vittorino enjoyed the evenings at the Y.M.C.A. At first some of the kids in the basketball program made fun of his Italian accent, but he took things in stride and soon won them over. He pitched in to help so much that he soon became a fixture as timekeeper for boxing and scorekeeper and even referee for basketball games.

After discussions with Art Nelson, he decided to go ahead in June of 1945 and volunteer for the White Plains auxiliary police despite his still sightly broken-English. He was surprised by a letter to report for an interview two weeks later. The officer that interviewed him, Lieutenant Gregory, asked him several questions and told Vittorino he would hear something within a few weeks. He gave no indication about Vittorino's chance for the auxiliary. Within two weeks Vittorino received another letter instructing him to report at 9 A.M. July fifteenth for a second interview. Vittorino came by the police department after work on July first and explained that he worked on the first shift. The Sergeant on the desk told him to take a seat while he called Lieutenant Gregory. After a short delay Lieutenant Gregory called back and had the Sergeant ask Vittorino if he was ready to interview now. Vittorino said yes.

The Sergeant sent him to the second-floor conference room for his interview.

Vittorino sat waiting for fifteen or twenty minutes before the door opened and a tall officer entered. He did not offer his hand.

"Good afternoon, I'm Captain Richard Nelson."

"I am Vittorino Sabatini."

"A damn Guinny and a Jew, too. What makes you think we want the likes of you on our force?" Asked Captain Nelson, looking very skeptical.

"I have goals I want to pursue; this is the first step."

"Answer my question, why should we want you on our force."

"Because I am totally reliable. I am willing to do any job to help the police department and I respect the badge worn by the White Plains police officers."

"What if you were told to go clean the latrine?"

"I would do it. If I may ask Captain Nelson, what is a latrine?"

"What are the goals you want to accomplish?"

"I want to become a police officer. That is step number two."

"What is step number three?"

"I am trying to locate two men that murdered members of my family in Italy. Being on the force as an officer would help."

Smiling Captain Nelson held out his hand and Vittorino shook it hard.

"Yes, you are everything my brother said you are, cool, unnerved and determined. I like that in an officer. I am going to recommend you for the auxiliary. I recommend you change your service station job to the night or evening shift, if you can, that way you will be able to attend some classes and get into the field sooner. Give yourself about six months on the auxiliary before you apply to be an officer. You will receive a letter in the next few days confirming what I have said."

"You are Art's brother?"

"Yes. Art told me all about you. The first part of the interview was a little test to see if you could remain calm. You see, in the field an officer must keep his wits about him and remember his training. You passed the test. If you had got mad or rattled, you would not have been recommended. And by the way the latrine is where officers relieve themselves. Don't worry you won't have to clean it. We have a cleaning staff."

The next day Vittorino asked to be put on the third shift. His request was granted, and he started the next Monday. He reported to the White Plains police department on the second Monday in August,1945. He attended traffic school and basic officer training courses held by the White Plains police department. Two weeks later he started to work assisting and accompanying officers on their rounds. He was often used during special events or when officers were on vacation. He liked the work and followed Captain Nelson's advice to put in for a regular officer's job in February 1946 after he had six months experience as an auxiliary officer. He liked the auxiliary but three months after submitting his application he had still not been called for an interview. He suspected it might be because when he first volunteered, he had such a heavy Italian accent that he was overlooked.

He wrote home to his family regularly. Guido had remained single. Marcus was nearing marrying age but was still not even engaged. Guido wrote often and always finished his letters with a plea for Vittorino to come back to Italy, something Vittorino longed to do, but he wrote that he felt he would one day get a break that would lead him to Fontana and Bellheimer.

Vittorino had kept in touch with Lt. Arturo who wrote that Italian extradition warrants had been issued for both Fontana and Bellheimer along with a German warrant for Bellheimer.

It was suspected that the pair assumed different identification in the U.S. Lt. Arturo wrote that Fontana was so vicious that he felt it was just a matter of time before something, a crime of some sort would surface.

The Memorial Day weekend was a favorite time for officers to take a week of vacation to visit the New Jersey seashore. Both Atlantic City and Ocean City were always crowded signaling the unofficial start of the summer tourist season. On May twenty eighth Vittorino received a call for seven days of evening duty in downtown White Plains due to vacationing officers. He was delighted to hear he would be paid, something that had never happened before. When he reported he was given a badge instead of an armband. The watch commander Lt. Jim Arnold jokingly told him to keep his Italian nose clean, that he was trying to get him on the force full-time. He also told Vittorino the night stick was just for show, and he was not to use it unless his or his partner's life was in danger. Vittorino was assigned with a regular officer, Eric Jones, to do traffic duty as required and patrol on foot in an area where a festival including carnival rides was taking place. It looked to be an assignment like several others he had as a volunteer.

The sights and the aroma of all kinds of food, buttered corn, cotton candy, sausages and especially grilling hot dogs and hamburgers filled the air. Vittorino loved hamburgers and purchased one, so did his partner. They found a spot at a table near the carousel. Halfway through the burger Vittorino heard a cry for 'Help' then 'Stop thief'. He turned in time to see a man running and clutching a purse. Both officers jumped to pursue. Vittorino quickly sprinted ahead of his older and much heavier partner. He ran on ahead and as he closed on the purse snatcher he turned and threw the purse at Vittorino. It missed and Vittorino pointed it out to his fellow officer who stopped to pick it up and catch his breath. Vittorino caught up to the would-be thief who stopped and brandished a knife. Vittorino closed to within a few feet then drew his baton from his belt. "Put down the knife," he said "You're through. My partner's coming and he has a gun. Now drop it." The thief complied and Vittorino ordered him to the ground. He kicked the knife out of reach and handcuffed the thief. By the time his partner arrived he had the thief back on his feet and the knife wrapped in a handkerchief in his hand. His wheezing partner was full of 'Way to Go's'.

They walked the thief back to the same area. The woman identified her purse and agreed to make charges at the station. Vittorino sat the would-be-thief at the same table they had occupied earlier. After he was seated, he heard a voice say, "Not bad for a guy from Veranza." Vittorino looked around and saw former Army Captain Albert Johnson. He immediately jumped up and hugged him. Johnson responded with a return hug and then held out his hand. Vittorino shook it heartily.

"I heard the shout but was on the other side of the carousel, did you catch him yourself?" Asked Johnson.

"No."

“Yes,” said his partner. “He had him before I caught up, and that’s the way it’s going to be reported.” Then he left for a callbox to report the incident.

“Well good for you, how long have you been a police officer?”

“I’m not really an officer, yet. I’m just here to help, I’m police auxiliary.”

“Some helping out, do you mind if we talk while you are waiting for your partner?”

“No, please sit down.”

“We’re passing through on our way back to Nashville, Tennessee from a vacation in Niagara Falls.” His wife Lori and five-year-old son Mark joined them, and Johnson introduced them to Vittorino.

“My husband has spoken of you and your family many times,” said Lori.

“That’s right, I have kept up correspondence with Lt.- now Captain- Arturo and through him kept up with Guido and Marcus.”

Vittorino’s partner returned and Vittorino introduced him to the Johnsons. He did not elaborate on their connection, saying only Johnson had been helpful in Italy when things were very tough, and he needed a friend. They agreed to meet the next day at a nearby restaurant, the ‘SKY HOOK’.

The next day Vittorino and Johnson talked of old times in Italy. Johnson asked Vittorino what kind of luck he was having finding Fontana and Bellheimer. Vittorino told him about the chase to New York where they disappeared. Johnson thought about things for a moment then talked about some possibilities.

"You know New York is a great place to lose anyone that might be looking for you," said Johnson.

"Yes, I know it's so big. I've checked everywhere I can think to look, police stations, bus stations, railroad stations, post offices and many other places. No one remembers seeing either of them. As far as I can tell neither has been arrested."

"They will be very careful for a long time, but Fontana's old itch will make him strike again and we know his signature."

"His signature, what do you mean?" Asked Vittorino.

"What he does when he finishes murdering someone, Fontana's signature is cutting off ring fingers. He will make a mistake and we will nab him and Bellheimer".

"We?"

"Yes, we. I'm with the U.S. Federal Marshals now. I requested all the information I could get on them. The Italian authorities have warrants out for them through INTERPOL. The Germans have one out for Bellheimer. All federal agencies have been alerted. It's just a matter of a slip-up."

They talked at length. At first Vittorino felt they were probably still in New York. Johnson said he believed the trip to New York was a precaution and a diversion. Why else would they come? No one knew of any contacts they might have in New York.

Vittorino thought then asked: "What should I do if this is true?"

"How long do you think it will be until you go through the police academy and are officially an officer?"

"Lt. Arnold said I will hear something within a week."

"Then here's what you do. Keep observing things here, newspapers, radio, post office bulletin boards, etc. And make sure you pass the police academy, it's not easy."

"I will."

"When you complete one full year as an officer call or write me. If you want, I can help get you on as a U.S. Marshal. It will give you access to more national crime information, and this is important, I can assign you to help investigate if we think a crime may be linked to those two."

"Yes, yes, I will do this and maybe next summer I can be a Marshal."

"First you must be an officer in good standing for a year to make it easier to hire you. Now, you must not talk to anyone about this plan. White Plains may not like hiring and training you just to lose you to the U.S. Marshals."

"I will as you say, 'keep this under my hat.'"

They exchanged telephone numbers and Johnson gave Vittorino his home address. He explained to Vittorino he already had his address from Arturo and had planned to visit him in White Plains on this very day. Vittorino looked amazed, almost stunned, that this man would come looking for him. They parted, Vittorino to do his evening duty and Albert Johnson going home to Nashville.

True to his word, Lt. Arnold called Vittorino into his office the next Friday. Vittorino was scheduled to start as a full-time officer at the end of June 1946 and start the six weeks course at the police academy the first week of July. The appointment was conditional that he passes the police academy final exams both physical and paperwork. He thanked Lt. Arnold for his support and said he would do his absolute best. His best was good enough for eighth place in a class of thirty graduates. The ceremony was held on August twenty first.

Though he was a new type of beat cop, mostly riding with his partner and occasionally directing traffic, he loved the job and gained a reputation as a fine new officer. He learned a whole lot about human nature. The police procedure was, when talking to the public, try to get to the heart of the problem, listen to what is being said, don't be too quick to judge, and always try to solve the problem in the field.

As a rookie cop Vittorino was assigned to the evening shift from 2PM to 10PM. His partner, Bill Blaise, was a ten-year veteran on the force and preferred the second shift.

"I like second shift, sometimes things get chaotic, but I like to stay busy, and the shift seems to go quicker. You never know what's going to happen. Standing in one spot directing traffic for hours doesn't interest me," said Blaise.

Blaise considered himself an expert on human nature and enjoyed negotiating with people to resolve issues. Vittorino, too, found himself settling squabbles between merchants and customers, husbands and wives and sometimes between neighbors in the crowded apartment buildings. Rarely did they find it necessary to arrest someone for 'poor behavior' as Blaise called it. The exceptions were assault, especially husbands on wives and of course crimes such as robbery or burglary. They wrote traffic tickets, but only for the worst offenses, drunk driving, excessive speeding and running a red light. Slow rolling stops were not considered a problem but complete disregard for a stop sign earned a driver a ticket.

Lt. Arnold routinely briefed officers at shift change about precinct news. One evening in December he warned the officers about a tip they received.

"In conclusion gentlemen we have received a tip about a major heist possibly going down tonight in White Plains. We are not sure of the exact nature of the heist but with it being the holiday season it could have something to do with retail shops or warehouses since they typically carry large inventories this time of year. Check anything you think is unusual activity. Be careful out there, the word on the street is this is an armed bunch that won't go down easy. Good luck this evening and good hunting. That's all I have. Any questions? None? Good."

Vittorino and Blaise went outside to their patrol car. Once inside Vittorino asked Blaise, "Have you had any dealings with this type of situation before?"

"What do you mean this type of situation?"

"I mean crooks we know are armed and probably won't go down easy."

"Well, if you are asking me if I've ever run into a bad bunch before, the answer is yes, I have. But a good show of force is usually enough to stop any gun play."

"That's nice to know."

"Don't worry. It's probably a false alarm."

Always being careful, they did extra checks on delivery trucks, shop back entrances and people that seemed to be in the wrong place at the right time. Nothing unusual happened to them or any other officers on their shift.

The next day at the shift change briefing Lt. Arnold repeated the previous day's tip and reminded them to be very cautious.

"I'd feel better if somebody'd got arrested last night," said Blaise as they began their shift. "I don't like something that was supposed to go down not happening. It keeps me on edge."

"Yeah, I know what you mean."

Their shift progressed until 8:30 when they received a call on the radio that they had to work over another 4 hours until 2AM.

"Damn, somebody must have called in sick or something," said Blaise.

"Maybe it has something to do with the tip from yesterday," said Vittorino.

"Could be, I guess," said Blaise. "Let's get a cup of coffee and something to eat."

They ate and by 9:30 were back on patrol.

"Do you think we ought to change our patrol?" Asked Vittorino.

"Yes, why not. We just might catch somebody that knows our routine," said Blaise.

With that in mind they started their late patrol. At 10:00 PM when they would normally be going off duty, they entered the alley behind Sterling Jewelry Store. There was a panel truck with 'Girard' visible on the closed left rear door. The right panel door was open and a man in coveralls was loading some boxes onto a two-wheel hand truck. Another man came out of the jewelry store rear door with a hand truck loaded with boxes. Neither man paid much attention to the patrol car. The second man approached the truck and appeared to tell the van driver to start the truck, which he did.

"Looks like Girard is making a late delivery," said Blaise.

"But why take boxes out of the store?"

"That's a good question. Radio headquarters with the details of our position and what we see. I'll check this out."

Vittorino got on the radio and Blaise started walking to the truck. When he got within thirty feet of the truck the man loading the boxes turned around with a gun in his hand. Blaise tried to pull his weapon, but the gunman shot him before it cleared his holster. Vittorino was still on the radio.

"Officer down behind Sterling Jewelry Store. Blaise is shot. I'm going to return fire. Send backup and an ambulance," he shouted into the mike.

The second man was loading the last of the boxes when Vittorino got out of the patrol car. "Halt, drop your guns," he said from behind the open patrol car door.

Both men turned and fired at Vittorino. Several of their bullets stuck the car door and one hit Vittorino in the right ankle. He returned fire striking the one in the coveralls first then hitting the second man. Both men went down. The man in the coveralls threw his weapon aside, but the second man was able to keep shooting. He got up and attempted to get in the back of the van, but Vittorino shot him again. The van started to move but Vittorino closed the patrol car door and ran forward taking careful aim at the left rear tire. He hit the tire and took careful aim at the right tire. He missed but the driver stopped the van and got out with a shotgun, firing quickly. Several pellets hit Vittorino at the same time and he fell backwards. He returned fire from the ground hitting the driver who spun around and fell backwards, sitting with his back against the truck.

"Drop your weapons," shouted Vittorino. The driver complied. Vittorino limped slowly to him. "Turn over," he said. The driver did and Vittorino handcuffed him and threw the shotgun aside. He walked to the rear of the truck where both men were now laying in the alley. He searched them both for weapons finding another pistol taped to the ankle of the one in coveralls. He turned them both on their stomachs.

"I'm bleeding to death," said the man in the coveralls.

"An ambulance is on the way," said Vittorino.

Vittorino went to Blaise who was conscious and sitting up in front of the patrol car.

"Where are you hit, stomach or heart?"

"In my right hip and side. It feels like I have some broken ribs. What about you?"

"Right ankle and some pellets in the chest and arm. How much are you bleeding?"

"Not too bad, I'll be alright. Good shooting."

"I wish it was before you got hit," said Vittorino as he sat next to his partner.

"I never dreamed it would go down like this," said Blaise.

"Me too."

They sat together for a few minutes before backup entered the alley from both ends with sirens blaring and red lights flashing. Officers bailed out of both cars with guns drawn. They checked on the wounded officers and handcuffed the two men lying face down at the rear of the van. One officer retreated and called for at least two more ambulances.

The first ambulance arrived, and Blaise was loaded onto a stretcher and into the ambulance. Vittorino climbed in behind. Two more ambulances arrived and took the three wounded thieves to the hospital.

Both Vittorino and Blaise were operated on for their wounds. Blaise it turns out had been shot in the side and it broke two ribs one of which grazed his lung but didn't puncture it. The bullet to his thigh went straight through, missing the femoral artery. Vittorino's ankle was broken but he still managed to climb out of the ambulance into a wheelchair. He had one shotgun pellet in his chest, two in his left arm and two in his shoulder.

Blaise was hospitalized for ten days. Vittorino was out in five days. Both men left the hospital on crutches. Both men received commendations for their efforts. Blaise swore his was a gift, but that Vittorino's was well deserved claiming he saved both their lives.

"He was cool under pressure, like he had ice in his veins, he's my partner," said Blaise.

"I'll tell you I didn't feel cool, for sure, after that shotgun blast."

All three of the thieves lived and were charged with burglary, theft over $1,000 and attempted murder.

Vittorino stayed at his apartment for another few days then resumed volunteering at the 'Y'. After another week he returned to the doctor's office where he asked about his ankle.

"How long before I can return to work?"

"It will be at least another three weeks before you can return to patrol. You will probably be able to return to desk duty after another ten days off. That's what I am going to put in my report," said the Doctor.

"Do you think I can travel?"

"It depends. I won't clear you to drive."

"I would like to go to Italy to see my family. I've checked on the airfare and schedule. I would fly to Newfoundland then Iceland then Paris to Rome. It would take about a day and a half."

"As long as you don't drive and don't carry a heavy suitcase it will probably be Okay."

Vittorino took a written copy of the doctor's report to the precinct and asked to speak to Lt. Arnold who reviewed the report and invited Vittorino into his office.

"Good to see you Vittorino," said Lt. Arnold.

"Thank you, sir."

"It looks like we can expect you back for desk duty in about ten days and back on patrol in about three weeks. Is that what you wanted to see me about?"

"In a way. What I wanted to know is if I could travel to see my family in Italy while I am on this injury leave. I would add vacation time so I could be gone for between three to four weeks."

"Has the doctor cleared you to travel?"

"Yes, as long as I don't drive, he said I could travel."

"Wait here, I'll be right back," said Arnold. He walked across the hall to Captain Nelson's office. "Captain, I have an unusual request that I would like to grant officer Sabatini."

"What is it?"

"He wants to use his medical leave to go home to Italy."

"How much medical leave does he have left?"

"Three weeks at least, if we wait to bring him back for patrol duty and about ten days if we bring him back for desk duty. He wants to add vacation time so he could be gone for between three to four weeks total."

"You have my permission to grant him the three weeks medical leave with the understanding that he will be coming back for patrol duty and one week's vacation time with the stipulation that he reports to the doctor at the end of four weeks. That should work and I believe with what he did it's fair for all parties. What do you think?"

"I agree."

Lt. Arnold went back across the hall to Vittorino. "You are granted three weeks medical leave and one week of vacation with the stipulation you report to the doctor for clearance for patrol duty at the end of four weeks."

"Thank you, Lt. Arnold."

"You're welcome, good luck and I hope you have a wonderful trip home."

"Thank you again sir."

Vittorino went to a local travel office and booked a flight to Rome for two mornings later, January fifth and for his return three weeks and three days later. After lunch he went by Blaise's house to check on him and tell him his plans.

At noon on January sixth, he arrived in Rome. It was a warm sixty-two degrees, about thirty degrees warmer than New York. His father and brother were waiting for him at the airport. After hugs all around they took a train into Rome and from there they took a bus as close as they could to Veranza and from there they loaded into the family cart pulled by a new younger horse. In Veranza, they stopped at the fountain across the street from the Mayor's cafe. Marcus filled a bucket with water for the horse and after he drank Guido gave him some grain. They went in mayor Davinti's cafe to order a spaghetti dinner.

Mayor Davinti came out to greet the family. "Hello Guido, hello Marcus and how are you Vittorino?"

"I am fine, Mayor and how are you?"

"I am fine. Did your father tell you about getting the property back in the family name?"

"Yes, he did. We are all very grateful, Mayor."

"You are quite welcome." Turning to his wife he said, "Bring us a bottle of our best red and there will be no charge for their lunch and if it is permissible, I would like to eat with them today."

"Of course, Mayor, you are most welcome," said Guido.

The meal was spaghetti with meat sauce and sausage cooked to perfection by the Mayor's wife. The sweetness of the sausage was offset by the garlic in the sauce, a combination Vittorino had not quite experienced since he left Italy.

"That's the best spaghetti dinner I've had since I left here over two years ago."

"My wife makes the sauce and the noodles, all I do is add the sausage," said the Mayor.

The meal progressed with Guido and Marcus complimenting the food, also.

When the first bottle of wine was gone the mayor ordered a second. He started to order a third, but Guido stopped him. "Mayor Davinti you are too kind, but I think we better get Vittorino home, he has been traveling for nearly two full days. You have been a very gracious host and we can't thank you enough."

"Papa is right your honor; I am very tired."

"My thanks, too," said Marcus.

"You are welcome. Vittorino make sure you come back before you return to the U.S.," said the Mayor.

"I will your honor and thanks again."

"The Mayor was certainly gracious," said Vittorino.

"Yes, I think it's because we were on the same side at the end of the war," said Guido.

"I am anxious to see the farm."

"It's not a great time of the year, but that's good since you are with us," said Guido.

They drove the rest of the way in silence. When they reached the farm Vittorino asked his father to take the cart to the family cemetery so he could pay his respects. Once there all three men went inside the old fence and visited the graves of all the family members. There were new headstones for the seven that had been murdered. Vittorino walked around and touched the headstones of each of them. Tears streamed down his cheeks, and he turned bleary eyes toward Marcus and Guido and realized they reacted the same.

"It is very difficult to think about the loss we have all suffered. I miss them so much I can't even explain it. I would give my life in exchange for one more day with them," said Guido.

"So would I Papa," said Vittorino.

"And I," said Marcus.

After a few more minutes they returned to the house. Marcus took care of the horse and the other livestock while Vittorino unpacked, and Guido started a fire in a new wood stove connected to the fireplace.

After unpacking Vittorino joined his father in the living room. "Does the stove heat better than the fireplace?"

"Yes, much better and with much less wood. I put in just a little wood to take the chill off for this evening."

"I can feel the warmth already."

The three of them talked until nearly midnight. Guido and Marcus asked question after question about America. Vittorino did his best but didn't always know the answer.

The next morning Vittorino slept late due to fatigue and the time change from New York. When he got up Guido and Marcus were already outside working. Guido left him a breakfast of biscuits and cheese with two hard boiled eggs under a cloth covering on the kitchen table. He put some wood in the kitchen stove and re-heated the coffee. After breakfast he took a cup and the coffee pot to the veranda. The vines had been trimmed for the winter and the sun shining through warmed him as he sat on the old bench. After an hour or so Guido and Marcus returned for lunch. Guido washed up and prepared a sandwich of goat's meat and cheese with milk for lunch. When he finished, he called his sons inside to eat. He said the prayer and they ate. After the meal they went outside to smoke their pipes, something Vittorino hadn't done since he left.

"It feels so good and warm in the sun," said Marcus. "What's the weather like in New York?"

"Now it's wintertime like here, but colder. Also, the air is clearer here, but that's true all year long. I didn't appreciate how lucky we are not to have a lot of factories and so many cars close by. Imagine Rome with three or four times the cars and factories polluting the air. It creates a lot of smog.

"Smog? What is smog?" asked Marcus.

"Smog is a kind of light smoky fog. It's hard to describe and can make it hard to breathe when it's bad, but that doesn't happen often."

"Papa, are both of the other houses rented?" Asked Vittorino.

"Yes, one for cash and one day a week labor from the husband or the oldest son. The other one is paid for by the wife preparing lunch and supper meals for us every day except Monday and cleaning the house once a week. Of course, we provide the food we eat and tell her what to cook."

"That sounds like a good deal for everyone concerned," said Vittorino.

"It is."

The next week went by quickly. News of Vittorino being home traveled quickly and he had several visitors including The Planner and the head of the underground forces he fought for with Guido. Vittorino was happy to see them all especially The Planner who he was very anxious to tell that he had everything figured for the trip to the U.S. correctly.

One day he was sitting on the veranda talking to the Chief of Police for Veranza when an Army truck pulled into the yard. Vittorino stood and walked to the edge of the patio. He greeted a friend that emerged from the truck.

"I see you are no longer Lt. Arturo," he said.

"Yes, you are right I am now Captain Arturo."

"Come sit on the veranda with me."

"I would have been here sooner, but I had a meeting in Rome."

"I'm glad you had to wait because you are here now."

"What happened to your leg?"

"An accident before I left from America."

"Is it very bad?"

"The ankle was broken but now it is healing good."

"Are you home for good?"

"No just a couple more weeks."

"I had hoped you were home for good."

"No there's still business to tend in America."

"Did you get any leads on Fontana or Bellheimer?"

"No not really except I do know they docked in New Orleans just as The Planner figured they would. Then they took a bus bound for New York. I followed them a few days behind but never caught up. I'm still looking for them."

"I understand you are a police officer, now."

"Yes."

"Do you like the job?"

"Yes, very much and I get to check the latest information for anything that points to them. Captain Johnson came to see me, he's with the U.S. Marshals now. He says after I get in one year as a police officer he can get me a job with the U.S. Marshals, too. That way I will have access to all the federal information that comes out about Fontana and Bellheimer that we don't see at the local level."

"Has Fontana done anything in the U.S., I mean any crimes?"

"Not that we know of, yet. But Johnson says he will. He believes Fontana enjoys killing and it's only a matter of time before he gets careless and is caught."

"I hope with everything in me he is caught and hopefully hung," said Arturo.

"I agree."

"Well, I can't stay long, I just kind of snuck up here to say hello. When you get back to the U.S. we can start writing again. In the meantime, I will try to get back here to see you again before you leave. When is that going to be?"

"I will be leaving here in about two more weeks. I hope to see you again before I must leave."

"I will be back before then. Maybe we can meet in Veranza when I inspect the station there on Friday the twenty fourth?"

"Yes, that's fine, I don't have to leave from Rome until the twenty eighth. Maybe we can have supper at the mayor's cafe. He was very nice when we stopped on my way home from the U.S."

Vittorino spent the next several days visiting friends on neighboring farms where he was invariably invited for lunch before he went on to the next one where he was invited for supper. Some of the friends were Jewish but most were Roman Catholic. Religion was not a problem. They had been friends and neighbors for generations.

Vittorino had been using his ankle as an excuse for not going to synagogue but since he was well enough to visit friends his father asked about synagogue.

"Will you be going to synagogue with us on the sabbath now that you are able to travel easily?" Asked Guido.

"No father, I don't go to synagogue."

“Why son. Surely you believe in God.”

“Where was God when our family was murdered?”

“God cannot stop every evil deed that is done. You must have faith that you are loved by God,” said Guido.

“I am sorry, Papa. I ask, ‘When will God deliver Fontana and Bellheimer to me or to others that look for them?’ I have not seen God do this, at least that would be something. Something I could believe in, something good. Retribution for their sins.”

“God will punish them. You must believe or you will be empty and unhappy.”

“I believe it is up to men to punish them right here on earth.”

“I will pray to God that you will change your mind my son.”

“I don’t know what to say, Papa except I love you and Marcus and that’s all I feel strongly about right now. Perhaps things will change, I don’t know. What I do know is the day we buried our family I swore that I would find the men responsible and punish them.”

“Revenge is a hard thing to carry with you. Maybe you should consider at least talking to a Rabbi.”

“Maybe someday Papa. Maybe someday.”

On the twenty second The Planner, who everyone now knew as Maurice DeVenito, again stopped by the farm. Vittorino told him about the get together with Arturo at Mayor Davinti’s cafe on the twenty fourth and invited him and the Traveler to

"Thank you, Guido. Now here's a surprise. This dinner is complimentary to all of you, my good friends."

There were genuine protests by all to pay for the meal. After the final courses were eaten, and some more wine drank, everyone said their good-byes and left for home.

Guido and Vittorino were a little unsteady getting in the old cart, but Marcus who only sipped his wine, was fine and drove the old horse home.

Vittorino was up and about more and more, and the next few days went by quickly. On the morning of the twenty eighth Guido prepared breakfast and a lunch for Vittorino to take with him on his trip. Marcus prepared the horse and cart while Vittorino prepared to leave. Guido came into Vittorino's bedroom and spoke softly to him.

"Son, I know your heart is heavy about what happened that black day, but will you please promise me to give some thought about what we spoke when you first came home?"

"Yes, Papa I have been thinking a lot about what you said and when I can, I will go to synagogue and speak to a Rabbi. I don't know how I will feel, but I will do this when I feel like I can."

"Thank you, son, now it's time to leave so you can catch your bus. But before we leave will you promise me that if you catch this Fontana and his partner Bellheimer, or if you determine it will do no good for you to keep trying, you will come home?"

"Yes, Papa."

With those final promises made Guido and Marcus took Vittorino to meet the bus and sent him on his long journey back to New York. Two days later he visited the doctor and had his cast removed from his ankle. The doctor gave him three more days recuperation before he was to return to patrol. He returned to desk duty the next day.

Blaise returned to work the next week and they returned to patrol duty as partners.

In July of 1947 Vittorino applied to be a U.S. Marshal with Albert Johnson's blessing and recommendation. He took some tests, scored well, and was put on a list of qualified applicants. Johnson assured him he was well qualified and would likely be chosen soon. In August he was interviewed by the Atlanta office. After a second interview In September, he was hired beginning October first. He liked the U.S. Marshal job as much as being a police officer, though he missed the camaraderie of being on the police force. In December an officer in the Nashville office came to Johnson requesting a transfer to Atlanta. Johnson called the Atlanta office and they agreed to let Vittorino transfer in exchange for the Nashville agent. Vittorino began working with Johnson in January 1948. The first thing he did was send out a request to all U.S. Marshal Offices that if anyone knew of a crime committed where the victim had a ring finger severed to please contact him at his new office. He included an explanation about his family.

CHAPTER TWENTY-ONE

After reading Fontana's fake credentials, it took Jeanette a day and a half to come to terms with his confession to her. During that time, she thought about the previous contact she had with an Italian doctor, Giuseppe Montanari, before the war and wondered if there was a connection. After another day she decided to meet with Fontana again. She called and they agreed to meet at the park. She had her questions ready.

Why was he here? Had he contacted her because of her campus position? What did he want from her? What was their future together? What about Doctor Montanari?

He said he was in Ithaca by chance. He also claimed they met by chance, and he had no way of knowing her position. He said he did not know a doctor Montanari. He claimed he wanted nothing from her, only her love. Their future he claimed was dependent on him being accepted as a legitimate psychiatrist in the U.S. He showed her several letters he claimed were responses to inquiries he made at Medical Schools regarding his requests. All were rejections. Some cited the war. Others stated Medical School policy. All had postmarks from the city of the University contacted. All, of course had been written by Fontana and mailed by Bellheimer. One was from Olivier and Barnwell University. It was very carefully crafted using the correct names and policies, something he knew she could and would verify. It, like the others, was a firm rejection leaving no possible recourse. They had lunch together at their favorite cafe. She said she would call him.

Later in the day he and Bellheimer met again. Bellheimer again pressed him to approach her for help. Fontana refused the direct approach.

"I have spent a long time, nearly a year, pursuing her. She is in love and wants to get married. The only question now is whether she will take the bait and run with it. She thinks she knows the entire situation. She has to be thinking about a solution. She's in a box. The next move must be from her. She will move one way or another. It's best for us if she suggests the solution. That guarantees it long term. If I push too hard or if we try to use force, that is a short-term answer, one that will eventually lead to discovery. Remember I not only need documents I need her here to attest to the credibility, at least for a few years."

"And then what?"

"And then we no longer need her, and she disappears."

Another week went by before Jeanette called him to meet again. This time they met in her apartment. She started all business-like indicating he was to take a seat. She sat directly across the table. She began to speak, choked up and paused to regain her composure. Then, with a coolness he had rarely seen the last few months she continued.

"I have thought things out the last couple of weeks. I have wondered if you have been honest with me or using me. I still don't know, only time will tell I suppose. I have been contemplating whether to help you obtain a license or not. If I do and someone finds out I will lose my job and maybe worse." She looked at him for some sign of reassurance.

"How can you help, I don't understand?"

"I have access to most of the documents necessary to create Leonard Franklin, M.D. Psychiatrist, graduate of Olivier and Barnwell University."

"I'm at a loss for words. You can do such a thing?" He asked in faked astonishment.

"Yes, but I want to know what our future together would be if I do this." Her voice cracked and her lower lip and hands trembled.

"I want to marry you of course. We have to think this out very carefully. I'm stunned I need a moment to think," he said continuing to feign astonishment. He got up and began to pace around the small kitchen.

"If I do this, and I'm not saying I will, it will be very complicated. Would you want to be licensed as Franklin or Beresi," she said struggling to regain her composure.

"Neither one."

"Why not?"

He sat back down and said, "The Fascists have long arms and many agents. Since none of the Medical Schools would help me, I planned to change my name again for the last time, to make the trail completely cold."

"But the Fascists in Italy have been defeated, surely they can't come here after you."

"Don't kid yourself, just because Italy has surrendered doesn't mean the Fascists are all going to disappear. They have put a price on my head, they will try to find me," he said and looked around acting nervous.

"Have you thought of another name?"

"Yes, I have. It's a little different but I like it. It's purely American."

"What is it?"

"Elliott Rose. With a name like that and my license I would feel safer. Leonard Baresi could disappear." He smiled broadly and raised his arm to mimic an airplane taking off.

"I like it, too. What about a middle name?"

"I haven't thought about that. Any suggestions?"

"Hmm, I don't know. How about Michael."

"Elliott M. Rose. Sounds good to me, let's go with it," he said.

"I still have to think about all this. I don't know for sure if I can do this or if I even want to, it's very risky." She paused. Her eyes were glassy. She took a handkerchief and dried her cheeks. "I've never even thought about doing anything illegal in my whole life."

"Look, I understand, we're talking about a future aways down the road. You do what's best for you. Don't worry about me, I'll get by."

"I know. Let's part for now, okay? I'll call you when I've had time to think things out completely."

"Okay." He got up and kissed her on the forehead and left.

A week went by, then another. He began to doubt he would hear from her again.

During the third week she called and invited him to her apartment.

When he arrived, a large manila envelope was sitting in one of the kitchen chairs. She asked him to sit across from her at the table. She was again business-like but smiled more readily. Her hands shook as she moved the envelope from the chair to the table.

She paused to regain her composure. "I've spent a lot of time praying about what to do. My conscience tells me one thing, my heart another. I have decided to gamble with my life and possibly my very soul. I pray that God will forgive my sins." Their eyes met. Hers were green and full of tears, she wiped them with a handkerchief as they spilled down her cheeks. His were deep black and showed no emotion.

"Things have been so great between us I'm putting my future in your hands. Now open the envelope."

He did. He couldn't help being amazed. At no time did he expect such a quick response from Jeanette. He went through all the documents. It was all there. Everything necessary for Dr.

Elliott M. Rose to be an M.D. with a Psychiatric Residency from Olivier and Barnwell University. Every piece of paperwork, every signature on every document. He looked at her. She was smiling a poignant smile, tears streamed down her cheeks.

"You know what this means? This means you have the identity you need. It also means I must resign from my job."

"Please." He protested, "In order for us to go on you must remain until I can establish a credible identity in the U.S."

"I've done all the back-up paperwork. You should have no problem."

"There are always skeptics. People check references. I need you to run interference until I get established. Then we can get married." He took her hand in his, then walked around the table and hugged her where she sat.

"I can only do my best. I don't see every inquiry." The smile was gone. Her shoulders drooped and she looked very sad.

"I will let you know when to expect one. Please stay on at the business office," he said in a pleading voice.

"For how long?"

"A couple, two to three years until I, we are established. Then you can join me. In the meantime, I will correspond and visit you. You won't regret this."

"I hope not."

They had a quiet dinner together. Both were looking forward to the future, but for different reasons. They discussed where he should seek a position as a psychiatrist. She suggested a small hospital in Baltimore. He said he would look into it.

It was now the first week of September. He spent the next few days sending out inquiries. He sent them exclusively to Veterans Administration Hospitals because he knew they were still trying to catch up to the demands made by the war. Many were on campuses of larger general hospitals. He received three positive responses. The first and most promising was from Pittsburgh. The V.A. Hospital was on the campus of Monroe General Hospital. The response included a request for references and included a telephone number to call.

He met with Jeanette. She gave him three references, all at Olivier and Barnwell. He had hoped for a better variety, but as a fictitious professor and part-time university doctor he responded first with a return telephone call. He was invited for an interview.

On October twelfth he met with officials of the V.A. Hospital at Monroe General. It was obviously a start-up situation. They did not have a psychiatrist on the staff and only had two other M.D.'s, both of which were also on Monroe General's staff. Dr. Christopher Wright was Monroe General's clinical director. He questioned Rose about his clinical experience since it appeared from his resume to be very limited. Dr. Rose explained that he liked his position at Olivier and Barnwell but felt he could contribute more by working with veterans that suffered trauma from the war. His answers were well rehearsed and well received. After the interview he was asked to lunch with Dr. Wright and Mr. Lawrence Caldwell the V.A. Hospital Director. The lunch was in the hospital cafeteria and certainly not up to Rose's personal standards, but he ate with gusto and tried to be very engaging. Mr. Caldwell seemed impressed with Dr. Rose personally but not with his experience. He said they would check out his background and he and Dr. Wright would confer. Dr. Rose said he understood and would be happy to provide them with any additional information they needed.

Mr. Caldwell left the luncheon ahead of Wright and Rose explaining he had another meeting to attend. Dr. Wright remained very cordial. He said he would call Rose in a few days. He emphasized he would be the one with the most input about hiring for the new position. They shook hands and parted.

Rose was elated. He had everything set at Olivier and Barnwell. Jeanette could answer routine questions and put off calls to the college. 'References!' They would be out or busy. She would have them call back or give out their 'home' telephone numbers. One was a new line at Fontana/Rose's apartment another two lines were at Bell's apartment. Rose drove straight to Ithaca.

When he got to his apartment, he called Jeanette. She had not received any calls from anyone inquiring about Rose. The next day Rose received a call from Dr. Wright and gave himself a glowing report. Bell received a call on each phone line. He also gave Rose excellent references. The next day was Friday. There was no call from Wright, which Rose reasoned meant that Wright and Caldwell were meeting to confer about him.

He was right. Dr. Wright met with Caldwell. Caldwell wasn't sure about Rose, but Wright was……. he needed help. He could rely on Monroe General to help with physical problems but not mental problems, they didn't have a staff psychiatrist and neither did Wright and he needed one. He pressed Caldwell. "What the hell. If he doesn't work out, we can always terminate him," said Wright. Caldwell caved. The call to Rose came Tuesday morning. They offered him $22,500 to start with a promise for periodic increases. Dr. Wright was very gracious he said he would look for suitable housing for Rose if he liked, through a real estate person.

Rose agreed to the salary and the help locating suitable housing. He said he would give a notice suitable to the University since it was nearing the end of the fall semester. They agreed on December 15, 1945, as Rose's starting date.

Rose called Bell with the news. They met and discussed plans for the move. They agreed that Rose would rent a house and Bell would follow later.

The appointment so soon surprised Jeanette. Her congratulations were a bit stilted.

"Don't you realize what this means?" He asked.

"I think I do."

"Well, I hope so. This means we are a giant step closer to our goal about marriage."

The conversation helped but she still seemed skeptical. "How do I know you won't just leave me here?"

"Believe me Honey, all I need is two to three years to get well established with some references besides Olivier and Barnwell. Then we can be together permanently."

"It's going to be a long two or three years."

"It won't be so long. We can visit each other."

Just then her cat Hercules came strolling through the room. Rose reached out to stroke him, but Hercules dodged his hand and ran to his box.

"I don't know why he doesn't like me."

"He senses you don't like him."

"But I do, I do."

"He senses the opposite. Come here boy," she said, but Hercules left for the bedroom.

The next few weeks went by very quickly. Wright called and made arrangements for Rose to meet with a real estate agent regarding several houses he had screened. Rose came and selected a house on Second Avenue in Verona, a suburb of Pittsburgh. It was a three-story house with two actual apartments, one on the first floor and one occupied the second and third floors. Rose rented the whole house. The upstairs would be for Bell. The location was perfect. The neighborhood was old, but the houses were well maintained.

Rose settled in and a few weeks later Bell arrived. He applied for a maintenance position at a local convalescent home. He gave Rose as a reference and was hired after Rose gave a glowing referral about his work as an independent repairman.

When Bell arrived, Rose had a few assignments for him.

"I want you to get us each an extra Pennsylvania driver's license."

Bell stood up and looked at Rose mystified. “Why? We can just exchange our New York licenses.”

“Because we need to shield our names Rose and Bell in case something goes wrong.”

“Wrong with what?”

“Our extracurricular activities. We can’t have them here in this house, it’s too risky. We need a whole second identity and another place. New cars, too.”

“Look, if you just want sex, we can hire a woman or two. Don’t worry I can find them,” said Bell.

“You know that sometimes things get out of hand, and we can’t take chances here. One mistake could ruin everything. We need another place where houses aren’t so close together.”

“I’ll get the licenses first,” said Bell clearly frustrated.

“Make sure you use different addresses, nothing in Verona.”

“The name on mine will be George Drum. I’ve thought about yours. You still have a slight accent. We need to give you a name that goes along with an accent. I’m thinking Lars Nelson. If anybody asks you can claim to have been brought up in Denmark, just outside of Copenhagen. Then your accent won’t matter, but you still need to work on it.”

“Another thing, when we’re at the other place, even looking for it, or the garage where we exchange cars, we need to disguise ourselves. I’ll wear a heavy dark mustache and bushy eyebrows. I’ve got a light goatee and mustache for you.”

Pittsburgh Suburbs Along the Allegheny— —1940's Era

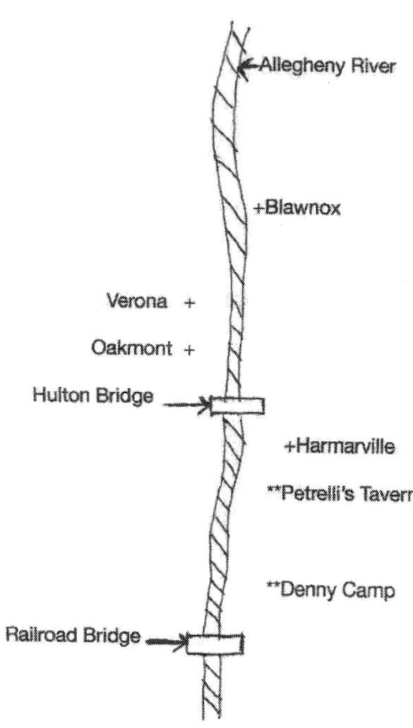

Within a week Bell made the connections for the licenses. Next, they each purchased another car. Bell got a '36 Ford coupe and Rose got a '39 Packard. Under disguise, Bell rented a garage where they both felt it would be safe to swap cars without suspicion, or even more important being seen. The garage was just a couple of miles away near the river in the nearby town of Oakmont.

Bell's next assignment was to find another house. A private place where Rose could feel secure. He checked out several places advertised in the newspapers, but none seemed quite right. He was on his way to check out another ad when he saw a sign with an arrow that simply said 'For Rent' on the shoulder of a highway near Harmarville a town across the river from Oakmont and Verona.

A boy was loading newspapers onto his bicycle nearby. Bell stopped and asked, "Is that sign for a house nearby?"

"Yes," said the boy. "It's across the railroad tracks, just follow that road on the right. You'll see another sign on the other side."

"Thanks."

"You're welcome".

Bell went about a hundred yards on a sandy dirt road before crossing several railroad tracks. On the other side a 'For Rent' sign pointed to the left. He went a short distance before coming to another 'For Rent' sign near a driveway on his right. It pointed to a yellow house with white trim well off the road. He drove to the house, got out, and walked around it. It had a large, level yard with grassy areas on all sides. He peeked in the windows and was able to see just enough to tell the first room was a kitchen and the second was a living room and both were furnished. At the rear of the house there was a large, covered porch. From the porch he walked left along the riverbank a short distance to the top of a set of thirty or so wooden steps that went down to a grassy area that extended out another fifty or so feet to the river. There, directly opposite the steps a wooden dock bobbed slowly in the water. He took a final glance around then walked to the sign in the yard and wrote down the phone number, VA-8246. As he wrote, the same boy delivered a paper to what looked to be the last house on the road. He turned his bike around and started back. When he got closer Bell walked toward him and hollered. "Hey there, do you know who owns this house?"

"Yes, the Jacobs brothers."

"Do they live nearby?"

"Yes, they live in the house where I just left a paper, but they aren't there now, they're at Red's Place."

"Where is Red's Place?"

"You go the other way on this road until you come to a white and blue building that sits close to the road. In front of it are cottages trimmed in different colors. The Jacobs brothers were inside the main building earlier."

"Thanks again," said Bell. Then, "What's your name?"

"You're welcome. My name's Micky. What's yours?"

"Lars Nelson."

Bell got in his car and drove towards Red's Place. The land was nearly level and though the road was never far from the railroad tracks, a low hill, more like a mound, rose on the right side hiding them from view. All the buildings were on his left between the road and the riverbank. Along the way he passed several houses and two other places with clapboard cabins. One had three cabins and no main building, another had two rows of three cabins each and a main building with the sign, Lily's, on it. Both places had 'Cabins for rent' signs in their yards. A little further on he came to the place the boy described. The main building was fairly good sized and sat just off the road. There were two rows of four cabins each between the main building and the riverbank. He parked and walked around to the front of the building. It had a large full length covered porch with two chairs and a small table on each side of a dark blue door. Bell climbed the steps, crossed the porch and knocked on the door.

"Come in," someone said from inside.

He entered a large room painted to match the exterior's white with blue trim. It had several tables, either red or blue, covered by oilcloth tablecloths of various designs and colors. The chairs were all either blue or red. Several feet from the door on his left was a coin-operated bumper pool table, to his right near the side wall was a shuffleboard.

A narrow galley style kitchen stretched halfway across the back of the building from the right side. It had a refrigerator, a stove, and a large cooler along the back wall. Above the cooler and stretching a couple of feet beyond were three open shelves holding dishes and various sized pots and pans. Below the shelves a countertop ran to the right side wall. A low gas flame heated a large pot on the stove. The low front kitchen wall was straddled by a gray linoleum covered countertop and separated into two parts by an opening a few feet from the right side. A faucet from a sink stuck up behind the countertop. A red-haired man with a beer in one hand stood in the kitchen opening. Several people, men and women, sat at a large round table near the kitchen. They all had a beer in front of them and two men were eating.

The man standing in the kitchen doorway spoke. “What do you want?”

“I’m looking for Red’s Place and the Jacobs brothers.”

“I’m Red. Abe and Ike are at the table.”

“I’m Abe Jacobs,” said a large, over six foot tall, man that got up and shook Bell’s hand. “That’s my brother, Ike, that’s trying to digest some of Red’s chili,” he said pointing to a considerably shorter but stocky man that waved and said “Hi”.

“My name’s Lars Nelson. The paper boy said you owned the house for rent down the road.”

“That’s right. Would you be interested in it?”

“Yes, I walked around the outside. I’d like to see the inside.”

Ike got up and shook Bell’s hand. “I would have got up sooner, but I wanted to finish the chili while it was still hot.”

"I understand."

Red spoke up again. "Can I get you a beer or a bowl of chili or a sandwich?"

"Not today, but if I rent the house, I'd like to be able to come back sometime."

"You're welcome back anytime."

"Ike, do you want to take him, or do I have to?" Asked Abe.

"Either way we have a bet first," said Red. He produced two pieces of galvanized pipe each about a foot long and threaded them together. When they were as tight as he could get them by hand, he put a pipe wrench on each piece.

"Okay, you say no matter how tight I get these two using the wrenches you can move them one quarter inch tighter with your bare hands, is that right?"

"Yes," said Abe.

"I'll bet two dollars you can't do it," said Red. "Any other takers?"

"I'll bet a dollar he can't," said a man named Monk.

"I'd like to have more bets than that. What about you Roy?"

I'll bet two dollars you can't. Red I sure hope you ate your Wheaties this morning," said Roy.

"Lars, you want to bet?" Asked Red.

"I'll bet one dollar he can."

"I'll take that bet."

Red tightened the pipes, straining for all he was worth. He carefully removed the wrenches and laid the pipe down on the bar. He took a pencil and made a mark across the joint where the pipes met. Then he drew an arrow indicating the direction to tighten the pipes.

"I see you've seen this before," said Abe.

"No, but the arrow makes sure you tighten, not loosen."

"Hmmm. You're pretty smart Red." He picked up the pipes and tried to tighten them, but they didn't budge.

"Give me another beer Red," he said.

Red dropped his hand into a cooler, opened another beer and handed it to Abe. He took two large swallows then tried again. The blood vessels on his arms and hands and even his face and neck looked like they were going to explode. He set the pipe down and said, "Measure it."

Red measured the distance. "Damn, you moved it three eights. I don't see how, but you did." He handed Abe two dollars and then Bell one dollar. "How did you know he could do it?"

"I didn't. I just thought he probably did it before."

Picking up the pipe Roy said, "Well I'll be damned, I thought it would be impossible," and then paid Abe. So did Monk without saying a word.

"Do you want anything before we go look at the house?" Ike asked Bell.

"No."

"Then follow me."

At the house, Ike opened the front door and they walked into a small kitchen. It had a sink and stove on the left side with cabinets above, a table and four chairs in the middle and a small refrigerator and more cabinets on the other side. There were large windows for light on each side of the door.

The kitchen had a wide center archway leading to a small living room. A chair and low table with a reading lamp were on the right sidewall. A couch on the left sidewall had a table and lamp at each end. On the rear wall an enclosed gas heater sat well to the left of the open doorway to the hall. Ike opened doors as they went down the hall. The first was to a small bedroom furnished with a double bed, a nightstand with a lamp and a small dresser with a mirror. Next was a bathroom with a commode, a shower, and a sink with a medicine cabinet above and finally a second bedroom slightly larger than the first but furnished the same. A door at the end of the hall opened onto the large, covered porch with three wicker chairs, a round metal table and a swing.

Ike concluded the tour with a short walk to the steps leading down the riverbank to the dock. "That's our dock, you can keep a boat there if you like. Now what do you think of the place?"

"I like it. What are the rental terms?"

"Sixty dollars a month due the first of each month and a fifty-dollar damage deposit that we will either return when you leave or use to fix any damage to the property. There is no lease just month to month rental."

"I'll take it."

"If you want it now, you can have it for twenty dollars for the rest of February plus the fifty-dollar damage deposit. One thing this is a quiet community, and we want it to stay that way. Abe and I live in that last house near the railroad bridge. It's almost exactly like this one except it has a wood stove instead of a gas heater and the kitchen door and windows face this way." He pointed to the house across the field.

"There won't be any problem."

"Good." Ike went to his car and came back with a receipt book. He filled out a receipt for seventy dollars and gave it to Bell along with a set of keys. "Good luck," he said.

Bell handed him the money and said "Thanks, I like this place already." He turned and went through the house locking both doors. He drove to the garage in Oakmont to change cars then to meet Rose in Verona.

"I rented a place across the river."

"I hope it meets all our requirements."

"I'm sure it does. It has a large yard and backs up to the river."

"How much."

"Sixty a month plus a fifty-dollar damage deposit."

"I want to see it after dark."

After supper Bell took Rose to check out the house. He went through it slowly then walked to the riverbank. "This is good, really good. The big yard helps with privacy and the river nearby can be handy. The house is small but has two bedrooms, that's good. It's all good, better than I thought we could find. The possibilities here for some relaxation and extra-curricular activities are really good." He stood at the riverbank without saying anything for a few minutes. He smiled broadly at first then followed that with a sneer that suggested some deep thoughts.

Both Rose and Bell lived a quiet life in Verona. They each became semi-regulars at local restaurants in both Verona and Oakmont and each kept pretty much to himself. Their neighbors considered them a little odd, but harmless recluses. Rose made no real friends at the V. A. or Monroe General Hospital and Bell made none at the convalescent home.

Rose impressed both Wright and Caldwell with his knowledge and dedication to patients, many of whom wrote glowing reports about him (at his suggestion). He also went to see Jeanette every few weeks and wrote or talked to her at least weekly. She pressed him about their marriage plans. He countered that he needed another step up as a clinical director in a hospital.

Their lives at the house across the river in Denny Camp were completely different. They gradually brought clothes and food to the house and began staying more and more on weekends. By mid-March they were pretty well established in the house. Rose always wore a thick, dark reddish-brown mustache and thick bushy eyebrows. Bell wore a light mustache and a goatee. At Rose's insistence they did everything possible to keep their dual lives separated. Both had some plastic surgery when they first came to the U.S. Not a lot, just enough so they wouldn't be easily identified by any old photos.

Both men frequented the speakeasies in Denny Camp, sometimes together and sometimes alone. One evening Bell was walking along the riverbank when a woman in panties only burst through a door saying “Stop, you bastard.” A man in his underwear with a large knife in one hand and a bottle of whiskey in the other followed her cursing loudly. They ran slowly around the house, twice.

“Come here you bitch. You’ll do what I say or else.”

“The hell with you,” she answered and crouched behind Bell.

“Oh, a new boyfriend,” he said as he approached.

“I don’t even know him. But he’s better than you.”

“I’ll slit your damn throat if you don’t do what I want.”

“Screw you.” Then to Bell in a low voice, “He’s drunk, he’ll go back inside in a minute,”

After a minute of staring and drinking he dropped the knife and staggered inside.

The woman, who tried to cover her bare breasts with folded arms, appeared no worse for wear and completely calm.

“He gets that way when he’s drunk. Wants kinky sex and stuff. I don’t mind but when he pulls out a knife, I leave. What’s your name, honey?”

“Lars Nelson. What’s yours?”

“Helen Butler. His name’s Bill. When he’s sober he’s a real nice guy. But when he’s been drinking for several days he gets kind of crazy. Do you live nearby?”

“I rent a house down the street.”

“Oh, the one owned by the Jacobs?”

“Yes, that’s the one.”

“Maybe I’ll sneak down there some night,” she said in a low voice.

"If you do make sure no-one sees you."

"Don't worry, if I do, I'll go down our steps and come up yours after he's asleep. Where are you headed now?"

"To Red's place."

"Oh, Whiskey Red's. He's one of my favorite people. Have a good time," she said and walked back inside.

He continued his walk along the riverbank to Red's. When he got there three men and the paperboy, Micky, were pitching horseshoes. He said "Hi" and walked past the cabins to the main building.

Once inside Red said "Hey Lars, how's it going, want a beer?"

"Not bad, and yes. I was walking along the riverbank and the strangest thing happened. A woman ran out of a house, chased by a man with a knife in one hand and a bottle of whiskey in the other. He chased her around the house twice, cursing the whole time. Then they both stopped. He cursed and threatened some more, took a couple of swallows from the bottle, and went inside."

"Were they both about half clothed?" Asked Monk.

"Yeah."

Everyone laughed. "That's Wild Bill Butler and Helen. He's been chasing her around that house for years," said Red.

"I think he meant to kill her."

"I don't doubt it. But she's faster than him and if push came to shove, in the shape he gets in sometimes, I think Helen can whip him," said Monk.

"I don't know. I watched from the riverbank. After he went inside she talked for a minute then went in too."

"They live right next to Charley there," said Red indicating a man wearing glasses that appeared overdressed in a coat and tie.

"That's right. He's been scaring the hell out of my wife for years," said Charley.

"Won't the police do anything?"

"Not much except talk. Helen won't press charges and Wild Bill sobers up and apologizes to everybody and things go back to normal for a while. Actually, he's a hell of a nice guy when he's not on a bender. He's got a short wave set and talks to people all over the world, all the time day and night. Hell, he speaks three or four languages better than most of us speak English. You can't help but like him."

"Doesn't he work?"

"Doesn't have to. He's got some patents to do with electronics. He says he won't ever work again."

"What about her."

"She started out years ago as his housekeeper, then she moved in with him. Hell, nobody knows if they're married or not and I don't guess it matters much."

Bell stayed a while sipping on his beer. He met a few more people, a couple named Ralph and Irene that lived just two doors from Red's place and another couple Johnny and Mabel that lived a little ways in the other direction. After a while the guys pitching horseshoes came in and had a few beers. Micky had a Pepsi and a sandwich.

"Who won pitching?" Asked Red

"Hell, that kid's pretty damn tough to beat," said Jerry a large overweight man smiling and shaking his head.

"I told you to take him as a partner," said Monk.

"I thought you were shitting me. Now I know better."

Bell stayed and drank three beers his self-imposed limit. He walked back home, purposely on the road this time. He thought of the possibilities if Helen did what she said.

Back at the house Bell told Rose about Wild Bill and Helen.

"What do you think about Helen?"

"She's about fifty something and not too much to look at, but I'm sure she'll show up some night. I just can't say how game she'll be."

Rose liked card playing and most evenings a low stakes game of knock rum or poker could be had at Red's place. The usual players were Red, Monk, the Jacobs brothers, Roy, and Micky for knock rum only. Red, Micky's stepbrother, wouldn't let him play poker. Occasionally Pete or Johnny played if their wives weren't present.

Rose and sometimes Bell joined in the game if there was room. Five players were the limit on knock rum and six on poker.

They were playing knock rum one evening in early May, Red, Ike, Monk, and Rose when Micky came by and asked to play.

"You have to have at least three dollars table stakes. Do you have it? Asked Red.

"Nah, I only have one fifty."

"I'll loan him two dollars," said Ike.

"You know the rules. No loaning money in the game," said Red.

"I'm loaning him money before he gets in the game."

"What about it," said Monk "As long as Ike doesn't take money off the table, I don't see any problem."

"Me neither," said Ike.

"What about you, George," said Red to Rose.

"I say let him play."

"Okay, play," said Red.

The game commenced. Right away Micky knocked. His hand of seven was low and he collected from them all. He knocked with six and won again. The third time was too much for Red. "I told you guys not to do this," he said.

Rose had been staring at Micky on and off since the first hand. Micky began to feel uneasy and after a few more hands he repaid Ike and left still ahead another two dollars.

About that time an attractive woman in her late thirties or early forties entered the room.

"Can a gal get a drink around here?" She asked.

"If she has the money," said Red.

"What have you got?"

"What do you want?"

"I'll take a highball with whiskey and seven up," She said and sat down near the game.

"I can handle that."

"You own this place?"

"That's right, I'm Red. What's your name?"

"Mary Ann."

Red introduced everyone.

"Are the cabins for rent?"

"Yes, we're re-doing them. Would you like to take a look?"

"Yeah, when I finish my drink.".

The game continued and she exchanged some light banter with the players. She finished her drink and said, "I'm ready to see a cabin now."

Red finished the hand then escorted her to the first cabin on the left.

"We've been running water and electricity to the cabins. This is the first one done," he said as he let her inside. It had two rooms. The first was a kitchen and living room combined. Behind it was a bedroom with a small bath.

"All the conveniences of home," she said.

"Absolutely."

"How much?"

"One dollar a night or five fifty a week."

"I'll take it for a week."

She gave him a ten-dollar bill. "Don't forget I owe you for the drink."

"I won't. Are you coming back inside?"

"No, I'm tired."

"That's six dollars total," he said and handed her four dollars. "You can park in front of the cabin if you like."

"Okay, thank you," she said and closed the cabin door behind him.

Red went back inside the building.

"She's quite a looker," said Monk.

"Did she rent a cabin?" Asked Ike.

"Yeah, for a week."

"If I had known she was coming I would have saved Lars and George's house for her," said Ike. Everybody laughed.

"Something's strange about her. I just can't put my finger on it."

"What's so strange?" Asked Monk.

"I mean she just shows up out of the blue, orders a drink, then rents a cabin for a week, that just seems strange."

"Count your good fortune," said Rose.

"Yeah, I just hope she isn't trouble."

"Red, I see you have an airplane tied to your dock. Did you fly in the war?" Asked Rose.

"Yeah."

"In Europe or the Pacific?"

"Europe"

"He was an Ace," said Monk.

"An Ace? What exactly is an Ace?" Asked Ike.

"An Ace is a fighter pilot with at least five kills," said Monk.

"What aircraft did you fly?" Asked Rose.

"P-38s and P-51 Mustangs. Now let's drop it. No-one's a hero here. Everyone just did their jobs, so let's forget it."

"Do you give rides in your airplane?" Asked Rose.

"I have on occasion."

"If you go again sometime and I'm around, I would like to go with you. I'll pay for the ride."

"Maybe."

About 10PM the group broke up. Rose was the last to leave. Mary Ann was sitting outside on the porch.

"Nice night," she said.

"You make it even nicer," said Rose.

"You think so, huh?"

"Yes. I think you make it nicer and could make it much nicer."

"Maybe."

"Well, if you would like company some night, I live in the yellow house just past the track crossing."

"I'll remember that."

"Good," he said and left for home.

When Rose got home, he walked around to the back porch. On the way he noticed a light on in Bell's bedroom. Once on the porch he filled a glass with water from a pitcher they kept in a small refrigerator they added. After a few minutes he heard some muffled voices from inside the house. He went to Bell's bedroom and opened the door. Bell and a woman were sitting naked in bed, propped up by pillows.

"This is Helen," he said.

Helen pulled a sheet up to her chin.

"So I see. I'll leave you kids alone," he said and closed the door. A few minutes later he returned stark naked.

"My turn," he said.

"Like hell it is," said Helen as she got out of bed near the far wall.

"Excuse me my dear," said Bell as he got out on the other side.

Rose climbed in the bed. He held out his arm palm up in an exaggerated genteel way and said, "Come sweetheart."

"What the hell do you think you're doing?"

"Waiting for you."

She looked at Bell and said, "Aren't you going to do something?"

"I'm going to get a drink. Have fun."

"I'm not doing anything with you. I'm leaving."

"What do you think Wild Bill would think of this situation?"

"You wouldn't dare tell him," said Helen stopping in mid-stride.

"Not if you get back in bed. Otherwise?"

"Damn you," she said. She stood there for a moment longer then got back in bed. "What the hell," she muttered as she turned to Rose.

A little while later Rose joined Bell on the porch.

"Is she coming out?"

"Yeah. She said she would like a glass of white wine first."

Bell opened the refrigerator and poured her a glass of Chardonnay.

"Take it to her. Then maybe she'll drink it and come out here with us. Treat her nice and she'll be back."

"You think so?"

"Yeah. She got back in the mood after you left."

The next day Micky stopped at Red's on his way to pick up his newspapers.

"Why did you leave so early last night?" Asked Red.

"George Drum."

"What about George?"

"It's his eyes. They make me feel like he's trying to burn a hole in me."

"What?"

"He's scary."

"George? How?"

"I just told you. I think he could kill someone without batting an eye."

"No way. George is too good natured." Red shook his head while he wiped off a table.

"I think that's an act. I've seen him look at people. Last night it was me. I don't like him. I don't like to be around him," said Micky giving an exaggerated shiver.

"Okay, okay. Just keep it to yourself."

A few days later-on a Saturday-Mary Ann stopped by Rose and Bell's for a visit.

She knocked at the door and Rose answered.

"Mary Ann, the beautiful, come on in."

"Don't you have some place we can talk outside?"

"Sure." said Rose and he took her around to the back porch.

"Where's your car?"

"Still at Red's. I like to walk."

"Oh good, so do I."

She stayed a couple of hours, chatting with Rose. They swapped some personal history, his was all lies.

She left about 6 PM after a promise to return. At the end of her week at Red's, she extended for another one.

Rose came down to Red's after work one night and she was sitting at a table on the big porch drinking a highball. He pulled up a chair. Micky came by and Rose asked him to bring him a beer.

Red wouldn't let Micky serve alcohol, so he did it himself.

After Red went back inside Rose asked Mary Anne about her plans. "Are you going to stay with us for a while longer?"

"I paid Red for another week. After that's up I'm leaving."

"I'm sorry to hear that. Maybe you'll come by for another visit before you leave?"

"I'll try."

"Please do, can I buy you another drink?"

"No, I've had my limit."

They sat for a while then he went inside and drank another beer.

"Did you get anywhere with her George?" Asked Monk.

"Nope, afraid not." he said and left by the side door.

The last day of her paid up time, she packed her car as if to leave then gave Red $1 for one more night. That night she drove to Rose's place and knocked. This time when he answered and invited her in she accepted the invitation. It was obvious she had been drinking. He offered her a burger and she ate with him on the back porch. She had a few more drinks and he told her he wanted to show her the house. When they reached his bedroom he reached out and pulled her close to him and forcibly kissed her on the mouth. She did not respond, but instead put her hands on his chest in an attempt to move away.

"I know I've had a lot to drink, but I don't want to go to bed with you. I'm engaged to get married. I came to Red's because I needed time to think, to be sure."

"And screw around," he said as he pushed her on the bed.

"No. Please."

"There are no 'no's' left."

She attempted to get up, but he slapped her hard in the face knocking her back on the bed.

Shielding her face with her hand she said, "Please don't do this I don't want to sleep with you. This is rape."

"We're past that now. I'm going to do something I enjoy even more than sex."

He hit her again, this time in the stomach. While she was gasping for breath, he opened the nightstand drawer exposing a large knife. She saw the knife and started to scream but he began choking her. She grasped his hair in her left hand, pulled his head down, then punched him in the nose and grabbed and twisted his left ear.

He punched her in the face, but before he could hit her again she put her arms up and the blows bounced off. He stopped, his lips curled back showing his teeth, then he growled and bit her left arm just above the wrist. She pulled her arm away and he hit her face again.

"Gina, I told you not to entertain my father."

"I'm Mary Ann," she managed to shout between gasps for air.

He choked her again, grabbed the knife and stabbed her in the stomach.

"Gina, you whore, you took advantage of me before I was eighteen. Now you bitch you won't have any more benefactors," he said and dragged her by the hair to the foot of the bed.

"Please, I'm not Gina, I'm Mary Ann. Please." She tried to get away, but he stabbed her again. She spit up blood. He raised her head in front of the mirror and slit her throat. She looked at him with sheer terror in her eyes then slumped forward from the bed to the floor.

"You bitch. You should not have entertained my father as a benefactor."

He reached down and cut off her ring finger. "My first souvenir."

When he looked up Bell was standing in the room.

"Are you alright?" He asked. His lips trembled and his hand shook as he took the knife from Rose.

Rose sat on the bed and looked around in a daze.

Bell said "Look, we're going to have to get her out of here, and her car, too."

Rose kept babbling about Gina and his father. Bell took the sheets off the bed, doubled them, and rolled Mary Ann in them. He went to his car and got some light rope that he tied around the body. Then he helped Rose take off his bloody clothes. He took Rose to the bathroom and put him in the shower. The cold water seemed to bring him around.

Bell waited until Rose got dressed. Then he took Rose's bloody clothes and put them in a large paper bag. He put the paper bag in the back seat of Rose's car. Next, he put Mary Ann's body in the trunk.

Rose sat outside on the porch while Bell cleaned up the blood in the bedroom. He used several towels and washcloths but finally got it clean. He put them in the washing machine and ran it on cold water to get out as much of the blood stains as possible.

At midnight Bell approached Rose.

"Look I have an idea where we can take her. When I was looking for a house to rent I went to a place in the country, if it's still vacant we can bury her there. I put a shovel in your car. Follow me in your car and we'll drop hers somewhere on the way. I'll take off the license plates."

"They'll still figure out whose car it is," said Rose.

"Yes, but it will give us a few days."

Bell put on gloves then got in Mary Ann's car and drove it out to the country. He pulled onto a side road then got out of her car. It sat at the edge of a steep ravine, he removed the license plates and he and Rose pushed it over the edge. They got in Rose's car and Bell drove to the house he had gone to before. The 'For Rent' sign was still in the yard. He pulled the car around the house. They took Mary Ann's body into the woods behind the house. Bell told Rose to take the car and come back in an hour. He dug a shallow grave among the trees.

He was at the roadside when Rose slowly approached. Rose stopped and Bell got in to drive. Rose seemed fully coherent.

"Did you bury her good?"

"As good as I could. There were a lot of rocks and roots. I put loose leaves over the spot. I think it will be alright. I put your clothes under her."

They drove home and Rose slept, exhausted. Bell didn't sleep for a long while. He put a pistol under his pillow and locked the bedroom door.

The next morning Bell checked the towels and wash cloths. Most of them came clean enough to dry on the clothesline. Those that didn't he laid out in the grass to dry. When they did, he burned them in an old barrel that had been used to burn sticks and trash. He threw the license plates in the river.

They expected any day to hear that Mary Ann's car had been found but didn't.

They both frequented Red's place but didn't hear anything unusual about Mary Ann only a couple of comments like Monk's.

"Red whatever happened to that good looking gal Mary Ann?"

"Damned if I know. She paid up and left."

"What about you George. I saw you talking to her on the porch one day?"

"That was the last time I saw her, but man was she ever good looking."

"What do you do for a living, George?" Asked Roy.

"I work for Western publishing, a subsidiary of Dent books. We do the printing for a lot of paperbacks."

"Does it pay pretty good?" Asked Red.

"Yeah, not bad. But it keeps me on the road a lot. I spend a lot of time in motels. I have a small apartment in the city, too. That's why I like it here so much, it's relaxing."

"What's Lars do?" Asked Pete.

"He's a dry-cleaning fluids salesman. It keeps him on the road pretty much, too."

Bell paid the house rent and Rose supposedly rented a room from him. It surprised no-one that they were gone during the week but usually one or both showed up on the weekends. Several other places in Denny Camp were rented or owned by people that came only on weekends or for the summer. It was as Rose said 'relaxed living' for most. They made it a point to go their separate ways a lot of the time. They both went to Sam's and Sarah's frequently as well as Lily's. Both of them liked Red's place, actually nicknamed Whisky Red's, the best. Bell took up horseshoes and got pretty good at it. Everyone played really well, even fourteen-year-old Micky. Rose played a lot of bumper pool, often playing with Red for quarters. He never won or lost much, Red saw to that, he made his money on the ten cents it cost to start the game. Both men liked to play shuffle board, often with Monk and Roy or Pete, for beers.

Every now and then somebody asked Red about that good looking Mary Ann, but Rose and Bell never did.

One Saturday afternoon in October they were walking along the riverbank. When they got to Red's he was just coming out of the main building with a beer in his hand. "George, you still want to go for a plane ride?"

"Yes."

"Well go get yourself a beer and leave a quarter on the counter. Bring me another one, too."

Rose got the beer and joined Red on the dock.

"Micky come down here and untie us."

They got in the plane. It was a two-seater. Micky untied the plane and pushed it away from the dock. Red started the engine and the plane moved farther away from shore.

"You might want to put on that seat strap."

"Sure, don't worry I will."

Red pulled back on the throttle. The engine coughed then the plane took off. They headed down the Allegheny toward Oakmont. Red circled around to get some altitude then came back by his place. He dipped the wings as a salute like he always did. He had one beer between his legs. He took a huge swallow then said, "Dead soldier." He turned the plane on its side, dropped the empty bottle out the window and opened another one, again putting it between his legs. He took a big gulp then said, "Hang on."

"How high are we?"

"Look at the altimeter, about 2,000 feet."

"Here we go," he said and put the plane in a steep dive at the Hulton Bridge spanning the river between Oakmont and Harmarville. When it looked like they might hit the bridge Rose asked, "Can you still get it over the bridge?"

"Not now," said Red and he flew under the bridge.

"Damn, you scared the hell out of me Red."

And he took a long swallow of beer.

"Here we go 'round again," said Red and this time he just barely cleared the bridge.

He flew farther down the Allegheny to Blawnox before he put the plane into a deep bank. He came back past Verona then Oakmont then past Denny Camp on the opposite bank.

"That was one hell of a ride."

"We're not done yet."

He went farther upriver gaining altitude then circled back toward the railroad bridge spanning the river near the end of Denny Camp.

"Here we go. Give me that cork in the ash tray," he said. Then "Better stick your finger in the bottle so you don't get too wet. Make sure your seat strap is good and tight."

He dove the plane directly at the railroad bridge and at the last possible second turned it upside down and flew it under the bridge. He flew it upside down past his place then righted it, circled the island in the middle of the river then landed and taxied to the dock where Micky tied the plane.

"Let's get out, that'll be ten dollars."

Rose still had his finger in his bottle and just sat there.

"You crazy bastard. I'll never get in another airplane with you."

"You wanted a ride. I believe you'll remember this one."

"I just hope I didn't shit myself," said Rose as he got out.

"You gave him the full double-barrel treatment didn't you," said Monk laughing when they reached the top of the steps.

"Mostly."

"Mostly? Mostly, you crazy bastard. I might have shit myself. I'm going to check."

—————

The next year went by pretty quietly. Helen visited the house on weekends when Wild Bill went on a bender. That kept them both pretty happy.

Bell took up visiting Sam's place more and more. He had a small two room cottage and sold beer out of his kitchen. He also went more often to Sarah's, an older white-haired heavy-set woman that had three cottages. She tried to rent out the other two but seldom had any luck. She kept two dogs, Pat and Molly, that Bell got along with pretty well. The trouble with Sarah's was that she didn't have an indoor toilet which meant that after a few beers a trip to the outhouse between the road and railroad tracks was often necessary.

Everybody played the numbers. It was addictive. Some, like Sarah, even had dream books that gave numbers based on dreams. Bill Flinn was the numbers man. He made his rounds every night. Some places gave him a beer, at others he had to pay. He called Denny Camp his 'beer route'. He often said he was lucky to break even.

Bell genuinely liked the weekends at the house by the river. He worried about Rose losing control, but he seemed to be doing pretty well. In the fall of 1947 Bell started going to Pittsburgh for a pair of prostitutes a couple of times a month. They all partied most of the night then Bell took them back the next day, usually making a date for the next week or two. This worked out well enough for months until after one visit in July when Rose turned up with gonorrhea. He visited a doctor in Oakmont where he received a shot of penicillin, then a booster a few days later.

"I guess that's the end of the girls coming out," said Bell.

"No. They probably got shots by now. We'll wait a couple of weeks to be sure."

A month later Bell picked the women up and brought them back to party.

Rose asked his girl if she had taken care of the gonorrhea and she said yes.

"When did you get your shot?"

"A month ago. I got checked again last week, I'm all clear."

They followed their usual routine early in the evening. At about midnight Bell's bedroom door was swung open hard enough to hit the wall. Rose turned the light on and walked straight to the woman's side of the bed. She barely woke up before he hit her with a hammer and started stabbing her.

"Stop, damn it," said Bell.

"Too late now. I'll teach these bitches to give me gonorrhea."

"Damn it Rose, don't you realize that some asshole had to give them gonorrhea?"

"I don't care. I feel better. Now let's go. We're going to take these two downstream and drop them in the water."

He cut off the woman's ring finger, then did the same to the one he left in his bedroom. They wrapped the women in sheets and took them to the back porch. Rose went to the steps and turned off the dock lights. They carried the women down one at a time to their small, fourteen-foot fishing boat.

"Bring a couple of fishing rods," said Rose.

"What for?"

"Cover."

They took the boat down river, powered only by a trolling motor. Rose carried out the acting, fishing from the bow. What they didn't notice was someone fishing from Red's dock. Micky was sitting between Red's plane and a boat owned by Blackie, a local cop visiting Red's. Micky saw the boat go by. He thought it was Bell and Rose but wasn't sure. He saw one of them casting out into the river. The boat was moving very slowly in the middle of the channel.

After they went by Micky put the catfish he caught in a bucket. Then he took them to Sara's where he gutted and filleted them. He slipped into Sara's kitchen and put the fillets in her refrigerator, then went home.

Rose and Bell took the women downstream below Harmarville then dumped their bodies overboard. They returned home about 3A.M.

A month later in late September the body of one of the women was hooked by a fisherman near Blawnox, a small town across the river from Verona, not far from where they were dumped. It was noted her ring finger had been severed.

———–––

Vittorino had let it be known when he came on board the U.S. Marshals that if anyone heard about something like that happening to give him notice. On September 28th he received a teletype from Pittsburgh.

To Vittorino Sabatini, Nashville office. Per your request for notification, a body with a severed ring finger has been recovered from the Allegheny River near Blawnox, a suburb of Pittsburgh.

Vittorino brought the teletype to Johnson.

"I'd like to go to Pittsburgh to help with the investigation."

"Let's wait to see what the local police come up with," said Johnson. "If they have any hot leads or completely the opposite we'll see. We can't just bust in on their case."

"But this is Fontana's M.O. It's what I've been waiting for."

"I know. I know. Just wait."

On October sixth another teletype came in.

To Vittorino Sabatini, Nashville office. Per your request for notification a second body with a severed ring finger has been recovered from the Allegheny River near Blawnox, a suburb of Pittsburgh.

Vittorino again brought the teletype to Johnson.

"I'd like to go to Pittsburgh to help with the investigation. If I have to take vacation time, I will. This may be the mistake we've been waiting for them to commit."

This time Johnson acquiesced. "Okay, but first contact our Pittsburgh office to see if it's alright with them and the locals. If it is, pack your bags and go."

Vittorino called Pittsburgh, they said they had no problem with him coming. They called the Blawnox police, who said they welcomed any help by the U.S. Marshal's office.

The next day, October seventh, Vittorino left for Blawnox. Johnson told him he had one week to turn something up or return to Nashville. He got to Blawnox about 9 P.M. on the eighth. He immediately went to the Blawnox Police department. There was only one officer on duty.

The detective in charge of the investigation was on loan from the Pittsburgh P.D. and had gone home for the day. Vittorino asked where he could get a room and was told to go to Oakmont across the Allegheny for a good room. He found his way across the Hulton bridge to the Oakmont Inn where he booked a room for three nights. After eating he studied a map of the area.

The next morning Vittorino went back to Blawnox where he met the detective in charge, Sgt. Robert Kessler.

"Sergeant Kessler, I'm Vittorino Sabatini of the U.S. Marshals. I'd like to do whatever I can to help with the homicide investigation about the brutal murders of the two women."

"Good. I'm happy to get some help. The F.B.I. is supposed to be sending a forensics team here soon. They're undermanned just like everyone else, but I believe they're going to devote a whole investigative team to the effort to catch the murderer or murderers. Something about the possibility of fugitives from Italy and Germany."

"Yes, that's right. The one that removes the ring fingers was a Major in the Italian Army named Fontana. His partner was an officer in the German Army. They committed numerous crimes in Italy, including the murder of seven members of my family. I followed them to the U.S. but lost their trail in New York. Italy and Germany have issued fugitive warrants for them."

Stunned by Vittorino's information Kessler said, "That clears up a lot of questions I had, thank you,"

"I'm glad. Now can you give me an update on where the investigation stands?"

"It stands the same as it did when I started, no real leads. All I have is the locations where the bodies were discovered and the coroner's reports that state the cause of death for both women was a blow to the head, possibly by a hammer, and multiple stab wounds. The ring fingers were removed from both bodies. The coroner estimated they had both been in the river for at least a month and neither body had marks to indicate they were weighted down, but both bodies were pretty banged up which the coroner believes may be due to getting caught up against something for a while."

"Has anyone come forward to claim either body?"

"Not yet. The theory is they may be prostitutes."

"Do you have any idea where they may have been dumped into the river?"

"Nothing conclusive,"

Vittorino laid out his map. "Can you show me on the map where the bodies were found?"

"Right here for the first one," said Kessler, indicating a spot on the map just a little upriver from Blawnox. "And a little downstream for the second one about here, at Blawnox,"

"How far away is this dam across the river?"

"It's about five miles upriver just above Harmarville."

"Do you think the bodies could have gone over the dam?"

"It's possible, but I think it's more likely they were dumped between here and the dam. If you have any suggestions to help get things rolling I'm willing to try just about anything," said Kessler.

"One thing we can do is check the riverfront on both sides of the Allegheny. Somebody might have seen something unusual, and we might pick up a lead or two," said Vittorino.

"I agree. I know Verona and Oakmont the towns on the opposite side of the river fairly well including the police and the clubs. I think I can cover that area in two or three days at the most. I suggest we ask Blawnox police to do Blawnox and you start near Harmarville and work upriver. We can both do above the dam if necessary."

Vittorino agreed. Kessler asked Blawnox for help and a police car for Vittorino.

Blawnox police loaned Vittorino a police car and on Friday afternoon they started canvassing the riverbanks for leads.

Kessler started in Verona working his way toward Oakmont. Vittorino started in Harmarville. His first stop was at a series of apartments along the riverbank. He dutifully stopped at each one to ask if they had noticed any unusual activity on the river or its' banks for the last month or so. No one seemed to know anything important. Next, he stopped at Petrelli's tavern just past the Hulton bridge. The proprietors were friendly but didn't know of anything unusual. They suggested he try Werner grounds and Denny Camp.

"There's a lot of houses right on the riverbank. A lot of people fish and go boating and water skiing. There are three railroad crossings, the first one's about a quarter mile from here, on the right," said Mr. Petrelli.

Vittorino ate a sandwich at Petrelli's then went on to the first crossing. He was surprised by the number of tracks to cross. Once he crossed, he turned right to make sure he got to the end of the road before he started back. He worked the houses the same way noting the response of all the residents and listing the ones not home for a later visit. By Friday night at eight o'clock he had covered all of Werner Grounds. He couldn't drive into Denny Camp because posts prevented driving between the two campgrounds. He did walk through and stopped at the first few houses. The people at the first house didn't know of any unusual activity. The people at the second house weren't home. At the third house a large older man named Sam invited him in. It was a two room cottage that had several people drinking beer and one boy eating ice cream, all in the kitchen. Again, he asked the same question. No one remembered anything unusual, then the boy, Micky, spoke up.

"I don't know what you call unusual, but I was fishing off the dock at Red's after midnight about a month ago and a boat with two men fishing came trolling by."

"Do you know who the men were?" Asked Vittorino.

"No, not for sure, I think it might have been George Drum and Lars Nelson, at least it looked like it could have been their boat. It was real dark and all I could see were silhouettes."

"Is there anyone else it could have been?"

"Oh sure, a lot of times people go up the other side of the island then come down on our side. That could have happened. I don't know, it's just that I don't see many boats go by that late?"

"Did the boat come back?" Asked Sam.

"I don't know I quit fishing. I picked up my catfish and took them up to Sara's. I cleaned them and left them in her fridge. We ate them the next day."

"Did you walk home along the riverbank?" Asked Sam.

"Yes."

"Did you see any boats on your way home?"

"No."

"Who's Sara?" Asked Vittorino.

"She's a lady that rents out cabins farther up the road," said Sam.

"Thanks. I'll check the rest of the grounds tomorrow."

"So you're with the U.S. Marshals," said Sam as he walked outside with Vittorino.

"Yes."

"I used to be a Pittsburgh cop."

"I thought maybe you were by the way you questioned Micky."

"Old habits are hard to break. Any luck so far on the two women?"

"No. Not much that's why I'm out here checking."

"Well good luck. Do you want a beer or some water before you go?"

"No thanks. It's been a long day. How do I get back here to start tomorrow? I walked through from Werner Grounds this evening."

"You bypass Werner crossing and go on to the next one, that's Denny Camp. After you cross the tracks make a right and just keep coming until you get here," said Sam.

"Thanks again, maybe I'll see you tomorrow."

Early Saturday morning after breakfast Vittorino resumed his canvassing of Denny Camp. Even earlier Bill Butler got his itch for a drink. At first he resisted, remembering previous problems. But after a while as the urge grew stronger, he reasoned that this time things would be different. He would just have a few and keep things quiet. By the time Helen got up at nine A.M., Bill had reasoned himself through a pint of Scotch and Wild Bill began to emerge. By eleven he was on a full-scale bender, walking around the yard in his underwear carrying a bottle of whiskey in one hand and a large knife in the other. He cursed Helen and ordered her inside. She refused. He started to chase her. They went around the house at a slow run the usual two laps then Bill stopped for a drink and to catch his breath. They walked around one more time, with him cursing her the whole way. Finally, he stopped near the steps to the dock and after thoroughly cursing her he pleaded with her to come inside where he would 'put her out of her misery'.

Helen again refused and he dropped the knife and went inside.

After a few minutes Helen went inside and found him on a couch. She took the bottle of whiskey and covered him with a sheet. She sat on the back porch a little while then went down the dock steps. She turned left at the bottom in the direction of George and Lars' place where she believed she would be welcomed.

When she got to the steps to their house Ike Jacobs was doing some work on his boat and saw her. They exchanged greetings and she went up the stairs while Ike continued working. Ike had seen her sneak up the stairs before and had a good idea where she was going.

Helen went directly to Rose and Bell's back porch where she stopped and knocked.

collect for the week's papers. It was sort of a reward for putting the paper in the box instead of throwing it on the ground.

Abe's back was to the window, but Micky saw Ike holding his side and running to the house with Bell and Rose chasing.

He pointed and said "Abe, Ike's coming. He's hurt and they're chasing him."

Abe turned around and saw Ike being chased by Rose and Bell.

"Run for help Micky."

He jumped up and ran to help his brother. They met on the back porch where

Ike collapsed in his arms. Bell was close behind him.

"They killed Helen Butler," Ike gasped.

Bell picked up a piece of firewood and swung it at Abe who dodged. He then hit Ike who had fallen to his knees when Abe ducked. Rose ran at Abe with his knife. Abe ran to the kitchen. He tried to get in the knife drawer below the cabinets, but Rose came after him from one side and Bell came from the other side. Bell hit him with the firewood and Rose stabbed him. It was all over in less than thirty seconds.

Micky was outside backing his bike away from the kitchen door when Rose saw him.

"Get Micky," he said to Bell.

"Why, it doesn't matter now."

"More time."

Bell burst through the kitchen door just as Micky was about to get on his bike.

Micky saw Bell coming and dropped his bike. He ran across the field ahead of Bell. When he reached the riverbank he jumped as far down as he could then ran the rest of the way to the bottom. Bell took the steps as fast as he could but lost ground to the boy who was already up and running. Bell chased him for a short distance then ran back to the steps. He climbed as fast as he could then ran to the Jacobs house. Rose was coming off the Jacobs back porch.

"Did you catch him?"

"No. He was too fast. We have to go."

"Look two more fingers," said Rose as he held them for Bell to see.

"Why?"

"Because you hate Jews."

"Not them, I liked them."

"Is there anything here that identifies you as Bellheimer?"

"No, all I have to get is my gun and some clothes. What about you?"

"Nothing. I have to get my keys and my finger jar."

"Hurry, I saw a police car come in earlier. Let's take the Packard, it's faster," said Bell.

———

At Red's Vittorino was having a bowl of chili and a beer after interviewing Red and his wife Jean along with several customers when as he would say later, "All hell broke loose".

Micky came up the steps from the dock hollering. "Help. They need help," he said as he ran into the main building.

"Who needs help?" Asked Red.

"The Jacobs, they're killing them."

"Who is?"

"George and Lars. I was there. Lars chased me but I got away."

"Where?" Asked Vittorino.

"The other end of the grounds. This may be who you're looking for," said Red.

"I'll go check things out," said Vittorino.

"Not without me, Ike and Abe are my friends."

"Me, too," said Monk.

"Everybody stay here," said Vittorino as he raced for the car.

"Like hell we will," said Red.

Four of them piled in the car, Vittorino, Red, Monk and Micky.

"Stay here Micky," said Red.

"No."

"No time to argue, we'd all just follow right behind you," said Monk.

Vittorino started for the Jacobs.

Red described where it was as they rode, "The Jacobs brothers have the last house on the grounds. Lars and George live in the yellow one right before you get there. They could be at either place or gone by now."

———————

Rose and Bell ran across the field to their house. Rose went inside and got his jar of fingers. He picked Helen's finger off the floor and added it to the jar along with the two of the Jacobs brothers. Bell got his pistol and met Rose at the Packard. Rose started the car and headed for the crossing.

———————

As they came down the road Red spotted the Packard coming toward the tracks.

He pointed, "That's them."

"I'll block the entrance to the crossing. Everybody out on this side when we stop," said Vittorino.

He pulled the car up on the slope to the tracks, blocking the entrance.

Everybody got out on the left side.

"Down," said Vittorino. He stood at the hood of the car with his pistol aimed at the oncoming Packard.

"Damn one minute too late. Hold on we'll have to ram it. When we get close, shoot," said Rose.

Just before the Packard hit the police car both Bell and Vittorino started shooting. Bell hit Red, who was standing beside Vitorino, and Vittorino hit Bell. When the Packard rammed the police car it slid sideways onto Vitorino's left foot knocking him down. He couldn't get all the way up.

Rose and Bell bounced around inside the Packard. Rose got behind the steering wheel again and backed the Packard up. He rammed the police car again and this time he kept the Packard pushing against it moving it farther sideways. He backed up again and managed to drive across the tracks out to the main highway where he turned left on his way to Oakmont. By the time they got as far as Harmarville the Packard was overheating, the radiator had been pierced and steam poured out.

"Look there's Bill Flinn's car outside Petrelli's," said Bell.

Rose parked in front of Flinn's car and went inside. "Hi Bill," he said.

"Hi, yourself. What the hell happened to you?" Asked Flinn.

"Never mind. I need your car, give me the keys."

"No way."

Rose put Bell's pistol in his side. "Now. I don't have time to argue."

Bill reached in his pocket and handed the keys to Rose.

"Now bartender hand me your phone," he said. Once he had the phone, he yanked the wire from the wall. "Do the same thing to the pay phone Bill," he said.

Flinn walked to the wall at the far end of the bar where he grabbed the receiver on the wall phone and pulled on it until it disconnected.

"Now no one comes outside for five minutes, or I start shooting."

Rose walked calmly to the door then ran to Flinn's car, a '47 Ford. Bell was already inside.

"Take off your beard and mustache. I'll take off my stuff, too."

It took a minute or two, but nobody came out. Rose started the Ford and drove across the Hulton Bridge to their rented Oakmont garage. He helped Bell inside and into Rose's '40 Olds. He backed out the Olds and pulled in the Ford. He cleaned up the disguise pieces and put them in his pocket. They drove to Verona and Rose pulled into the garage behind the house on Second Avenue. Bell stood as upright as he could walking into the house. Once inside the house he collapsed. Rose immediately began to work on his wound, ripping off his shirt and applying pressure to stop the bleeding. Next, he got out his medical bag, which he never used, and some ether which he kept on hand for other reasons. He got Bell to his bed and cleaned the wound and his instruments with alcohol. He administered ether to Bell and began to probe for a bullet. He found it after a few minutes and removed it before Bell woke up. It had lodged against the shoulder but did not appear to break the bone.

———————

Back at the crossing, the second time the Packard rammed the police car Vittorino's foot came free. They all scrambled out of the moving car's way. Vittorino had a difficult time standing and couldn't get another shot off before the Packard was out of range. The bullet that hit Red creased the top of his arm barely piercing the skin.

Monk walked to the other side of the car and said "It's not drivable, the fender's pushed into the tire and it's flat. The right front door is going to have to be replaced. The good news is I don't see any leaks from the radiator."

Red dabbed at his wound with a handkerchief and said, "I'm going to the Jacob's." Monk went with him.

Vittorino hollered, "Be careful not to destroy any fingerprints. I'll be there as soon as I radio Sgt. Kessler."

Micky started to go with them until Vittorino said, "Stay here Micky you can help with their description."

He called Kessler and told him what happened then added "I think it would be good to set up roadblocks."

"I agree, in Oakmont and Blawnox. What kind of car were they driving?"

"A dark gray Packard that's severely damaged. They'll probably steal another one as soon as they can. Hold on and we'll give you a description of the occupants to broadcast." He turned the radio over to Micky and he gave a description of Rose and Bell.

"Is that good enough?" Asked Vittorino.

"Yes, I'll get right on the roadblocks and get these descriptions out on an A.P.B."

"Good."

Vittorino and Micky jogged to the Jacobs where Red and Monk discovered Abe dead in the kitchen. Ike was unconscious but still alive on the back porch. Monk propped his head up with a pillow.

Red was on the phone. "Operator this is an emergency we have one man dead and another seriously wounded. Please send an ambulance with blood plasma to number thirty-nine Denny Camp in Harmarville."

"That's number thirty-nine?"

"Yes, thirty-nine."

"Okay, I'll report it right away."

Vittorino quickly noticed both men's ring fingers had been severed.

"That confirms it. It was Fontana and Bellheimer."

"What confirms it?" Asked Monk.

"The severed ring fingers. Fontana likes to take trophies of sorts."

"Who are these guys?" Asked Red.

"They're fugitives from Italy and Germany."

"What did they do before this?"

"They're murderers. They killed people in Italy, and we suspected and now know they've killed in the U.S. The FBI is after them, too."

"Then why isn't the FBI here?" Asked Monk

"I'm sure they'll be here as soon as they can. That's why we need to be careful about fingerprints. They'll dust things down completely."

"The ambulance should be here for Ike soon. I suppose we should call the coroner for Abe," said Red.

"Yes, and the Harmarville police. Now let's check out the other house. Is it that yellow one across the field?"

"Yes. That's where Ike was running from when I saw them chasing him," said Micky. "They were my friends. They were good to me. I'm so sorry about Abe. I hope Ike lives." He stood shaking.

Red put his arm around Micky. He had to use a handkerchief to dry his eyes. "They were good friends to all of us. I hope Ike makes it, too."

Turning to Vittorino Red said, "It's the Jacobs' rental house and it's just like this one except the kitchen door faces the front not the side."

"And it's heated with gas not wood," said Monk putting a throw from the couch on Ike to keep him warm.

"Yeah, that's right," said Micky sitting on the floor beside Ike.

Monk and Micky stayed with Ike. Monk called the Harmarville police and the coroner.

Vittorino and Red went to the other house. Inside they discovered Helen's fully clothed body in the living room. Blood was splattered on the wall and floor and one table in the living room. A large wound was visible on her forehead and another wound in the back of her head. Both wounds had oozed blood on her body and the floor where she laid. Her ring finger had been severed. A hammer with blood on it was beside her body.

Red sat down on the couch. "This is Helen Butler. She lives with her husband Bill in a blue and white house not far from here. Sometimes he goes on a bender, and she has to shift for herself, so to speak, for a few days. She wasn't perfect that's for sure, but none of us are. It's a damn shame they murdered her." He shook his head and looked at Vittorino before continuing. "These aren't men, they're animals."

Vittorino continued to examine the crime scene, "From the looks of things, I'd say something to do with Helen went wrong and your friend came upon what was happening and was stabbed to prevent him from going to the police."

Again Vittorino cautioned not to touch anything. He phoned Albert Johnson in Nashville. Johnson called a friend in the FBI to alert them about the situation. The next day they sent a forensics team to Denny Camp. They fingerprinted everything including the cars. They promised the US Marshals, and specifically Vittorino that they would receive copies.

Vittorino stayed around interviewing people for two more days. It was obvious to all the investigators that Fontana and Bellheimer murdered at least four persons while staying in the little yellow house. The FBI put Rose and Bell on their ten most wanted list and promised to forward to Vittorino any information they obtained about them.

It was several weeks before Ike Jacobs was able to leave the hospital. He sold both houses and rented a cottage from Red until he could find another house in Denny Camp. Wild Bill Butler went on a bender for several weeks until he was finally put in jail for disturbing the peace. For months Micky had nightmares about the murders and Bell chasing him. It was months before the owner of the garage in Oakmont checked to see if anyone was still using it. He went inside and found Bill Flinn's car. He reported it to the Oakmont police, and they contacted Bill. When the Oakmont police found out who stole it from Bill, they called in the F.B.I. They checked it for fingerprints and impounded it for another month before returning it to Bill.

CHAPTER TWENTY-TWO

The close call at Denny Camp convinced Rose to live a quiet life in Verona. He also continued to see Jeanette every few weeks and wrote or talked to her at least weekly. She continued to press him about their marriage plans. He countered that he still needed another step up as a clinical director in a hospital. In late 1948 he gave her an engagement ring.

In January of 1949 the Louisville, Ky. V.A. Hospital sent out notices that the Clinical Director for Psychiatric services position was vacant, and they were accepting applications from qualified candidates. Rose talked to Dr. Wright and Mr. Caldwell, and they offered their support if he applied. He talked to Jeanette and worked out some details. He rented a small apartment in Ithaca and Bell had three telephone lines installed. He applied for the position in Louisville and received a call to interview. He sent Bell to man the phones in Ithaca.

The hospital was smaller than the one in Pittsburgh and it was actually about ten miles southwest of Louisville just outside of Sharpsburg, KY. He was met in the lobby by the outgoing Psychiatric clinical director Dr. Andrew White. Dr. White escorted Rose on a tour of two psychiatric wards. There was little happening on the wards. Rose had little to say and volunteered no suggestions for change, believing such comments would not please Dr. White. When the tour was concluded White and Rose conferred in White's office for about an hour. No probing questions were asked, and no criticism was made by Rose. White then took Rose to the Hospital Administrator, Mr. Jacob Heart. The three met for a little while before Mr. Heart indicated he wanted to finish the interview alone.

Heart asked several penetrating questions. Rose sensed Heart was not satisfied with White. He asked Rose about his assessment of the wards. Rose said they were not as clean as he would like, there were too many patients with nothing to do and too many ways to commit suicide, such as curtain drawstrings hanging down and hooks on the backs of bathroom stalls and in closets. They discussed supervision and the role of the clinical director. Rose was ready and gave his opinion on possible improvements he picked up observing Dr. Wright in Pittsburgh. At the interview's end Heart seemed impressed and said he would follow up on Rose's application.

A few days later Dr. Wright and Mr. Caldwell received calls from Mr. Heart. The next week Rose was re-interviewed by Mr. Heart. At the conclusion of the interview Mr. Heart offered to take Rose to lunch.

"While we're at lunch I'll show you the town. That is if you have time."

"I have time. By the way why do they call the hospital the Louisville V.A. when it's about ten miles away in another town?"

"Originally it was on the campus of another hospital in Louisville and named Louisville V.A. hospital. Since the new hospital was so close to the city the name was not changed. Personally, I prefer living in Sharpsburg, but I like recruiting like it's in Louisville. Let's go now, I think you'll like the town."

They drove less than a mile to the huge town square and Mr. Heart drove slowly around it. The center of the square was dominated by the county courthouse a two-story red brick building. It had a wide entrance on all four sides and was surrounded by a huge lawn with large trees that provided shade for benches along the wide sidewalks that led from the courthouse to another wide sidewalk with benches that ran next to the streets that surrounded the square. Diagonal parking spaces went all the way around the square. Across the street from the courthouse were the town merchants; five and dime stores, drug stores, banks, law firms, beauty shops, barber shops, department stores and several restaurants.

As they drove around it became apparent to Rose that something special was going on. The parking spaces next to the courthouse sidewalk were completely filled, mostly with cars and pickup trucks but there were quite a few larger trucks and even a few horse and mule drawn wagons. The pickup trucks were backed in as were some of the cars. They all had things for sale, everything from shotguns, rifles and pistols to rabbits, coon hounds and women's bonnets. Baby ducks and chicks seemed to be everywhere. One man had a cow for sale. Another had goats. There were horns from Texas longhorn cattle for sale on the hood of one car. A woman was demonstrating an old manual sewing machine that had a price tag of three dollars on it. At one spot women had an assortment of dolls dressed in homemade clothes and hung by strings on an aluminum pole that had many side arms that got shorter towards the top. Each side arm had several short stubby arms that held the dolls. Everybody was selling or trying to sell something. On the courthouse lawn lay preachers worked the crowd. Some had microphones and some just spoke loudly to anyone that would listen. Most but not all, had collection plates close by their feet. Also on the lawn were buskers doing tricks or playing in small bands. Girl Scouts sold cookies. Some churches had tables under the trees where they sold used clothing and crocheted items. To stop and spend a couple of minutes at each place would have taken at least a full day.

"What's going on?" Asked Rose.

"First Monday."

"First Monday?"

"Yes, Trade Day. Every First Monday of the month the town has Trade Day. People bring stuff to sell or trade."

"But don't the merchants get upset. I mean people selling things to each other instead of buying from them?"

"No. No new merchandise can be sold or traded. Just used stuff or homemade things like crocheted sweaters or gun racks. Everybody knows the rules. Of course, the animals are different. The merchants do quite well on First Mondays. As a matter of fact, First Monday actually gets started the Saturday evening before during the warm summer months. Everybody enjoys it including me. I like to walk around myself and sometimes I even find something to buy. Would you like to walk around for a few minutes before we eat?"

"Yes."

Heart parked on a side street, and they walked back to the square.

"I think you'll find just about everything you could possibly want here including local entertainment."

"I believe it."

They walked along the sidewalk on one side of the square with both men obviously enjoying themselves. Rose stopped several times to pet hunting dogs but they either growled and showed bared teeth or whimpered and tried to get away.

About mid-way they slowed to listen to a lay preacher that was halfway between the sidewalk and the courthouse. He didn't have a microphone but did have a strong voice and had gathered a crowd of twenty or so people listening intently. At his feet was a small round wicker basket with a few coins and a dollar bill in it.

"This is my church, and you are all welcome. Come," he said looking out over the gathering, "I don't mean I own this property, of course I don't. I preach in a building about ten miles from here in Farley. Most of the people there are saved. But here, many have never heard the word of the Lord," he said as he raised a Bible in his right hand until it was just above shoulder height. Slowly he turned his head to look at it and as he did the crowd looked, too. "Every thing you need to know about life is in this book," he said as he angled it slightly to the right and slowly moved it so those on that side of him had a better view. Slowly he returned it then passed it to his left hand and did the same thing. He lowered the Bible to his chest and embraced it with both arms. He moved quickly back and forth in front of the growing crowd always seeking to catch their eyes with his. "Every good thing is in this book. And every bad thing is in this book. Praise is in this book and scorn is in this book. Love is in this book and hate is in this book."

Certain he had their attention he slowed his movements and looked at his assistant who picked up the basket.

He was really rolling now, working the crowd, looking at each one in turn, always seeking their eyes with his. His mind raced (Maybe I can convince a few lost souls to come to our church. Maybe we can have a baptism or two.)

Words were flowing and his voice was raised. "Genesis tells the story of how God formed the earth in six days and rested on the seventh, the Sabbath. The story of Adam and Eve is in here. God formed Adam from clay and Eve from one of Adam's ribs. Eve ate the forbidden fruit. Cain slew Able. The story of David and Goliath is in this book. Battles and wars won and lost. Moses leading his people out of bondage in Egypt and delivering to them the ten commandments. All that and more is in this book."

Looking out over the crowd and a few more in the street that had stopped to listen he said. "But even more important to me as a Christian is the story of Jesus Christ our Lord and Savior, he came in the body of a man with the power of God."

He paused for a minute to gather his changing senses.

Speaking slowly and deliberately lowering his voice he said, "I feel the presence of Evil here today."

The crowd responded by looking around to see the Evil. Not able to identify it, they returned their attention to the preacher.

Heart and Rose continued to listen and walk closer.

He raised both arms to shoulder height and in a slightly louder, teaching tone he continued, "Evil hides the truth and masks itself. Sometimes it even appears as good. I feel the Evil is closer," and he cast a searching look at the crowd that had swollen since the sermon took on a dark side. Suddenly in a booming voice he said, "The power of the Lord is in me today. I feel Evil as I have never felt it before. There is the Evil," he said and pointed a crooked finger above the crowd at Rose.

Rose and Heart look at each other and laugh. Heart says, "I'm afraid you are vastly off course. This is a doctor friend of mine. He is a good and decent man."

Full of righteousness the preacher said, "I stand on the truth of my convictions."

Dr. Heart says, "Let's go Dr. Rose, he'll be passing the collection basket any minute now."

They walked away at a faster pace, but the preacher continued to point, and as Heart said, the collection basket was passed around and hardly a person in the crowd failed to contribute.

Heart led Rose to his favorite restaurant. It sold 'plate lunches', catfish, bar-b-q, baby back ribs, chicken fried steak and several others. All plates came with two sides and a salad, and the price ranged from $1.50 to $3.00.

Heart had the catfish and Rose tried the ribs. They both ate heartily, and all the time Rose watched the square.

"Well Dr. Rose what do you think of our little town?"

"Amazing. Simply amazing. I've never seen anything like this in my whole life. Whether you offer me the job or not I'm coming back here on a First Monday that's for sure."

At the end of the ride back to the hospital Mr. Heart told Rose he was impressed with his credentials and references, and he would be hearing from him in a few days.

On Friday Heart called Rose and told him he had been authorized to offer him the Clinical Director position at a salary of $34,500 per year plus a house on the hospital grounds.

Rose accepted the offer and gave the customary two weeks' notice. He told Mr. Heart he could not report before April fifteenth and Heart agreed.

—————

There had not been any calls to Olivier and Barnwell. Or to any of the lines Bell had installed. Bell paid the extra month's rent for leaving the apartment early and terminated the lease. He also discontinued the telephone lines. Everything had been done with cash. Nothing could be traced to Rose or Bell.

Rose went to see Jeanette in Ithaca. She was surprised and elated to see him. They made love. She fixed dinner and each had a glass of wine. Jeanette said since there were no calls to Olivier and Barnwell or the reference lines, that it was no longer necessary for her to be at Olivier and Barnwell to cover his tracks. He agreed.

"So when can I join you? When can we get married?"

"Right now I don't feel like getting married."

"But you promised we would get married when I no longer had to stay at the college," she said piteously.

"I know, promises don't always happen." He said without emotion.

"We've been going together for over four years. I've been waiting and living a lie for four years."

"I know, things happen."

He looked at the cat. It was older now. It was sleeping in its box near the table.

She started to cry, "Please, please." Then she was crying hard. "Please don't do this to me. I've told everyone we're getting married. I'll look like such a fool."

"I told you things happen. Plans change." He said again without emotion.

She stopped crying, just an occasional sob. "I'm not crying so much about you as I am for being such a fool. For doing all the things I did to cover your trail. You used me. For four years you used me and now you don't need me. I think I might just undo what I've done."

"You wouldn't like the results."

"How do you know, maybe I would."

"You wouldn't like it at all," he said. He got up from his chair and walked to the cat's bed and before it could run he reached and caught it by the fur behind its' neck and the tail. The cat screamed and looked terrified.

"Now, do you want to see this cat's head in one hand and body in the other?"

"No. Please. I was just angry. I won't do anything."

"How can I be sure?"

"I swear it."

He dropped the cat then walked over to Jeanette. He put one hand on her throat and one on the side of her face. "Understand what I said about the cat can happen to you, too."

She nodded. She looked into his eyes and a chill came over her, one so strong it raised goose bumps on her arms.

"Now you tell everyone that we had some disagreements and we decided not to get married. That's all you do. If you do more, heads will roll."

"I'll do as you say just don't hurt us." The love she felt was suddenly gone, replaced by fear.

She watched from the kitchen door and was glad when he left. She had been preparing for the possibility of a break-up for some time and now that it happened she felt relieved, as though a great burden had been lifted from her shoulders.

The next morning, she thought about undoing what she did to help him but realized the consequences would be severe. Besides she reasoned he must know what he's doing, or he would have been fired instead of being promoted. And she thought about what she saw in his eyes the evening before and was afraid.

She followed his instructions and let it be known that she and her fiancé had a falling out and agreed not to get married.

She returned to a routine similar to the one before she met Fontana and relished the time she spent with old friends doing things she loved.

CHAPTER TWENTY-THREE

Rose seemed to enjoy his position at the Louisville V.A. Hospital. He made improvements where he could. The wards were cleaner, and he made an effort to get patients active as he had promised Mr. Heart prior to coming on board.

In the back of his mind though he was concerned about Jeanette. And as Bell kept reminding him almost daily, she could put a monkey wrench into everything if she confessed to falsifying so many documents for him. So, in late March of 1950 he decided she would have to go. He made arrangements for a week's vacation in early June.

He left Louisville for Ithaca on June 9th. He stayed in Erie, Pa. for one night. The next morning he donned a full disguise. He put on a reddish-brown mustache and a full beard. He wore workman's clothing, old blue jeans, brown calf length boots, a black and white plaid shirt and a dusty brown hat. In the late afternoon of the 10th he arrived in Aurora, a small town Northwest of Ithaca on Cayuga Lake, and had supper at a small cafe. After supper he went a short way out of town to the Aurora marina where cabins and fishing boats could be rented. He rented a cabin and a boat for three days. He took the boat and searched the nearby shoreline until he found a spot that he felt was secluded enough for his purpose. He returned to the marina and spent the night in the cabin.

The next morning he put on the same clothes and drove South towards Ithaca. At Kings Ferry he stopped at a general store where he purchased some concrete blocks and a large quilt he pretended to admire so much he couldn't do without it. Further on he stopped at a hardware store in Lansing where he purchased a roll of galvanized wire. He arrived at Ithaca about 7PM and went straight to Jeanette's apartment. Just as he thought, her car was in the driveway and the apartment lights were out which meant she was probably on a date with Worth or out with friends. He left for about an hour to put gas in the car and get a bite to eat.

He returned just after dark. He put on a pair of gloves, quickly gathered up a hammer, the quilt, some tools to jimmy a lock and slipped around the old house. Wooden steps led from the sidewalk to Jeanette's apartment on the second floor. He climbed the steps and tried his old key in the door. Disappointed, but not surprised it no longer worked, he quickly loosened the porch light bulb, so darkness cloaked the landing while he worked to open the door. Before going inside, he replaced the loose bulb with a burned out one and then stepped inside very quietly. He strode silently to the old cat's

noisy outboard, he used the trolling motor to move the boat away from the dock. Once the boat was well out into the lake, he started the motor and went to the spot he picked out the afternoon before. He shut off the motor and dropped anchor. The sky was cloudless, and the bright, nearly full moon shone a golden reflection on the water. He wrapped wire around the quilt as tight as he could and attached two concrete blocks, one at the chest and one just below the knees. He slid her body along the metal seat and swung her legs over the side. He hesitated for a few seconds, then rolled her body into the water and said, "Bon voyage my dear it's been a real pleasure."

———————

Things were going well for Rose when in March of 1951 he attended a psychiatric conference in Lexington, hosted by the state. At the conference he arranged to meet Dr. Robert Pierce Chairman of the Board of Directors at Hardin Mental Asylum, a facility that had an opening for a Superintendent/Clinical Director. At first, they only talked about mutual medical interests. After Dr. Pierce mentioned that Hardin needed a Superintendent/Clinical director, Rose asked him about the hospital and the duties of the position. Dr. Pierce explained that the Superintendent was the hospital C.E.O. and as the Clinical director closely supervised the medical staff. He invited Rose to visit the hospital the next week and Rose accepted.

Dr. Pierce personally took charge of a long tour, including several buildings and key personnel. At the end of the tour

Pierce told Rose he thought he would be a good fit for the hospital.

"If you are interested, and I hope you are, send me a current resume that I can present to the board."

"I must admit it certainly is tempting. I'll send my resume as soon as I can."

" Good, I'll look forward to receiving it soon."

Rose went back to Sharpsburg, updated his resume, and sent a copy to Pierce who then presented it to the board on the 15th. They were impressed by Rose's credentials and agreed to a meeting as soon as Pierce could arrange it. Pierce called Rose and he agreed to meet with the board the next week.

The board only asked simple questions. They seemed as much interested in his personality as his medical knowledge. When the interview was over Pierce told Rose he would be in touch in a few days. The board voted unanimously to offer Rose the job if his references checked out.

Dr. Pierce called Dr. Heart at the V.A. hospital In Sharpsburg and Dr. Wright and Mr. Caldwell at the V.A. hospital in Pittsburgh. All three gave Rose a good reference. Dr. Pierce called Rose a week later and offered him $45,000 a year plus a house on the grounds to take over Hardin Mental Asylum as the Superintendent/Clinical Director. Rose stalled for a few days then accepted. He reported for duty on April 20, 1951.

Rose moved quickly to establish complete control. He rearranged staff supervisory duties to mirror those at Sharpsburg and Pittsburgh. Within thirty days everyone was well aware that Dr. Elliott Rose was in charge and expected results.

———————

At Sharpsburg on the First Monday in July, the Reverend Ethan Caldwell started talking with the bible held tight to his chest. "Good morning, folks, I'm the Reverend Ethan Caldwell. I preach Sunday mornings and Wednesday evenings at the Farley Community Church. I believe it's really going to be a hot one today. It's almost too hot to talk about anything except something that's very important and that's what I'm here to talk about today, something very important, your salvation and my salvation. You know you can't get to heaven at the bus stop, or the railroad station or by driving your car. But you can get to heaven if you follow what's in this book." He held up the Bible and continued, "The Bible tells you what is important. It's fundamental. Today, through passages in this Bible, I will tell you how you can be born again."

The words were flowing, and his voice was booming out over the crowd. He looked at his assistant who picked up a woven basket, with a few coins and a dollar bill already in it and started it through the crowd.

Looking out over the crowd and a few more in the street that had stopped to listen he said, "But even more important to me as a Christian is the story of Jesus Christ the....................." His eyes wandered across the street, and he stopped preaching in mid-sentence. A chill ran up his spine. A bearded man was watching him from a sidewalk bench. They stared at each other for a moment, then the man stood and walked to the corner and turned down a side street.

"Are you alright Reverend Caldwell?" The assistant asked.

"Reverend Caldwell are you alright?"

"What?"

"I said, are you alright?"

"Yes, I'm fine. Folks, thank you for your attention. We have to leave a little early today, but if you'll come to Farley Community Church next Sunday, I'll continue this lesson. Thank you for coming."

"Ralph gather up things and let's go," he said as he started to leave.

"What is it Reverend Caldwell? You look like you saw a ghost. You're white as a sheet."

"Nothing. Nothing's wrong."

They moved through the crowd and every so often Reverend Caldwell stopped to look back.

——————

After he turned the corner, the bearded man signaled for another to join him. "That's him. He spotted me. Follow him but be careful not to be noticed. Don't worry if you lose him, we know where his church is and his name. I'd like to have his home address."

"Why bother, he's no danger to us? Besides with the beard and the clothes you're wearing he couldn't possibly recognize you from before."

"I tell you our eyes met, and he recognized me. He's got to pay for pointing me out as evil when I was with Heart."

"I think it would be better to forget it."

"No. I can't. Call me later when you get back."

"Look, it's too soon to do anything about that. What if he tells his assistant you were here today in disguise and you kill him right away? It would blow our cover. You need to wait a couple of years at least so nothing is connected to you."

"I agree, I'll wait. But I still want his address."

"Okay, I'll get it."

CHAPTER TWENTY-FOUR

In the spring of 1951, a teletype came over the wire in the Nashville Regional Marshals office from the U.S. Marshals Regional office, Syracuse, New York. It was addressed to Vittorino and read: As you requested, we are notifying your office that local authorities have a woman's body with a severed ring finger. It was found in Lake Cayuga near Aurora, New York. It floated to the surface and was discovered by two fishermen two days ago, April 16. They have not yet been able to identify the body.

Vittorino immediately took the teletype to Albert Johnson. Johnson reviewed the teletype and asked, "Where is Lake Cayuga?"

Vittorino pulled out an Atlas and they found Aurora and Lake Cayuga on the map.

"I think what we need to do is ask the Syracuse office to keep getting updates from the local authorities and pass them on to us. Call that office and explain about the Italian and German warrants and the reason you are so interested."

"What about me going to Ithaca?"

"I think it's best at this point to let the local police and the local Marshals office handle things. At least until we know more about the situation, such as the name of the deceased," said Johnson.

Vittorino called the Syracuse office and explained to deputy marshal Bill Kohler why the Italian and German warrants were issued and why he was so interested in the body with a severed ring finger. Kohler said he would offer to help the local authorities and keep Vittorino informed of any developments.

A week went by without response. After two weeks Vittorino called Kohler. He was apologetic, but said he had no news. The local authorities were checking missing person identities and trying to use dental records to make a positive I.D. Kohler assured Vittorino they were moving as fast as possible.

On June 10th Vittorino received a call from Kohler.

"Vittorino?"

"Yes."

"This is Kohler. We have a positive I.D. on the body."

"Who is it?"

"Jeanette Strube, she is from Ithaca, New York. She has been missing since June,1950. She was a clerk or secretary at Olivier and Barnwell University. She was in her late 30's, 38 I believe, unmarried."

"Any suspects in the case?"

"Just one so far. A boyfriend, John A. Worth, he's a professor at Olivier and Barnwell University. He began seeing her again a few months before she disappeared. He is known to have a temper. Does any of that ring a bell?"

"No. What do you mean began seeing her again?"

"They were an item and then broke up for a few years, then started dating again."

"How tall is Worth?"

"He's above average height, about 5'11" or 6 feet."

"With a temper."

"Yes. That's all we have for now. The locals are checking him out. His background, how bad a temper he has, etc."

"Okay. The guy I'm interested in is about 6' tall. I'll send you a picture for comparison, and one of his partner. They are both wanted and are both ruthless."

"I'll keep you posted," said Kohler.

Okay, thanks."

Vittorino sent the pictures by airmail. A week later Kohler called again.

"Vittorino?"

"Yes, is this Kohler?"

"Yes, bringing you up to date."

"Good, what's happening?"

"First, Worth doesn't match either picture. Not even close."

"Any more news?"

"Yes, Worth doesn't look to be the murderer."

"You sure?"

"We're about as sure as we can be with a homicide this old. Worth's temper may be considered bad in his circle but not in the general population, he's actually a pretty quiet guy. No arrests of any kind."

"Anyone else possible?"

"Not really. I talked with the family. She was engaged to another guy, but he moved to Pittsburgh about five years ago. They stayed together a couple of years but then split up. She told her parents it wasn't working for either of them, so they mutually agreed to call off the engagement. The parents couldn't recall his name, they never met him. They say Jeanette said he was very meek. They don't believe he had anything to do with the murder."

"Okay, thanks for letting me know what's happening."

"If I find out anything more, I'll let you know."

"One more thing, it would help to learn the name of the guy that went to Pittsburgh or where he went to work there."

"I'll try."

"Thanks again for the update."

"You're welcome."

Vittorino and Johnson discussed the latest information. Vittorino sensed Fontana was the killer, so did Johnson.

"I don't think you going there would help much if anything. It looks like the locals and Kohler have done a good job with little or nothing to work with besides dead ends. If it's him he will strike again. We will wait him out."

CHAPTER TWENTY-FIVE

In June of 1952 the U.S. Marshals office in Louisville, Kentucky sent a teletype to the Nashville office. It read: As per the request of your agent Sabatini about any body(s) found with a severed ring finger, one such woman's body has surfaced in the Ohio River near Shepherdsville. Please contact agent David Martin of our office for more information if desired. Vittorino immediately took the teletype to Captain Johnson who agreed that Vittorino should contact agent Martin for any additional information available. Vittorino called the Louisville office.

"U.S. Marshals Office, may I help you?"

"This is Deputy Marshal Vittorino Sabatini of the Nashville Office. I would like to speak to David Martin, please."

"Hold, please I'll transfer you to him."

"Hello. This is Deputy David Martin. I thought you might be calling, Vittorino."

"Yes. Thanks for keeping me in the loop. Just where exactly was the body found? I mean on which side of the Ohio?"

"It was found on the Kentucky side, but the Indiana police have been notified, also."

"Any luck on an I.D.?"

"Not yet. It could have come from just about anywhere upstream, the currents in the Ohio are very strong."

"Any idea how long it was in the water?"

"Long enough for it to be picked practically clean. The preliminary estimate from the Medical Examiner's office is at least months, maybe longer. I know why you are interested in any body showing up with a severed ring finger. I'll keep you up to date with any information we come up with."

"I would appreciate it if you would ask your boss if he would mind if I came up there and looked over everybody's shoulder for a few days."

"Hold on, I'll check."

After a few minutes he returned. "Captain Reed says you are welcome to come up and lend a hand."

"Thanks. I'll try to arrange my schedule to come up as soon as possible, hopefully tomorrow, good-bye and thanks for notifying our office."

Vittorino asked for and was granted time to help identify the body and pursue any leads in the case. He helped local and state police in both Indiana and Kentucky search missing persons reports as far back as June of 1951. They checked with individuals and families on both sides of the Ohio to determine who was still missing and came up with a list of eighty people from an area ten miles downstream from Shepherdsville to about ten miles upstream from Louisville. They obtained dental records for seventy three of the eighty and checked them to those of the body and identified it as Joan Bleecher of Louisville, missing since December 1951. They checked all the dental records to make sure there wasn't another perfect match and again interviewed the other seven families to see if they knew about their loved one's dental records. All seven families said their family member either had no dental work or nothing as extensive as the body's.

Vittorino was part of the team that investigated Miss Bleecher's death. They determined that she lived a relatively quiet life. She was in her mid-twenties and worked at a local shoe factory where she was a quality assurance inspector. She was well liked and had dated two men at the factory, both of whom seemed particularly distressed to learn she had been murdered. Neither had a clue as to who would do such a thing, and neither was dating her when she disappeared. Background checks failed to turn up anything suspicious about the men. Neither man was the size of Bellheimer or Fontana and their features weren't close.

They interviewed other co-workers and came up with nothing. They checked her friends and none of them knew her to be dating anyone at the time of her disappearance. It looked like a dead end, but Vittorino took this to indicate the murder was committed from outside Miss Bleecher's circle of friends and co-workers, and he believed it was the work of Fontana. Miss Bleecher's apartment had been rented to another woman a month prior to the discovery of her body. Vittorino received permission from the woman to check it for fingerprints, which he did with the help of the local Marshal's office.

They also fingerprinted the new tenant and the members of her family and friends that had visited the apartment. These prints along with the prints of Miss Bleecher's family and her known visitors including former boyfriends were given to a fingerprint expert and checked against the prints Vittorino and the marshal's office found in the apartment.

When the expert finished he found one set of finger prints from the left hand of what he believed to be a man that did not match any of the prints from the known visitors of either woman's family or friends. Vittorino identified those prints as having come from the interior frame of the apartment door. He had two photocopies of the set made, one for his office for future reference, and the other set he sent to the FBI with a request to match them with the prints of Fontana and Bellheimer from Pittsburgh.

Though he couldn't be sure, Vitttorino believed there was a very good chance the prints belonged to Bellheimer or Fontana.

The investigation continued until all possible leads had been checked and rechecked and Vittorino returned to Nashville where he and Johnson discussed the case.

"I believe the murderer was Fontana. Nothing was discovered to dissuade me from that," said Vittorino.

"I agree it could very well be Fontana."

"It's so discouraging. It looked promising in the beginning but ended up being another dead end."

"Look, for only the third time in eight years something has happened, a body with a severed ring finger has surfaced and you found fingerprints that could very well be tied to Fontana or Bellheimer. So far, they have been very careful. They have new identities; they may have even had surgery to help change their appearance. But wherever they are, they're probably growing more confident in their ability to avoid capture. If they reach any position of power they'll make a mistake or an investigator will notice something. It may be small, maybe even a hunch, but it will happen. And you want to be around when it does."

"You're right, it will happen, and I want to be around when it does."

CHAPTER TWENTY-SIX

In August of 1953 a teletype was received in the Nashville office about another body with a severed ring finger found in a shallow grave near Pittsburgh, Pennsylvania. Missing persons reports failed to turn up an identification.

A story was printed in the Pittsburgh Press about the discovery and the fact that a necklace containing a locket was found on the body. A picture contained in the locket was well preserved and printed in the paper along with a picture of the locket. The woman's family came forward to identify the picture and the locket. The police used the information plus dental records to positively identify the body as that of Mary Ann Hostetter of New Kensington, Pa. She disappeared in May 1946.

Vittorino went to Pennsylvania to investigate, but the trail was cold, and no suspects were turned up. However, it reminded him of Jeanette Strube's long lost engagement to the man who went to Pittsburgh in1946. He was determined to find out who that man was.

He asked for and received a week's leave and drove to the Syracuse office. He reviewed the file on Jeanette and became convinced the mystery man may indeed be Fontana. He contacted Jeanette's friends and showed them a picture of Fontana and Bellheimer. No one could identify Fontana or Bellheimer but one of her friends said that Fontana had some similar features to the man engaged to Jeanette. She thought his name was Leonard Roberts, or Leonard Fredericks, but she wasn't sure. She knew he moved to Pittsburgh but didn't know where he worked or if he was still there.

The last person on his list to interview was Professor John Worth. Worth like the others was cooperative.

"Professor Worth I have an old photo of two men I would like you to look at in connection with the murder of Jeanette Strube," said Vitorino.

"Sure," said Worth.

Vittorino gave Worth the pictures of Fontana and Bellheimer.

"Do you recognize either man?"

"No, I'm afraid not. Besides I've seen these photos before."

"Do you remember the name of the man that Jeanette was dating after she and you broke up?"

"I'm not sure, it's been about eight years ago. Let me think for a moment. Hold on, I think his name was Leonard Franklin or something like that. I'm pretty sure that's right."

"Did he have an accent of any kind?"

"Nothing particularly striking. I mean I don't know where he came from, but he didn't seem to have a foreign accent if that's what you mean."

"Yes, that's what I meant. Thank you, Professor Worth, for your help."

"You're welcome, are you any closer to finding her killer?"

"No sir, but we're still working on it."

"I hope you find him."

"Me too sir, me too."

Vittorino was delighted. He believed he was right about the Pittsburgh-Ithaca connection and went to Pittsburgh to check it out. He went to the telephone company and asked for their help. They agreed to check their current records and to go as far back as 1946 to see if a Leonard Roberts or Leonard Fredericks or Leonard Franklin had been a customer. In the meantime, he went to the local library and reviewed all their old telephone books as far back as 1950. Neither Vittorino nor the telephone company had any luck. So Vittorino went to the local utilities, water, gas and electric and asked them to check their records. Again, he had no luck. He left Pittsburgh convinced that neither Leonard Roberts or Leonard Fredericks and maybe even Leonard Franklin existed, but that Jeanette Strube had somehow been entangled with Fontana and it had cost her life.

When Vittorino got back to Nashville and talked it all out with Johnson they decided to do a timeline and determined that Fontana and Bellheimer (more than likely) arrived in

New Orleans in 1944 but instead of going to New York City, they went to Aurora or maybe even Ithaca where Fontana met Jeanette Strube. In 1946 he went to Pittsburgh, Pa. for a job and in May of 1946 he murdered Mary Ann Hostetter. In August of 1948 they murdered two women believed to be prostitutes. In October of 1948 they murdered Helen Butler and Abe Jacobs. In June of 1950 he went back to Ithaca to murder Jeanette Strube. Then, they theorized, he murdered Joan Bleecher in December 1951. But the big question was, of course, where was he now? Was he still in Pittsburgh or had he moved South to Louisville after the 1948 murders and shootout with Vittorino.

"I believe he is in the Louisville area," said Vittorino.

"I do, too but let's not get locked into only one scenario. He could be somewhere upstream from Louisville, or he could have moved on again."

———

In March of 1954 Sheriff Will Scott of Rhodes County, Kentucky attended the FBI Training Center in Quantico, Virginia. Deputy U.S. marshal Vittorino Sabatini was also in attendance. They sat near each other in class. Each was a good listener and a good marksman. They got to know each other and talked about interesting cases. Scott had very little to contribute since he was from such a low crime county. After listening to Vittorino talk about his experiences, Scott invited him to visit Rhodes County. Vittorino said he would as soon as he could.

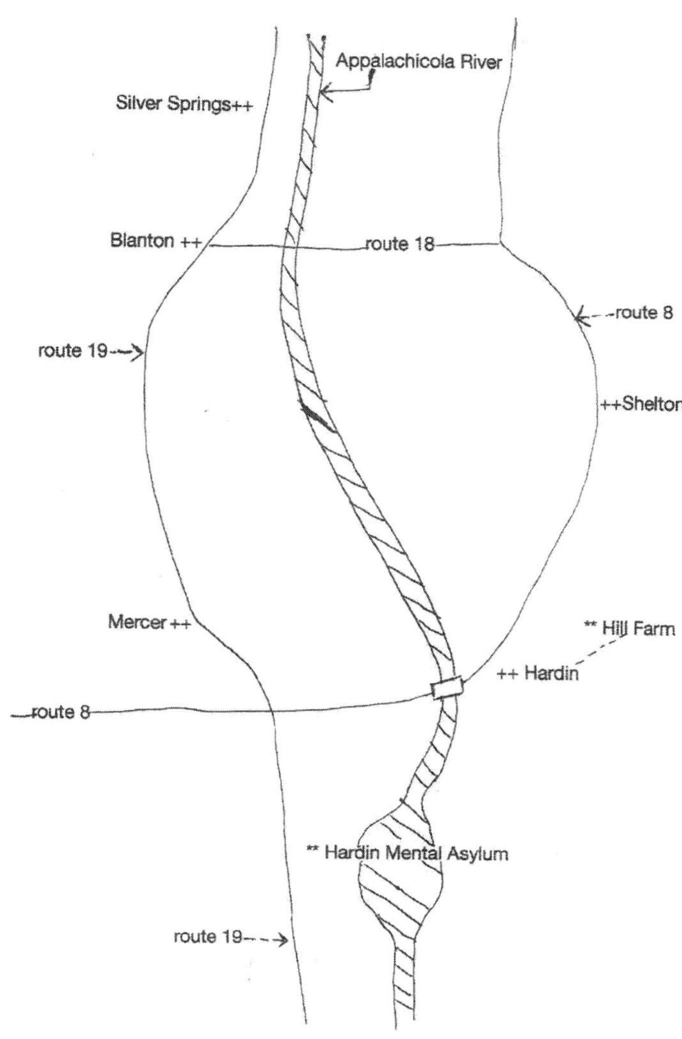
Rhodes County
Appalachicola River
Silver Springs++
Blanton ++
route 18
route 8
route 19
++Shelton
Mercer ++
** Hill Farm
++ Hardin
route 8
** Hardin Mental Asylum
route 19

CHAPTER TWENTY-SEVEN

Diane

On the morning of April 17, 1954, the phone rang in the Blanton office of the Rhodes County, Kentucky sheriff's office.

Deputy Will Carter lifted the receiver and heard sounds of a struggle: A woman said loudly, "Diane stop that. Help please, we can't hold her much longer. She's bleeding. We need help."

"Yes, ma'am, who are you?"

A second woman's voice roared loudly in the background "Ooohh, ooooh dammmn youuuu let me loo-oo-ooose! I hate you! Let me do it, damn you let me go!"

Then a man's voice, "We can't. Please stop honey, you'll hurt yourself."

Then yelling directly into the phone the first woman's voice: "Damn you! Aren't you coming?"

"Yes, ma'am. Where are you?"

"What?"

"Where do you live?"

More sobbing then, "I……don't …..we're….. trying…… to…… hold. Oh, God! I can't think," followed by loud crying from the second woman and finally a pause.

"Ma'am just tell me where you are!"

The line went dead for a few seconds, then, "This is George Cleary 116 Smith Street. Please hurry."

"Have you called an ambulance?"

"No, we caught her before she could cut herself too bad. But she said she's going to 'finish the job.' We need some help."

"Okay, I know Diane. I'll be there shortly." He called the main sheriff's office in Shelton to let them know what was happening then grabbed his hat and a light jacket from the hall tree in the corner of his small, cramped office.

Deputy Carter drove through Blanton as fast as he could. Traffic was light and the siren wasn't necessary. He arrived at the Cleary's less than five minutes after he received the call. He parked on the street then hurried up the sidewalk and onto the porch to the front door. He rang the doorbell and a male voice said, "Come in!"

Will opened the door and walked into a wide foyer. He saw Mr. and Mrs. Cleary on the living room couch with their daughter Diane, each one of them held one of her arms.

"Thank goodness you're here, we couldn't hold her much longer," said Mr. Cleary.

He had his left leg across Diane's to help hold her on the couch. She was struggling and crying. She cursed her mother and father: "You bastards, let me go, I'll be good."

Will moved quickly to the couch. He spoke quietly and calmly, "Diane this is Will Carter. We were classmates in school. Do you remember me?"

"Go to hell. Leave me alone. All you men are bastards."

Mrs. Cleary was crying and looked exhausted. Diane gave a strong heave and pulled her right arm free from her mother's grasp. Will quickly grabbed it and held it for a few seconds before handing it back to Mrs. Cleary. He pulled his handcuffs from behind his back and snapped one on Diane's right wrist. Diane tried several times to kick him, but he avoided her feet and deftly helped her parents roll her towards her mother. When they had her face down on the couch, he pulled the handcuffed arm to her back. Her father pulled his daughter's left arm back for the deputy to handcuff. Once she was handcuffed, Will looked at her left wrist.

"She doesn't appear to be bleeding bad. Do you have any gauze pads we can use for a bandage?"

"I'll get some," said Mr. Cleary walking toward the hallway.

"He caught her just as she started to cut herself," said Mrs. Cleary still nervously shaking. "What do we do now?"

"Well," said Will. "Do you truly believe she will try to do it again?"

"Yes, I do," said Mr. Cleary returning with the pads.

"Then we need to take her to Hardin Mental Asylum for treatment."

"No," screamed Diane. "I won't do it again. I promise. Please don't take me there."

Diane had slipped onto the floor and was on her knees facing the couch. Will held her while her father applied a gauze pad to her wrist and wrapped a bandage around it and tied it. Once the bandage was in place Will pulled Diane to her feet and held her securely.

"Mr. Cleary one of you needs to follow me to H.M.A. near Hardin."

He looked at his still-struggling daughter and said, "I'll go. I know where it is."

Mr. Cleary followed Will to the Asylum. When they arrived at the main gate a security guard stopped the cars.

"Are you here to admit a patient," he asked.

"Possibly, I don't know if she will be admitted or not."

"If you are armed you will have to leave your weapon in the trunk of your car to proceed. No one is allowed on these grounds carrying a weapon, it's the law."

"Yes, I know, I've been here before," said Deputy Carter as he exited the car and put his pistol in the trunk and locked it.

"Okay, I'll call Admissions and tell them you're on the way."

"Thanks. The man in the car behind me is this woman's father. Please let him through. He's not armed."

"Sure," said the guard and after a quick check of Mr. Cleary's car, waved them both on through the gate.

At Admissions two staff members met Deputy Carter. One spoke, "I'm Jessica Holmes. Will you help us take her inside? The nurse has already paged the Doctor."

"Okay," said Deputy Carter and he opened the rear door to help Diane out.

She was sitting next to the door. Her head hung down nearly to her chest. He spoke gently to her, "Diane, you remember me. I'm your old friend Will Carter. We used to pass notes to each other in school. I'm just trying to help you." Diane lifted her head and her eyes met Will's. For a fleeting moment she smiled, then her head dropped to her chest, and she cried. When he reached in for her arm she cringed and avoided his hand.

Mr. Cleary was standing behind him and said, "Let me try." He moved forward to the open car door and said, "Honey, you know I love you and I would never let anyone harm you. Please let us help you out of the car."

She raised her head and said, "Oh, Daddy, I wish I was your little girl again."

He looked up at the sky for a few seconds and one at a time took the palm of each hand and rubbed his eyes to clear them. Then looking in his daughter's eyes, in a near whisper said, "You'll always be my little girl, always."

"Oh, Daddy. Can I really be your little girl again, please?"

"Yes, you can be my little girl again. Forever."

"Thank you, Daddy," she said and leaned toward the door where he reached in and helped her out.

Outside the car, they stood together, her arms handcuffed behind her, her head touching her father's chest, his arms were around her, one hand held the back of her head, his face nestled in her hair near the top of her head. They stood for a minute then he led her into the Admissions building.

Inside the Admitting area a man wearing a white coat greeted them, "I'm Doctor Steve Carmine. Are you the young lady's father?"

"Yes, I'm Ted Cleary, I'm here with my daughter Diane. We're from Blanton."

"Please have a seat I'll be with you in a moment," said Doctor Carmine. Then turning to Diane, "Please sit down so we can chat."

Diane slowly looked around the area at her feet then back at the Doctor, but she did not move.

"Okay, let me get you a chair," said Doctor Carmine as he reached for one and sat it behind Diane.

Diane's eyes followed him, and she stared at the chair.

"Now there won't you please sit," he said and gestured to the chair with one hand and touched her shoulder with the other. Diane looked from him to the chair then sat.

Dr. Carmine said, "I'm Doctor Carmine and I'm going to ask you some questions. Think of it as a game. Answer every question that you can."

"I know your name is Diane. What day is today, Diane?"

No response.

"Do you know what year this is?"

No response.

"Do you know who the President of the United Sates is?

No response.

"Do you know your name?"

No response.

Diane's eyes were glassy, and saliva dribbled from her mouth and off her chin. A nurse wiped it off.

Dr. Carmine spoke to Diane, "I'm going to ask the Deputy to remove the handcuffs. Will you promise me you will sit still?"

Diane didn't respond. Deputy Carter removed the handcuffs.

Dr. Carmine spoke to Mr. Cleary, "Can you tell me what happened to her?"

"Yes, I walked into the kitchen just as she was trying to cut her wrist. I was able to take away the knife and got her into the living room. I called my wife from the bedroom, and she called the Sheriff's office and helped me hold Diane. Deputy Carter came, and we brought her here."

"Did anyone or anything traumatize her today or any time recently, the last few days perhaps?"

"Not that I know of."

"Well then, I believe admitting her is the best thing for her. You will need to sign the commitment papers. As soon as you do she will be taken to a unit and given a sedative to help her calm down. I expect her to be much better after a short stay."

"How long do you think she may have to stay?"

"There's no way to tell now, but I would say she could be ready to leave in a few weeks if things go well. But I emphasize that it depends on how she responds to treatment,"

"When can we visit her"?

"I would call in a few days to see if she can have visitors," said Dr. Carmine.

"Don't worry," said the nurse. "We'll take good care of her."

"I hope so," said Mr. Cleary. He paused then repeated "God, I hope so." Tears welled in his eyes and his hand shook as he signed the admission forms.

After Diane was taken to a unit Mr. Cleary and Will walked outside.

"Thank you, Deputy Carter. I appreciate the way you handled the situation."

"Glad I could help. I've always liked Diane. I hate to see her this way. Hopefully they will be able to help her so she can get back home soon."

"She hates this place. She was here before, about a year ago. She said they do things to her."

"I suppose they have to for treatment."

"She says 'other things not treatment things' but she won't elaborate."

"Well, I don't know about that. I would have to have something specific. Something for a formal complaint." He shook hands with Mr. Cleary and left him standing in front of the ADMISSIONS sign at the main building.

On his way back to Blanton Will stopped in Hardin to see a fellow deputy, Buford Hill. He parked his patrol car in the shade of a Live Oak tree then quickly crossed the sidewalk and entered the deputy's office.

"Hello Buford," he said.

"Hey Will. What are you doing here in Hardin?"

"I just delivered a young lady to H.M.A."

"How'd it go?" Asked Buford, then "Have a seat."

Will sat in a chair opposite Buford's desk and said, "It wasn't too bad, but I wanted to talk to you about it."

"Shoot," said Buford "Anything unusual?"

"The girl's been there before and begged not to be taken back."

"I can understand that. Was she suicidal or homicidal?"

"Suicidal. I've known her since we were in grade school together. She was okay until we got to junior high. Then it was like a light switch turned something off. She went from straight A's to barely scraping by. In high school it got worse. She started hanging out with a different crowd, drinking, smoking pot, and stuff."

"What kind of stuff?"

"Well, she was, is, awfully pretty and was kind of free spirited. That's all I'll say about that."

"Okay, I got you."

"Anyhow, after she was admitted her father, Mr. Cleary, and I walked outside. He said Diane said they did things to her at the Asylum, non-treatment things, but she wouldn't say what. I told him I had to have something more to go on for a complaint."

"Alright," said Buford. "I'll make a note on that. Her last name still Cleary?"

The next morning a different orderly made the last of the night shift checks on Diane. She made a note in her chart that she was 'awake and no longer struggling'.

Diane asked to be allowed to go to the bathroom. The orderly talked to the new unit nurse who read the night shift's complete notes. She agreed it would be okay. The two of them went to check on Diane and take her to the restroom, but it was too late, she had wet herself and was again tearful, but coherent.

"I'm sorry I couldn't hold it any longer," she said.

"I understand" said nurse Bratcher as she loosened Diane's restraints. "Will you behave if I let you go on the unit so you can take a shower?"

"I'll be good."

They escorted her to a bed in a ward of twenty women. She was given a change of clothes from a small gym bag her father had brought that was next to her bed. Diane seemed bewildered.

Nurse Bratcher spoke softly, "Come with us, we'll take you to the showers and after you clean-up we'll take you to breakfast."

After the shower and breakfast Diane was allowed to go to the unit dayroom. She sat through two hours of cartoons on a portable screen. Then she watched two women fight. They rolled around on the floor cursing, screaming, and hitting at each other. It took three orderlies to pull them apart. She watched as they struggled before each was taken to a control room and strapped down.

Lunch came. Everyone, staff, and patients, ate at tables for four set up in the ward dining room. The food wasn't the best. Vegetable soup, one half a baloney and cheese sandwich, a glass of milk and a chocolate chip cookie for dessert.

After lunch Diane again visited the day room. More cartoons, then T.V. on a very small screen. The Howdy Doody show came on. When some of the patients complained, an orderly said it was the only channel on at that time of day. Diane watched for a while then went to bed to rest. She slept until an orderly woke her for supper. Another plain Jane meal she thought, but was surprised to get a plate of spaghetti, garlic bread, salad, a glass of tea and a piece of apple pie for dessert.

After supper it was back to the dayroom where there was nothing to do but stare at the walls and read magazines. T.V. again in the evening, then bed. In the middle of the night Diane was wakened by someone trying to kiss her. She was groggy from the sleeping pill she had to take but managed to push and scream. An orderly came running and dragged the would-be lover away, but most of the ward woke up and it was a couple of hours before things quieted down enough to sleep.

Sunday was more of the same listlessness on the ward, but Diane did talk to a Social Worker named Mary Ann Humble. She asked Diane routine questions about her life, her health, her family, her job, and the anxiety that caused her to try to take her own life.

Diane told the truth; she just didn't tell everything. She was working at the box factory in Blanton, she liked her job and co-workers, her health was good, she lived with and loved her parents. Her anxieties were many, she was afraid at night, she worried about losing her job, getting pregnant, going to heaven and many smaller things, about her clothes, her education and what other people thought of her.

Mary Anne asked her to tell what specifically had triggered the incident two days ago and the one a year earlier. Diane said she wasn't sure. Mary Anne made some notes in Diane's chart and concluded the interview.

Diane made a friend, Evelyn Baker, a fellow patient who came in the day before Diane. She was a big girl, very heavy. She told Diane she had been there before, too. They talked a long time about their lives in and out of H.M.A. They exchanged address and telephone numbers and each promised to keep in touch after they got home.

About 10A.M. Monday morning the day shift nurse had Diane brought to the Dutch door in the middle of the nurse's station, a pentagon shaped reinforced glass structure from which most of the unit could be observed. Diane was introduced to Dr. Charles Emery a psychologist. Dr. Emery took Diane to the same interview room used by Mary Anne Humble the day before. Dr. Emery reviewed Diane's chart then asked her pretty much the same questions as the social worker. Then he added some more.

"Why do you think you're here?" Asked Dr. Emery.

"I cut my wrist with a kitchen knife."

"Do you remember being here before?"

"Yes, I do."

"Who is the president of the United States?"

"President Eisenhower."

"What day of the week is this?"

"Monday."

"Are you still afraid?"

"Yes."

"What are you afraid of?"

"I don't know, everything I guess."

"Do you like or dislike men?"

"I like some men, but not all?"

"Do you enjoy or not enjoy sex?"

"It depends, if it's with someone I like very much then I try to enjoy it."

"Are you bisexual or a lesbian?"

"No."

"Have you ever had sex with another woman?"

"No."

"What about a family member. A brother, an uncle your father or stepfather?"

"Why are you asking me all these crazy questions? They don't make sense."

"Why do you think I'm asking these questions?"

"I guess to figure out why I did what I did?"

"You mean, why you tried to take your life two times in one year?"

"Yes."

"That's exactly right. We, you, and me, need to find out why you tried to take your life so we can work to help you. Do you think that's a good idea?"

"Yes, I do."

"Good, then we're off to a good start. I'm going to make some notes before I forget my thoughts. While I'm doing that, I'd like you to think about anything you need to tell me. Okay?"

"Yes."

Dr. Emery wrote in Diane's chart for a few minutes then said. "Have you thought of anything?"

"No, I haven't."

Other technicians may talk to you. You will meet with the whole treatment team later in the week. This interview is finished, thank you for your patience," said Emery.

On Tuesday Diane and Evelyn met early and talked a lot. They both wanted off the Acute unit. Diane tried to watch TV when it was on but had a hard time concentrating. Every few hours she was given medicine that made her sluggish and sometimes she fell asleep sitting in the dayroom and once on the commode.

The nurses and orderlies on the acute unit had their hands full trying to keep things as calm as possible. Fights broke out daily, sometimes more than once. Patients tried to find ways to kill themselves which was difficult considering they weren't allowed to have belts, shoelaces, blade shavers or any hard surface items. The most common things were attempts using a piece of clothing, such as a bra to hang from a ward clothing hook. One girl almost succeeded after faking she took her sleeping pill, then waiting until everyone was asleep, she slipped out of bed then put one end of her bra on a hook next to her bed and wrapped the other end around her neck. She might have made it, but another patient woke up and screamed. The most unusual attempt was when a woman closed the door to a bathroom toilet stall then clogged the toilet with towels, flushed the commode, stuck her head in the water and flipped her feet over her head to the wall behind the commode. She would have drowned for sure, but an orderly heard her gurgling and saw water coming out from under the stall door. They got her out, gave her C.P.R. and saved her from drowning.

"Damn." One of the orderlies said "Now I've seen everything. That was close. If you're not nuts when you start to work here if you stay long enough, you will be. Damned if I don't think I'm getting close to going over to the other side."

Wednesday. After Tuesday's excitement Wednesday seemed rather uneventful.

Diane tried to remain as calm as possible. She was interviewed by nurse Katherine Varone and social worker Mary Ann Humble, again. They asked probing questions and

Diane opened up more to each of them about her life. But the one who really pushed her was Dr. Emery. He had the unit nurse bring Diane to the interview room and began to talk softly.

"I think we should sit at the table facing each other. Is that okay with you?" He asked.

"Yes," she said and sat at the opposite end of the long table.

"I want you to close your eyes and speak your thoughts out loud. Go all the way back to your childhood as far back as you can remember. Okay?"

"Yes, I'll try."

"I remember a birthday party. We had paper hats and little noise makers. We played games, everyone was laughing and having fun, it was great. I remember my first pair of roller skates, they were adjustable, anyone could slip them on their feet. A key fit the skates so they could be tightened to fit your shoes. I loved them. I remember walking and holding my dad's hand. He is so gentle. He never gets real upset. The carnival, we went to a carnival in Shelton, I rode the kiddie dips and tilt a whirl with my sister. Then we rode the ponies. My sister's pony stopped halfway around the loop, that's all the ride was, a long loop. She was so mad because her pony wouldn't go. My pony, named Doe, kept turning around and going back and forth instead of stopping at the end of the loop. I kept passing her, first going one way then back the other way. Everyone was laughing and enjoying watching us until the ponies finally went to the end and stopped. I remember the first day of first grade, my mama took me. Some of the kids were crying, their mothers sat in the tiny chairs with them. I didn't know what all the fuss was about, the teacher was very pretty and very friendly. In third grade we had a Halloween party. I was a princess, I wanted to be a pirate. Valentines day parties were always fun, every year."

Diane stopped talking, tears filled her eyes and she sobbed quietly, almost silently.

Dr. Emery gently probed her with questions, but she wouldn't or couldn't answer. He knew it was time to stop, if he continued to press her, she might never open up completely. He concluded the interview by asking her "Is there anything you want to ask me?"

"Just one thing, am I going to get off this ward soon? It's a terrible place. I'm afraid here."

"The treatment team will meet tomorrow. We'll call you in and you can speak to us. Then we'll decide on a plan of treatment. That's all I can say for now. Thank you for talking so openly. Goodbye for now."

"Goodbye."

The full treatment team met at 9:30 a.m. every Tuesday and Thursday reviewing and presenting reports on at least five and sometimes as many as a dozen or more patients. The team consisted of the unit day shift nurse, a social worker, recreational therapist, psychologist, and an M.D. if one was available. Notes from orderlies entered in the chart were presented by the unit nurse. Security reports were also reviewed if they involved a particular patient meeting with the team.

Patients were called and had to wait in the unit day room until their turn. Diane fidgeted in her chair near the interview room while she waited for her turn to meet with the treatment team. She was third on the list. Her new friend Evelyn was first. She wasn't in the interview room long. She soon came out with a dejected look on her face and sat next to Diane.

"How'd it go?" Asked Diane.

"Who knows? They just kind of reviewed my behavior and my interview answers with different members of the treatment team, especially any that they found unusual. They said they'll review my progress again next week. I guess that means I'm stuck here and stuck on this damn unit for at least another week."

Diane cringed. "I hate to leave you, but I want off this unit. The people here are crazy."

After she said that they looked at each other and laughed out loud so hard they both had to wipe their eyes.

The second interview didn't take long and after another fifteen minutes or so Diane was called into the interview room. Dr. Emery gestured to a chair at the opposite end of the table.

"Please sit down," he said.

"Thank you, sir."

"How do you feel?"

"Fine sir, I think I'm ready to go home."

Dr. Emery then asked each person that had interviewed or otherwise interacted with Diane to report what they had observed.

The day shift nurse, Katherine Varone, said Diane was very difficult on arrival but had slowly improved. She noted Diane was not violent toward staff or other patients. Mary Anne Humble, the social worker, said she also did not see Diane as a danger to others but felt she could still be a danger to herself. She agreed Diane was improving but felt she still needed to be at H.M.A.

The only comments Dr. Williams had was that he had been called for a shot on admission and since then he had one contact with her during which he had prescribed medication.

Dr. Emery said he agreed with Mary Anne Humble. "You're doing better, but I believe you need close observation for at least one more week. Then we'll talk about a discharge plan including transfer to another unit. I'm making a note now to interview you again next Tuesday. Katherine, would you make this room available for 2 P.M. Tuesday?"

"Yes."

"Do you have anything you would like to say?" Asked Dr. Emery.

"Only that I feel much better. I don't want to hurt myself anymore. I would like to go home or at least transfer to another unit."

Dr. Emery said "You may return to the day room. I'll see you at 2 P.M. Tuesday. Good day."

Diane left the treatment room and sat down beside Evelyn in the day room.

"Well?" Said Evelyn.

"I'll be here at least another week. I'll see Dr. Emery again Tuesday at 2 P.M. "

"That's right after me at 1:30."

"I don't understand. They all said I wasn't violent towards anyone. Why would they think I needed more close observation? I'm not going to even try to kill myself anymore."

"Who knows what they're thinking. I guess it's the old CYA," said Evelyn.

"CYA?"

"You know 'Cover Your Ass' in case something goes wrong."

"I get it, but it's not right."

"Yeah, but they have all the keys, all the control. We'll just have to be good little girls so we can get the hell out of this place or at least off this unit."

"I guess you're right."

"Come on," said Evelyn. "Let's re-read some of the magazines."

Friday and the weekend went without a major incident concerning either Diane or Evelyn. The staff even moved Evelyn to a bed next to Diane's.

At 1 P.M. Tuesday Dr. Emery came onto the unit and went straight to the interview room. The first patient was soon called. Then it was Evelyn's turn. She wasn't gone long. When she came out, she walked straight to Diane and said "I'm going to 'K' unit. Dr. Emery said if everything works out okay, I should be discharged in a couple of weeks, three at the most."

"Good. I hope it's sooner rather than later."

"Me, too. Good luck. I don't know when I'm moving, hopefully today. If we're lucky maybe we can both go to 'K.'"

"You don't have to wait on the team meeting on Thursday?"

"No, Dr. Emery said he would arrange the transfer to 'K' himself."

Diane waited trying to appear patient. She was nervous, biting her fingernails and cracking her knuckles. Finally, Dr. Emery called her into the treatment room.

"Good afternoon, Diane."

"Good afternoon, Dr. Emery."

"How do you feel?"

"I feel fine, everything's okay except the medicine makes me feel sluggish and sleepy."

"Maybe we can cut down on the doses."

"That would be good."

"Now, are you feeling anxious? You did when you first came here."

"Some but not nearly as much."

"On the last interview you answered all the questions truthfully except one."

"All my answers were truthful."

"Yes, I believe so. What I mean was you did not answer one of my questions. To understand you better and even for you to understand yourself better it is very important to answer all questions truthfully. Do you understand?"

"Yes Dr. Emery, I'm trying."

"I know, let's try again."

He then reviewed all the questions and answers from the last interview. At the end he said "You did not answer one of the questions about sex. 'Were you forced or coerced into sex with someone at an early age?'"

Diane sat still. A tear rolled down her cheek. She looked at the floor. She tried to talk but her voice quivered, and she stopped. She tried again and managed to whisper "Yes."

"Was it forced or coerced?"

"Forced."

"About how old were you?" Asked Dr. Emery going slow trying to get Diane to continue.

"I was 13. I was in the 7th grade."

"Was the perpetrator a family member or a stranger?"

"A family member."

"Male or female?" He asked, continuing to go slow.

"Male."

"If you can, describe the incident. It will help to get it all out. Also, how it made you feel."

"My mother gave me a loaf of bread to take to my Aunt Bess and Uncle Elmer's house. They just lived a block away. Aunt Bess is my mom's sister. She wasn't home, only Uncle

Elmer. He answered the door and told me to take the bread into the kitchen. I did. He followed me and before I could put the bread down he started kissing me. I didn't know what to do. He pushed me down to the kitchen floor. I was wearing shorts, he pulled them off. I tried to put them back on, but he grabbed them from my hands and threw them. I begged him to stop, but he wouldn't. (Her voice became a whisper.) Then my panties. I tried to turn to the side, but he held me and got on top of me. I tried to get him off, but he was stronger than me and got inside of me. When he finished, I was crying. At first, he said he was sorry, then he got mad. He said it was my fault, I dressed too sexy. He said he would tell I kissed him and took my clothes off."

"Have you ever told anyone else about this?"

"No."

"How do you feel about telling it now?"

"Somehow, I feel better. Like a burden has been lifted. I guess I should have told my parents, but I was ashamed to tell anyone, and I was afraid my dad would shoot him."

"Where is your uncle now?"

"In California, I guess. They moved shortly after he did that to me. After a couple of years they divorced, and Aunt Bess came back home. As far as I know he's still there."

"Dr. Emery should I tell my parents what happened?"

"That's a tough question. There is no cookie cutter answer. You must ask yourself several questions."

"What questions?"

"Do you think it would help you to tell them what happened, maybe further lift the burden you've been carrying?"

"I think so, but I don't know."

"Do you believe this incident profoundly changed your life up to this point?"

"Yes, I do believe it did."

"Do you think they will understand how this affected you from that day forward and how it changed the lives of all of you?"

"I think so, but I don't know for sure."

"Those are some things to consider."

"But what do you think?"

"I've always felt it is best to face your problems than it is to hide from them. If you are straightforward with them, it may help all of you. You'll never know otherwise."

"Dr. Emery do you think my uncle doing that to me is the reason I'm here?"

"Yes, it is my professional opinion that incident is the principal reason why you are here. It caused most if not all the emotions that have caused you to need the help, we are trying to give you. Without that incident I don't believe you would ever have been here."

"Dr. Emery I don't know if I can explain the effect this had on me and through me them. Would you be willing to help me explain that to them?"

"I would be willing to help, but I would want to talk to them prior to you telling them what happened, to set the groundwork, so to speak."

"Thank you, Dr. Emery, I feel much better about things now."

"All right, that's good. I believe you're on the road to recovery. Now, I'm going to assign you to 'H' building. I will tell the treatment team. It will not be necessary for you to meet with them."

"When will I move?"

"How does Friday sound?"

"Great, thank you."

"Good-bye for now. I'll continue to meet with you while you're on 'H' unit."

CHAPTER TWENTY-NINE

Diane moved to Building 'H' on Friday May 1st. It was a relief to be off the Acute ward. The next Tuesday she met with her new treatment team for the first time and after reviewing her chart the team decided to let her have two hours of free time on the asylum grounds and by the next week she had the run of the grounds on the provision that she report in to her unit at noon and 6 P.M.

On the sixth of May Dr. Emery met with Diane's parents as a prelude to Diane telling them about the incident involving her uncle Elmer. They met in the unit 'H' interview room.

"Mr. and Mrs. Cleary I'm here with you today because Diane asked me to meet with you and try to explain why Diane has had so many emotional problems since she was a young girl."

"Well, we certainly appreciate you Dr. Emery," said Mr. Cleary.

"To start I would like to say that I believe we have had a breakthrough in her treatment. She has finally faced the reason for her emotional behavior all these years."

"Just what is it, I think we would like to know," said Mrs. Cleary.

"She was abused by a family member when she was in the 7th grade. That abuse left emotional scars that she has tried, unsuccessfully, to live with ever since. As is so often the case, the perpetrator blamed it on her and said he would tell everyone she caused it to happen."

"Who abused her and what happened?" Asked Mr. Cleary.

"She was sexually abused, actually raped, by her uncle Elmer, it happened when she was thirteen years old".

"My god, my baby was raped by Elmer. Did you hear him Charles? Did you hear what he said?"

"Yes, that no good son of a bitch. I'll find that bastard and kill him."

"That's not the answer. That's another reason why Diane didn't tell you at the time. She was afraid of Elmer's lies and your reaction to what he did."

"Oh my god then it's my fault, too."

"No, your reaction is the same as most fathers in that situation. What we have to do now is concentrate on what's best for Diane now and for the rest of her life."

"What can we do to help her?" Asked Mrs. Cleary.

"You can start by meeting with her in a few minutes. Give her a hug, tell her you love her. I don't know if she will want to tell you the details of the assault. If she does, fine, if not that's fine, too. Frankly, I doubt that she will want to. But remember this, don't pressure her for details and remember it was not her fault. That's what's important here today and from this day forward. Remember, neither of you should dig for details, and no threats against Elmer. That will keep the wound open and do more harm. Do you both understand what I'm saying?"

"Yes," said Mrs. Cleary.

"I do, too. But what about going to the police?" Asked Mr. Cleary.

"It's probably not a good thing after all these years, and it will just put Diane through more pain. Besides seven years is the limit for sexual assault in most states and I believe it is in Kentucky. Remember we want Diane to heal. She has made the first important step, support her, understand her, love her but don't harp on things. Are there any more questions?"

"No. I think you have made it clear we are to be there for her but not to pressure her or do anything to make it more difficult. One more thing, though should we tell her aunt Bess what happened?" Asked Mr. Cleary.

"Use this simple rule of thumb. Will it help Diane or can it possibly make it harder for her to heal. What do you think?"

"I guess it may do more harm. I can't see it doing any good," said Mr. Cleary.

"I agree. I believe what she says or what we have discussed should stay between us. I will send Diane in to talk with you in a few minutes."

"Thank you, Dr. Emery, we appreciate everything you have done," said Mr. Cleary.

Dr. Emery left the interview room and sat next to Diane in the day room. She was clearly anxious about meeting with her parents.

"Don't worry, everything's going to be okay."

"How much did you tell them?"

"I told them basically what happened, who did it and why you didn't come forward before. I believe they understand. You can choose to tell more details or not, it's strictly up to you, today and in the future. They know that and accept that."

"I don't want to go into any details with them."

"Then don't. Now go, they want to see you."

Diane went to meet her parents, feeling good about herself and wanting to talk to them for the first time in years. It started out like Dr. Emery suggested, hugs and 'I love you' all around, and tears.

Diane wiped her eyes. "Dr. Emery said he told you what happened a long time ago."

"Yes, now we know what has been going on, what you have been going through for so many years and we just want you to know that we love you and want to do anything we can to help make you happy," said her father.

"That goes for me, too dear," echoed her mother.

"Just having you two as parents and understanding is what I need."

"We'll always be here," said her father. "I'm just sorry we didn't figure out things a long time ago."

"Let's not get into that kind of stuff. I just want to rebuild my life the best I can without dwelling on the past."

"Absolutely, I think we all want that," said her mother.

The unit nurse came in and said, "Visitation is up for today, I'll have to escort you off the unit."

"Oh well honey, we better do as she says but we'll be back soon. I love you" said Mr. Cleary.

"Good-bye sweetheart, I love you and I'm so glad things are working out," said Mrs. Cleary.

"I love you both," said Diane and hugged them both.

CHAPTER THIRTY

The treatment team's trust in Diane and the encouragement she received from Dr. Emery and her parents gradually gave Diane confidence in the future. She no longer hated to be at H.M.A. but instead accepted the time as a necessary part of healing.

The only thing disturbing to her was she and Evelyn both felt they were being watched too closely by at least one guard and another unmarked car as they walked the grounds. Evelyn was quite a bit heavier than Diane and didn't like to walk as fast or as long. That left Diane walking alone after lunch most days. Some afternoons a Security car circled and sometimes slowed up to her walking speed. She tried not to react and would move to an area with sidewalks that didn't border streets. Another car, one without any Security markings circled the grounds late every afternoon. The driver kept the car a few feet behind her as she walked. She made a point of not looking at the car. Finally, after about a week or so the car pulled up close to her and the man driving said, "Hello, I'm Doctor Rose the superintendent, I see you out here every day. You must have the run of the grounds."

She stopped to answer. "Yes, I do."

"Well, they are beautiful grounds."

"Yes they are. I really enjoy walking around. It helps me concentrate," she said and continued her walk.

"Anything that helps is good for you," he said and drove off.

The next day he pulled close again. "You look very lovely today. Your stay here must be helping you."

"Yes, I believe it has helped me," she said and got on a sidewalk that led under some trees and continued in a large circle in an open area.

"Good-bye," he said and drove off.

The next day he was back again. "Have you ever gone down to the dock?"

"No, I didn't know there was a dock."

"Have you noticed if you follow this street for a couple hundred yards a gravel road leads off to the left?"

"Yes, but there's a gate across the entrance with a sign that says for maintenance crews only or something like that."

"That's true, normally we don't allow patients in that area but since you have the run of the grounds and seem so calm, I believe it would be alright if you go around the gate. The road leads to a dock where we sometimes take patients fishing. It's a nice place to relax. The lake looks beautiful from there and it's so calm."

"I'm afraid I might get in trouble with my treatment team and lose my privileges."

"If anyone says anything just tell them to check with me," he said and drove away.

Diane went down to the dock and spent the remainder of her free time there before checking in at 'H' unit.

Dr. Rose continued his patrol of the grounds, eventually ending it at his house. Shortly after he arrived, he received a call from Bell.

"I saw you talking to the blonde again today. How did it go?"

"Fine. I told her she could go down the gravel road to the dock. That's where you pick her up the next time she goes there."

"Don't you think it's kind of risky? You know she probably has to be back at her unit by six."

"That's to our advantage. You tell her you don't have any instructions about her having permission to be at the dock, so you have to take her back to her unit. But instead, you take her to building 'I' and keep her there until it's dark enough to bring her here. Then we have some fun with her."

"Until you kill her."

"That's the plan. But that's way down the road. She's too good looking to be in a hurry."

"Okay, but I don't like it."

"You worry too much. We had fun with the other one, didn't we?"

"Yes, but I'd rather get another toy from off of the grounds."

"You can do that, too. As a matter of fact, we're going to have some of your countrymen coming again pretty soon. We'll need at least one more. But I want that blonde. Now get back to work so no one gets suspicious about what you're up to."

"Okay, okay," said Bell as he hung up.

The next afternoon Bell made it a point to watch for Diane walking. About 4:30 he saw her walking with Evelyn and cruised past pretending not to be interested. He passed the road that went to the dock and continued on until he came to a bend in the road then stopped beyond it and waited to see if they would be walking that way. No-one came. At 5:45 he doubled back and drove down to the dock. He found Diane there by herself. He pulled up to the dock and stopped. He got out and walked up to Diane sitting on a bench looking at the lake.

"What are you doing here?" He asked.

"Just enjoying the view."

"Don't you know this is off limits to patients that aren't with staff."

"Doctor Rose said it would be alright if I came here."

"Then let me see your pass."

"I don't have a pass. He just said to mention his name."

"Let's go check, come with me. Get in the car."

He drove around for a while to the more remote areas of the campus, feigning security checks, until dusk when he took her to the side entrance of 'I' building. He had previously unscrewed the light bulb above the entry to make it difficult for anyone to see what was going on.

"This isn't my building."

"It doesn't matter. I have to check out your story to see if you keep your grounds privileges."

He got out of the car and went around to the other side. He got Diane out and held her by the arm as he led her to a side door where he used a key to open it.

"Now follow me."

Diane followed him inside. And disappeared.

On the second floor of 'K' building Evelyn looked out just as the security car pulled to the side of building 'I'. The light was poor, but she saw Diane get out of the car and go with the guard into the side entrance of the building. She turned back around and finished packing, wondering why Diane would be going into building 'I' with a guard. She was in a hurry; her parents were waiting downstairs to take her home.

After pouring a cup, he turned off the stove and the kitchen light and slipped into the darkness and onto the full length covered back porch. Ed and Bill the farm dogs had heard him stirring in the house and were waiting on the porch. They were a mixed breed, brothers from the same litter with the square head of a Labrador retriever but a lighter body and medium size. They had reddish brown coats and looked identical except Bill had a white diamond shaped spot behind his left ear. After he patted them sufficiently, they went out into the darkness to patrol the grounds near the house and barn.

A storm was threatening nearby and every so often lightning flashes lit the sky and the area between the horizon and the porch. "Dear God, I do love this place so," he said aloud, as the barn, chicken house, spring house and the fields and trees, in turn were lit. During the flashes he managed to count all seven of their cattle. They were the herd for now, one bull and six cows all of which were due to calf any day. He also saw their two milk goats head into the pen attached to the right side of the barn. He stood listening to light rain on the tin roof and enjoyed a second cup of coffee.

He was a large man at six feet four inches tall and two hundred and sixty pounds. He had put on about ten pounds each of the last two years and knew he had to lose it. His job demanded it. His hands swallowed most men's hands, and his arms and shoulders were huge. His shoes were size thirteen. His waist at forty-four inches was large but not excessively so. He had a square chin, a slightly hawk-like nose, and a tall and wide forehead. His face was lightly freckled around hazel eyes and he had dark red hair.

His very size was an asset in his job. Where other deputies might have a problem stopping a fight or performing other duties such as serving divorce papers or arresting a drunken driver, Buford's mere presence seemed to calm things. Even arrest warrants rarely caused a problem and if one did it didn't last long. For all his size he was a gentle man especially with Mary, his wife of over thirty years, but nobody, nobody with common sense that is, messed with him.

With the break of dawn, the rain stopped, and he moved to one of the porch chairs and pulled down across his lap the wide leather Sam Browne belt he had draped around his neck. He took an awl from his pocket and skillfully cut another hole in the belt to make it fit his increased size.

Finished, he took the belt back inside and put it on the counter next to the door. Back on the porch, he pulled a pair of rubber galoshes on over his cowboy boots. With the light of dawn, he proceeded with a clean milk bucket to the barn some one hundred or so feet from the house. As always when he or Mary ventured outside, he was joined by the ever faithful, ever protective Ed and Bill. After a few steps at his side, they seemed to sense all was well and left to continue their early morning patrol. The goats saw Buford coming and began their piteous naah, naaah, naah baying, anxious for their morning feed and milking.

Buford entered the barn and flipped a switch that turned on two bare light bulbs hanging from the ceiling, each bulb

"Sure, honey. I'll hold off cooking the eggs until you come back. By the way how did things go out there today?"

"Oh, fine. It's a good thing George is coming tomorrow. Becky's almost dry. Marilyn's doing fine though. I put almost a full bucket in the spring house."

He walked to the bedroom and changed into his uniform. Minutes later he joined her at the table for a breakfast of one egg, one biscuit, three strips of bacon and a cup of black coffee.

"Wow," he said. "When I said I needed to diet to lose weight you took me serious."

"Yes, I did. This is it for breakfast. I packed you a sandwich and an apple for lunch."

"Oh well, I asked for it. This won't take long," he said as he began to eat.

A few minutes later he rose, bent over and kissed her on the cheek. "Goodbye. I'll try to be home on time this evening."

On this the fifteenth day of May 1954 he listened patiently to Mary voice her almost daily concern as he headed to the patrol car parked in the driveway.

"Honey, remember, don't do anything that will get calls to Sheriff Scott's office."

"Don't worry I won't".

"No tickets to the 'wrong people.'"

"Don't worry. I know and I won't. Relax, I know how hard it is to get a good job and I don't intend to lose this one."

"Good Sweetheart," she said. "I love you."

"I love you, too. More than you could possibly know."

As he walked to the patrol car parked in the driveway he thought about their exchange and the unspoken meaning behind it. The jobs he'd had and lost. Some were true dead ends like the mill closing after giving five years of his life and the department store in Shelton where he worked for three years selling everything from shoes to suits to furniture. The owner had to close because business dried up when money got tight. He worked on various government projects during the 30's, the C.C.C., W.P.A., and P.W.A.. Anything to keep food on the table. He remembered too well those prayers, the ones most all poor people made: "Thank you God for this food that we may all be fed and thank you God for Mr. Roosevelt and please God watch over our President." When the war started, he tried to join but was too old so he did the next best thing, he went to work in a defense plant in St. Louis. He sent money home to Mary and his daughters every two weeks. After the war the plant cut way back and he was 'laid off' never to be rehired. He returned to his hometown, Hardin. Jobs were scarce. They lived off their savings and the part-time work he and Mary could find. The farm provided food and some much-needed income. In '48 he got a job as a milkman. Life was looking up again until '52 when the big national dairies made their moves out of the big cities and the Hardin Dairy Co. went out of business and he was again out of a job. In the summer and fall of '52 his first cousin, Will Scott, ran for and won the election for sheriff. Buford worked hard in the campaign and when it was over he asked for a deputy's job. Scott agreed to hire him.

He even sent Buford to the state police training academy to learn police procedures. Buford loved the job and after a stint of over fourteen months in Red Fern he put in for a vacancy in Hardin and transferred March 1st, 1954.

No Honey he thought as his mind raced over the past, you don't have to worry. No screwups, nothing is going to mess this job up, nothing. He got in the patrol car, a black and white '54 Ford, started it and drove the six miles to the Hardin office. When he got out of the car he heard a familiar shout, "Run Buford Run" from a former classmate at Hardin High. It was a shout that always brought a smile to Buford and the person that said it. It was a reference to a football game nearly forty years earlier. Buford was a lineman, both offense and defense. Hardin High was playing Shelton High a much bigger school from Shelton the county seat. The game was winding down in the 4th quarter with Shelton six points ahead and driving for a clinching touchdown. The ball was on the Hardin twenty-yard line with a minute and ten seconds to go. Lee Crandall the Hardin coach called his final time out. He gathered his team around him and challenged his tired players to get the ball back.

"You get that ball back and we'll win this thing. They're going to try to run it. Everybody play the run first," he said.

Shelton lined up. The quarterback handed the ball off to the halfback. Buford saw the play coming and wrapped up the back and ripped the ball loose. It rolled around on the ground and Buford reached down and picked it up. He started running. He managed to get to the sideline and picked up a couple of blockers. He got hit from the side and back by just about every Shelton player on the field, but he kept going. Hardin players and fans screamed "Run Buford Run" and he did all the way to the end zone for the winning touchdown. Hardin won by one point. Hence the familiar shout "Run Buford Run". He loved hearing it and always waved.

Buford was new to the Hardin sheriff office but knew the territory and the people very well. The town was small, Main Street held most of the town's businesses and stretched out for about a half a mile with side streets running off on both sides. The local branch of The Rhodes County Farmer's Bank, a two-story brick structure, dominated Main Street in the center of town. There wasn't a town square but the bigger retail businesses were closer to the bank. There was an Uncle Ben's variety store, Ralph's tire and battery shop, Mildred's flower shop and a scattering of restaurants. A gas station stood at each end of the business district. One was flanked by the local farmer's market where on most Thursdays from spring thru fall Mary had a stand. She sold produce when it was ripe, fresh eggs, baked goods and canned fruit and jellies. Occasionally she finished a quilt or a hand crocheted Afghan. Across the street from the market was Wayne's feed store. Near the service station at the other end of Main Street stood First Baptist Church, across the street Hardin Methodist Church conducted services. One half block off Main Street the Hardin Cafe was a local favorite and across the street from the cafe was the local Hardin County Sheriff's office. Since Hardin had less than 5,000 people it shared deputy Hill with Mercer another even smaller town about five miles West. The Appalachicola river flowed between the towns and in places bordered Hardin.

It was Mid-May, a beautiful spring day and after consuming his sandwich and apple a little early, Buford decided to clean the office. He started with the lone cell in the very back. He swept the cell clean then opened the barred window for some fresh air. Next he swept the restroom and the office front. About noon he went to lunch at the cafe across the street. After some lively banter with the cook, Reed, and the waitress, Millie, he made a routine patrol through Hardin and Mercer then returned to his office and did some paperwork. He resumed cleaning and finished mopping the cell floor and was about to start on the restroom when the phone rang.

"Rhodes county sheriff's Hardin office deputy Buford Hill speaking can I help you?"

"I hope you can," said an unfamiliar voice. "I'm John Shaker the Administrator at Hardin Mental Asylum. I'm calling to report an elopement from our facility."

"How long ago and who?"

"The patient's name is Diane Cleary. I'm afraid it could be more than twenty-four hours ago."

"Can you describe the patient, sir?"

"Of course. A white female twenty-three years old about five foot three inches tall, blonde hair and she weighs about 140 pounds so I'm told."

"Where and when was she last seen?"

"She was last reported seen when she came to her unit to report in just before lunch yesterday. That would be about noon or so. I don't know if she was seen later or not. She has the run of the grounds as long as she reports in at noon and 6 P.M. As far as I know she did not report in at 6 P.M."

"Okay, I'll be out there as soon as possible. Who should I contact for more information?"

"Jack Mitchell the Assistant Superintendent for Patient Services. He will provide you with what you need. A guard will meet you at the entrance gate and take you to him. Goodbye."

"Goodbye." Buford hung up and immediately dialed the sheriff's office in Shelton.

The deputy assigned to day duty at the main office was named Bean. He was average height but tremendously overweight, something he was trying to correct on the sheriff's orders.

The phone rang several times before he was able to get to his desk to answer it. He was a little irritated that Margie, the receptionist, didn't get it so when he answered he was out of breath.

"Sheriff's office" he half wheezed as he spoke. "Deputy Bean here."

"String, this is Buford."

"Damn it Buford don't call me String. Do I look like a string to you?"

"No, but the sheriff calls you that and I just thought String was your nick name."

"Well, it ain't. Sheriff just thinks he's funny that's all. My name's Robert. Now what in hell do you want," growled Bean.

The entrance road ran for about a quarter of a mile before it ended at the main campus road which ran both left and right from a circular grassy area containing a fountain and the U.S. and Kentucky state flags. A large two-story building was on the other side of the circle. A sign in front of the building said ADMINISTRATION BUILDING. Buford stopped the patrol car at the stop sign and asked, "Is that where Jack Mitchell's office is?"

"No, make a left on the main road, that building has Personnel and Accounting and stuff like that."

They turned left and came to a place where the road made a large circle. There were buildings on the outer edge of the circle.

"What are all of these buildings?"

"They're patient living quarters."

"Damn. How many patients do you have here?"

"It varies. There's between fifty and seventy-five to a building and there's eight buildings. The first one on the right with the ADMISSIONS sign in front holds the Acute units where new patients are placed until they are ready to be discharged or stepped down to one of the other buildings. Turn right after the third building."

Buford did. There were several buildings along the road. The first sign said FOOD SERVICES, the next one said PROFESSIONAL SERVICES BUILDING.

"That's where Mr. Mitchell's office is, pull into a Visitors parking space," said Lanier indicating the Professional Services Building. "That small building is for Arts and Crafts, and that last building is the gym. The Motor pool is farther on down the road. You can't see it because of the trees."

"Is that all the buildings?"

"No. The warehouse is to the right back at the fountain where we turned left to come here, so is the laundry. There are other small buildings that hold maintenance equipment and things like that and the Superintendent, Doctor Rose, has a house on the grounds. It's a real nice white two story that sits off by itself on a side road between the warehouse and the Administration building. Some other staff members have houses on the grounds, too."

"Anything else?"

"About a quarter of a mile past the motor pool there is a dock on the river. Sometimes staff and patients fish from it. That pretty much covers it."

"I had no idea this place was so huge."

"Most people don't until they come here as a patient or a visitor."

They got out of the car and Lanier led the way to a door on the right front of the building. Inside, they went directly up a flight of stairs to the second floor and a short way down a hallway to an office marked 'Assistant Superintendent for Patient Services'.

The door was open. What looked to be a secretary's desk was just inside on the right. Several feet further inside there was a door to another office. Muffled voices could be heard inside.

Lanier knocked on the door. A short, slightly overweight woman with dark brown hair that looked to be in her late 30's or early 40's opened the door.

"What is it?" she asked.

"Deputy sheriff to see Mr. Mitchell," said Lanier.

"Oh," she said to Buford. "I'm Ruth, Ruth Randolph. I was just leaving, he's all yours."

She gestured towards a rather thin faced man with gray hair sitting behind a large wooden desk. He had taken off his suit coat and his tie hung loose around his neck. He rose to shake hands with Buford as he came into the room.

"Don't be too hard on him deputy," she said.

"I won't."

"See you Monday, Jack," she said as she left.

"Yeah, Ruth, Monday," said Mitchell.

"Mr. Mitchell?"

"Yes, please call me Jack. And you are?"

"I'm deputy Buford Hill."

"And you've come about the elopement?"

"Yes. I was told by Mr. Shaker you were the person I needed to talk with for more information."

"What do you already know?"

"Her name is Diane Cleary, she's a twenty-three-year-old blonde about five foot three inches tall and weighs about one hundred and forty pounds. Is that correct?"

"Yes, and from what staff have told me she is quite attractive."

"I understand she is from Blanton. Is that correct?"

"Yes, she's from Blanton, about twenty miles North of here."

"Why was she here. Was she dangerous to others or only to herself?"

"She was brought in by a deputy from Blanton because she tried to commit suicide. She cut her wrist and lost some blood. That was a few weeks ago."

"The guard that brought me to you said he had checked the local roads as far as she could have possibly walked by now."

"That's right. We always call home to see if the missing person has been heard from or has turned up at home. If not, Lanier checks the roads in all directions from the hospital."

"Who calls the patient's home?"

"If a social worker is on duty then that person makes the call. That was done late yesterday and again today."

"Is it always Lanier that drives the roads?"

"No, not always. If he's not here someone else heads up the search. The grounds are thoroughly searched then a security guard and another staff member are sent out to search the roads. Sometimes volunteers, staff members, help. The guard that brought you here, Lanier, is our Chief of Security. He's very conscientious."

"Where do you think she went?"

"That's hard to say. Hopefully she headed for home. Sometimes they go to a friend's house. If she was hitch hiking she could have got a ride or maybe she called a family member to meet her off campus."

"Does that happen often?"

"Everything happens here."

"Do you have a phone number that I could have to reach her family?"

"Yes, like I said we've already contacted them, no luck."

"I'll need that number."

"Sure," said Mitchell. He picked up a single sheet of paper and handed it to Buford.

"This is everything, other than her medical record, that we know about her."

Buford looked at the paper. "Do you have a picture of her I could have?"

"No, we don't make pictures when a patient is admitted."

"Has she ever been here before?"

"Yes, it's all there. Including all the staff she had contact with, nurses, social workers, doctors, psychologists, everyone including extension numbers and buildings they work in. She was in Building 'H'. My numbers are there, too, work and home. Actually, she had the run of the grounds and was ready for discharge. She was doing really well."

"Then why would she run?"

"That's always a great mystery. Mostly it's just impulsive."

"Any chance of foul play?"

"On the grounds?"

"Yes."

"Well, you never know, but I doubt it. There would be a better chance off the grounds on her way home. Lanier will probably check on her in a day or two."

"You mean go to her home in Blanton?"

"Yes, he will probably go. He usually does if the social workers or other staff are very concerned. Do you need any more information?"

"Just a couple more questions. When did the facility discover she was missing?"

"Sometime after 7 P.M. yesterday, she didn't make her check in."

"How often was she supposed to check in?"

"Twice a day, noon and 6 P.M. Like I said she had the run of the grounds."

"When was the last time she did check in?"

"About noon. It's all on that sheet."

"Sounds like someone slipped up."

"Yes," said Mitchell looking irritated.

"One more thing, if I want to contact a staff member do you mind if I just contact that person or do you want me to go through your office each time?"

"It's okay to contact them directly. We've nothing to hide."

"Okay, thanks. We'll put out an A.P.B. on her."

"Goodbye," said Mitchell.

"Goodbye."

They shook hands. Mitchell went back to his paperwork and Buford walked into the hall. He was on his way down the steps to the first floor when he heard some talking. As he got to the outside door he saw it was Lanier and another guard. Buford walked outside and started to get in his patrol car then thought better of it. He turned to Lanier and said, "May I have a word with you?"

"Sure," said Lanier walking toward Buford, "What do you want?"

"Mr. Mitchell said you will probably drive to Blanton to check on the missing woman to make sure she made it home okay."

"That's right, if a social worker or other staff are worried about her, I'll check on her."

"If you do when will that be?"

"Well tomorrow's Saturday. It's my day off so I guess it will be tomorrow if they're concerned."

"If you go would you call me? I'd like to go with you. To save a trip by myself."

"Sure, but why?"

"Just want to sew up loose ends. Here's my card it has my office and home numbers."

"Okay, if I go, I'll call."

"Thanks."

Buford drove to the main road, stopped, and got his pistol out of the trunk. Then he turned left, continuing South on 19. He turned down one side road after another until he was sure he had gone farther than the woman could have walked. He then headed back towards Hardin. He passed by the asylum entrance then continued on for a few hundred yards before he came to a house on the left side of the road. He pulled in the driveway and drove to the front of the house. He no sooner got out of the patrol car when two kids, a boy, and a girl, came running.

"Hi," said the girl. "I'm Megan, this is my little brother Billy."

"Hi, are your parents home?"

"Yes," said Megan. "I'll get them" and she ran inside the house.

A couple of minutes later a tall man wearing a short sleeve shirt, blue jeans and work boots appeared.

"I'm Jacob Boone," he said. "These are my children Megan and Billy. What do you want?"

"I'm deputy Hill," said Buford extending his hand which Boone quickly shook.

"I'm looking for a woman that left the asylum yesterday before being discharged and apparently hasn't show up at home yet. I was wondering if any of you saw her. She's a white female, early 20's, blonde, average height and apparently very pretty."

"I work at the asylum. I knew about the elopement, but I didn't know she was still unaccounted for."

"Well, she is. What do you do there?"

"I'm a security guard."

"Oh good, then you would be working the grounds."

"Yes, I was on the first shift. I didn't see her on the grounds."

"Have you or any of your family by any chance seen a young woman on the road?"

"No, I've already checked with my family. None of us saw her."

"I'll bet the Weathers got her," said Billy.

"Who are the Weathers?"

"Don't pay any attention to him. The Weathers are the people that live in the next house on the way to Mercer. They're not the friendliest but they seem alright," said Boone.

"They're weird," said Megan.

"Yeah," said Billy. "When we walked back home from town today, I heard something when we were on the path behind their house. It sounded like crying."

Buford turned to ask Megan. "Did you hear anything?"

"No, but I believe Billy 'cause I've heard stuff like that other times when we walked the path behind their house."

"They've got rich imaginations," said Boone.

"Thank you, sir, I'll be on my way."

He left the Boones watching from their porch. By the time Buford got to the Weathers place it was dusk. His headlights shined on the house as he came up the driveway. Walking up to the house he noticed there weren't any lights on in the front part of the house. He pushed the button for the doorbell. After a minute or two without anyone coming to the door he pushed it again, twice. A minute later the door opened slightly, and someone spoke from the darkness.

"Who are you and what do you want?"

"I'm deputy sheriff Buford Hill and I would like to talk to you."

The door opened wider, and Mrs. Weathers came out onto the porch. It was apparent to Buford why the Boone children thought the Weathers were weird. Mrs. Weathers was dressed in black from head to toe. She had on a black long-sleeved blouse, a fully pleated black skirt and leggings tucked into black high-topped boots. Her hair was black and topped by a black beret-looking hat of some kind. She glanced to her left and then to her right.

"What is it you want?" she asked.

"Are you Mrs. Weathers?"

"Yes."

"Good. I'm looking for a young blond headed woman that may have been walking or hitch hiking on the road yesterday. She left the Hardin Mental Asylum without being discharged. Have you or any of your family seen anyone that fits that description?"

"No," said Mrs. Weathers. She turned and started to re-enter the house.

"Hold on a minute. What about your husband and family?"

"There's only the two of us. I'll check with my husband," she said and went back inside.

A moment later she returned. "Neither of us have seen anyone. Like I said there's just the two of us, we have no children and no-one else lives here. Goodbye".

"Goodbye," said Buford as he headed for his car.

Buford continued to search the side roads along route 19. Continuing North he soon came to Mercer. He stopped several times to make inquiries. No one admitted seeing Diane. He drove past Mercer going up and down side roads and stopping at houses and any businesses along the way. Satisfied Diane didn't come that far he turned back South on route 19 and turned East on route 8 toward Hardin. In the middle of the bridge over the Appalachicola he pulled the car to the side and stopped. He put the lights on park and turned on the right turn signal. Once outside the car he walked to the rail and began to shine a powerful flashlight on the water, first near the center of the river then along both banks. Satisfied nothing looked unusual he crossed the road and did the same thing on the other side, then drove on to Hardin.

He stopped several times on the way, no-one remembered seeing the young woman. At his office he reported in to the sheriff's office in Shelton. Sheriff Scott agreed it would be futile to search any more that evening and agreed that if the guard Lanier went to the woman's home, Buford should go with him to help close what was now a missing persons case. If Lanier didn't go, then Buford should go alone.

Saturday morning after milking the goats, feeding the chickens and picking some squash and radishes from the garden for Mary, Buford was sitting at the kitchen table enjoying his second cup of coffee when the phone rang. They were on a party line, so he listened for their ring, one long ring followed by three short ones. He answered after the second complete series of rings.

"Hello."

"Officer Hill is that you?"

"Yes, who's calling?"

"This is Lanier. I'm going to Blanton to Miss Cleary's home. You said you wanted to come with me if I went."

"Yes, I do," said Buford. "Where and when can I meet you?"

"I can be at the sheriff's office in Hardin in about thirty minutes. Is that okay?"

"Yes. I'll meet you there."

"Okay, bye."

"Bye."

"Buford finished his cup of coffee then took a quick shower before leaving. He made it to the office just as Lanier was arriving. Lanier was in a security car so Buford got in and they left. The trip started with each man talking about his background, his family, his schooling and how he came to his present job.

After about ten minutes they became less talkative and finally grew silent. After another twenty or so minutes they were getting near Blanton and Buford started talking again.

"Did you know Miss Cleary?"

"Not really, I just saw her walking around on campus."

"I understand she's a pretty woman."

"She's pretty alright, from what they tell me she charmed just about everybody."

"Who?"

"You know, the doctors and the patient staff. That's how she got the run of the grounds."

"That's what they say?"

"That's what I say, I talked to several people, and they couldn't believe she just walked away like she did."

"Does that happen often? I mean fool the staff?"

"I didn't say she fooled the staff."

"That's the way it sounded."

"Didn't mean that. Meant she was nice, pretty and friendly. It seemed to be her nature's all I meant. Anyhow, every now and then a patient elopes. Hardin is a mental asylum not a prison except for maybe the Forensics ward. There's some very dangerous characters there. But she didn't seem dangerous to the staff, more suicidal."

As they came into Blanton Lanier started talking again. "I don't think it's far now. Her house is on Smith Street, 116."

They came to a red light and stopped. Then they went two blocks farther and Lanier made a left onto Smith Street. They passed the houses slowly. Large, old, once elegant houses. Some were now in a neglected state, 116 was one of them.

They stopped just before reaching the house and observed for a few minutes. There didn't appear to be any activity going on inside or in the back yard. A new Ford was parked out front. They walked to the house and climbed the steps to the large wooden porch. Before he knocked Lanier spoke. "If she's here they'll probably deny it at first until I explain we're not here to take her back with us. We'll be able to tell by the way they act if they're trying to hide her."

He knocked on the door and tried the bell. The bell didn't ring. After a few minutes he knocked again. After the second knock a woman with graying hair, that appeared to be in her mid-to-late fifties, answered the door. She was wearing a flowered house dress with pockets in the front. Her shoulders drooped and she was a little unkempt. She looked tired, very tired.

"You're from the asylum," she said as if to confirm what she saw.

"Yes, ma'am. I'm Lanier Dixon. Is Miss Diane Cleary here?"

"No. I was hoping you had her with you or had some news." She looked around them at the car to make sure Diane wasn't in it.

"No, she's not with us. We checked the road on the way here. She wasn't walking or hitch-hiking."

"I can't believe it," said Mrs. Cleary. She took a small handkerchief from a pocket and lifted her glasses to wipe her eyes. Readjusting her glasses she said, "I just can't believe this is happening. Would you men like to come inside?"

"I don't think so," said Lanier.

"Maybe just for a minute," said Buford.

Lanier gave him a hard look and shrugged his shoulders.

They went inside. The house was quiet. Mrs. Cleary sat and offered them to sit, also.

Lanier spoke first. "Mrs. Cleary we're not here to take her back or anything like that. We just want to make sure she's alright."

"I understand. If she was here I would tell you, but she never did come home. We're worried to death about her. My husband's upstairs asleep. He's been riding the roads looking for her, all night last night, until early this morning."

"Mrs. Cleary is there anyone who might have come to the asylum to pick her up? A boyfriend or relative. Anyone you can think of?" Asked Buford.

Mrs. Cleary thought for a moment then said "No, she isn't dating anyone right now and her brother is away in the Air Force."

"You just said she wasn't dating anyone 'right now', does that mean she had been dating recently?"

"Well, she did date a guy recently. Just once though. She didn't care for him so she wouldn't go out with him again."

"Do you know his name?"

"I think his name was James or Jacob or something like that. No wait it was Jeff. That's it Jeff. I remember Jeff. Jeff Carpenter because she said, 'You know Mama like a builder'. She said he worked at the box factory. Do you think he may have picked her up?"

"We don't know, anyone else you can think of?"

"No."

Buford pulled a card from his pocket and handed it to her. "If you do give me a call."

She stared at the card. "You're not with the asylum," she stated. "You're a deputy sheriff, is that right?"

"Yes, Lanier asked if I wanted to ride here with him."

"Oh," she said. "I'm sure the asylum will call again. They called this morning and said they would check back again tomorrow."

"Remember if you think of anyone else or anything else I might want to know about please give me a call. Okay?"

"Yes, I will."

They left Mrs. Cleary standing on the large porch when they returned to the car.

Once inside the car Lanier turned to Buford with pursed lips and staring hard. "I try not to upset people. That's why I wanted to do the talking just to find out if she was here or not. I could tell she wasn't here, so I wanted to leave without upsetting anyone. You upset her. I could see it on her face."

"It's my job to" …. Buford started to say.

"To upset people. That's your job?" Asked Lanier in a louder, more heated tone.

"No. It's my job to find out what happened to Diane Cleary," Buford fired back.

"And you do that by upsetting her mother?"

"I tried not to upset her. That's why I came with you instead of alone. If I did I'm sorry, but maybe putting her or her husband a little bit on edge, one of them might think of something or somebody that's important to help find out what happened to Diane. That's my job to get a picture of what happened."

"I know what didn't happen. She didn't come home. That's what I came to find out, if she was here, and she's not," said Lanier.

"That's right. But I came to find out more and we did find out something interesting."

"Like what?" Asked Lanier calmer.

"Like Jeff Carpenter."

"She said Diane only dated him once."

"Yes, that's true, too. But what she actually said was she wouldn't go out with him again. She said Diane didn't care for him and wouldn't go out with him again. Without setting off alarm bells and pressing her, it sounded to me like he tried to date her again, but she refused."

Lanier hesitated a moment, thinking, then started the car.

"Let's go to the box factory, that is if you have the time."

"I have time."

"Good it's just a little farther out 19."

They drove to the box factory in silence. When they got there Lanier parked the car. Buford went to go inside by himself. He was met at the door by a security guard. He explained who he was and who he wanted to see. The guard took him inside and looked at the company roster to see where Carpenter was working. He wasn't. He called in sick the last three days.

Buford asked for Carpenter's address. The guard refused. Buford explained the situation explaining that Carpenter could possibly help.

"If you won't tell me his address, can you at least give me a phone number?"

"It's probably in the book anyhow," said the guard.

He searched through the employee roster until he found Carpenter's number.

"It's Colfax 5-1209."

"Thanks. Now can I use your phone?"

"Oh hell, why not?" Said the guard getting more friendly and more curious.

Buford dialed the number. The phone rang several times. No answer. Buford asked if the guard had a regular phone book. He did and handed it to Buford. Buford looked up Carpenter's name and checked the number to make sure it was him. He wrote down the address. He thanked the guard. Then acting like it was a throw away question he asked, "Do you know him?"

"Just at work and to see him around town."

"What's he like?"

"I don't really know him."

"Was he impressive to be around?"

"Not really. But he does have a look about him sometimes."

"What kind of look?"

"I don't know exactly. Sort of one of those looks when someone feels like you're wasting their time."

"When?"

"When the guys come in for their shift, they have to have their I.D. badges to show. We have to spot check. He doesn't like to be checked. He has that look."

"Mean?"

"More like he could get mean."

Buford thanked the guard and hurried to the car.

Lanier cranked the Ford. Buford asked him to go to Carpenter's apartment. Lanier didn't want to go but finally agreed.

When they arrived Buford knocked on the apartment door but no one answered. He tried the nearest apartments, but no one answered there either. Back at Carpenter's apartment he stuck his card in the doorframe next to the handle. On the back of the card he left a message to give him a call at the sheriff's office 'collect'.

When they arrived back in Hardin they talked for a few minutes. Lanier agreed to pass on any new information he received about the woman's whereabout and said he would keep his eyes open for anything unusual at the asylum.

CHAPTER THIRTY-TWO

Sunday after church Buford and Mary went fishing near the bridge across the Appalachiacola. He tried to relax but his mind kept coming back to Diane Cleary's disappearance.

"It doesn't make sense," he said to Mary. "She just disappeared without a trace, nothing."

"Maybe she'll turn up. You said Lanier said they often do."

"I know. I just think something could be wrong this time. I hope not, I sincerely hope not but nothing adds up."

"Give it a little time something might happen to clear things up."

"I hope so."

Monday May 18.

At the Hardin Cafe, Reed Wilson finished scraping the grill, wiped off his cooks spatula and put it below the countertop. As he untied his apron he looked around at the nearly empty cafe and announced to no one in particular. "I'm on break be back in fifteen."

"Wait Reed," said Millie "I've got another customer coming. Its Bill Hearn he'll want to eat. He's outside now."

"You take care of him. You know how to fry an egg."

"That's not fair Reed."

"Life's not fair honey."

Reed walked through the cafe door out onto the sidewalk. He pulled a pack of Chesterfields from his shirt pocket, took one out, lit it and inhaled deeply. Smoke rolled out his mouth and both nostrils as he walked across the street to the deputy sheriff's office.

Inside he sat in a chair next to Buford's desk and asked, "How'd your physical go Thursday Bufe?"

"Not worth a shit."

"Why?"

"The first thing they did was weigh me and take my blood pressure. That got Doc's attention. He told me I had to lower my blood pressure and lose fifty pounds. He reminded me it was forty pounds last year."

"What were your readings?"

"265 and 152 over 100."

"Wow. Everything else okay?".

"Why hell no. I told him sometimes my right nut hurts and when I go to take a piss by the time I find my pecker and get it out I damn near piss my pants. A couple of times I've dribbled in my shorts."

Reed-laughing, "What did he say?"

"Same thing 'lose weight'. Then he gets ready to do the finger wave and tries to be a comedian. While he's lubricating the glove's middle finger he says, 'You know Buford ten percent of American men claim to enjoy this procedure'. I told him 'Don't get your hopes up Doc, this ain't romance to me. I'm in the other ninety percent'. Then he checks and says I have a swollen prostate and it's probably why my nut hurts."

Reed red faced and laughing harder, "Did he give you any medicine?"

"The quack gave me two prescriptions, one for my blood pressure and one for my prostate."

"It doesn't sound too bad. I mean the physical results," said Reed smiling broadly.

"The hell you say. When this report hits the sheriff's desk there will be hell to pay. At least a good ass chewing or maybe a suspension. He warned me last year to make some progress, and I have—in the wrong direction. I've got to turn things around to make it to retirement. I'm getting too old to get another job."

"How old are you, Bufe?"

"Listen you skinny little shit, I told you to stop calling me Bufe. My name's Buford and I'm 55 trying to make it to 65 so I can get out of this rat race and die in peace at 66 or maybe 67 or 68 if I'm lucky. Now get the hell out of here I've got work to do."

"Okay, okay." Said Reed heading for the door.

About 10:30 Buford called the main sheriff's office in Shelton. Margie the receptionist answered. Buford asked to speak to deputy Bean. When Bean answered Buford told him he needed permission to follow up on something in Blanton.

"It's about the missing woman from the asylum. I need to go back to contact the guy who dated her last. Will you ask the sheriff. He said he wanted to close this case. She's still missing as of this morning. I spoke to the head of security and the man over Patient Services. No one has seen or heard anything."

"Yeah, I'll get back with you asap."

"Thanks."

"Sure."

At about 11 Buford's phone rang. He started to answer "Deputy Buford Hill…"

Bean interrupted his spiel. "This is Bean. Sheriff Scott said go ahead. He said do whatever you feel you need to do to close the case. When are you leaving?"

"Soon, very soon."

The sheriff also said to keep him informed of any important developments. 10-4."

"10-4."

Buford called Lanier again. "Are you going back to Miss Cleary's home?"

"No, no sir. Mr. Mitchell and Doctor Rose said to let it go, she could be anywhere. So, I let it go."

"Who's Dr. Rose?"

"He's the head of the facility."

"Anything ever happen like this before?"

"Yes we've had elopements that never did turn up before. But they usually don't live nearby. Sometimes out of state."

"Usually pretty young women?"

"Well sometimes, but not always young women."

"Any young men?"

"I guess so."

"Any haggard old women or old men elope and not be located?"

"Not that I recall. Look I have to go now we're having trouble on one of the units and I have to go help out."

"Okay. If you hear anything let me know. That's not just a request this is an official investigation."

"I will. Goodbye."

"Goodbye."

Buford hung up and pulled out a small pad from his breast pocket and spent several minutes writing notes. He then flipped back through several pages and sat down the open pad. He picked up the phone and dialed a number from the pad.

"Hello" said a woman's voice.

"Mrs. Cleary, is that you?"

"No, this is not Mrs. Cleary. Who's calling?"

"This is deputy Buford Hill. Mrs. Cleary gave me this number to call about her daughter Diane."

"This is Beverly Swint, Diane's sister. My mother's lying down. She's very tired. Is there any news about Diane?"

"No. I'm coming to Blanton in a little while to check on a few things. I'd like to come by in about an hour or so if that's possible."

"I suppose so."

"Thank you, goodbye."

"Bye".

Buford walked to the patrol car, got in, started it and headed West on route 8 then North on 19 towards Blanton. On the outskirts of town he checked his pad for directions to the Cleary's. He then went directly to 116 Smith Street. He rang the doorbell and a pretty blond woman about 30 answered the door.

"Hello," he said. "I'm deputy Hill, I called earlier."

"Yes, I'm Beverly please come in."

"Is your mother or dad here?"

"Dad's at work. He works at Morningside Boats. He's a fabricator whatever that is. Mother's lying down and I'd rather not disturb her."

"I see. Maybe you could help me. I would like to know more about Diane's friends, old boy friends, anything you think may help. Also, I'd like to have a recent picture of her."

Beverly went to a desk at the far corner of the room. She picked up a framed picture of Diane. She took the picture out of the frame and handed it to Buford.

"Thanks. It's hard to work on a missing persons case without a picture."

"Well, mother told you about that weasel Jeff Carpenter. He tried to force himself on Diane. Called her a nutcase, stuff like that. She got away from him on their first and only date. Said she couldn't stand him."

"Anyone else. Any old boyfriends trying to reunite with her?"

"No. None that I can think of."

"What about good friends, close friends?"

"Well, there's her best friend Marlene Hart, but we contacted her and she said she didn't know anything anymore. Marlene's married now with two kids. She said she didn't know much except where Diane was hanging out, at the Lucky Horseshoe sometimes."

"Lucky Horseshoe, is that a bar?"

"It's a bar in a bowling alley, a big bowling alley about twenty or so lanes. Very busy."

"Can you give me Marlene's address and telephone number?"

"Sure. Let's see if it's in this phone book. You're lucky, VA-82868, 114 Oliver Street. That's two blocks over from here—just down the street and make a left." She gestured which direction to go from the house.

"Can you tell me what made her suicidal?"

"No. I have no idea. We're very worried about her. Do you think there may be something wrong? I mean do you think something bad may have happened to her?"

"No, I don't suspect anything. We have to look into missing persons cases. I don't know why I'm checking so close. Something keeps pushing me. I'm sure it's nothing."

"It's horrible not knowing if something has happened to someone you love. So please keep trying to find her or what has happened to her, and please, please keep us informed as much as possible," said Beverly with tears in her eyes.

"I promise, I'll do my dead level best."

The sneer was gone.

"You're sure?" Asked Buford looking askance at him.

"Positive. Why?"

"She's missing. That's why."

"Look, I swear to God I haven't laid eyes on her for at least three or maybe four weeks, maybe more." He reached inside the room and set his beer down.

Acting heated Buford questioned him.

"Where were you last Thursday?"

"Work, I guess."

"You guess wrong."

"You're right. I took three days off to go camping so I could do some fishing."

"Where?"

"On the river near Silver Springs. Thursday, Friday, and Saturday."

"Anyone go with you?"

"No. I went by myself."

"Anyone see you there?"

"I don't know. The only person I saw was at the bait shop. She might remember me."

"For your sake, she better. If you have any information about Diane now or in the future give me a call. Here's my card."

"Sure. I will. I promise." Said a visibly shaken Carpenter.

Buford turned and walked to the girl waiting at his car. "What's your name?"

"Darlene Metcalfe."

"What do you know about Diane Cleary?"

"Not much. I met her at the Lucky Horseshoe a few times. She was fun."

"Do you know anyone she was dating or hanging out with?"

"No, I really don't."

"What's your relationship with Carpenter?"

"Nothing now. He asked me to come by today and I did. It was a mistake. He has a hard time taking 'no' for an answer. I'm glad you came by so I could get out of there easier."

"Do you know anything about Diane's disappearance?"

"No. Absolutely not. I haven't seen her for a while."

"Here's my card. If you hear anything give me a call. Anything, okay?"

"Sure. Can I go now?"

"Yes. Just remember, anything."

Darlene left. Buford got in his car, but he left the door open and spent the next twenty minutes or so sitting sideways with his feet out resting on the curb. He had his note pad out and every now and then wrote in it. Then he would pause and look off into the distance for a few minutes before looking at the pad and writing again. Finally, he put the pad away and drove down main street looking for the Lucky Horseshoe. He found the bowling alley/bar. He checked the door, the sign said 'closed Mondays', open Tuesday-Saturday 4pm-midnight, Sunday open 5pm-10pm. He stood for a minute trying to decide whether to go to Silver Springs or back to his office. He got back in the Ford. After a few more minutes of thought he headed South on route 19 toward his office. He arrived at 7:30 and was hungry. He called Mary and asked if she had eaten, and she said 'yes' so he said he would eat at the diner across the street. She offered to reheat supper, but he said no. He said he would be home in another hour or so. They hung up and he walked across the street to the diner.

The diner was about to close. Reed and Millie were long gone. The second shift, Charley the cook and Virginia the waitress, were chatting behind the counter when he came in. It looked to Buford like plans were being made, especially since Charley's hand was somewhere below Virginia's waist.

"Hello Buford," said Virginia "what can I get you?"

"Oh, just a burger and a piece of pie. Maybe some coffee."

"The works on the burger?" Asked Charley.

"Yes, and apple pie."

"Sorry, all we have left is chocolate," said Virginia.

"That'll do."

Charley brought him some fries with his burger.

"They'll just go to waste."

"Thanks."

He ate in silence with his thoughts. No other customers came in. Every now and then Virginia came by to fill his coffee cup and check on him. Strange case he thought, things sure are strange. Few real leads, only Carpenter. I'll check on his alibi tomorrow and visit the Lucky Horseshoe. By 8:30, the cafe closing time, he was finished and on his way home to Mary.

Tuesday, May 19.

Buford left for the office early, about 6:30 AM. After some routine paperwork he went to the diner to get some coffee and breakfast. He sat down on a stool at the far end of the counter. Millie was at the cash register just inside the door. She reached inside the glass counter and pulled out a pack of gum. She handed it to a customer and said, "Total is $1.75."

The customer paid her then walked back to his spot at the counter. He laid his quarter change next to his empty coffee cup and walked out the door waving as he left.

Millie came to take Buford's order. She deftly handed him a menu with one hand and set a cup of coffee in front of him with the other. She stood waiting.

"I'll take two eggs over medium and some home fries."

"No meat?"

"Not today."

"What about toast?"

"One slice."

She wrote the order then put it under one of a series of clips near Reed's grill.

Buford opened his notepad and reviewed his notes.

Reed walked Buford's breakfast to him and asked, "What are you studying so hard?"

"I'm reviewing my notes about a woman that's missing from Hardin Mental Asylum. They say she eloped, but she hasn't made it home, so now it's officially a missing persons case."

"What do they mean 'eloped'?"

"She had the run of the grounds and was supposed to check in twice a day, at noon and 6 PM. She made the noon check-in but not the one at 6 PM. They assume she left for home with a six-hour head start, either hitchhiking or called someone to meet her. I'm not so sure. She should have been home for several days by now."

Reed stood there for a moment thinking, then said "Sounds familiar."

"What do you mean?"

"Same thing happened two or three years ago."

"How do you know?"

"Well, her boyfriend plastered pictures of her everywhere trying to find her, then trying to find out what happened to her. As far as I can remember they never did find out anything. The deputy before you, Tom, should have left a file on her."

"I remember that now, I'll check," said Buford as he started to eat his eggs and home fries.

"Do you think maybe something happened to this woman you're looking for?"

Asked Reed as he freshened Buford's coffee.

"I don't know, it's possible."

"Have any good leads?"

"Not really. Thanks for the information. I'll check to see what Tom left in the files."

"Sure, anytime." Reed trudged back to the always waiting grill.

Buford finished his breakfast and pondered about the new information Reed had given him. His mind raced. Why haven't I checked the files? A good deputy would have. Hadn't String (Robert) told him that elopements happened before, the first time he called the main office? Need to start thinking more like a detective or at least more like a deputy, he thought.

He laid down a quarter by his cup and walked past the register and through the cafe door to the sidewalk. One good thing about the diner, he thought, the breakfast was always free.

Buford walked to the patrol car. He stood there undecided about what to do first. Check Carpenter's alibi or Reed's new information. He decided he had to check Carpenter's alibi first. He got in the Ford then radioed the main office. Margie answered the radio. He told her his plans so Sheriff Scott would know his whereabouts. Then asked, "Margie how long have you worked in the office."

"Oh, just about 18 years. I'm working on my third sheriff. Why?"

"I'm checking on a missing woman, an elopement from H.M.A. and I need some help. Things just aren't adding up."

"Okay, how can I help you?"

"I would like to know about any similar cases, any open or dead file cases."

"Do you want just the county or beyond?"

"Anything that's interesting or unsolved."

"I keep an auxiliary file on my own. It has cases from all over, even a few from out of state but along the rivers or main highways. You want me to send it to you?"

"Yes. When can I get it?"

"This afternoon. I'll send it by courier if Sheriff Scott okays it. If not, then in tomorrow's mail."

"Wait, I'm coming up Route 8 this morning. I'll stop in and pick it up. Okay?"

'Yes, see you then. 10-4."

"10-4."

Buford started the Ford and turned it North on Route 8. Twenty minutes later he arrived at the main office. He parked around back and came through the rear entrance, the one reserved for employees. He was greeted by two other deputies. One, Oliver Horton was from the northeast part of the county. His office was about ten miles North of Shelton in Red Fern.

"How goes it, Buford?" Asked Oliver.

"Fine Ollie. How about you? What're you doing here?"

"I'm fine, just picking up some forms and a new ticket book. How about you?"

"Margie has a file for me, then I'm going to check on an alibi in a missing persons case."

"I saw the notice about the woman missing from the asylum. Any word on her yet?"

"No, not yet."

"They have a way of surfacing one way or another."

"Yeah, so I hear." He continued through the open bull pen of desks towards the front. He noticed Sheriff Scott's office door was closed. He reached Margie's desk located behind the chest high main public receiving counter.

"Hi Margie. I'd like to take that file with me for a few days. Okay"

"Sure, just don't forget where you got it. I want it back."

"I guarantee you I'll return it. I see the sheriff has his door closed, big meeting going on?"

"No, he's talking on the phone to a friend he made at Quantico, a U S Marshal. He's coming to visit with us tomorrow, I think."

"Where you headed now?" It was Robert.

"I'm going to see if anyone saw a certain camper near the river last Thursday and Friday."

"Aren't you making a little too much out of this?" Asked Robert with an air of authority. "She'll turn up, they usually do. You might be needed in your own area."

"Sheriff Scott said for me to close this case ASAP. He said do whatever I thought needed to be done. That's what I'm doing."

"Where near the river?"

"Near Silver Springs. I'm just trying to find out something while people's minds are fresh. Nothing more. See ya." He picked up the file, thanked Margie and returned to his patrol car.

He drove North then turned West on route 18, crossed the river, then turned North again on route 19 in Blanton. He continued towards Silver Springs a wide spot on a side road that led to Carpenter's camping spot on the West Bank of the Appalachichola. He knew the area fairly well. He stopped at the

Early Bird Market and Bait Shop. He walked inside and to be friendly stopped at the soft drink cooler and pulled out a Pepsi. He almost bought a candy bar but remembered his weight and decided to pass. Behind the counter a pretty dark-haired woman about thirty-five or so waited next to the cash register.

As he approached, she asked "Is that all. Don't you need some bait or something else?"

"I do need something else, some information. By the way, I'm Buford, what's your name?"

"I'm Ella. What kind of information?"

"About a man. A man named Jeff Carpenter. He says he camped on the river for two days last week. I thought maybe you might have seen him."

"I don't know about the last name, but I do remember a guy named Jeff."

"When did you see him. Was it here at the bait shop?"

"Yes, he said he wanted to get to know me better."

"Did he get to know you better?"

"No. Not my type."

"When was he here?"

"Thursday morning fairly early about nine or so for bait, and Friday afternoon for a sandwich and some snacks. He said he was going to spend one more night and then head home."

"What did he look like?"

"He was tall, had dirty, greasy looking long brown hair. No cap, just long hair. He looked like he could be mean or at least hard to get along with."

"Do you remember what he was driving?"

"Yeah, an old beat-up Ford pickup. Does that help?"

"Yes. That clears that up."

He finished the last swallow of the Pepsi and placed it in the case with the empties.

"How much?"

"Seven cents."

He gave her the change. "Thanks for the info."

"You're welcome."

Buford walked to the screen door, pushed it open and walked to the patrol car. In the car he pulled out his pad and made a few notes. He started the Ford and headed towards Hardin. Along the way, in Blanton, he stopped at the Lucky Horseshoe. They had just opened for business. He made his way to the bar and spoke to the bartender. He said some of the regulars had heard about Diane's disappearance but none of them seemed to know anything about it, as far as he could tell. Buford asked him what she was like when she was there and he said she was really nice, she didn't get loud or anything like that. He descried her as a 'kind of a free spirit'. But he did say that every now and then when the blues hit her she wanted to drink alone, didn't want to be bothered by anyone. He couldn't remember her going home with anyone or dating any of the regulars.

Buford stayed another hour or so talking to some customers. They all seemed to like her and were genuinely concerned about her disappearance. None had anything of importance to add to what the bartender said. He gave them each one of his cards and left a few extras with the bartender. He went to his patrol car, made a few notes, and headed to Hardin. It was early evening when he reached his office. He went inside and opened the folder Margie gave him.

CHAPTER THIRTY-THREE

Vittorino arrived at Sheriff Scott's office about 10 AM.

"Good morning," he said smiling. "I am Vitorino Sabatini here to see Sheriff Scott."

"Yes, I'm Margie, we have been expecting you. I'll buzz the sheriff and let him know you're here." She turned, clicked on the intercom, and spoke. "Sheriff, Mr. Sabatini is here."

"Good, I'll be right out."

Sheriff Scott came quickly to the counter and shook Vittorino's hand.

"Good to see you, Vittorino."

"Nice to see you again, too."

"This is our do everything receptionist Margie."

"Yes, hello again Margie, I'm glad to meet you, too."

"Me, too Vittorino," said Margie smiling broadly.

"Let's go to my office."

"This is the area for three of our countywide deputies," Scott said as he made his way through the desks behind the counter. "The other desks are for other deputies to use when they're in the area, and sometimes state police or federal officers need a place to work for a while."

"This is deputy Robert Bean. He, along with Margie, pretty much handles day to day business. Robert this is Vittorino Sabatini of the US Marshals office in Nashville."

"Nice to meet you," said Robert. He put down a folder to shake hands.

"Nice to meet you, too," said Vittorino again smiling broadly.

Scott continued to his office with Vitorino close behind.

Robert walked to Margie's desk and said, "He seems like a nice guy to me."

"Wow! I'll say, nice and so handsome."

"I thought you might notice that" said Robert grinning.

"What woman wouldn't. I need a fan," said Margie smiling and laughing as she waved a folder in front of her face.

Once inside his office Scott sat at his huge desk and offered Vitorino a chair.

After a few moments Scott sensed the seating was too formal.

"Let's move to the table over there," he said, pointing to a low marble table and four chairs.

After moving he said, "That desk area is too business like for a friend."

"Thank you. I appreciate being regarded as a friend. Sometimes visitors can take up time and be a nuisance. If you are too busy today just say so and I will leave. The last thing I want to do is get in the way."

"Of course you're a friend, I really enjoyed our time at Quantico. My invitation to you to visit was sincere. How have you been?" Asked Scott smiling.

Leaning forward with his elbows pressing on the arms of the chair Vittorino answered, "I have been fine, I really like Nashville. The people are friendly and so are the fellow officers, but I still miss the friends I made in White Plains."

Leaning forward in his chair Scott said, "I can understand that." Then gesturing with open arms, "I guess I'm lucky I've lived in this county my entire life and most of it within ten miles of this office."

"Yes, you are very fortunate."

"Any news about the men you are pursuing?" Asked Scott leaning back in his chair.

Leaning back, Vittorino shook his head quickly back and forth then answered slowly and in a quieter tone, "No it's very disappointing there hasn't been any new information about them recently. I have chased down a few leads, but nothing sticks. I'm afraid the near miss in Pittsburgh may have made them more careful. This country is so huge they could be anywhere by now."

Sensing the tone change Scott said, "Everything has been pretty quiet here lately, too. We have a lot of little things here in Rhodes County but nothing earthshaking. The only interesting case right now is about a missing young lady."

"What are the circumstances?" Asked Vittorino leaning forward in the chair.

"A young woman, about twenty-three was reported missing from Hardin Mental Asylum on the fourteenth of this month."

"That's interesting. Any evidence of foul play?"

"No. She was just about ready for discharge. She had the run of the Asylum grounds. The staff reported her as an elopement."

"What exactly is an elopement?"

"The way I understand it an elopement is when a patient leaves before a final discharge."

"Does this happen often?"

"Not too often, but it does happen. They usually turn up at their home before long."

"When does your office investigate?"

"Usually after the patient is missing for twenty-four hours."

"Any luck on this one?"

"Not yet. Our deputy in Hardin, Buford Hill is investigating. Hey, let's have some fun. I have free access to a local gun range. Would you like to do some target shooting?"

"Sure."

"Fine. Let's go. I've been practicing, waiting for your visit," Scott said rising to leave.

They left for the range and afterwards went to lunch at Sonny's a local restaurant. When they finished eating Vittorino pulled out his wallet to pay for lunch.

"Put your money away. You're my guest, besides it's not necessary. I'll just leave a good tip. We watch this place pretty close; my lunch is always free here at Sonny's."

"Your deputies, too?"

"No, there's too many."

When they returned to the office Scott resumed his place behind the big desk and Vittorino again took a seat in a chair facing him.

Vittorino, sensing Scott needed to do some work said, "I guess I better get going it's a pretty long drive to Nashville."

"I'm really glad you came even if you did score better on the targets," said Scott as he got up from behind the big desk to shake Vittorino's hand.

"Just my day, I guess," said Vittorino grinning. "Next time, you come to Nashville. We'll try it again."

"Sounds good to me."

Vittorino held his hat in one hand then shifted it to the other, he looked down at the floor then raised his eyes to Scott and said, "Do you mind if I check with your deputy Hill from time to time on the disappearance of the young lady?"

"No, not at all. But why?" Asked Scott somewhat perplexed. "Surely you don't think there's any connection between an elopement here and the men you're after."

"Probably not." His voice grew soft and his expression thoughtful. "I've been told I sometimes grab at straws. But I have to, I owe it."

Ohio showing the pictures along the way, but decided for the time being he would be better off talking to the staff at H.M.A. that had worked with Diane.

He called Lanier and asked if he had any more information about Diane. Lanier said no. Buford asked who he thought would know the most about Diane. Lanier said the unit nurse or social worker would probably know the most. Buford thanked Lanier then called Jack Mitchell.

He had the list of the personnel that Mitchell had given him and asked him to make them available to interview. Mitchell seemed surprised at Buford's interest but told him if he came out that afternoon, he could interview all the day personnel. He explained there was little activity on the second shift and virtually none on the third shift. Buford insisted on seeing the second shift personnel, too. Mitchell told him to come about 1:00 PM that way he could overlap first and second shift personnel. Mitchell said he would make the arrangements for Buford to use the interview room on the Acute unit. Buford thanked him and continued reviewing the file Margie loaned him.

At precisely 12:50 PM Buford arrived at H.M.A. A guard named Bell met him at the guard shack. He told Buford to go to the women's Acute unit 'A', in the Admissions Building. Before going any farther Buford deposited his revolver in the patrol car trunk. He then drove to the Admissions Building, inside he approached a desk with an INFORMATION sign in the lobby. There he rang a bell. A tall nurse came out of an office. He told her who he was, and she said she had a list of people to see him. She took him to a small room down the hall. There were several people sitting in chairs in the corridor outside the room. The nurse gave Buford the list she had. Buford thanked her and began comparing it to the original list Jack Mitchell had given him the day they first met. The latest list had all the names on the original list plus a few more. Satisfied, Buford began interviewing staff.

The first interview was with the day shift Acute nurse Katherine Varone. He asked her the same basic questions he asked them all. What was Diane's state of mind? Did she seem to be recovering well? Was she aggressive or a risk taker? Were you surprised by her elopement? Was there anyone they could think of who might help her leave? Was there anyone that might be a danger to her? He then asked the same questions about Naomi Shepherd. Most of the people on 'H' didn't know Naomi because she wasn't on that unit, but the Acute personnel did. They described her progress on Acute as similar to Diane's. Her personality was similar, too. Not aggressive and not a risk taker.

Buford was gradually able to form a strong opinion about Diane. She was not aggressive toward others; she was not a risk taker. Her mind was becoming clearer every day. She was anxious to get home, but the people on 'H' unit were very surprised she had eloped.

Mary Anne Humble, a social worker that had a lot of contact with Diane, said Diane knew she was about to be discharged and felt good about her stay at H.M.A. this time. She reiterated what several staff members had said that it didn't make sense for Diane to elope so close to discharge.

The last, and to Buford most important, interview was with Dr. Charles Emery. Buford went into the hall and said, "Dr. Emery, I'm Deputy Buford Hill would you please come inside and have a seat?"

"Certainly." Said Dr. Emery. He came inside and sat in a chair directly across from Buford. He put both elbows on the chair arms and clenched his hands together, fingers interlocked, about chin high. It was a pose he often used to emit an air of calmness.

Buford had his open note pad in front of him and leaned back in his chair as he spoke, leaving his right arm on the table, pencil in hand over the pad, "Dr. Emery I'm here investigating the disappearance of Diane Cleary. Would you mind answering a few questions about Diane?"

"I surmised that was what this interview was about. I'll be glad to help in any way I can."

"Thank you. Dr. Emery are you a psychologist?"

"Yes, I am," he said and removed his elbows from the chair arms and sat up straighter.

"Dr. Emery did you work much with Diane Cleary?"

"Yes, I worked with Diane the whole time she was here. I felt she made great progress and had such success in therapy that she would never be back as a patient. I was shocked at her elopement. It didn't make a damn bit of sense."

"Did you also work with Naomi Shepherd?"

"Yes, she seemed to make good progress too. She was pending discharge and felt good about the world. Naomi's elopement didn't make a damn bit of sense either." Then he looked at Buford, drew his head up slightly and seemed to look past him. A strange 'knowing' look came over his face.

"What is it?" Asked Buford.

"Nothing."

"I know that look on a person's face, it means something. What is it?"

"Well, the similarity of the two disappearances have been gnawing at me. Neither elopement makes sense, and they both disappeared into thin air."

"My thoughts exactly. Any more thoughts Doc?"

"No, except I hope you get to the bottom of all this and find Diane. Do you think there may have been foul play?"

"Right now, I have no evidence of any. Do you think there may have been some sort of foul play?

"I have no way of knowing, but the circumstances do seem strange."

"If you do have any more thoughts, give me a call. Here's my card. I've given everybody one."

"I will."

"By the way when Naomi got off the Acute unit where did she go?"

"Unit L."

"You sure?"

"Yes, quite sure."

"Thanks Doc, I appreciate your input."

"You're welcome."

Buford sat and wrote in his pad, (his second one on Diane Cleary's disappearance), for another thirty minutes or so. At five o'clock he walked outside the Admissions/Acute services building and walked over to the Professional Services building. He went directly to Jack Mitchell's office. The outer door was open, he walked to Mitchell's door and knocked.

"Come in," said a voice inside.

Buford did. "Hello Mr. Mitchell."

"Hello deputy Hill. Were you able to interview everyone?"

"All that were here today. You have two scheduled for tomorrow about 9AM. I'll be here to see them then."

"Good. Will that wrap things up?"

"For now. I may want to re-interview some, and there are some others I may want to talk to."

"Why the re-interviews, and who else?"

"Sometimes people remember things better after a first interview. I can probably do some of that over the phone after they have time to think about things."

"I may want to talk to some or all of the security guards, but I guess that falls under John Shaker's area."

"Yes."

"I don't know yet, but I may want to interview some of the people that worked on 'L' unit, and the Acute unit when Naomi Shepherd disappeared."

"Why?"

"Because I'm investigating both disappearances. I'll review my notes from the people I interviewed today that happened to be on one or both units when Naomi was here, along with the original investigation made when she disappeared."

With his face growing red with anger and without mincing words Mitchell stood up and stated flatly, "We don't have time for all this. I'll have the two ready at 9 AM. That's all I can promise."

"Mr. Mitchell please understand something, these disappearances are important. If I ask to interview an employee, it will only be if I can see a possible benefit. But also understand this, if I want to see an employee, I will. Is that clear?"

"Is that a threat?" Asked Mitchell less heated.

"No, I'm telling you the way it is. There are laws about obstructing an investigation. Now I'm asking you, can I expect your full cooperation going forward?"

"Well, since you put it that way, yes you can expect my full cooperation," said Mitchell sitting back down.

"Good."

"Look, I'm just frustrated. It's been a long, bad day," said Mitchell shuffling some papers.

"I understand my days aren't exactly peachy all the time either."

Mitchell stood and extended his hand to Buford. "I guess we're on the same team."

"Absolutely," said Buford shaking Mitchell's hand.

Buford went back to his office to review his notes while they were still fresh. A couple of notes from interviews stuck out. He mulled them repeatedly.

First, Mary Ann Humble was the social worker for both patients. She was very attractive and very friendly. She answered all the questions quickly except one: 'Do you know of anyone who might be a danger to her'. She stumbled a tiny bit when asked that question about both Diane and Naomi. Ruth Randolph the director of Social Services had a similar reaction. Although both said 'no' Buford wondered about their answer. He decided to give them each a couple of days to think about things and then call them at home.

He again reviewed Tom Sargent's file on Naomi's disappearance. Nothing unusual stood out except one note at the end. "I have interviewed all the staff that worked with Naomi Shepherd. None saw any reason why she would elope especially since she was close to discharge. Her family felt the same way. I have canvassed friends and acquaintances, and no one has seen her,"

Tom's official report to then sheriff Giles was in standard form, stating the facts as Tom knew them and included the statement.

Sheriff Giles and sheriff Marcum of Stewart County then issued a joint statement to the press stating the investigation in both counties was ongoing and asking for any information the public had about the disappearance.

There wasn't anything official in Tom's file, but Margie had made some notes about a couple of calls from a woman or women that believed Naomi never left H.M.A. None of the callers gave a name or phone number and were eventually thought to be 'crank' calls. The case was not closed but the investigation was stopped after an official review by the State Police who had assisted the sheriff's offices during the investigation.

After breakfast and before leaving for work Buford told Mary he anticipated a late evening and not to bother fixing supper for him. But he did call to check on her and told her he loved her very much. As always, she said the same to him and told him to be careful.

Buford gave a big sigh and went across the street to the diner. There were still a few customers eating and chatting. Buford made his way to his customary seat at the counter.

"Hi, Buford, what can I get you?" Asked Virginia.

Before he could answer Charley said "Tonight's special is catfish. Want a plate?"

"Yes, I'd appreciate it, and some cold lemonade if you have it Virginia."

"Coming right up," she said.

Buford ate pretty much in silence. A few "Hi, how are you doings" were the only conversation he had. His mind wouldn't stop thinking about work.

——————

"The reason goes back a long time. I'll give you my work and private phone numbers. I'd appreciate it if you would keep me informed."

"Sure, sure. But it would be better if you called here, we have budget restraints. Also, it's getting pretty hectic, the state police are supposed to send an investigator down to review what I'm doing. You know CYA."

"Okay. I'll call you, thanks again."

Buford included the call in his report to Sheriff Scott. The rest was a recap of facts only, no speculation about the interviews.

Buford no sooner finished the report when a state police patrol car pulled up across the street and parked in front of the diner. A couple minutes later a tall, lean, looking man with a long thin face and light brown hair came inside. Buford knew him from his first duty station in Red Fern.

"Hello Matt. Long time no see."

"That's true. How're you doing these days Buford?"

"Not bad. I guess you're here to see what's happening?"

"Yes, and to help if I can."

"Let's go have a cup of coffee across the street. I haven't had time to make a pot."

"Sounds good."

They entered the diner and Buford ambled to his favorite spot. Millie came with a pot of coffee and two cups. Buford introduced Matt and added, "Just coffee for me, Millie."

"Me, too."

"So, what's happening?" Asked Matt.

Buford explained what he had done so far on the case from the first time he was called until this morning.

"Sounds to me like you're covering the bases pretty good. I have a couple of days free time. What can I do to help?"

Buford knew Matt was a good guy, but he also knew he was there for a reason and his free time was probably assigned to Buford's missing person's case.

"Well, I was going to spend some time, maybe even two or three days going up the Appalachichola and the Ohio rivers. I have an array of missing persons pictures I'd like to show to people, primarily businesspeople. People that run service stations and diners, places like that."

Matt asked what pictures he planned to use. Buford told him about the five.

"Why more than just the two missing from H.M.A.?"

"Well, there's always the possibility that there is a serial killer responsible for the deaths and disappearances. A U.S. Marshal called me earlier today asking about this case. He asked me to keep him informed. I know it's a long shot showing these pictures around, but I believe it's one worth trying. I have no true suspects, only hunches,"

"What about this Jeff Carpenter?"

"I don't believe he had anything to do with it. Too good an alibi."

"Well, if you have a spare set of pictures, I have two days I can help."

"I think so," said Julie. "Me, too," said Susan.

Buford got both of their names and home phone numbers as well as their work number.

He finished up by telling them either he or another officer would be in touch with them and to maintain silence about their conversation. They wanted to know why of course, and he just told them it was a police matter. He thanked them both and left them each one of his cards before he left.

When he got back to Hardin Buford called Matt about the picture I.D. made by the cashiers at Chuckey's. Matt was truly excited and said he would have the state investigators on the case follow up on the potential lead. They agreed to stick to their original plan to get back together at 9 AM. Saturday morning.

Buford and Matt both spent the next day showing pictures to roadside businesses without any success. Buford retuned to Hardin dead tired and discouraged. He finished another report and sent it to Scott's office.

At home Mary tried to cheer him up. She had a nice chuck roast for supper and an apple pie for dessert, both favorites of his. Buford ate almost mechanically. Normally he would have raved about the supper and the pie, but not today.

"What's wrong honey, still no leads?"

"Yeah, still no leads."

"At least you got a lead on that other case."

"Yeah. Hopefully the state boys will figure something out."

"Was she young and pretty?"

"Yes, I believe she was."

"What was her name?"

"Joan Bleecher".

"What do you plan on doing next?"

"Going in early tomorrow and reviewing everything again. Then I'll meet with Matt, he might have some suggestions. Beyond that I don't know, except I have a couple of people at H.M.A. I'm going to re-interview."

"Why?"

"It's a feeling I got when I interviewed them originally. It was a social worker and the head of Social Services. They both seemed to be holding something back. It's probably nothing." His voice trailed off.

"Your feelings are usually right."

"Yeah, let's hope for one more time. Right now, I just want to go to bed."

Matt met with Buford early. By 9:30 they finished briefing each other and began to discuss the case in general.

"Do you have any plans about pursuing this further?" Matt asked and started walking around the room. He pulled a pack of Pall Malls from his shirt pocket and lit one.

"Yes, I'll keep working on it if that's what you mean."

"I meant any specific plans,"

"Well, I have two people at the Asylum that might have been holding back a little when I interviewed them. Beyond that I want a little more information before I interview some others."

"In what way were the two holding back? Do you think it's material?"

"I don't know. For all I know it might be just my imagination."

"Well what about it?" Asked Matt, standing at the front door he had cracked, and blew smoke outside. After a couple more puffs he put the cigarette out on the sole of his shoe and threw it outside to the curb.

"I asked everyone the same questions. These two kind of stumbled on the same question."

"What was the question?"

"Can you think of anyone who might help her leave or that might be a danger to her?"

"What did they say?"

"They both said 'No.'"

"Then why are you suspicious?"

"Because my gut told me something at the time."

"Why have you waited to talk to them again."

"To give them time to think about it."

"When do you plan to ask them again?"

"I thought about doing it this morning. Over the phone."

"Why over the phone. Why not in person?"

"I think they'll be more comfortable answering over the phone and at home, too."

"You ready to do it now?"

"Yes. I'm ready. They should both be off duty. This may shock 'em a little. Here goes."

Buford dialed Mary Anne Humble's home number. Matt was on the office extension.

"Hello," said a woman's voice.

"May I speak to Mary Anne Humble please?"

"This is Mary Anne."

"Mary Anne this is deputy Buford Hill. I interviewed you the other day. I'd like to ask you another question if I may."

"Yes, go ahead," she said sounding a little bit annoyed or deflated, Buford couldn't tell which.

"Mary Anne, it seemed to me you may have wanted to add a little to one of your answers in the initial interview. Is that possible?"

"Maybe, I don't know."

"The question was 'Can you think of anyone who might have helped her to leave or may have been a danger to her. By her I mean Diane Cleary or Naomi Shepherd. When I asked that before you seemed like you might have wanted to add something to your simple 'no'. Is that right?"

There was a long pause. What Buford later referred to as a pregnant pause. Buford waited for another moment then continued. "What is it Mary Anne. Spill it."

"Well, it's probably nothing. I don't want to be telling tales or getting myself in trouble."

"Don't worry. You won't get yourself in any trouble."

"It's Doctor Rose."

"What about Doctor Rose?"

"It's the way he looks or rather leers at young pretty women."

"Did either of these girls complain to you about him?"

"Both of them mentioned him talking to them as they walked the grounds. He would ride along side of them in his car. It happened more than once to each of them. I remember Diane said he was spooky, and Naomi said she asked him to leave her alone. It's all in my notes. I reviewed them after I talked to you the first time."

"Did either of them say he did anything physical or asked them to get in his car?"

"No."

"You said 'the way he looks at or leers at pretty young women.'"

"Yes. That's right."

"Did he ever make any advances towards you or any other staff member that you know about?"

Silence.

"What about it Mary Anne?"

"Yes, me. He tried hard to seduce me. I finally told him if he didn't stop I would go to personnel. He stopped."

"Is there anything else you wish to add Mary Anne?"

"Just this. Both Diane and Naomi said a guard sometimes followed close behind them in a security car when they walked."

"Did they know who the guard was?"

"No,"

"Did either of them mention about him trying to talk to them or asking them to get in the car."

"No."

"Is there anything else you would like to mention?"

"No, I've said enough already."

"Thank you Mary Anne you've been very helpful. If you think of anything else, you have my card, good-bye."

"Good-bye,"

Buford and Matt sat looking at each other for a minute then Buford said "I think it's time I talked to Ruth Randolph she's the director of Social Services. How about you?"

"I agree."

Buford looked at his list of numbers, then dialed Ruth Randolph's home.

"Hello." Came the answer.

"May I speak to Ruth Randolph?"

"This is she."

"This is deputy Buford Hill, I interviewed you about the Diane Cleary and Naomi Shepherd elopements."

"Yes, I remember."

"I'd like to ask you another question if I may."

"Sure, go ahead."

"It seemed to me that you may have wanted to add more to one of your responses. I'd like to give you that opportunity now."

"Okay, like I said, go ahead ask."

"Referring to the elopements of Diane Cleary and Naomi Shepherd the question I thought you might have wanted to add something to your initial response was 'Can you think of anyone who might have helped her leave or that might have been a danger to her."

A short pause then, "Not really. Nothing more than speculation."

"What kind of speculation. If there is something, spit it out."

"Well, it's nothing specific. Both girls told me they felt uneasy walking the grounds sometimes."

"Did they say why?"

"Yes, one of the guards made them feel uneasy."

"How".

"He would ride close behind them, then look them over when he passed."

"Which one?"

"Neither knew the guard's name. He always had his name tag covered. He was on second shift though and he was white."

"Anything or anyone else?"

"I remember Diane asking about Dr. Rose."

"What about him?"

"She mentioned him riding beside her a lot. Then he started trying to talk to her as she walked. She said she felt like he was undressing her. It made her feel uncomfortable."

"Anything else?"

"No. Like I said it's probably nothing."

"Thank you, Ruth. If you think of anything else, you have my card."

"Please don't get me in any trouble."

"Don't worry I won't, Goodbye."

"Goodbye."

Buford spent several minutes making notes before he looked at Matt.

"What do you make of that?" He asked Matt.

"I don't know. Maybe nothing, maybe a lot."

"Yeah. The shit just got deeper."

"Remember one thing, feelings usually end up not counting for much."

"Yeah. I know, especially my feelings, but this is two for two. And it sure makes me wonder about the good Doctor Rose and a guard."

""You have to be objective. Now what's your plan?"

"I'm not sure. I feel like I have to check out Dr. Rose but somehow not make a big deal out of it. And the guards, especially the first and second shift guards on duty the day Diane disappeared."

"I agree, when will you do it?"

"Monday. That gives me today and tomorrow to come up with a game plan."

"Well, I need to leave."

"Will you be making a report on your visit here?"

"Yes. Don't worry I'll be saying you are on top of things and working hard to find out exactly what happened. Now I've got to go."

They rose and shook hands.

For the next two hours Buford reviewed all his notes on the case as well as Tom's notes about Naomi. At 12:30 he closed his folder and walked across the street to the diner.

"What will it be Buford?" Asked Millie.

"A hot roast beef sandwich with home fries on the side and a piece of apple pie."

"You want gravy on the fries, too?"

"Yeah sure, why not? How about a side salad, too."

"What to drink?"

"Lemonade if you got it."

"We got it. Water, too?"

"Yes, thanks."

Millie brought the lemonade and water then said, "Buford you have a farm, isn't that right?"

"Yes."

"Is it big?"

"It all depends on what you consider big. Ours is about 35 acres."

"That's pretty big to me. Got any dogs?"

"Yeah two, Ed and Bill."

"Funny names for dogs. What are they like?"

"They're real good farm dogs. Just the right size and temperament, about 50 pounds each and are real protective of the place and us too, especially Mary."

"What kind are they?"

"They have square heads like Labradors, but I believe they're half chow and half traveling man. We got them as pups from the animal shelter in Shelton. They're brothers from the same litter. They're both a solid red color, real pretty. The only difference is Bill has a diamond shaped white spot behind his left ear. We really love them. They're special. Why are you so interested?"

"We're thinking about getting a dog."

"They're great pets."

"That's what everybody says."

After a little while Reed came rambling over to Buford with his food. "Any luck on the missing persons case?"

"Not much yet, but I'm still hopeful."

"Well, good luck."

"Thanks, I need all the good wishes I can get."

"Hi Buford, hi Mary," he said. They both said "Hi" and he continued.

"Buford, a woman called the office this morning wanting to talk to you."

"What did she want?"

"She didn't say much. She said she had some important information about Diane Cleary she wanted to talk to you about. I tried to get her to tell me what the information was, but she wouldn't say. She said it had to be you. I thought I might run into you here so I wrote her name and number down and told her I would get in touch with you today." He handed Buford a slip of paper.

"She say anything else?"

"Just that you can reach her at home today or tomorrow morning. She's from Sleighton about 30 miles East of here."

"Thanks Charley, I'll give her a call. Have a good shift."

"I hope so."

Buford stared at the slip of paper. The name on it was Evelyn Baker.

"Something important?" Asked Mary.

"I don't know, but I hope so. We need a break. All I have now is other people's feelings to go on. I'd rather have facts. I've eliminated the only good suspect I had."

"Only good suspect? Do you mean you think she could have been kidnapped or something?"

"Yes. But I can't prove that or anything else right now. Just speculation so far."

They finished their lunch without much small talk. Buford's mind was on work.

At home Buford tried to call Evelyn Baker but she was out with a friend. He left a message with her mother that he would call her between 8:00 and 8:30 Monday morning.

On Monday morning, a loud clap of thunder woke Mary. She looked at the clock. Quarter past six! She nearly jumped out of bed. She went to the dresser, checked her hair, brushed it, then put on her house coat. She was about to rush to the kitchen until she smelled bacon frying. She stopped hurrying and began to get dressed. She was tall, about five foot six and still shapely at less than one hundred and fifty pounds. Her face was a little on the long and thin side but neither ears or nose protruded. Her eyes were dark blue with laugh lines at the corners from so much time spent outdoors. Her forehead was a little high, but she compensated for that with naturally curly hair the color of ripe wheat. Like Buford, she had a light smattering of freckles. At 55 she could still turn heads walking down a city street or country road. Though big, she was dainty. Her only rough feature was her hands. She worked hard on the farm. Years of experience had taught her not to take the good times for granted. She knew they sometimes ended abruptly and then the 'butter and egg' money as they called it, had to get them through the tough times.

She put on her favorite house dress and after a trip to the bathroom went to the kitchen. Buford was cracking eggs into a bowl. She snuck up and hugged him from behind, laying her head against his broad back.

"How's my favorite farm hand?" She teased.

"Your favorite? I didn't know there was anybody else."

"There's a couple of cowpokes outside named Ed and Bill."

He laughed. "Yeah, they are special."

She set the table and he filled their plates with bacon, scrambled eggs, home fried potatoes, and toast. She poured the coffee, and they sat down to eat.

After breakfast he put on his uniform and after a kiss good-bye left for work.

Buford stopped at the diner for a quick cup of coffee. It was past 7:30.

"Anything else?" Asked Millie smiling.

"No. Not today."

Reed finished cleaning the grill then ambled down to Buford.

"Any news about the missing girl?" He asked as he took a towel and made a swipe at the counter to remove some crumbs.

"No, not much."

"How long has she been missing?"

"This is May twenty fifth and she has been missing since the fourteenth so that makes her missing for eleven days."

"Was she pretty?"

"Yes, very."

"Seems strange doesn't it," said Reed shaking his head slightly.

"What."

"That it's always a pretty one."

"Yes, I've thought the same thing."

"No clues, huh?"

"None to speak of."

"Do you think there's foul play I mean this is two in two years from the asylum," said Reed in earnest like he was trying to get a 'yes'.

"I don't know. Nobody does. That's one reason I'm investigating."

Reed wanted to talk more but Buford had enough. He slipped a dime by his coffee cup and left.

In his office Buford reviewed the questions he had for Evelyn Baker then called the number Charley gave him.

"Hello," said the voice at the other end.

"Hello. This is deputy Buford Hill. You left a message for me yesterday, I mean if this is Evelyn Baker."

"Yes, I'm Evelyn. I called about Diane Cleary."

"What do you know about Diane."

"I was at Hardin Mental Asylum the same time as Diane. We became friends, I saw her right before I left on May fourteenth."

"Where did you see her?"

"I was looking out the third-floor window near my bed and I saw a security car stop and a guard get out. He got Diane out the other side. He held her by the arm and took her inside a side door. He used a key to get in."

"What time was this?"

"About 7:00 or 7:30 at the latest."

"That would make it about dusk. Not very good light."

"It was light enough for me to see."

"What makes you think it was Diane?"

"The hair, the long blonde hair and the clothes."

"Did you see her face?"

"No, the angle wasn't right. But I still believe it was her."

"What building did the guard take her into?"

"I."

"Are you sure it was I?"

"Yes, I'm sure."

"Why didn't you come forward before?"

"I didn't know she was missing. I called her home yesterday and spoke to her mom. She told me about Diane being missing and gave me the numbers for you and the main office in Shelton. I called them all. The deputy in Shelton said he would let you know I called."

"He did. One more question. Did you recognize the guard who had her by the arm?"

"No."

"Was he white or black?"

"He was white."

"Are you sure?"

"Yes, I'm sure."

"Is there anything else you can tell me about Diane?"

"No, not really except one thing. I saw her earlier on the fourteenth and we walked together. I don't believe she eloped, it doesn't make sense because she knew she was about to be discharged."

"Anything else you want to say?"

"Only this, one of the guards rode beside her a lot and the Superintendent gave Diane the creeps. He was always trying to talk to her when he made his rounds in his car."

"Did she ever say he tried to get her in his car?"

"No, she never said that about him."

"Do you know which guard rode beside her?"

"No, he always had his name tag covered."

"Would you be willing to write a statement if I need it?"

"Sure."

"Thanks and goodbye," said Buford.

"Good-bye. I hope this helps and I hope you find her."

"I hope so, too and good-bye again."

Buford mulled over the conversation. Diane being escorted into building 'I' didn't make sense. Dusk could be a good time to make her disappear. But into another building? Why?

"Hell," he wondered out loud. "Am I trying to connect dots that aren't even on the page?"

The phone rang and before he could even answer he heard "Buford this is Bean. Sheriff Scott wants you to report three times a week, Monday, Wednesday and Friday, as long as the Diane Cleary case is open. Also, if you come across anything really big he wants you to phone it in immediately. You got that?"

"Yes. I've got it."

"Anything new about it?"

"I'm trying to pull the pieces together. I'll detail everything in my report today."

"Did that state boy help?"

"He helped but didn't turn up anything."

"Are you making any progress at all?"

"Yes, I'm eliminating possibilities and adding new ones. Like I said I'll detail it in my report today or Wednesday."

"Okay, I'll pass it on to the sheriff, 10-4."

"10-4."

The phone rang again.

"Sheriff's office Deputy Hill speaking, can I help you?"

"Deputy Hill this is officer Sabatini. I'm calling to check on your case."

"Why?" Asked Buford, irritated.

"Well, I said I would."

"Why?" Asked Buford even more irritated.

"What do you mean why?"

"I mean why do you want to know. You're not being honest with me. Maybe I can help you and maybe you could help me, but you only want to pick my brain and not volunteer any information. I don't like that."

"Well, you know I asked Sheriff Scott if I could check in with you and he said it would be okay."

"I'm deputy Hill. You're not leveling with me, and I want to know what's up."

"Look deputy Hill I'm going to be near the Kentucky border this morning, suppose I come on up to your office. I can be there about noon or so. Then we can discuss things. How about that?"

"That sounds better, I'll see you then. In the meantime, I've got work to do."

"Okay."

"Good."

Vittorino hung up and went to see Albert Johnson.

"Captain, I need to go on up to see Deputy Hill today when I'm near the Kentucky line. I need to explain why I'm interested in his missing persons case."

"I think you're grabbing at straws."

"Maybe so. I don't know. It's just a feeling in my gut."

"This is about the tenth feeling in your gut you've had about this."

"I know, but Pittsburgh panned out and I believe if I don't do this and miss out on some information……". His voice trailed off.

"I still think you're grabbing at straws again."

Irritated, Vittorino replied a little heatedly, "Right now straws are all I have to grab at. The trail grows colder and colder. I really believe I need to talk to this deputy. If I need to I'll take vacation time."

"Alright go. But unless something solid happens I expect you here tomorrow."

"I'll be here."

He left 30 minutes later. He headed straight up 31W, then back roads when he got close to Rhodes County. He got to Buford's office at 12:30. He parked right outside then walked in.

"Hello officer Hill," said Vittorino smiling.

"Hello yourself," said Buford rising from his desk to shake hands.

"I believe you're right I need to level with you."

"I'd appreciate that. Have a seat and let's hear it."

Vittorino leaned forward in his chair, his demeanor was professional.

"I suppose you noticed I have an accent."

"Yes, my guess is you are Italian."

"That is correct, and Italy is where I will begin. My family is Jewish. We have a farm in Italy. My father and I were in our village making arrangements to leave Italy because it was no longer safe. The Fascists and Nazis were committing crimes, some just to gain money and some against people because they were Jews."

"After making the arrangements we went home and found our family murdered. Seven people. Only my younger brother Marcus survived. My mother, grandmother and grandfather, uncle and aunt and two cousins had been shot while we were in our village."

Buford looked astonished. "My god, I'm so sorry. What a horrible thing to happen."

"Later we found out who did this, it was an Italian Major named Fontana and a German Lieutenant named Bellheimer with about a dozen German soldiers. First Fontana murdered my grandfather with his pistol then Bellheimer ordered the machine gunner to open fire. They systematically walked among those shot and finished killing anyone still alive. My brother Marcus managed to feign death."

"The major forced four Italian soldiers to lead them to the farm. The ruse was so that they could conscript me into the Italian Army. Fontana tried to get the Italians to shoot my family, but Lieutenant Arturo refused the illegal order."

"Couldn't the Italian soldiers do anything to stop the shooting?"

"No, they were also covered by the machine gun and the dozen German soldiers. They were lucky to leave before Fontana realized they could possibly be witnesses against them."

"Did they bring charges?"

"Oh yes. But at the time in this part of Italy the Germans were in charge. Fontana and Bellheimer claimed my family were armed and resisted and Arturo refused an order to help put down the uprising. Arturo asked for an investigation and presented his statement and statements from the three other Italian soldiers that were there. The Italian police in our village also tried to bring charges against Fontana and Bellheimer but the German soldiers were shipped out and the Germans said it was a legitimate act of war."

"I am truly sorry for the loss of your family," said Buford. Empathy was on his face. "I had no idea, and again I am truly sorry."

"Fontana is a true monster. He cuts the ring fingers off his female victims. To shorten this story, I will tell you this, I followed them to the U.S. and have been trying to capture them."

"I take it they are still alive and still at large?"

"Yes, and still murdering people."

"So, you think they or one of them is involved in this elopement? If so, how?"

"I don't know that. I just heard about your case when I visited Sheriff Scott. My boss Albert Johnson thinks I'm grabbing at straws. I probably am, but that's all I have."

"Has anyone seen these two in the U.S?"

"Yes, we had a shootout in Pittsburgh. I believe I wounded Bellheimer. They got away after murdering two more people that day."

"Wow. These are really dangerous men, but I agree with your boss, I think it's a stretch to think they are involved in this elopement. But then again wait a minute. There actually have been two elopements where young pretty women ready for discharge have never shown up at home."

"Two?"

"Yes, one about two years ago."

"Do you have anything to go on?"

"Not much. Just speculation, no real evidence. But the information you just gave me could open another can of worms."

"Now that I've leveled with you, do you have any more information?"

"Yes, a few things. I showed some pictures of missing women along route 31W North from here. I got a hit on one. Joan Bleecher, one of the women found with a severed ring finger. I was working with a state trooper. He turned the information over to the state investigators."

"Yes, Joan Bleecher. We believe Fontana and Bellheimer were responsible. Where did you get the hit?"

"At a Chuckey's where Campground Road meets 31W. The cashiers said she was being held forcibly by the arm. They weren't sure they could I.D. who had her."

He checked his notes and handed a slip of paper to Vittorino. "Here these are the names of the cashiers who saw Joan Bleecher."

"Thanks, I'll ride up there and talk to them. You said a few things."

"Yeah. I'll get to the rest but now I have a few questions for you," said Buford.

"Go ahead."

"This Fontana and Bellheimer what do they look like?"

"Here's a picture of them taken in '43 or '44," said Vittorino handing it to Buford.

Buford studied the picture. He started to hand it back, but Vittorino waved him off.

"I have many copies."

"How tall are they?"

"They're both pretty tall. Fontana's about six feet, Bellheimer's almost as tall. Both have brown hair. Fontana's is darker than Bellheimer's. Fontana has dark brown to black eyes. Bellheimer's are light blue, quite the Nazi color."

"Do you think they could have had plastic surgery to change their appearances?"

"They have plenty of money, so they could have. But probably just enough to alter their appearance not completely change it. That and Bellheimer's accent would have sent up red flags."

"I agree. But if they had surgery, it could make it hard to use an old picture to make an I.D."

"I know. That's one of the problems. In Pennsylvania they obviously used mustaches and beards to mask their appearances."

"Do you have a picture of them in their disguises in Pittsburgh?"

"No. They were very careful to avoid any cameras."

"What did they do in Italy."

"Fontana was a liaison to the Germans in Italy. Like I said he was a Major in the Italian Army the last year or so before he disappeared. He and Bellheimer had a scheme going to throw people off their land by saying they owed back taxes or were enemies of the state. Then they bought the confiscated land and resold it. Before that he worked for the Fascists in a court prison system. He claimed to be a doctor. We checked on him. He was in pre-med at the University in Naples, but he didn't get far in med-school. He passed himself off as a doctor to the Fascists, there was some doubt about whether they believed him or didn't care as long as he did his work, which was obtaining confessions."

"What about Bellheimer?"

"He's a typical Nazi henchman. A former member of the Hitler Youth in Germany. He, like Fontana, likes to kill, especially Jews. You must understand one thing about both of them. They are pure evil. Fontana was the leader in Italy and probably still is over here. They have avoided being caught for a long time. My boss says they'll make a fatal mistake, they haven't yet, but they nearly did in Pittsburgh."

"So, are the ring fingers Fontana's only souvenirs?"

"The only other one I know about was my grandmother's peacock broach. I have a picture of her wearing it. Let me show you."

"That's some large broach," said Buford leaning forward to get a good look at the picture.

"Yes, and it's decorated with emeralds, rubies and sapphires."

"Very beautiful, I hope you get it back from the son of a bitch."

"I will. Now, what else do you have that may interest me?"

"All I have is indirect or circumstantial, actually some is just sort of hearsay regarding Diane Cleary and the other young woman, Naomi Shepherd, that eloped and was never heard from again. She disappeared in May 1952 no clues, nothing."

"What is the information?"

"Before they disappeared both women told social workers that a guard made them nervous, maybe even scared on their walks on the grounds. Also, both women said the

Superintendent, Doctor Rose, made them feel uneasy. Diane said he would follow along in his car when she was walking, trying to talk to her. She told the social worker it was like he was undressing her."

"It might be interesting to know the Superintendent's background, especially since he's a doctor."

"Of course, but to find out I need an excuse to check his personnel record. So far, I haven't been able to come up with one. Same with the guard. Right now, the only way I know to get the records is to run a bluff and that puts me on pretty shaky ground. If there's no connection and the Superintendent finds out and makes a big enough squawk it could cost me my badge or at least a suspension.

The first thing I'm going to find out is who the guards were that were on duty the evening Diane Cleary disappeared. This morning I found out she was seen that afternoon at the dock. Another patient left her there and saw a security car going in that direction."

"That's not much."

"No but things add up. Later that evening the same patient was packing up to leave when she looked out her third-floor window and saw a security guard take a patient she believes was Diane into building 'I'. That doesn't make sense because Diane's building was 'H'. She's willing to sign a statement about what she saw."

"It sounds like you're on to something, but it's still not hard evidence."

"Maybe not, but it's pretty damn close. After all the dead ends, it's all I have to go on. Now tell me more about your killers' tracks."

"Well, the only trail is bodies with severed ring fingers. The first two were women found in the Allegheny River near Blawnox, a suburb of Pittsburgh, in September and October of 1948. I went there and we almost caught them red handed in a shootout after they murdered another woman and a man. In June of 1951, the body of Jeanette Strube, a clerk from Olivier and Barnwell University in Ithaca, New York was found. She had been in lake Cayuga near Ithaca since June 1950. Then in June 1952 Joan Bleecher's body surfaced in the Ohio but you know about that."

"Yes."

"There was one more body found with a severed ring finger. In August of 1953 Mary Ann Hostetter's body was found in a shallow grave near Pittsburgh, Pa. She was reported missing in May 1946."

"None of the local police departments have been able to track down the killers. The F.B.I. has an open investigation, they're stymied, too. They keep me informed because of my family's connection to the case."

"So let me get this straight," said Buford as he started making notes in his pad. "There are seven murders you know about in the U.S. Mary Ann Hostetter, in May 1946 and three women and a man in September and October 1948 all from near Pittsburgh, Pennsylvania. Jeanette Strube from Ithaca,

New York in June 1950. And Joan Bleecher in December 1951 from Louisville, Kentucky and they all have severed ring fingers, is that right?"

"That's pretty much it," said Vittorino.

"Hmm," mused Buford. "That means the killer or killers were in or near Pittsburgh from at least May 1946 to October 1948. In Ithaca, New York in June,1950 and in Louisville in December 1951. Is that right?

"As far as we know, except we know they rented a house near Pittsburgh in April. 1946," said Vittorino.

"Does the F.B.I. have any hard evidence like fingerprints?"

"Yes, they have a print from a door frame in Louisville, and multiple prints from their house and cars in Denny Camp near Pittsburgh. They all match. I have photocopies of the prints myself."

"And you're interested in the disappearance of the two women here because you think they are somehow linked to those crimes?"

"My boss says I'm grabbing at straws, but straws are all I have. I've been grabbing at straws since 1944 and right now I just feel they may be relaxed enough to make a big mistake. I don't know if they're linked to your case, but now you know enough about them that you'll know if things are adding up and I hope let me know."

"Don't worry. That can of worms I talked about makes my own suspicions about the guard and the superintendent here a lot more plausible. I'm working on a plan to find out more about them. If I even suspect anything involving Fontana and Bellheimer I'll call you right away. Who knows, I might develop a plan to eliminate them or nail them. I'll have to think about it."

"What do you think happened to the two women?"

"Well, I can't prove a damn thing, but I don't believe either one eloped. I think someone at the hospital got them. I believe Naomi's probably dead. I don't know about Diane, hopefully she's still alive."

"You're pretty sure, aren't you?"

"Right now, it's only a hunch, but a pretty strong hunch."

"Fontana is very clever. He might even be able to pass himself off as a doctor. With pretty young women here it would be hard for him to resist the temptation if he thought he could get away with it. All this is speculation of course, but let's keep in touch. Here's my card," said Vittorino.

"You're right it's speculation, kind of wild speculation, but you never know, I'll keep these two in mind while I'm investigating."

"Goodbye and thank you."

"Goodbye and good luck."

Buford thought for a moment, New York, Pennsylvania and now Kentucky. It looks like they're moving South. Maybe Vittorino is grabbing at straws, but so would I if I was him. "Hell, I sure hope he finds those fiends," he said out loud.

CHAPTER THIRTY-SIX

While eating lunch at the diner, Buford decided on a course of action. He smiled as he thought about it. When he finished, instead of the usual quarter tip, he left a shiny new half dollar and walked out waving at Reed and Millie as he went.

In his office Buford dialed the asylum. The switchboard answered and quickly transferred him to Security. Lanier answered.

"Security. Lanier speaking, can I help you?"

"I sure hope so Lanier this is deputy Buford Hill."

"What do you want?"

"I need some information and I hope you will help me get it."

"I'll do my best, what is it?"

"I want to know the names of the guards on duty the day Diane Cleary disappeared. The morning and afternoon shift."

"I'll check the schedule and get back to you."

"Two things Lanier. One this is important, so I need It as soon as possible. The second thing is keeping this inquiry confidential. Now when can you get back to me?"

"If nothing happens in the meantime, I can call you back in fifteen or twenty minutes."

"Good I'll wait for your call,"

Buford waited patiently for Lanier's call. The fifteen or twenty minutes went by. Then thirty minutes, then an hour. Buford resisted the temptation to call again. Finally, the phone rang. "Sheriff's office deputy Hill speaking. Can I help you?"

"Deputy Hill this is Lanier, I'm sorry it took so long. There was a disturbance on one of the units and I had to respond. Also, there was a schedule change that day on the evening shift. I had to check timecards to make sure who worked the shift. The early shift guards were Greene and Boone. The evening shift was Roberts and Bell."

"What color are they?"

"Greene and Roberts are black. Bell is white, so is Boone."

"Thanks. Remember keep this to yourself."

"I'll have to tell my boss, Mr. Shaker."

"Okay. Can you transfer me to his office?"

"I can try, hold on".

A moment later a male voice answered, "This is John Shaker what do you want deputy Hill?"

"I just received some information from Lanier, and I want to keep it confidential. He said he had to report any inquiry to you."

"That's right. If it's important I'll keep it to myself."

“Well, it is, kind of. I don’t want anyone getting excited over routine questions.”

“No problem,” said Shaker.

“Well, I’d like to come out there tomorrow morning about 11 and interview the security guards that were on duty the afternoon and evening Diane Cleary disappeared.”

“I’ll have to check with Lanier to see who that would be.”

“I already checked there’s four of them, Greene, Boone, Roberts and Bell. It’s kind of important or I wouldn’t ask on such short notice. Do you think you could make them available?”

“Hold on and let me check on their schedules.”

A minute later he came back on the line and said “If you can make that about 1:30 I think we can arrange to have all four of them here close to that time. That’s close to shift change. They run screwy schedules in security, but I think that will work out for you.”

“Thank you. I appreciate your effort. One more thing, I’d like to talk with you while I’m out there.”

“Sure, see you tomorrow.”

“So long.”

Buford redialed H.M.A. When the switchboard answered he asked to be transferred to the Superintendent’s office. A moment later a woman with a pleasant voice came on the line.

“Superintendent’s office. May I help you?”.

“Yes ma’am you sure can. This is deputy Buford Hill of the Rhodes County Sheriff’s office. I would like to make an appointment to interview Dr. Rose sometime tomorrow afternoon.”

“Hold please,” said the voice. A moment later the voice said, “What would the interview be about?”

Buford answered, “About the disappearance of Diane Cleary on May fourteenth.”

He said disappearance rather than elopement on purpose.

“Hold again please,” said the voice.

In a moment she returned. “Dr. Rose said you need to check with Security and Patient Services. He wouldn’t have anything to add to their comments.”

“By the way, we’ve been going back and forth, and I don’t even know your name,” said Buford,

“I’m sorry deputy, my name’s Martha Brown. Will that be all deputy?”

“No ma’am. Tell Dr. Rose this. I’m making an official inquiry and expect his cooperation. I’d like to interview him tomorrow afternoon. It won’t take long, but it is important.”

Buford smiled as he waited for the next response. Nothing like stirring the pot he mused.

A few minutes later Martha came back on the phone. “I’m sorry it took so long. I had to rearrange Dr. Rose’s schedule to accommodate your request. Is 4:30 tomorrow okay with you?”

“Yes, I’ll be there, thank you.”

“You are welcome,” said Martha her voice still pleasant.

———————

It was about 2pm when Buford made the appointment to interview Dr. Rose.

After he agreed to meet with Buford, Rose decided he needed to head off any danger. He used his private line to call Bell.

Bell was at home and answered the phone. "Bell here. Can I help you?"

"Possibly, this is Rose. That deputy that's been snooping around wants to interview me tomorrow afternoon about Diane Cleary."

"I wouldn't worry about it. What can he possibly do, maybe ask a few questions? Besides I heard, unofficially, that he's going to interview all the security guards on duty the day the woman disappeared."

"When?"

"I don't know, maybe tomorrow. Probably before your interview."

"Well you better have your answers ready if he does interview you," said Rose.

"I will."

"Call me if you find out what he's after."

"Okay."

"The one from on the grounds here two years ago, how well did you bury her?"

"About three feet deep," said Bell. "Besides it was way out in the country. No-one's going to find her."

"Nobody better find her. We don't need any slip ups with this deputy snooping around."

"What about the other one?" Asked Bell.

"We can still play with her for a few more days, then it's 'bye-bye,'" said Rose.

"Are you going to have anybody over?"

"Maybe this weekend, I haven't decided. A lot depends on the interview tomorrow."

"Do you want me to stay away tonight?"

"Yes, you never know who's watching, I have to go now."

"Ari Viderci," said Bell. He put his hand over the phone mouthpiece so he could laugh at Rose's response.

"Stop that, one day you'll screw up saying that." He hung up and said aloud "Peasant Nazi bastard, one of these days you'll have to go."

Just before 5 PM Rose buzzed his secretary on the intercom.

"Get me State representative Duncan Sharp. Try his office first then home if necessary."

"Yes sir."

A few minutes later she buzzed Rose.

"Representative Sharp is on the line."

"Thank you, Martha."

"If it's alright I'm going home now."

"Yes, go ahead," he said then answered the phone.

"Hello Duncan, how are you."

"Just fine, how about you."

"I've had better days, that's why I'm calling."

Sharp didn't take the bait. He waited.

Finally Rose spoke again. "I'm being forced to do an interview with a local deputy sheriff tomorrow afternoon."

"What about?"

"County Sheriff office, deputy Mills speaking can I help you?"

"This is Representative Sharp. I would like to speak to Sheriff Scott."

"The sheriff has gone home for the day."

"I seem to have misplaced the Sheriff's card; can you give me his home number?"

"I'll need to call him first and make sure it's okay. He normally doesn't like to be called at home unless it's an emergency. I'll call right now while you wait if you want."

"I want."

A minute later deputy Mills came back on the line. "His home number is Vandyke 74168. He said it's okay to call."

"Thanks."

He immediately called Sheriff Scott's home number.

"Hello," said Scott.

"Sheriff Scott this is state representative Duncan Sharpe, we've met a few times at festivals and ribbon cuttings."

"Sure, how are you Duncan?"

"I'm fine but one of my constituents is upset."

"Someone get a speeding ticket?"

"No, it's more than that. Dr. Rose out at the Hardin Asylum says one of your deputies, Buford Hill, is insisting on interviewing him tomorrow afternoon about a woman's elopement. He says it's not necessary, that your deputy has interviewed everyone that had contact with the woman and even called some of them at home. He said he had no contact with her and has nothing to add to what's been told by Patient Services personnel. He also said he was bullied into the interview by deputy Hill saying it was an official inquiry. He would like the interview cancelled and for your office to wrap up the investigation as soon as possible."

"I don't know this Dr. Rose very well. I've only met him once or twice. He doesn't seem very sociable, what's your opinion of him?"

"I've known him for a couple of years, he seems alright. Everyone says he seems to be a good doctor, that's all I know." said Sharp.

"But you want me to call off this interview and wrap-up the investigation, because Rose is your friend. Is that right?"

Sharp was trapped and he knew it.

"What I'm doing is passing on information from one of my constituents. Nothing more."

"Well, you've done that. Anything more? Any particular action you want me to take?"

"I would like you to look into the matter."

"And do what?" Asked Scott trying to see how far Sharp would go.

Sharp thought for a moment then took the plunge.

"If you think Dr. Rose may be justified then do what he asks. That's what I want from you."

"Thanks for your call. Bye."

"Thanks for listening. Bye."

Scott thought for a few seconds, the words "may be justified" seemed to hang in the air. He made notes about

Sharp's call, a lot of them. His wife, Barbara, called him to supper. He strolled in and sat at the dining room table.

"Anything important, Will?"

"Representative Sharp. It seems that Dr. Rose the big wig at the Asylum doesn't like Buford sniffing around. Says he's more or less worn out his welcome."

"What do you think?"

"I don't know, but I did get one thing out of Sharp, he applied some pressure. If Buford's onto something, I'll let him go and if Sharp ends up on the wrong end of the stick I'll break it off."

"Are you going to call Buford tonight?"

"No, I'll call in the morning. I want to give this some thought."

"Didn't this Representative campaign against you?"

"More for my opponent, Charley Smith than against me. Sharp's real slick he doesn't normally stick his neck out."

"Then why now?"

"I guess because Rose let him campaign on the Asylum's grounds and kept his opponents out on the road."

"But that's unfair."

"That's just politics, Honey."

"Seems dirty to me."

"Me, too".

———————

On Tuesday the twenty sixth Buford got up really early, completed his farm chores, and was at the diner shortly after

Millie opened the door at 6:30. By the time he got to his stool Millie had coffee on the way.

"What'll it be?" She asked.

"The works."

"You'll have to be a little more specific."

"Sausage, couple of eggs, home fries and biscuits."

"Over medium?"

"Yeah, over medium sounds good."

Millie passed the order to Reed. Ten minutes later he delivered it to Buford.

"What's happening, Buford?"

"Nothing yet, but I hope it will."

"Any more on the missing woman?"

"I'm still working on it."

"Getting closer to solving it?

"I hope so, but you never know how things are going to turn out."

Buford finished eating and drank a second cup of coffee. He left his usual tip then waved as he headed for the door.

At his office desk he made out a short list of questions for Dr. Rose.

At about 7:30 or so the phone rang. He went through his usual answer, then Sheriff Scott spoke.

"Buford this is Scott."

"Oh, good morning sheriff."

"Buford, Representative Sharp called me last night. It seems the Superintendent at the Asylum feels he's being harassed into having an interview with you. What's the story?"

"Okay. I'm going to let you do your thing today. But I want a full report this afternoon or no later than tonight. Understand?"

"Yes, and I thank you Sheriff, I won't let you down."

"I hope not. 10-4."

"10-4."

After the conversation with Scott, Buford began to work in earnest.

He looked at the picture Vittorino had given him of Fontana and Bellheimer for possibly the hundredth time in the last twenty-four hours. Fontana was a little taller and Bellheimer was heavier built. Fontana's ears stuck out from the side of his head and his hair was darker. Maybe I'm nuts he thought, this is a one in a million shot, I hope I don't lose my badge over my actions. He returned the picture to his desk drawer.

He put on some thin surgical gloves and pulled three pastel blue envelopes from his briefcase. He took a moment to slightly wrinkle all the envelopes to give the appearance of being used. Next he took three identical pictures out of his briefcase. He wiped two of the pictures with a clean handkerchief and put one in an envelope marked with a tiny A in the lower back corner. He put another one in an unmarked envelope. The last un-wiped picture he put in an envelope marked with a tiny X. He then wiped off the envelopes marked A and the unmarked one. The one with the X he didn't bother to wipe. He put all three envelopes in his briefcase.

Next, he called the asylum and asked to speak to Lanier.

"Security, may I help you?"

"Lanier this is deputy Hill, I would like you to escort me to a building this morning,"

"Okay, when and what building?"

"I'd like to meet you about 11:15 at the guard shack."

"Okay, I'll meet you at the entrance."

Buford arrived at the Asylum a little early. At the guard shack he stopped to show his I.D. and put his revolver in the trunk. He recognized officer Boone, and they exchanged greetings.

"Are you still working on the elopement?" Asked Boone.

"Yes."

"I was supposed to meet Lanier here, do you know where he is?"

"That's him coming now," said Boone nodding at a Security car coming down the road.

Buford walked about 100 feet up the road and hailed Lanier to stop.

"Good morning, Deputy Hill, are you ready?"

"Yes, one thing I forgot to mention, I don't want anyone else to know where we are going this morning."

"I'll have to tell Mr. Shaker. What Building do you want to visit?"

"It's Building 'I' he said in a near whisper. Shaker's okay, nobody else, especially none of the guards."

"No problem, do you want to follow in your car?"

"Yes."

Buford followed Lanier to Building 'I'. When they arrived, he walked around to one end of the building.

"What do you want here?" Asked Lanier.

"I want to go in that side door," said Buford gesturing to the side that was visible from Building 'K'. That is if you have a key,"

"I do."

They walked to the door and Lanier opened it. They entered into a stairwell.

"Where do these steps go?"

"The up ones go to the main hall, it leads to the first floor unit."

"That's all?"

"Yes, that's all. The down steps go to the tunnel."

"Did you say tunnel?"

"Yes, I'll show you, come on."

They went down a series of steps to a landing then down some more to a door marked KEEP CLOSED AT ALL TIMES. The door was locked and when Lanier opened it they stepped into a wide, well-lit corridor that appeared to go a long way in either direction.

"What's the purpose of this tunnel?"

"It has two main purposes. First, it connects all the patient buildings and food service in that direction," said Lanier pointing to his right, "and the laundry in the other direction. About fifty feet or so down the hall on the left are two elevators. Food and clean laundry go up in one elevator and dirty trays, garbage and dirty laundry come down in the other one. It's the same way for all the patient buildings. Also, when we have tornado warnings patients and staff use the tunnels as safe areas."

"I see. Let's take a walk," said Buford.

They walked past the elevators. Both doors were open. A little farther on they came to a door marked STORAGE AUTHORIZED PERSONNEL ONLY.

"What's in here?" Asked Buford.

"Probably just maintenance stuff."

"If you have a key, let's see."

Lanier opened the door, and they went inside a well-lit room. There were several rows of metal shelves on either side of the door. Most of the shelves contained maintenance items and all had a thick layer of dust.

Buford walked straight ahead until he reached the end of the shelves. They stopped about six feet from the back wall. To the left was an old metal desk, on it was a roll of gray duct tape. The desk was covered in dust like the shelves, but the roll of duct tape was clean.

To the right was a rubber mattress. A blow-up type. It was clean, too.

"Isn't this cozy," said Buford looking around.

"Yeah, I had no idea," said Lanier staring at the mattress.

"Who all would have keys to this room and the outside door we came in?"

"Anyone with at least a sub master. That means all Security guards and lead maintenance workers, and anyone with a junior master such as Program Directors and anyone with a master key, Dr. Rose, Mr. Shaker, and Mr. Mitchell. That should be all."

Buford pulled a pair of rubber gloves from his pocket. He handed them to Lanier along with a ball point pen. "Here put these on then sign and date the duct tape," he said.

Lanier did it, then handed the gloves back. Buford put them on then picked up the roll of duct tape.

"Let's go," he said.

In the tunnel Buford asked, "If someone went to the laundry or food service after hours could they get out through either one?"

"If they had at least a sub or junior master."

"Thanks for letting me in, I have to go now."

"Any word on Miss Cleary?"

"Not anything earthshaking."

"I hope you find out what happened to her."

"Not so sure about the elopement, now?" Asked Buford as they started to leave.

"I don't know I've thought about it. It just doesn't make sense."

"No it doesn't. What we have discovered down here today may or may not be important, but it must be kept confidential."

"You know I have to tell Mr. Shaker."

"Not this time Lanier. You can tell him we went in Building 'I' if you want, but you don't tell him or anybody about what we saw in that room."

"How am I going to avoid it?"

"I don't know, that's up to you. This is a police matter and as such will remain confidential. Is that clear?"

"Yes."

"Good."

Buford drove to the Administration Building. He was about fifteen minutes early for his meeting with Shaker. In the lobby he looked at a directory with names and room numbers. John Shaker's office was number 108. Buford took a chance it was on the left from the lobby. He was right. The door was closed so he knocked. A secretary opened it. "Sorry, if we leave it open everybody wants to stop. Can I help you?"

"I'm here to see John Shaker."

"You are?"

"I'm deputy Buford Hill."

"Okay, I'll tell him you're here."

She knocked on his door and then went inside.

A moment later she emerged and said "Go right in deputy Hill. Mr. Shaker's expecting you."

"Thank you," he said and went on in.

Shaker was busy writing something so Buford waited for him to finish. In a minute Shaker put his pencil down then got up to shake hands with Buford.

"Green and Boone should be here in a few minutes. You can interview them in the office across the hall. Roberts and Bell are on second shift today. I left word for them to come as soon as they get squared away on their shift. That should be around 2:30."

"Thanks," said Buford then continued "There's something else I want to see. That's the confidential part I spoke about."

"What is it?"

"I want to see some personnel records."

"Whose?"

"You, Jack Mitchell, Dr. Emery, and the four guards I'm interviewing today."

"I'm not sure I can do that. Those are confidential records."

"This facility receives state and county funding. That makes those public records. You can and will release them to me. You can stay in the room with me while I look at them if you like. I won't take a single piece of paper from any of the files."

"I think I better contact our attorney."

"That's fine. Talk to him, but I'd appreciate it if you didn't tell him which records if you can avoid it."

Mr. Shaker's secretary came in. "There's two Security guards to see you," she said.

"Thank you, Sara," he said. Then to Buford "If you'll follow me you can interview them now."

They walked into the hall. Two uniformed guards were sitting on an old deacon's bench.

"This is deputy Hill. He wants to interview you today."

"Who do you want to start with?"

"Mr. Greene."

Mr. Greene got up and followed Buford into the room.

Buford offered him a seat.

"Mr. Greene I'm here today to interview just a few people, namely the Security guards that were on duty the evening Diane Cleary disappeared."

"Okay."

"Now you had the shift that goes off at 2:30 PM, right?"

"I don't know. I don't remember what day she eloped, or what time I got off."

"It was May fourteenth. You worked that day with Boone. I got the schedule from Lanier."

"Oh, okay. If Lanier says so it must be right. It's just we are on rotating shifts and sometimes it's hard to remember."

Buford opened his briefcase and handed Greene the envelope with the small x on it.

"Take a look at the picture in this envelope. Did you see this man May fourteenth on the Asylum grounds," asked Buford.

Greene opened the envelope and took out the picture. He looked at it carefully. "No, I don't recall ever seeing this man on the grounds."

"Do you remember anything unusual happening on the grounds on or about that day?"

"No, I don't remember anything like that."

"Thank you. That's all. Send in Mr. Boone please."

Mr. Boone came in and Buford went through the same charade with him.

"I don't recognize this man, and I don't remember anything unusual happening on my shift that day."

"Thank you that's all."

Buford knew there was a thirty-minute shift overlap and Greene and Boone would probably tell Roberts and Bell what the interview would be about. He counted on it.

Mr. Shaker came in, "Our attorney says we don't have to give you the records, but you could subpoena them if we don't. So, I'm going to personnel to get them. We have nothing to hide."

"I didn't say you did. Let's check the list."

"You said me, Jack Mitchell, Dr. Emery and the four guards."

"And Dr. Rose. Skip you."

"You don't want mine, but you do want Dr. Rose's?"

"Yes. Did you tell the attorney which records I wanted?"

"Yes, I did. He said it didn't matter whose records."

"Good. I'd like to have them now."

Shaker stood in the room for a moment. He started to speak then stopped. Then he crossed the hall and started to go in his office, then stopped and went down the hall. A few minutes later he returned with all the records. He piled them in a chair.

At 2 PM the guards filed into Lanier's office for shift change. He had Greene and Boone make an oral report then gave them the form to fill out for the written report.

Lanier then spoke to Roberts and Bell. "After shift change you are to report to Mr. Shaker's office, deputy Hill wants to interview you. Greene you and Bell stay over until 3 PM to cover while they're being interviewed. That's all I have for now,

I've got to go to Admissions while you guys have shift change," he said, and left the office.

"What was the interview about?" Roberts asked Greene and Boone.

"Oh, he just had this picture of a man he wants to know if we saw the day that woman eloped," said Boone.

"Yeah, he has it in a wrinkled blue envelope. I'd say he's had it for a while," said Greene.

"That's it?" Asked Bell.

"Yeah, pretty much," said Boone.

At 2:15 Bell left and went to a pay phone to call Dr. Rose on his private line.

"Dr. Rose speaking, who's calling?"

"It's me, Bell. That deputy's interviewing every guard on duty May fourteenth, he's showing a picture of a man and asking if we saw him on the grounds that day."

"What did you tell him?"

"He hasn't interviewed me yet. Roberts and I are due next in about 15 minutes."

"Can you be sure he shows you the same picture he showed the others?"

"They said he has it in a wrinkled blue enveloped. That's what I'll look for."

"Study the picture a little bit, see what he says. If you think you can get away with it, you might say you saw him. Play it by ear."

"Okay."

"Let me know how it goes."

"Okay, I'll call."

——————

Buford closed the door for privacy while he looked at the personnel records. He glanced through Bell's record, nothing stood out except that he claimed a long history of employment in various jobs. The only one verifiable was as a guard at a V. A. Hospital.

Buford made notes on dates and places of employment including references. He was about to start on Rose's when Shaker knocked.

"Come in."

"The guards are here, who do you want first?"

"Roberts I guess."

Roberts came in and they exchanged greetings.

"Close the door, please," said Buford.

He walked Roberts through the same thing as Boone and Greene. Roberts didn't recognize the man in the picture either. Buford thanked him and told him to close the door and tell Bell he would be right with him as soon as he made a couple of notes.

As soon as Roberts left the room Buford put the envelope marked with an x back in the briefcase. He put on his rubber gloves then pulled out the envelope marked with an A and put it on the table. He carefully removed the picture, then stuck it halfway back in the envelope, face down, hoping to get a good print on one or the other.

He pulled out the picture of Rose and Bell that Vittorino gave him along with one he blew up in his home darkroom. He studied both, then put them back in his briefcase.

He opened the door then asked Bell to come in and take a seat.

Buford spoke first. “Mr. Bell, Diane Cleary a patient here at H.M.A. disappeared on the afternoon or evening on May fourteenth. I’m trying to wrap up a few loose ends. I’ll ask you the same questions I’ve asked the other Security officers that were on duty that afternoon.”

“Okay, go ahead,” said Bell.

“Do you remember any unusual activity that day, either by patients or visitors?”

“I don’t remember anything unusual.”

“Some people have suggested a kidnapper or someone with a grudge against H.M.A. may have been in some way connected to Diane Cleary’s disappearance. Would you take a look at the picture on the envelope. I’ve shown it to all three of the other guards on duty that afternoon.”

Bell picked up the envelope and pulled out the picture. He appeared to study the picture carefully, then put it back on top of the envelope.

“Do you remember seeing that person on the Asylum grounds?”

“Yes, I remember seeing him or someone that looks a lot like him on the grounds.”

"Was it the day Diane Cleary disappeared?"

"I don't remember what day it was, but it was fairly recently."

"Was he driving or walking?"

"If I remember right, he was walking."

"Did you stop him, or talk to him at all?"

"No, I just assumed he was a patient."

"Did you see him more than once?"

"I don't recall seeing him more than once."

"Is there anything you want to say about the elopement."

"No."

"Then that's all. Thank you, Mr. Bell."

"You're welcome, I hope I've helped."

"Yes, me too."

Buford did not offer Bell his hand like he did the other guards. Bell closed the door and left. Buford put the rubber gloves back on and quickly inserted the picture into the envelope. He wrote Bell on the left end of the envelope then returned it to his briefcase.

Next, he opened Dr. Rose's personnel file. There were only three former places of employment, the V.A. Hospitals in Louisville and Pittsburgh and a long history of employment as a professor in the School of Psychiatry at Olivier and Barnwell University in New York. He wrote down dates of employment, the name and phone numbers of the references given for each location, as well as the phone numbers of the institutions themselves. He took his time and went back through the file, checking and cross checking the information he wrote to make sure it was accurate. He closed the file then walked across the hall to John Shaker's office carrying all the files. The inner door to Shaker's office was open so Buford knocked on the door frame.

"Come in," said Shaker.

Buford closed the door, sat the files on a corner table, then sat in the chair Shaker had offered earlier.

"Thank you, Mr. Shaker for your help. I really appreciate it."

"You're welcome but I don't like being tricked."

"I don't know what you mean."

"I mean waiting until I talked to our attorney before requesting Dr. Rose's personnel record."

"That was an oversight, that's all."

"I don't believe that."

"I'm sorry you feel that way," said Buford.

"Did you find out any information from the Security officers?"

"Not much and even less from the personnel records, they're boring."

"Is that all you want from me, deputy?"

"No. I need you to keep the requests for the personnel records confidential, it's very important."

"I don't get it, you just said they were boring. If they're boring, why do you want me to keep the request quiet?"

"Because there's a few things I want to check out before anyone knows I'm checking."

"Fair enough, you can use my phone."

"Thanks, but I don't have the time to do the checking now. I'll let you know when I'm finished."

"I don't like keeping secrets about personnel at this facility," said Shaker.

"You're not keeping secrets about anybody, you're just helping in an investigation."

"I may report this to the people whose personnel records were requested," said Shaker.

"Mr. Shaker this is an official inquiry if you get in the way or try to be cute you could suffer some heavy consequences, is that clear?"

"Are you threatening me?"

"I'm telling you the best thing you can do for this facility, Diane Cleary and yourself is to do as I ask. Now do I have your word you won't mention this to anyone until I say it's okay?"

"Anyone?"

"Yes, anyone. Now do I have your word?"

"Yes, I guess so, but I've already told the attorney."

"Is he normally pretty closed mouthed?"

"Yes, very."

"I'm going to see him right now, what's his name and where's his office?"

"Ed Murray, his office is number 119 at the other end of the hall."

"Thank you again Mr. Shaker."

"I'd like to say you're welcome but I'm not sure about that."

Buford went to Ed Murray's office and got to see him immediately.

"Hello. Deputy Hill, isn't it?"

"Yes, said Buford closing the door. I'm not going to bullshit Mr. Murray. I recently requested some personnel records. I need that request kept quiet, actually confidential, have you told anyone about that request?"

"No, I have not."

"Good as an attorney you know about official inquiries. This is one. I want your word you will not mention that request until John Shaker calls you and says it's okay. Do I have your word Mr. Murray?"

"Yes, you have my word."

"Good, thank you Mr. Murray and goodbye."

"Good-bye deputy Hill."

It was about two hours before Buford was due to interview Rose, so he went back to Hardin to review what he learned over a late lunch at the diner.

When Bell left Buford, he immediately called Rose.

"Rose speaking."

"Well, I met with the deputy. It was just like Boone and Greene said, he had a picture in a blue envelope on the desk where Roberts left it. He asked me if I had seen him on the grounds."

"What did you say?"

"I told him I had seen him or someone that looked a lot like him."

"What then?"

"He asked if I saw him on the day Diane Cleary eloped and did I see him more than once. I told him I couldn't remember the date I saw him, and I only remember seeing him once. That was it except he asked if I wanted to add anything to my statement and I said no."

"Sounds good, my interview's at 4:30, give me a call about 5 we'll talk. Now get off the phone."

CHAPTER THIRTY-SEVEN

Buford decided not to go to the diner, instead he called.

"Hardin Diner Millie speaking, can I help you?"

"Millie, this is Buford I'm kind of pressed for time, do you think you or Reed could fix me a couple of burgers and call when they're ready for pick-up?"

"Sure Buford, the works?"

"Yeah, the works and thanks."

Buford reviewed the information he gathered from the personnel files and the interview with Bell.

He decided to skip the V.A. Hospital in Louisville and go straight to Pittsburgh. He dialed the number he had for Dr. Christopher Wright. A few minutes later a woman answered the call.

"Dr. Wright's office, Melanie Richards speaking. Can I help you?"

"I sure hope so, I'm deputy William Harris from Baltimore County, Maryland. I would like to speak to Dr. Wright if he is in today."

"Yes, he is. May I tell him what the call is about?"

"Certainly, it's about some references on a physician."

"Hold please," she said.

A few minutes later a male voice answered. "This is Dr. Wright what do you want with me, deputy?"

"I wanted to verify some information about a former employee and some references."

"And you are who?"

"I'm deputy William Harris from Baltimore County, Maryland."

"Very well deputy Harris what exactly do you want to know?"

"According to the information I have Dr. Elliot Rose worked at your facility from December 1945 to March,1949. Is that correct?"

"I would have to check on the exact dates but that seems correct," said Dr. Wright.

"How was your experience with him?"

"Dr. Rose did a good job while he was here."

"I have three other references I believe he may have given you. Can you verify them?"

"Possibly, what's this all about, like I said he did a good job while he was here."

"I do reference checks part-time. He's applied for another position here in Baltimore County. I'm checking out his references, that's all."

"Oh, well he was truly an excellent physician while he was here."

"That's great. I'd like to check about some other references while I have you on the phone."

"He came from Olivier and Barnwell University, he was a professor there," said Dr. Wright.

"Do you happen to have the names and telephone numbers of the Olivier and Barnwell University references?"

"Yes I do. Since I called about him I kept his application in my office after our Personnel Department finished with it. I'll have Melanie pull the folder, hold on a minute."

A few minutes later Dr. Wright resumed the conversation.

"What references do you have?"

"I have three Olivier and Barnwell references. Professor Worth telephone number 868-5261, Professor John Deal telephone 859-2301 and Professor Edward Smith 886-9201. I also have the main number for employee records at Olivier and Barnwell, 885-2195. Do any of these numbers jell with your references?" Asked Buford.

"Yes they all do. I have a note here though. These are all numbers given by a clerk in the Personnel Office when I called the Employee Records Office. I have a second note by the clerk verifying Dr. Rose worked there and giving me the direct numbers."

"Do you happen to have the clerk's name?"

"Yes, somewhere, I'm sure I would have asked for it and written it down. Hold on, here it is, Jeanette Strube."

"Thank you, Dr. Wright. You've saved me a lot of leg work."

"Remember, I said he was a good Psychiatrist."

"Yes sir, may I ask you to do one thing?"

"What's that?"

"Will you refrain from calling Dr. Rose until we've had ample time to complete our report for Baltimore County?"

"Certainly, we haven't spoken since he left and there's no reason to now. Goodbye."

"Goodbye and thank you again."

Buford dialed the operator again and asked for Information.

"Information, this is deputy Buford Hill I need the number for the Personnel office at Olivier and Barnwell University at Ithaca, New York."

"One moment please," said the operator. A moment later she came back on. "The number is Ithaca-5304 would you like me to connect you?"

"Yes, please."

It took a few minutes, but a woman answered.

"Olivier and Barnwell University, Ithaca campus Personnel Office can I help you."

"I hope so, I'm Buford Hill with the Personnel Department of Rhodes County Kentucky Psychiatric hospital. I'm checking out some references on a former Olivier and Barnwell employee. The position is for a Clinical Director at our hospital. I have three people I need to talk with, Professor John Worth, Professor John Deal and Professor Edward Smith."

"I'll connect you with Professor John Worth first. When you and he finish, have him ring this number back 828-7411 and I'll connect you with Professor Deal, and then Professor Smith."

"Thank you," said Buford.

A moment later a male voice answered, "Professor John Worth, can I help you?"

"Professor Worth, my name is Buford Hill. I'm a deputy with the Rhodes County, Kentucky Sheriff's office."

"Did you say you are a Rhodes County, Kentucky Deputy Sheriff?"

"Yes sir."

"What in the world are you calling me about?"

"In 1945 Dr. Elliott Rose gave you as a reference to a V.A. Hospital. According to the reference he was a Professor of Psychiatry at Olivier and Barnwell University for over ten years. Can you verify that?"

"Absolutely not. I have been here for over twenty years. I know every professor in Psychiatry here and at the New York City campus. There is not now, nor has there ever been a Dr. Elliot Rose in Psychiatry at Olivier and Barnwell University."

"You're certain?"

"Yes, I'm positive."

"Professor Worth did you know a Jeanette Strube?"

"Yes, why?"

"We are investigating a possible missing person. Can you tell me anyone that Miss Strube may have been dating in 1945."

"Yes, me."

"Anyone else?"

"Yes, a fellow with the last name Franklin."

"Any first name?"

"Let me think. Why is this so important?"

"I'm not sure, it may not be," said Buford.

"Now I remember, his first name was Leonard. Yes, Leonard Franklin, that's it.

I'm asking you again why is all this so important?"

"Like I said we are investigating a missing persons case that may or may not have some connection to Miss Strube's case. Professor Worth, I assume you are also Dr. Worth, is that correct?"

"Yes. Look, I was engaged to Jeanette Strube. If the two cases are connected and you find out who is responsible will you please let me know?"

"Absolutely. There's one more thing, I need you to keep this inquiry confidential otherwise it could jeopardize our investigation. Will you do that Dr. Worth?"

"Yes."

"Now, would you please ring 828-7411 to get me back to the Personnel Department?"

"Yes, don't forget let me know?"

"I will, thank you sir."

The calls to Professors Deal and Smith confirmed what Worth said about Rose. Buford also tried the Personnel Department to make absolutely sure Rose never worked there. They had no record of his employment at Olivier and Barnwell.

Buford tried the three direct numbers Dr. Wright was given.Two of the three were in service to homes of individuals. The third wasn't even in service.

"Damn, this is getting to be pretty spooky. It's beginning to look like my gut feeling is right. And so was Vittorino to be grabbing at straws," said Buford out loud.

When Reed came traipsing in with his burgers Buford was reviewing his questions for Doctor Rose.

"Hi Reed, I appreciate you bringing that over here, I'm near starved."

"It's okay, I wanted to get out for some air anyway. You look like you're working mighty hard."

"I am, but I"m going to take a couple minutes to enjoy these burgers, thanks again for bringing them over."

"Well, as keyed up as you were this morning, and then called in your lunch order we figured you must be on to something and pressed for time."

"You're half right anyway, I am pressed for time, and I need a little privacy."

"I guess that's my cue to exit, right?"

"Right Reed, I'm sorry. See you later and thanks again. Here, split this with Millie." He pulled out his wallet and extended a dollar bill.

"That's not necessary."

"Look you guys have been great to me for a long time, take it."

"You sure Buford?"

"Yeah, I'm sure."

"Thanks, and thanks for Millie, too. So long."

"So long."

"He dialed the operator and called Deputy U.S. Marshal Sabatini in Nashville. In a moment a woman answered. "U.S. Marshal's office, Deputy Gallagher speaking, can I help you?"

"Yes, I'm deputy Buford Hill from Rhodes County, Kentucky I'm trying to reach Vittorino Sabatini. Is he in today?

"Yes he is. He's with Mr. Johnson. Can I help you in the meantime?"

"Thank you, but I really need to speak to Deputy Sabatini. Will you please have him call me ASAP?

"Yes, I sure will. Oh, wait a minute here he is now."

"Sabatini here."

"Vittorino this is Buford, how are you?"

"Fine Buford, what's up?"

"The last time we talked you said you had photo copies of fingerprints from some of the crime scenes involving the killings with the severed ring fingers."

"That's right several from crime scenes in Pittsburgh and one from Louisville."

"Well, you better sit down," said Buford.

"Why?"

"Because I believe you grabbing at straws may have finally paid off. Your long hunt may be coming to an end. I believe I have a solid lead on who did those crimes and is responsible for the two missing women at the Mental Asylum here."

"A solid lead? What kind of lead?" He asked, excitement resonated from his voice.

"This morning I interviewed four Security guards, three of them were a smoke screen I was only interested in one of them. I put out some bait and he took it. He tried to steer me in another direction. I also tricked him to get his prints on a picture and an envelope. His name is Bell, I believe he may be Bellheimer. Then I asked for seven personnel records so I wouldn't spook anyone. I only reviewed two. Bell's wasn't conclusive, but I still believe he's one of them. The other one looks good at least for the locations and I believe the time of the murders in Pittsburgh and Louisville. I also believe one of them, probably the one I'm going to interview this afternoon killed Jeanette Strube in Ithaca, New York. I checked his references. They're okay for Pittsburgh but they're phony for Olivier and Barnwell University in Ithaca. That's where Jeanette Strube worked. Remember?"

"Yes, I always believed she was killed by Fontana. Damn, we just couldn't find him to prove it."

"I believe Dr. Rose, the head of Hardin Mental Asylum, used her to get him phony credentials from Olivier and Barnwell. Then when he was all set up and established good references in Pittsburgh and Louisville and no longer needed her, he killed her to eliminate a possible disgruntled lover. I truly believe it," he said excitedly.

"We figured Fontana was somehow connected to Strube, but we couldn't be sure. It was a dead end in Ithaca, and we had no way to find out what new name he was using."

"I interview our good Doctor Rose this afternoon. I'm going to act a bit of a buffoon. I'm sure Bell told him about a blue envelope with a picture that everybody already touched. So he shouldn't be worried about touching it or the picture. What they don't know is I used one envelope for the three guards before Bell, then I used a separate one on Bell to get his prints. I'm going to use another picture in a different blue envelope to get Rose's prints. I've carefully wrinkled all the envelopes to make them look the same."

"What can I do to help?"

"First, keep this under your hat until we get the prints confirmed. We don't need the FBI or anyone else snooping around. It could spook them for sure. And if I'm wrong, which I sincerely doubt, I'm the only one with egg on his face. Will you agree?"

"Absolutely."

"Once I get Rose's prints, I need you to check both his and Bell's to get a match on the prints you have. That will be the hard evidence we need."

"Okay, sounds good to me. And good luck."

"I'll call you as soon as I get Rose's fingerprints. I interview him at 4:30, I should be finished by 5:00. Will your fingerprint expert be ready this afternoon or tomorrow morning?"

"I'll call and ask the Nashville police to have him available."

"Okay, wish me luck. Goodbye, I have to go now."

"Goodbye and good luck."

At 415 Buford arrived at Hardin Mental Asylum, he stopped at the guard shack and put his revolver in his trunk. Bell was on duty.

"Good afternoon deputy Hill," he said.

"Same to you. I need to go to the Superintendent's office, can you direct me?"

"Sure, Doctor Rose's office is in the Admissions Building. Go to the Administration Building and turn left, you can't miss it."

"Thank you, officer Bell. You've been a big help today."

Buford started the patrol car towards the Admissions Building. He looked in the mirror. Bell was standing at the guard shack entrance door with the phone in his hand.

"Good boy," said Buford.

As soon as Buford drove off, Bell called Rose.

"He's on his way,"

"Now what about this picture and envelope?"

"He has a picture of someone they suspect of foul play. He keeps it in a blue envelope."

"I wonder why it's blue."

"It looks like a used envelope for a birthday card or something. Anyway, if that's what he asks you to look at, don't worry, at least four of us have already handled it."

"I'm still not sure about handling it."

"Suit yourself. Ari Viderci."

"Stop that, you idiot."

Buford turned left at the fountain and continued on to the Admissions Building. He parked in a visitors space, locked the patrol car and went in the main entrance. He stopped at the combination Information/ Switchboard and waited until the operator had a free minute.

"I'm here to see Doctor Elliott Rose."

She pointed to the hall on the left and said, "If you proceed down the hall to your left you'll see his office on the right."

"Thank you."

"You're welcome," she said and turned to answer a buzzing extension.

Buford glanced around the huge lobby. It was well lit and at its' center was a beautiful chandelier. The floor had a shine that reminded him of his days in the C.C.C. He thought the floor had just been buffed but he noticed an older man was plugging in a buffer's cord. He watched for a moment as the man deftly handled the buffer, then he turned down the hall and reached the door marked Doctor Elliott Rose, Superintendent. The door was open, so he entered and stopped at a desk just inside the door. The placard on the desk identified the woman typing as Martha Brown.

She looked up from her typing and said, "Good afternoon deputy Hill. Doctor Rose is in a meeting. He should be finished in a few minutes."

"Thank you."

"Would you like some coffee or water while you wait?"

"No thanks."

The minutes ticked by. At 4:30 Martha buzzed her boss on the intercom, "Deputy Hill is here for your appointment."

"Okay, we'll only be a minute longer," came the response.

Another minute later the door opened and out walked a familiar looking woman. She glanced at Buford, held out her hand and said, "We've met a couple of times before Deputy Hill."

"Yes, nice to see you again," he said and shook her hand.

"Martha, he said to send the deputy in. Do you have your handcuffs deputy?" She asked smiling.

"I don't anticipate needing them."

"I didn't mean for him. I meant for me. I always wondered how it would feel to be handcuffed."

"Not pleasant I assure you."

"I guess you're right," she said and left.

"She's a live wire. You can go in now," said Martha.

Buford walked in and Dr. Rose met him at the side of his huge desk. They shook hands.

"Please sit down," said Rose indicating a seat in front of his desk.

"Thank you for agreeing to see me on such short notice."

"I got the feeling I didn't have much choice."

"I'm sorry about that. I wanted to see you because I felt you might be some help in my inquiry."

Buford noticed Rose took a deeper breath as he sat back in his chair.

"How can I possibly help you deputy Hill?"

"Dr. Rose I'm looking at the possibility of the disappearance of Naomi Shepherd and Diane Cleary as connected."

"Goodbye, Doctor Rose."

They shook hands and Buford started to leave. "By the way that looks like some house you have here on the grounds."

"Yes, it is very nice."

"It's a nice-looking house but I didn't notice a garage."

"Yes, that's right."

"Doesn't it have a basement?"

"Yes, but not a full one, the rest is a crawlspace."

"That's kind of crazy."

"I agree, it would have been nice to have a basement with a garage."

"This is a beautiful office, you ought to see my little cubby hole. My office and the jail cell could both fit in this."

Buford stood there another moment to give it an admiring look.

"Well, so long again," said Buford.

"Goodbye, deputy," said Rose clearly out of patience.

"Goodbye, Martha," Buford said as he walked by her desk.

"Goodbye, deputy," she said.

He walked nonchalantly down the hall and passed the Information/Operator desk on his way to his patrol car. He hurried slightly to the gate where he stopped to get his revolver out of the trunk. Bell came out and spoke.

"How did the meeting with Dr. Rose go?"

"Good, I can see why he's so well liked, seems like a great guy to me. And man what an office he has. Have you ever seen it?"

"No."

"If you ever get a chance to see it, take it, it's really nice."

"So long," said Buford as he slid behind the steering wheel.

"So long."

Once on the highway Buford sped towards Hardin.

Bell watched Buford leave then called Rose.

"Rose speaking."

"Bell here. That deputy stopped here on his way out. You really snowed him. He really thinks you're a great guy. He couldn't get over your office, told me I should see it if I could."

"He's an idiot. I had to keep him on track, or he never would have finished."

"Did he ask about the picture in the blue envelope?"

"Yes. I told him I didn't recognize the man, which is the truth."

"When I identified the guy in the picture I thought he was going to pee in his pants. I'm sure he's going after whoever's picture that is."

"Good, now we can relax. I'll see you tomorrow night. Bring a costume we'll have some fun. Time to move on. Bye."

"Okay."

CHAPTER THIRTY-EIGHT

Buford called Vittorino as soon as he got back to his office. Vittorino answered, "U.S. Marshals office, Sabatini speaking."

"Vittorino, this is Buford I got Rose's prints."

"Do you think he suspects anything?"

"I don't think so, I acted like a real buffoon."

"Okay, you get the prints here and I'll get them checked out."

"Like the man said, time is of the essence. Can you meet me halfway this evening?"

"Yes I can, where"

"There's a Chuckey's on 31W just across the Kentucky border. I can be there in an hour and a half, maybe an hour and forty-five minutes at the most."

"Okay. I'll see you there."

Buford hung up and then called Mary.

"Hello."

"Hello honey. I've got good news and bad news."

"Give me the bad news first."

"The bad news is I'm going to be pretty late tonight. I have to drive to the Tennessee border. The good news is I'm going to meet Vittorino with the prints I wanted to get."

"Okay Sweetheart, be careful."

"I love you. Good-bye," he said.

"I love you, too."

He hung up and called the Sheriff's office in Shelton. Margie answered.

"Sheriff's office, Margie speaking."

"Margie this is Buford. Is Sheriff Scott in?"

"No, Buford he's gone to see about a bad wreck just outside of town."

"Okay. Would you tell him I called, and I got what I went after today and I'll call him later with the details. Tell him I'm on my way to meet Vittorino halfway to Nashville. Bye Margie."

"Okay Buford, bye."

Buford took a large manila envelope from his desk and put it in his briefcase along with another pair of rubber gloves. He went outside and started the Ford. He drove hard towards the Tennessee border. He reached the Chuckey's on 31W at 6:45, went inside and got three pieces of his favorite candy, the log rolls, then went back outside to wait for Vittorino. He was about to start eating when Vittorino arrived.

Vittorino literally jumped from his car to shake hands with Buford.

"Man am I glad to see you."

"Me, too. Let me grab my briefcase. We can sit at a table inside."

Inside a waitress asked if they wanted to order. "Not now," said Buford.

He opened the briefcase and turned it sideways so Vittorino could see the contents. He put on a pair of rubber gloves and removed two envelopes from the briefcase. He placed them on napkins on the table.

"This envelope has Rose's prints on it and so does the picture inside. Unfortunately, mine are on them, too. I couldn't avoid handling them in his office. I'll mark it," he said and wrote Rose on the envelope. He pulled the picture from the envelope and clipped the upper left corner. "Just in case they get separated," he said.

"This one's already marked Bell and only his prints should be on the envelope and the picture." He placed both blue envelopes in a larger manila envelope marked 'Buford' and handed it to Vittorino.

Finally, he pulled the roll of duct tape from another manila envelope in the briefcase. "This is different. I don't know whose prints are on this tape. It could be just a roll of tape a maintenance man left in a storage room. But it's possible this could be the tape one of them, probably Bell, used on Diane. I followed up on a former patient's lead and found this in a maintenance room. If it matches any of the prints you have, that's good. If not check it against the prints on the blue envelopes or pictures. I recommend checking it last to avoid any confusion," he said and placed it back in the envelope before he handed it to Vittorino.

"How long will it take to get the results?" He asked.

"I'll rush it as much as I can. Possibly by late tomorrow morning. Captain Johnson has already approved the work. It will be done by the Nashville police department, they're pretty darn good and fast."

"Let's roll," said Buford, then "Do you need any rubber gloves?"

"No, I have some with me. I'll let you know as soon as I have an answer. I agree let's roll."

They rose and shook hands. Buford put a quarter on the table then followed Vittorino out the door. Vittorino sped South towards Nashville and Buford headed North towards Hardin.

Buford arrived at his office about 9:00 and immediately called Sheriff Scott at his office in Shelton. Scott had gone home so Buford called him there.

Barbara Scott answered, "Hello, may I help you?"

"Barbara, this is Buford, how are you?"

"Just fine. How about you and Mary?"

"We're fine. At least I hope so, I haven't seen her since this morning."

"Here's Will, he's chomping at the bit to talk to you. Bye."

"Bye Barbara."

"Buford, what did you find out?"

"I found out we have one really cautious suspect and one liar," said Buford.

"Who's the liar and what about?"

"The liar is the security guard I suspected. He identified a man in a picture I showed him. He said he saw him on the Asylum grounds once and maybe on the day Diane Cleary disappeared."

"Are you sure he lied?"

"Absolutely. It was a picture of one of my neighbors. He's never been to the Asylum."

"And the guard made an I.D. Why do you think he did that?"

"I think he wanted to send me off in another direction, hoping the case would get cold."

"Okay, makes sense. Who's the cautious one?"

"Dr. Elliott Rose, the Superintendent."

"Damn Buford. You said yourself that all you had on him was circumstantial stuff from a couple of Social Workers. Do you have anything new?"

"It's true they raised my suspicion, so did Vittorino. But him trying political pressure to cancel the interview made me more suspicious. I'll tell you one thing. I had one hell of a time getting him to touch the picture of my neighbor. He did everything he could to avoid it."

"Is that it?"

"No. I checked their personnel files. Rose was definitely at the right place, job wise, to commit the murders at Pittsburgh and Louisville that Vittorino and the F.B.I. are trying to solve. I also checked his references at the Olivier and Barnwell Ithaca campus, they never heard of him. He's a phony. Jeanette Strube, another murder victim, was a clerk in the records office at Olivier and Barnwell. I believe he somehow persuaded her to get him phony University documents as a psychiatrist, and when she wasn't useful anymore, he murdered her. I'd bet a thousand dollars to a doughnut Rose and Bell are really Fontana and Bellheimer the two that murdered Vittorino's family in Italy. It all fits."

"That's a pretty good stretch, but you just may be right. I hope for everyone's sake you are."

"I'm sure I got both of their prints on the envelopes and pictures I gave Vittorino a couple hours ago. He'll have them compared to the F.B.I. fingerprint copies he has from the murder scenes. If they match, we'll know for sure."

"And if they don't?"

"If they don't, I'll have to review everything again. But I believe we have a real good chance for a match."

"Okay, write this up and send it to me tomorrow."

"Okay. Is that all?"

"That's it for now," said Scott and hung up.

He sat at the phone for a moment then walked into the kitchen. "Either I have one hell of a detective genius working for me as a deputy or one hell of a dreamer. I sure hope he's a genius, we need this case to pan out."

"I'm betting on Buford," said Barbara.

"I hope you're right. It will mean a lot to people here and to Vittorino's family in Italy."

CHAPTER THIRTY-NINE

Tuesday night Buford was so keyed up he barely slept. Long before sunrise Wednesday morning he got up and fixed a pot of coffee. After his second cup he met Ed and Bill on the back porch and gave them a good petting before starting his chores. In addition to the usual milk bucket he carried a burlap sack. In the dim pre-dawn light he filled the sack with over-size squash and zucchini from the garden.

In the barn he quickly filled the goat troughs with hay and topped them off with some of the just picked vegetables. While milking Marilyn he talked to keep her relaxed, "You know old girl you aren't putting out as much milk as you used to. Maybe in a couple weeks I should have George bring Jack back for a little romance. Would you like that? Aren't talking huh? I'll take that for a yes." He emptied her teats and quickly moved on to check on Becky. Her sack was nearly empty. He milked her quickly and felt her belly, "It won't be long before you're a mama again."

Satisfied with the milking he walked thru the goat door with the remainder of the squash and zucchini which he cut up and dispersed among the cattle. The goats quickly came outside to share in the bounty. He retreated back thru the goat door and set the bar. Next, he stopped at the garden and refilled the burlap sack with vegetables for Mary's weekly trip to the Farmer's Market. Ed and Bill joined him. He gave them their usual splash of milk before making the deposit in the cool spring water.

Outside the spring house he stopped at the white picket fence surrounding the family's hallowed ground. For a moment he stood there, then went inside. He stood silently, visiting memories; farm chores, hunting and fishing with dad, laughing and picking vegetables with mom on market day, hugging granddad's neck and hugs from grandma. He pulled weeds around the headstones and again stood still. He whispered, "Thank you. Thank you for my life." He stepped through and closed the gate. He put his head in the crook of his elbow and wiped his eyes with his shirt.

He returned to the house and went directly to the bedroom, dressed and kissed Mary on the forehead. She stirred and he said "I've done the milking and put a sack full of vegetables on the back porch. I have to go to work extra early today, I'll eat at the diner."

"Bye honey, be careful" she said.

"I will, bye."

At his office he completed the report Scott wanted and reviewed his case notes for the last few days. Convinced he was right; he went to the diner for breakfast as soon as it opened.

"Hello Buford, what'll it be?" Asked Millie as she poured him a cup of coffee.

"A couple of eggs and a stack of pancakes."

In a few minutes Reed brought his breakfast.

"Looks good. Thanks."

"You're welcome. How's the diet coming?" Asked Reed leaning on the counter and obviously wanting to talk.

"I don't know, I'm afraid to weigh myself."

Millie brought more coffee. "You know Buford I think you have lost some weight," she said grinning.

"I hope you're right, but I doubt it," he said shaking his head and frowning.

"Did you ever hear anything about that Doctor's report?" Asked Reed.

"Yeah. Sheriff Scott sent me a nasty memo. I have to lose fifteen pounds by next year's physical. If I don't, I could get a reprimand or maybe even fired."

"Sounds serious."

"Hell, everything's serious," he said as he slid the eggs on top of the pancakes and broke the yokes. Next, he poured syrup over the whole stack. "Just the way I like my pancakes," he said and started eating.

"Anything new on the missing girl?" Asked Reed.

"Some, I'm still working on it."

After a second cup of coffee, he checked his pockets and found a lonely quarter and left it by his plate. He got up to leave and said "Thanks guys. See you later, the breakfast was great."

"Glad you liked it," said Reed from the grill.

"Me, too, said Millie. I hope you have a good day."

As he walked across the street, Buford thought about the tips he left. He wondered if Millie kept them all or if they split tips some way.

At eleven fifteen Buford's phone rang. He answered and started his spiel but was cut short.

"Buford this is Scott, a couple of hikers found a partially exposed body this morning. It's off Cherry Hill Road directly across the lake from Hardin Mental Asylum. The hikers called the State cops from a resident's phone. They just called here. They're on their way to the site. Get down there as soon as you can. I'll have Al Wiggins with me."

"Okay. What about Eddie Evans he makes really good crime scene photos."

"He's coming, too, now get going."

"I'm on my way."

Buford was familiar with the side roads along the East side of the lake, but not by name. It took him a good twenty minutes to find Cherry Hill Road and another five before he came upon two state cruisers. He pulled up and stopped behind one. He took his briefcase, an old Army trenching tool and a hand trowel and started to walk where he hoped the crime scene would be. As he got to the second cruiser, he saw two young men inside. He opened the door.

"You two the guys that found the body?"

"Yes sir," said one.

"Where is it?"

"About a quarter of a mile that way," said one of the hikers pointing to the right front of the cruiser.

"Thanks."

"Why are they holding us like this. We didn't do anything," said the second hiker.

"Don't worry they'll be wanting you guys to give a statement, that's all."

"I have to pee," said one, the other one echoed "Me, too."

"See that restroom over there, it's disguised as a maple tree. I'll let you guys out to pee but hurry up."

They headed for the maple tree. A few minutes later, after he put them back in the cruiser, he started walking in the general direction pointed to by the hiker. Soon he heard some voices. When he arrived, he saw his buddy Matt and another officer standing by a partially exposed body.

"Hi Matt, what's up?"

"Hi Buford," said Matt extending his hand. "A couple of hikers reported this body. I just found out about it a little while ago. I radioed Sheriff Scott"s office. He said you would probably be here before him."

"Yeah, he called and said you guys had a body. He's bringing the county coroner."

"This here's patrolman Chester Goodson. He was first on the scene," said Matt.

Buford offered his hand, and they shook.

"I'm Buford Hill, glad to meet you."

"Same here," said Chester.

"I brought some tools to help finish uncovering the body," said Buford.

"We started, but noticed a ring finger was missing. I knew about that F.B.I. bulletin and radioed it in. I got a message back that they would be flying into Shelton and then coming here. They said they didn't want the body disturbed so we stopped," said Matt.

"I don't want to disturb it. I just want to finish uncovering it," said Buford.

"I'm just going by my instructions," said Matt.

About that time Sheriff Scott arrived with Wiggins and Evans.

"What's going on Buford?"

"Nothing, that's the problem. I want to finish uncovering this corpse, but Matt here says he has instructions to wait for the F.B.I."

"Why the F.B.I., Matt?" Asked Scott.

"Because it has a missing ring finger. We notified the FBI because of their bulletin about that. They don't want anything disturbed."

"Oh, I see. What do you think Buford?"

"I think if we are careful, we can uncover this corpse with no harm to the crime scene. Eddie can make pictures as we go along. If this is the person I think it is I'll be able to tell."

"I agree. What do you think Matt. How the hell will anyone know how far along we were before the missing ring finger was discovered."

"Okay I guess. Let's get started."

"Eddie start making pictures," said Scott.

Though they were good friends, Eddie the Rhodes County Courier reporter and photographer and Doc Wiggins the local general practitioner and part-time coroner were in many ways opposite in appearance. Eddie was dressed casually in blue Jeans and long-sleeved shirt. He was short like Doc but much heavier. His hair was gray. His face was rather compact with a narrow chin, small nose and close set brown eyes . His only real distinguishing feature was his left ear. It stuck out more than the right one. He claimed that was because for years he kept a pencil tucked between it and the side of his head. When he moved too fast in warm weather he breathed heavily and sweated easily as he was now after the short walk from the sheriff's cruiser.

Eddie stood at what they thought was the foot of the shallow grave and shot the first picture. He moved around and made three more, one from each side.

Buford kept his trenching tool and handed Scott the hand trowel. Matt had a shovel he carried in his cruiser's trunk for bad weather. They worked slowly and carefully. Patrolman Goodson offered to help, and Scott gave him the hand trowel.

Every few minutes Scott called a halt for Eddie to make more pictures and Al to look the body over. After about twenty minutes they stopped again.

"Doc, can you tell much about the body?"

Doc got up close to the shallow grave. He was a short thin man. His face was long and ruddy and topped by wavy brown hair. He liked seersucker suits and today's colors were beige and light blue. His collar was not buttoned, and his tie hung down a little from his neck, held in place by a clasp attached to a white shirt. When serious, as he was now, he kept his wire rimmed glasses near the end of his long thin nose so he could look thru the lenses for close work or above them for anything a few feet away or when he was talking directly to someone.

"Yes. I'm sure it's a female body and the right arm is broken. That's all so far."

"Son of a bitch," said Scott. "Keep going."

Deputy Bean approached the site huffing and puffing.

"Sheriff Scott we just got a call from Margie. The FBI has landed at the county airport. They'll probably be here in thirty more minutes. There's two agents coming, Will Carter is driving them here."

"Go back to the car and radio them. Tell them they better hurry we're about to wrap this up." Said Scott.

"Do you think that's wise?" Asked Matt.

"I figure it'll give them time to cool off a little before they get here," said Scott.

They continued the slow uncovering, stopping every so often for Eddie and Al.

They had just uncovered most of the skull when the FBI agents arrived.

The older of the two approached Scott.

"I take it you are Sheriff Scott. I'm Special Agent Mike Kennedy. This here's Agent Connors," he said and extended his hand.

"This is an FBI crime scene. I want you men to stop. We're in charge," said Agent Connors.

"Yes, I'm Scott. This is my Deputy, Buford Hill. That's our county coroner Al Wiggins and our crime scene photographer Eddie Evans. That's Matt Williams he's the State Policeman in charge of this district and that man is Patrolman Chester Goodson. As you can see we're about to finish uncovering this corpse."

"What do you want next, Doc?" Asked Buford.

"I would like the skull cleaned off very carefully. Eddie make a couple more pictures. Long shots and close ups," said Al.

"You got it," said Eddie and did as Al asked.

Buford walked to his briefcase and pulled out a two-inch paintbrush. He returned to the body and bent down to clean off the skull.

"I told you men to stop. This is an FBI crime scene. Don't you dare touch that body. We'll finish this," hollered Connors.

"What with, pixie dust?" Asked Matt.

"We'll finish with your tools," said Connors.

"Like hell you will," said Buford as he turned and started to brush the skull very meticulously.

"This is an FBI crime scene. If you don't stop I'm going to put you all under arrest," said Connors, red faced and livid.

"Don't get your panties in a wad. This is Rhodes County, Kentucky and right now this is a Rhodes County crime scene," said Scott.

"I'm warning you," said Connors.

"Oh, shut the hell up Connors. These men are just doing their jobs and as far as I can tell have done a damn good job.

I'm in no mood for a pissing contest over whose crime scene this is or isn't," said Special Agent Kennedy.

Buford let out a chuckle.

"You think that's funny?" Asked Connors.

"I think you're funny," said Buford.

He started cleaning the skull of the remaining dirt. When he got the top cleaned off Scott asked Al Wiggins to take another look while the body was still in the grave.

"What do you see, Al," he asked.

Al bent down close. "Blunt force trauma to the head. I can see two places. My guess is a hammer. It looks like whoever did this also slit her throat, there's a cut mark across the neck."

"Can you tell enough to make an I.D. Buford?" Asked Scott.

"I'll know in a minute after I finish with the dusting."

He turned the skull to the left and dusted the right side.

"Doc look at this. What teeth are missing on this side?" Asked Buford.

Al Bent over again. "There's missing molars."

"Damn it Kennedy this should be our crime scene," said Connors. He had moved next to Special Agent Kennedy.

"Eddie make some pictures of that," said Scott.

A moment later Buford turned the skull to the right.

"What do you see on this side Doc?"

"I see two teeth with crowns."

"Hold on." said Buford. He opened his briefcase and handed Al a piece of folded paper.

"Do the missing teeth and the crowns match this diagram, Doc?"

"Exactly, where did you get that dental chart?"

"I made it. I got the blank chart from my dentist and the information about the teeth from this woman's dentist."

"Well I'll be damned," said Matt.

"Now I've heard of everything. This damn deputy is also a dentist's assistant by telephone," said Connors.

He was standing right behind Buford who was bent over closing his briefcase. He stood up and looked at Connors who was smiling. He grabbed him by the lapels and pulled him close.

"One more sarcastic remark out of you and I'm going to put you in this grave."

"Easy Buford. He doesn't know much. Let him go," said Scott.

Buford released the visibly shaken Connors.

"Connors for the last time shut up," said Kennedy.

"Do you know who that is?" Asked Scott.

"Yes, this is Naomi Shepherd," said Buford.

"Well I'll be damned. Are you sure?" Asked Scott.

"Absolutely. And I'm sure who murdered her and did the other killings."

"What other killings?" Asked Matt.

"The ones with the missing ring fingers. The ones in the FBI bulletin. Vittorino gave me a heads up about these characters when he visited my office."

"Are you absolutely sure about this?" Asked Scott.

“I’m positive. We just need a fingerprint match for additional hard evidence. Vittorino’s working on that now”.

“Who? How?” Asked Kennedy.

“Naomi Shepherd was a patient that disappeared two years ago from the Hardin Mental Asylum. It’s located directly across the lake from where we are now. Vittorino Sabatini is a US Marshal from the Nashville office. For years he’s been pursuing the men that murdered his family in Italy. Buford tricked the suspects into leaving their fingerprints on some bogus pictures. I’ll let Buford explain things from there. It gets complicated, real complicated,” said Scott.

“The men the FBI is looking for are Fontana and Bellheimer. How do you know they are the ones you suspect. Can you tie it together for me?” Asked Kennedy.

“I’ll try,” said Buford. “For me it all started a couple of weeks ago. Another patient, Diane Cleary, was reported as an elopement, which means she left the hospital without being discharged. But she didn’t show up at home like eloped patients usually do. I investigated her disappearance as a missing person. The more I looked into it the more I came to believe something happened to her before she left the Asylum. That’s when I tied Naomi’s disappearance in with Diane’s because she never showed up anywhere either.”

“I interviewed all the staff that had contact with both patients. Vittorino visited and told me about Fontana and Bellheimer. At first it seemed like quite a stretch, and I didn’t think they had anything to do with the missing women. But the more I thought about it and the deeper I dug into things the more I became suspicious. But all I had was circumstantial evidence nothing that would stand up in court. That is until I bluffed my way into checking some Personnel records at the Asylum. I interviewed some guards one of whom I believe is Bellheimer. I also interviewed the Superintendent at the Asylum, Dr. Elliott Rose. I made some calls yesterday checking on Doctor Rose's employment application. They never heard of him at Olivier and Barnwell University. He's a phony. I believe he somehow convinced Jeanette Strube a clerk in the Records Office at the Ithaca Campus of Olivier and Barnwell to create some bogus Psychiatrist documents for him. When he established a work background in Pittsburgh and Louisville, she was no longer necessary, and he murdered her rather than risk being exposed by a disgruntled lover. I firmly believe Dr. Rose is Fontana and the security guard Bell is Bellheimer. Last night I gave Vittorino the fingerprints of both men to compare to the photocopies he has of the FBI prints from crime scenes in Pittsburgh and Louisville. If they are a match, and like I told Sheriff Scott last night I'd bet a thousand dollars to a donut that they will, then Dr. Rose is Fontana, and the Security guard Bell is Bellheimer."

"I don't believe this bull. We've been working on this case for years," said Connors.

"Vittorino Sabatini, that name rings a bell," said Special Agent Kennedy. "Didn't he nearly capture them in Pittsburgh?"

"Yes. They got in a shootout but Fontana and Bellheimer escaped," said Scott.

Deputy Bean came back. "Buford, I have a message for you from U.S. Marshal Vittorino Sabatini. He says to tell you, 'It's a match on all three sets. He said he and his boss Albert Johnson are flying up from Nashville. He wants to participate in the arrest. He said you would know why," said Bean.

"That's it, that's the hard evidence we've been waiting to get. Of course, Vittorino should be in on the arrest. That is if it's okay with you Sheriff. Matt, too," said Buford.

"I suppose you guys want in, too?" Scott asked Kennedy.

"Yes, we would like to be included," said Kennedy.

"Don't go trying to steal any thunder," said Scott.

"We won't. Don't worry I'm just glad they're going to be caught," said Kennedy.

"What about Connors, can he take orders from a Sheriff or his Deputy?" Asked Scott.

"He better. Hear that Connors?"

"Well, what about it. If you want in on this, you'll have to take orders without any bitching, griping or questioning. Will you do that," Scott asked Connors.

"Yes, I will. I had no idea you all had put so much work into this operation. I thought you were just trying to take over a crime scene on a case the Bureau's been working on for so long."

"Not 'you all' just two men. Vittorino Sabatini and Buford Hill. Nobody else," said Scott."

"Okay. Matt if you and officer Goodson will help Al and Eddie put the body on the stretcher, they'll take it to the morgue." Said Scott.

"We will," said Matt."

"Now. Before we leave, I want two things to be clear. No more communication to anyone by radio. If you need to call anyone wait 'till you get to our office in Shelton. Does everybody agree to that?" Asked Scott.

Everyone nodded.

"The second thing. Everybody has to keep their mouths shut about this operation. Period. This must come off as a complete surprise. No leaks to anyone, wives, girlfriends, no-one. If you have to call your boss, I want you to hold off until we are ready. Everybody agree?"

Everyone nodded.

"I'm going to call Judge Appleton and get him started on the warrants. I'll call from the house that's nearby on the road. Buford, you stop, too. I need you to name names and aliases," said Scott.

They left Eddie, Al and the two state troopers to complete their gruesome task. Scott hurried to the road and decided to ride with Buford. They drove about a half a mile to the nearest house, parked in the driveway and ran to the front door. Scott banged on the door. A man came out and quickly agreed to let them use his phone.

Scott called Judge Appleton, then he motioned to the homeowner for some privacy. Buford escorted him to the far end of the house and returned.

"Henry, this is Scott. I need some warrants today. Four of them. Two search warrants and two arrest warrants. I'm going to give this phone over to my deputy Buford Hill to provide the details. And Henry this is all very hush hush. You get my point, I hope."

"Of course, put him on."

Buford gave exact details to the judge.

"I'll be in my office when you get here," said the judge.

"Hold on, judge," said Buford and relayed the message to Scott.

Scott got back on the phone. "Henry, I want those warrants in my office in forty-five minutes, you deliver them. No bullshit. Make whoever types them up come with you and no phone calls to anyone. I don't want any slip-ups."

"Don't get smart-alecky with me," said the Judge.

"Look. This is the biggest thing to happen in this county in fifty years. Don't you screw it up and don't let anyone else have the opportunity to screw it up. I'm serious. Anybody screws this up won't be able to get elected dog catcher."

"Okay, Okay. I'll get the warrants there as fast as I can."

CHAPTER FORTY

"You were right," said Vittorino.

"About what?" Asked Johnson.

"You said they would make a big mistake and they did. Actually they made two mistakes, they got careless kidnapping two young women from the same facility and they underestimated Buford."

"How long before we land?" Johnson asked the pilot.

"About five minutes. We're coming to the airport now."

Deputy Will Carter was waiting when they arrived. They ran to the patrol car.

"I hope they're still waiting," said Vittorino.

"Oh yeah, they're waiting. Buford said you need to be there. Sheriff Scott's making the final plans now."

When Vittorino and Johnson arrived they were taken into a small conference room and introduced to the other officers that would participate in the operation. Sheriff Scott and Buford were in a larger conference room with Special Agent

Kennedy and Matt Williams going over some possible plans. Both Kennedy and Williams had called their superiors to tell them what was about to happen. Officer Williams arranged for State Police to be ready to assist.

When they were told Vittorino and Johnson had arrived, Scott had everyone transfer to the larger room. Johnson and Vittorino were introduced to Matt Williams and Special Agent Kennedy.

"Has everybody met everyone?" Asked Scott.

"Yes they have," said Bean

"This is a pretty quick pulling together of forces, for safety's sake I'd like everyone to stand for a few seconds and state your name and affiliation, I'll start."

It took a few minutes for everyone to reintroduce themselves.

"Okay," said Scott. "Buford, Officer Williams, Agent Kennedy and I have been doing some preliminary planning. We'll start with the physical layout of the facility. Buford will explain the diagram on the chalkboard."

Buford had a pointer in his hand. "This represents the guard shack at the entrance where we undoubtably will be stopped by at least one security guard, maybe two. If the guard Bell is at the gate, we will arrest him immediately. If not, we will show the warrants and have a guard call Bell's house to determine if he's there. If he answers, the excuse for the call will be that Lanier, the Chief of Security, wants to know if he can work a double shift the next day. Whether we can determine if he is there or not, one guard in a security car will be instructed to lead the way to Bell's house on the grounds. Marshal Johnson with deputies Harrison and George and Patrolman Goodson will park nearby and surround the house. Marshal Johnson, we would like you to be in charge of this portion of the raid. Try to persuade the guard to knock on the door. With the house surrounded have two men at the door with the guard. Any questions or suggestions?"

"Yes," said Johnson. "I've been on similar raids, and I have a suggestion for a change."

"Go ahead," said Buford."

"Leave the Security guard in his car. He's unarmed and will only get in the way at the door. I'll ride past Bell's house with the guard to get the best placement of our people. The guard can wait out of sight for a few minutes while we get in place. Goodson and I will slip up to the front door. The guard will pull the security car a little off center from the door. Bell should see the security car parked out front and open the door when we knock. We'll be ready, with weapons drawn," said Johnson.

"That sounds good to me, what do you think Sheriff Scott?"

"Yes, that sounds good, let's go with that."

"What if there's only one security guard at the gate?" Asked Bean.

"Then we'll leave a deputy to control the traffic. Marshal Johnson if Bell's not home leave the deputies and

Goodson to search the house for evidence and proceed to the Superintendent's residence. I'll give you a hand drawn map, okay?" Asked Buford.

"Okay," said Johnson.

"Let's continue on," said Scott.

"Okay," said Buford pointing. "The entrance road meets the main road at a circle in front of the Administration Building. We'll turn right and continue on until we make a left on the second street. The Superintendent's house is a couple hundred yards on the right. It's a white two story with a porch stretching completely across the front. The steps up to the porch and front door are about six or seven feet from the left side of the house. A sidewalk runs from the front steps around the right side of the house and all the way to the rear where there's probably an entrance to a kitchen. A chimney bulges out about ten feet back on the right side. I suspect it's to a fireplace in the living room. There's a long driveway with parking for a few cars on the right front side of the house. There's a screened-in porch on the left side of the house."

"I'll pick up from there," said Scott. "If we leave in the next thirty minutes or so we should get there about 6:30. We should still have plenty of light. No sirens and no blinking lights. When we get to the Superintendent's house, everybody hits the ground ready to do their assignment. Deputy Sweet you go around to the left of the house and secure the door from the house onto the screened-in porch. Agent Connors you and deputy Bloom go around the right side checking for any exits on that side or the back. If you find any, Connors you secure the first one and Bloom you continue on until you find another. If there aren't any more exits continue around and serve as back-up for deputy Sweet. Any questions or suggestions so far?"

No-one said anything.

"Deputy Bean if anybody is outside the house, we'll place them in custody in a secure patrol car. In that instance you will stay outside. We'll go in through the front door, hopefully it will be unlocked since it's on secure grounds. If not Will Carter, you and Special agent Kennedy smash it open with the ram. Get it out of your car when we arrive so there won't be a delay. Now everybody remember these are very dangerous men, surprise is our best weapon. We think if Diane's there she will be in the basement. If Bellheimer and Fontana are both inside there may be some shooting have your weapons ready. Any questions or suggestions?"

"I have one. Who goes first, second, etc.?" asked Special Agent Kennedy.

"Buford, you call it," said Scott.

"I'll go in first followed by Vittorino, then Matt, then Special Agent Kennedy, then Sheriff Scott. Once inside deputies Horton and Smith you check out the first floor. Deputies Reed and Lawrence check out the upstairs. I'll go down to the basement with the same people that followed me inside from the front porch. Remember none of us can dilly dally around. That's all I have Sheriff."

"One more thing, right before we get to the Asylum, I'll radio Margie and have the Hardin ambulance crew alerted and have two more sent to Hardin from Shelton. Margie will be on standby here in the office. Are there any more suggestions or questions? Voice them now or forever hold your peace." said Scott. "None? Here's a list of who goes with who. Check it to see who you are with and let's go."

———

Seven patrol cars descended on the gate at Hardin Mental Asylum at the same time.

Wide-eyed, Lanier held up his hand to stop the procession.

"What's up, Buford?" He asked.

"I'm not sure you really want to know."

"I know this, if you are coming on these grounds you have to leave your weapons in the trunk of your cars," said Lanier.

"Not today, take a look at these warrants we're going to serve," said Buford.

Lanier glanced at the warrants and was unsure about what to do.

"Lanier, this is Albert Johnson of the U.S. Marshals."

Johnson extended his hand. Lanier shook it.

"Lanier we can't force you to help us this evening, but you could possibly help keep someone from getting hurt," said Buford.

"I don't understand what you want me to do. The warrants say Bell and Doctor Rose," said Lanier.

"That's right. We want you to take Marshal Johnson and three other officers to Bell's house, that's all. Will you do that?" Asked Buford.

"Yes, but Bell isn't there, he's doing security at Doctor Rose's, they're having a party there tonight."

"How many other people will be there this evening?"

"Just two more, at least that's all I have on the list."

"Are they already there?"

"Yes."

"That doesn't change what we want you to do. Marshal Johnson will give you all the details when we leave, okay?" Asked Buford.

"I guess so," said Lanier.

"One more thing, Lanier have you been in Dr. Rose's house."

"Yes, to deliver papers and food from restaurants left at the guard shack."

"How's it laid out?"

"The front door opens to a big foyer. The living room's to the right. There's a dining room between it and the kitchen in back. The stairs to the second floor are straight across the foyer from the front door."

"What about the basement?"

"There's a hallway from the left side of the foyer. The basement door is at the end."

"Thanks Lanier you've been a big help to all of us here this evening," said Buford.

"I agree," said Sheriff Scott.

"Tell that guard in the shack if he calls anyone, anyone at all about what's about to happen he'll end up in jail for interference in a police operation," said Buford.

Lanier spoke to the guard then he and Johnson got in his security car.

"Let's go," said Scott.

———

At Rose's house the party was just getting underway. Two men in costumes were at a barbecue grill cooking steaks near the rear of the house.

In the basement Rose was speaking quietly to Bell.

"This is the last time to have fun with them, they're getting stale. Hell, one of them isn't sure who she is, it's time to say bye-bye."

"Let's turn them loose," said Bell.

"Are you crazy? They'd spill their guts, and we would end up in jail."

"We could always leave; we have plenty of money."

"No, I like this set-up."

"You like killing people for fun."

"You've done your share," said Rose.

"When I did mine it was for a cause, for the Fuhrer."

"Just keep telling yourself that. Get the girls ready, I have to get a good knife and check on Gunther and Wolfgang."

"*You* will have to get them ready. I won't participate in this, and I won't do the burying, either," said Bell.

"You'll do what I tell you."

"Not this time, not anymore. I'm done with this."

"Our guests expect a little fun, and then a little excitement," said Rose. He turned and went to two cages attached to the right side of the wall opposite the steps. "I'll get them going," he said. He stood in front of the cages, each contained a naked woman prisoner with a dog collar around her neck. He was wearing a Friar Tuck costume, a one-piece brown robe with a yellow rope belt, and nothing under neath. He pulled up the robe and said, "Here girls, this is what you'll be getting in a little while. 'Bye for now, I know you'll miss me, but I'll be back," and laughed.

Rose got a knife and scabbard from his second-floor bedroom and then went back downstairs to the kitchen. He opened the side door and spoke to two men grilling steaks nearby outside. "How are the steaks coming?"

"You better be ready to eat. The steaks will be done in less than ten minutes," said Gunther.

"Good," said Rose.

Next, he passed through the dining room to the living room.

———

Buford led the procession from the gate, he turned right at the Administration building then left onto the second street. When they stopped at the Superintendent's residence two men were in costume at a barbecue grill near the right rear side of the house. One appeared to be wrapped in a one piece beige cloth, the other one wore a Robin Hood costume. When the officers got out of their cars the man in the one-piece outfit started to run.

"Stop, or you're a dead man," said Scott.

It was effective, he stopped.

"Where's Rose and Bell," asked Buford.

Nobody spoke. "I'll ask you once more. Where are Rose and Bell?"

The one in the tights said, "They're in the basement."

"Bean cuff these two and get them out of the way," said Scott.

Sweet, Connors and Bloom had already left for the sides and rear of the house.

The rest hurried to the front of the house and through the unlocked door into the foyer.

Horton and Smith started the downstairs search and Reed and Lawrence went upstairs.

Fontana saw the patrol cars arrive and slipped down the hall to the door that opened to the screened in porch. He opened the door just as Deputy Sweet started up the porch steps. Sweet drew his revolver, but Fontana burst through the door and knocked him to the ground where he stabbed him in the left arm and ran. Sweet recovered and fired two shots before Fontana disappeared into the woods behind the house.

Fontana ran down a familiar path toward the lake. He dodged between trees and around bushes for several hundred yards to a place where the ground rose high above the water's edge. There he parted thick low hanging pine boughs that hid the crude earthen steps he used to reach a small aluminum boat hidden from the path above. He pushed the boat into the water and climbed aboard all in one swift motion. He straightened the motor in the water, adjusted the choke and pulled the starter cord. The motor sputtered then came to life and he headed the boat downstream and away from the shore. He pushed the boat as fast as he could for a few miles then pulled it into a side slew where he opened a duffle bag and changed clothes. He put on a plaid shirt, blue jeans and cowboy boots, all used items he had purchased at a thrift store in Louisville. He attached a hunting knife and scabbard to his belt. He reentered the main channel for another two miles until he came to a bend in the river. In the distance he could see a familiar house with steps leading down to a dock. He chose this house as part of his emergency plan because there were no others close by. As he approached he could see a man and woman on the deck and smoke rising above a grill. He choked the motor to make it run rough then smoothed it out, he did this several times to make it sound like he was having engine trouble. He pulled the boat beside the dock and tied it. He walked up the steps and was greeted by Sam and Ella Moore.

"Hello Dr. Rose," said Sam smiling and waving. "Having engine trouble?"

"Hello to both of you, and yes, I am having some engine trouble. I was wondering if I could possibly use your telephone?"

"Sure" said Ella. "Sit down and have a burger with us."

"Oh, I don't want to impose on you good folks."

"Nonsense, we have plenty. Don't we Sam?"

"Sure," said Sam and he turned to the grill near the deck railing.

"They do smell good," said Fontana as he walked over to where Sam was standing .

With one quick motion Fontana drew the hunting knife, put his left hand on Sam's left shoulder and plunged the knife into Sam's back below the rib cage. Sam's legs buckled and he fell backward to the deck.

Ella said, "Oh my God" and jumped up to run, but Fontana caught her before she reached the door to the house. He grabbed her by the hair and plunged the knife into her back the same way he did to Sam. Then he turned her around and slit her throat. She hit the deck and he removed her ring finger while she was still alive. Sam had gotten to his knees but staggered sideways and fell again trying to get to his feet. He still had the spatula in his hand when Fontana casually walked over to him and stabbed him again, this time in the chest. It was all over in less than a minute.

Fontana quickly dragged the bodies to the woods at the side of the house. He removed Sam's driver's license from his wallet and put it in his own. He searched Sam's pockets for car keys, but he didn't have them on him. He returned to the boat and removed the small duffle bag. He untied the boat then reached down and pulled the plug. He gave it a hard push out into the river.

He entered the house and found the car keys on a nightstand in the master bedroom. Next, he took some spirit gum from the duffle and used it to attach a dark reddish-brown beard. He topped off the disguise with a beat-up blue hat. He took a tube of lipstick from a nightstand and used it to leave a message on the dresser mirror.

Two things to remember —— You'll never catch me because I'm smarter than you and I play for keeps. FONTANA

He washed the blood off the deck with a hose from the side of the house, then locked the house and left with the Moore's car and Sam's identification. He headed the old Chevy South towards the Tennessee border and the small cabin he kept rented.

——————

The sound of Deputy Sweet's shots fired at Fontana prompted Scott to send help.

"Kennedy, you take Will Carter and find out what's happening outside," he said.

"Okay," said Kennedy and left.

"Buford, you've earned the right to go first," said Scott.

"Okay, let's go," said Buford.

Buford opened the cellar door. There was a lot of light, but he couldn't see anyone or anything. He started down the steps, halfway down he spotted Bell on his left standing beside a couch dressed in a cowboy outfit. Bell had his gun out and fired at Buford. The bullet hit Buford in the right arm. He returned fire and shot bell in the left shoulder knocking him to the floor. Bell dropped his gun and laid still.

Buford managed to move from the steps to a chair near Bell.

Vitorino picked up Bell's weapon and reached down and pulled him up.

"What are you doing here?" Asked Bell.

"We're arresting your sorry ass," said Scott, then "How are you Buford?"

"I'll live. But I can't raise my right arm."

"You're losing quite a bit of blood. Let me put a tourniquet on you."

Scott took off his belt and put it on Buford's arm above the wound. He found a piece of wood on the floor and used it to tighten the tourniquet. "Loosen it every little while, you know the drill."

"Where's Fontana?" Asked Vittorino.

"I don't know anyone named Fontana." Said Bell.

"This will help you remember," said Vittorino and he punched him hard in the face. Bellheimer was knocked to the floor. Vittorino picked him back up and asked him again, "Where's Fontana."

"I know no-one named Fontana."

Vittorino hit him again, this time Bellheimer went to his knees.

"Why do you do this to me," he asked.

"For my family you murdered."

"I don't know what you're talking about."

"You remember Veranza, Italy. You and Fontana murdered seven of my family."

Bellheimer looked up and smiled. "Too bad we missed you, Jew scum," he said.

"Don't tempt me you bastard, my mother-in-law is Jewish," said Matt.

"Where's Fontana?"

"I don't know."

Vittorino knocked him down again then looked at the other officers. No one tried to stop him.

"No one will stop you, Vittorino. Do what you want," said Scott.

Vittorino turned to Bellheimer again.

"I don't know where he is right now, he was here but went upstairs right before you came down."

Buford looked around the room. There were several mattresses on the floor. Blown up pictures of men having sex with women in dog collars were on the walls. Apparatuses that looked similar to devices used for torture in horror movies were attached to the walls and ceiling.

There were two wire cages attached to the rear wall to the right of the steps. Each contained a naked woman.

"Please help us," said the woman in the nearest cage.

"Where's the key?" Asked Buford.

"Behind you on a nail," said the woman.

Scott got the key and opened the first cage. "Somebody go upstairs and get some sheets or something to cover these women and get Bean to call an ambulance, and send in Eddie Evans," he said.

Horton and Smith were coming down the steps. "We'll take care of it," said Horton. They started back up the steps and almost collided with Kennedy on his way down.

"Deputy Sweet was attacked and stabbed, Will Carter and I brought him around to the front porch. He's losing blood," said Kennedy.

"Tell Bean to make that three ambulances at least," Scott hollered up at Horton.

"Okay," he said.

"Where's Connors and Bloom?" Asked Scott

"When we got there, they were helping Sweet. He had already told them which direction the assailant took off in. We swapped to save time and they went after him," said Kennedy.

"Vittorino, see if you can get this scum to tell you where Fontana is headed. Do whatever it takes," said Scott.

"No need for that. I'll tell you where he's gone. He has a boat hidden along the lake shore a few hundred meters from here. It's his emergency plan."

"Which direction from the back of the house?" Asked Vittorino.

"To the right," said Bellheimer as he collapsed in a chair.

"That's the general direction Sweet told us, "said Kennedy.

"Where will he go in the boat?" Scott asked Bellheimer.

"I don't know, probably to steal a car, if he can."

Horton came back down with some sheets. He gave them to Matt.

"Help me, somebody," Matt said as he went in the first cage.

"I will," said Kennedy.

"Miss, please stand up so we can wrap this sheet around you. You're safe with us," said Matt quietly and gently. She stood and they wrapped the sheet around her. She began to shiver and cry and sat on the cage floor.

"What's your name?" Asked Buford.

"Emma Lee," she said.

"Okay, Emma, it's all over you're safe, we're going to get you to a hospital as fast as we can."

Matt and Kennedy helped her up and out of the cage to a couch.

Buford went with Matt and Kennedy to the next cage. "Diane, your name is Diane, isn't it? I told your parents and your sister I would find you. You're safe with us, we're all law officers. Can you stand up, please?"

Diane tried to stand but fell back to the floor. Buford reached to help her, but she turned her head to the wall and cried.

"Please don't hurt me, I'll be good," she said.

"Nobody's going to hurt you. We'll make sure of that," he said.

"How are these two?" Scott asked.

Buford turned to him; his eyes were wet. "I think the best thing we can do is get them to a hospital. Diane can't even stand up."

Matt and Kennedy helped Diane to her feet where Matt put a sheet around her, then they helped her to the couch beside Emma.

"Where's the best place to get nurses here?" Asked Scott.

"Probably in Admissions, or the Infirmary," said Buford.

Reed and Lawrence came down to report.

"The upstairs is clear. Nobody's there," said Lawrence.

"Has anybody, besides Buford, been here before?" Asked Scott.

"Bean has, so has Will Carter," said Buford.

"Reed, you and Lawrence put cuffs on Bellheimer, hands behind the back and cuffs on his ankles, too. I want you two to take him to the hospital in Shelton. Search him now. Don't take any chances, and don't let him out of your sight. If he gives you any trouble, shoot him. Keep a tourniquet on him 'till you get to the hospital. Open it every now and then for a little bit. You know what to do. Keep an eye on him. Don't leave him alone with hospital staff while he's there. He's a very dangerous man. After they patch him up bring him to the jail and keep him handcuffed," said Scott.

Scott went upstairs and found Sweet in the living room with Will Carter.

"How's it going, Charley?" He asked.

"I'll be alright," said Sweet. "I got a couple of shots off, but I don't know if I hit him."

"Will, take Charley to Admissions and tell them briefly what happened here. Try to round up some clothes for the two women downstairs. If you can find a doctor have him look at Charley, at least to stop the bleeding. Bring a couple of nurses back with you." Said Scott.

A few minutes later Deputy Bloom and Agent Connors arrived back at the house.

"What happened, where did Fontana go?" Asked Scott.

"We followed whoever stabbed Deputy Sweet on a path through the woods. He must have had a boat hidden somewhere because we heard him start it and take off. He went off to the right, away from here," said Connors.

"Downstream," added Bloom.

"Bloom take the photo on the mantle downstairs and ask Buford if it's Fontana in the picture with Bellheimer," said Scott.

"Matt can you phone the State Police and have them put out the A.P.B. we discussed? And ask if they can send some officers to help."

"Yes, I'll get on it right away. The district chief said he'll have several patrol officers on stand-by."

Bloom came back upstairs. "Buford says it's Fontana."

"Good. Matt, you can use it for a description to the State Police. When you're finished give it to Deputy Bean for his call to the Sheriffs in Cumberland and McEwen counties to activate the roadblocks I discussed with them this afternoon. That should cover the roads leading from the river."

Johnson, Goodson and Harrison came in from Bell's house.

"What did you find out at Bell's," asked Scott.

"We found Bellheimer's diary and some Nazi photos and a few weapons, two pistols and a couple of knives. We sealed the house and posted a crime scene do not enter notice on the front door. I left Deputy George there. Lanier said he would alert the guards to keep people away. I told him to send any ambulances to this house," said Johnson.

Scott said, "We got Bellheimer but Fontana came upstairs just as we arrived. He slipped around to the side porch and attacked Charley Sweet with a knife. Then he ran to a boat he had hidden on the riverbank and got away. We need to get a manhunt started right away. We're setting up teams to look for him. Can you and Vittorino stay and help?"

"Sure, where do you want us?" Asked Johnson.

"Good. Everybody listen up," Scott said loudly. "I want two cars with at least two people to go down each side of the river tonight. Our deputies will team with anyone unfamiliar with the territory. Play leapfrog checking houses. Check with the residents for any unusual activity. He won't go far before he tries to steal a car."

"Marshal Johnson, I would like you and Vittorino to work with deputies Harrison and Carter when Carter gets back from the infirmary. You'll go down this side of the river."

"Matt can Goodson team up in a car with deputy Bloom?"

"Yes."

"Okay, then they'll go along with Horton and Smith back across the Hardin bridge and down that side of the lake. Start a couple miles downstream from the bridge, okay?"

"Sure."

"Before anybody leaves here take a look at this picture of Fontana," said Scott.

Then in a more normal tone he continued, "Bean where's Toga Man and Robin Hood?"

"They're in the back of my patrol car, I put 'em there when the shooting started."

"Move 'em to mine."

"What about us?" Asked Special Agent Kennedy.

"I'd like you to take Buford's patrol car and follow the cars going back towards Hardin but stop at the bridge. Make sure Fontana doesn't sneak by us up the river. If he sees red lights on the bridge, he won't try."

"Okay," said Kennedy.

"Okay everybody, make sure you get a good look at this picture before you leave, then go," said Scott.

Buford came upstairs and said "Sheriff Scott, I'd like to call Diane Cleary's parents. I'm sure it will relieve them."

"Sure, go ahead. Ask them if they want a patrol car to bring them to the hospital in Shelton. If they do, call Fred Taylor."

Buford was sitting at the telephone on the living room couch when they brought Bellheimer upstairs.

"Fontana will come for you Deputy, you and your family, he'll know you did this to us," said Bellheimer.

"Get that no good bastard out of here before I shoot him again," said Buford angrily.

"He will come, deputy," he shouted as they led him out.

Buford called the Cleary's. Mrs. Cleary picked up the receiver. "Hello."

"Mrs. Cleary, this is Deputy Buford Hill, I'm calling to tell you we have Diane and she's safe. She will be taken to the hospital in Shelton for any treatment they think is necessary."

"Oh my God." Then heavy relief crying and, "Oh thank God, our prayers have been answered. Thank you, deputy Hill, thank all of you," she said and again began to cry. In another minute she said, "I'm sorry I'm just so relieved."

"That's understandable. She's going to need some recuperating, but I believe she'll be alright."

"When can we see her, Deputy?"

"I don't know but it will probably be an hour or so before we get her to the hospital."

"We'll be there as soon as we can."

"Would you like us to send a patrol car to bring you to Shelton?"

"Yes, we don't see to drive as well at night."

"Okay, it should be there shortly. Good-bye."

"Bye."

Buford immediately called Fred Taylor who was manning the Blanton office.

"Hello. This is….

Buford cut in, "Fred, this is Buford. Sheriff Scott wants you to go to 116 Smith Street and pick up Mr. and Mrs. Cleary. Take them to the hospital in Shelton. Okay.?"

"Yeah, Buford. What's up?"

"Mr. and Mrs. Cleary will explain. 10-4.

10-4.

The first ambulance arrived and took Emma Lee to Shelton.

Deputy Will Carter returned with Deputy Sweet, followed by two nurses.

"There was a doctor in the Infirmary he cleaned Sweet's wound and gave him a tetanus shot." Said Carter.

"Where is he?" Asked Scott.

"In the patrol car."

Okay. We'll put him in an ambulance when it gets here. I need you to go with Vittorino or Johnson down this side of the river checking houses."

"Where do you want us?" Asked one of the Nurses.

"You're needed in the basement, Diane Cleary's down there pretty badly traumatized. Bean take her there. I'd like the other nurse to look at my Deputy's wound."

"I'm okay for now," said Buford.

"Let's see, I'll be the judge of that, Deputy Hill. Where are you hurt?" Asked Nurse Bratcher.

"Oh, hi nurse Bratcher, I got shot in the arm," he said as he pulled off his shirt.

She cleaned his wound with some alcohol and covered it with a large bandage.

"You need a doctor to probe for a bullet or fragments. You also need a cast on that arm and a tetanus shot." She fixed a makeshift sling out of gauze and helped him put it on.

"I'm going downstairs to help with Diane." She said.

"Thanks," said Buford.

"You're welcome."

The second ambulance arrived and had to wait while the nurses worked with Diane. They finally got her dressed and calm enough to get on a stretcher and into the ambulance. Nurse Bratcher went with her to the hospital.

"No siren, just your flashers," said Buford.

The third ambulance arrived.

"Buford the ambulance is here for you and Sweet," said Scott.

"I can ride back in a patrol car," said Buford.

"You've lost a lot of blood. I insist you ride back in the ambulance."

"Okay."

"Bean seal the house as a crime scene. You'll have to stay until I can get some relief for you. I'm going back to help the State Police get the manhunt going," said Scott.

"Yes sir."

CHAPTER FORTY-ONE

The local newspaper and radio stations were immediately notified about the capture of Bellheimer and the manhunt for Fontana. Soon reporters from the local media were joined with reporters from the surrounding states and even network television and national newspapers carried the story.

The day after the raid Sheriff Scott felt pressured and decided to have a press conference. Officers from all the agencies that participated in the raid were available to speak. It was held in the Shelton High School Gym.

Eddie Evans acted as a moderator to get things started. "I'm Eddie Evans, reporter for the Rhodes County Courier, I've been asked to be a sort of M.C. here today. This is an unusual case to say the least. Lots of people had parts, small and big," he said dramatically. "We'll let several people speak and be available for questions.".

Before Eddie could continue one of the reporters shouted, "What about the FBI Did they solve it?"

Special Agent Kennedy approached the microphone. "I'm Special Agent Kennedy of the F.B.I. It's true we have had an ongoing investigation involving Fontana and Bellheimer for several years. Unfortunately, they always managed to elude capture by us and by local and state police in several states. Our role in Rhodes County was limited to helping with the raid and providing photos of fingerprints from other crime scenes. I believe they were a help. We did not do any local investigation in Rhodes County."

"Thank you, Special Agent Kennedy. Sheriff Scott, would you like to say something?"

"Yes, thank you Eddie. First of all, I want to say this, deputy Buford Hill is primarily responsible for solving this crime and saving two young ladies lives. With the exception of Vittorino Sabatini of the US Marshals who followed them from Italy and provided the information about Fontana and Bellheimer to Buford and was a great help getting fingerprints checked, the rest of us were just in on it at the end."

"Any questions for Sheriff Scott?" Asked Eddie.

"I know Bellheimer's in custody, but Fontana got away. How did that happen? Was it a screw-up?" Asked a Louisville Dispatch reporter.

"We believe it was just bad luck that he saw us arrive and slipped out a side door just as a deputy arrived to cover it. He attacked the deputy with a knife and stabbed him in the shoulder before fleeing. He had a boat hidden several hundred yards away and used it to make his escape downstream," said Scott.

"Was there a big delay before going in the house?"

"No, not at all. We knew surprise was very important. We hit the ground moving. The operation was well planned. According to Bellheimer, Fontana had just gone upstairs to secure a knife and check on the grilling. Like I said it looks like it was just dumb luck he got out the side door before we could cover it."

"Do you think he was going to use the knife on his captives?" Asked a St. Louis Sun reporter.

"We'll never know for sure, but one of the captives said she heard him say he was going to cut off their fingers after he murdered them."

"Do you consider the raid a failure?"

"I would say the raid was a limited success. We caught Bellheimer and freed two captives, possibly saving their lives that very day. We also found a recent picture of Fontana and it will be printed in newspapers all over the country, not to mention updating the old photos for law enforcement agencies. I regret that Fontana got away, but I believe that overall, the raid was a success, albeit limited. His elaborate scheme as a psychiatrist was unraveled by Deputy Hill's diligent investigation. I believe he'll never be as confident of his situation again."

"What about the two other men you captured at the scene? Are they wanted anywhere?" Asked a Memphis Star reporter.

"No-one in the U.S. has contacted us, but Germany or Italy may want to question them and possibly extradite them for war crimes. We'll be turning them over to the Feds either today or tomorrow."

"Thank you, Sheriff Scott. Vittorino, something?" Said Eddie handing him the microphone.

"Yes, thank you Eddie. Seven members of my family were murdered in Italy. Fontana and Bellheimer were responsible. Captain Johnson helped me get to the U.S. to pursue them and he helped me get in the U.S. Marshals where I could keep up with what was happening nationwide."

"Didn't you get into a shootout with them in Pittsburgh?" Interrupted a Nashville Banner reporter.

"Yes, they murdered two women near Pittsburgh. I was helping local police in that investigation the day they murdered two more people, a woman and a man, and stabbed another victim. A local boy witnessed them chasing the man who was stabbed and lived. His brother sent the boy for help and was murdered trying to fight them off. Bellheimer chased the boy, but he managed to get away and ran to his brother's house where I was conducting interviews. I had the brother and others take me to the scene, but Fontana and Bell were trying to escape and we got in a shootout. They rammed the car I was driving and managed to get away. That was the closest I got to apprehending them. I kept trying and never gave up hope. They kept changing names and locations. They even had some plastic surgery and used other disguises.

I met Sheriff Scott at Quantico. He invited me to visit him at his office in Shelton. At the time I didn't realize how important that visit would prove to be. He told me about a case Buford was working on about a woman missing from the Hardin Mental Asylum. I met with Buford, and we discussed his case and Fontana and Bellheimer. Though possible, there didn't seem to be any definite connection. Little did we know Buford would tie it all together. Now we must find Fontana. You guys can help by keeping the story going and his picture in the newspapers. Thank you."

"Thank you, Vittorino. Buford it's your turn," said Eddie.

"Thanks Eddie. First let me say this; It took a lot of people to accomplish what we have so far. The FBI and local police got crime scene prints from Pittsburgh and Louisville. Margie, Sheriff Scott's do everything receptionist, loaned me a file she kept about missing persons. I reviewed it and found some interesting comments. There was a so-called elopement two years earlier where the woman was never heard from again. I studied that file along with Diane's case. Things just didn't add up for an elopement. Nothing seemed to make sense. I followed every lead I had. I couldn't find any evidence that Miss Cleary eloped. I began to believe she didn't leave the Asylum grounds at all or if she did it was against her will.

I kept digging. I re-interviewed some staff. Two staff members mentioned how Diane and Naomi felt about a Security guard and the Superintendent. That alerted me to the possibility that two men could be involved. Early on, during his visit to my office to discuss the Diane Cleary missing person case, Vittorino told me all about Fontana and Bellheimer and what monsters they truly are. Who knows, after his visit maybe they were in the back of my mind all along. I don't know. But I do know this, after it looked like two people were after the women it made it more plausible that they could be Fontana and Bellheimer. Finally, I decided to try something new to eliminate or confirm Dr. Rose as Fontana and Security guard Bell as Bellheimer. It worked as much as I hoped it would. It turned out to be the key that unraveled everything.

Two more things then I'll shut up. First, I believe Vittorino Sabatini's dedication, to find Bellheimer and Fontana was crucial to this investigation. And his foresight to get photocopies of crime scene prints from the FBI made possible a quick match with the Fontana and Belheimer prints I obtained, probably saving the lives of the two captive women. Second, Sheriff Scott gave me a free hand to investigate. He received some political pressure to stop the investigation, but he never interfered. He backed me all the way. Thank You."

"Deputy Hill, I noticed your arm's in a sling. How did that happen?" Asked a Knoxville News reporter.

"Bellheimer shot me in the arm. I returned fire and shot him in the shoulder."

"Followup, please. How long were you on the missing persons case before you began to suspect that Rose and Bell were really Fontana and Bellheimer?"

"That's difficult to say. When you are investigating you have to go by facts. In this case the true facts were hidden or disguised. As I said before, Vittorino's visit and help were very instrumental. If he hadn't visited my office and told me about Fontana and Bellheimer I'm not sure I would have put it all together."

"Deputy Hill. If the facts in the case were obscured, how did you dig them out." Asked Edward Bain of the Atlanta Star News.

"I interviewed the guards on duty the day Diane disappeared and got Bell's fingerprints on a bogus picture and envelope. And I interviewed Fontana and got his prints on another picture and envelope. I also investigated their backgrounds prior to being hired at Hardin Mental Asylum. I couldn't tell much about Bellheimer his employment was too sketchy. Fontana turned out to be a phony and that also tied him to at least one other murder."

Sheriff Scott came forward and Buford handed the microphone to him.

"Thank you, Buford. That's all for now folks he has a hospital date for possible surgery. I hope you folks keep this story going with Fontana's picture in the papers and on T.V. Thank You for your attendance."

As Buford walked off the stage the two FBI agents were waiting for him. Special Agent Kennedy spoke first. "I guess it would be almost impossible to get you to leave Hardin, but I want you to know this, you're the type of person we want at the FBI. I'd be honored to recommend you for the service if you would consider it." He extended his hand and Buford shook it with his left hand.

"Thank you, that makes me proud to hear that," he said.

As he let go of Kennedy's hand, Agent Connors stepped forward. "Buford," he said then stopped. "Buford I'm sorry and glad, too. I'm sorry I acted such a fool at the crime scene. I mean that. But I'm glad I was in on the planning and the raid itself. I realize now how important every person working an investigation can be. I'll not forget it, or you. When I get stuck, I'd like to be able to call you, if I can."

"Sure. Don't beat yourself up too much. Remember, the best conversationalists are the best listeners. In our line of work that's real important to remember. Good luck on your search for Fontana, and feel free to call or drop by anytime at my office in Hardin or at our farm. Both of you."

Immediately after the press conference Deputy Bean took Buford and Mary to Louisville where it was determined he needed surgery on his right arm. He stayed in the hospital for three days. Mary stayed at a nearby hotel. Both of them were under the protection of Rhodes County deputies during their stays in Louisville.

The third day after the raid it was discovered how Fontana got away. The Moore's son Thomas couldn't reach them by phone, so he called and asked the Sheriff's office to check on them. Deputies Bean and Bloom discovered the bodies. The gruesome scene was officially recorded by Eddie Evans and Doc Wiggins. Several other reporters still in Shelton covering the manhunt were allowed to visit the scene. The brutality to the Moores was evident and though all wrote of the murders, none of their newspapers printed pictures of the victims' bodies.

Sheriff Scott put out a statement: "The bodies of Sam and Ella Moore were found this morning in the woods near their home. We strongly believe they were murdered by Fontana (alias Dr. Rose) so he could use their car, a '48 chevy, license number V45287, in his escape. The Moore's residence was checked the night of Fontana's escape. There didn't appear to be anyone home. No car was present, and the house was locked. There was no evidence of a struggle or signs of foul play. Apparently, Fontana performed his gruesome acts and cleaned up afterward so it would appear the Moores were not home and no one would look for their automobile which he stole along with Mr. Moores driver license. Our hearts go out to their son Thomas and daughter Rebecca."

The search of Fontana's residence yielded a treasure trove of information. It was determined by Fontana's phony documents and a journal he sometimes kept, that Buford and Vittorino were right about his relationship with Jeanette Strube, and how he got her to help him. He also wrote of the killings he was suspected of and others where the victims had not yet been discovered. Along with the written evidence officers found a jar containing eighteen ring fingers. Vittorino's family broach was also found and returned to him. The newspapers kept up the drumbeat for Fontana's capture for weeks calling him 'A True Monster'. The state put out a $5,000 reward for information leading to his arrest. But he continued to elude capture and after a few weeks national interest faded, and only local newspapers and radio stations reported on the story.

Buford took Bellheimer's threat about Fontana to heart and kept a gun at home for Mary's protection. He even took her practice shooting in the back pasture. He was determined to see that nothing happened to her. He called several times a day to check on her. The dogs were separated during the day, one was kept outside the house and one inside with Mary. Both dogs were kept outside at night.

CHAPTER FORTY-TWO

The Farley Community Church was in the center of town, it's preacher Reverend Ethan Caldwell resided alone on a farm a few miles away. His house was simple, a living room at the front, a hallway down the left side with a bathroom, bedroom, and kitchen off to the right from the hall. At the end of the hall the Reverend had turned a large closet into a room where he worked on his sermons. It had a small bookcase, a desk and chair. At the top of the bookcase a large, bejeweled silver cross with rounded ends sat on a homemade wooden mount. It had been his grandmother's and was a prize possession.

After the raid on the Hardin Mental Asylum Fontana decided it was time to settle the score with Caldwell for calling him evil. He purposely donned the same clothes and beard he wore two years earlier when Caldwell spotted him watching while he preached. He drove to the Reverend's farm and parked his car in the long graveled driveway out of sight from the house. He got a machete from the back seat and approached the house from the blind side. He located the telephone line and cut the wire. He walked to the front door, knocked loudly, and stepped to the side out of sight.

Reverend Caldwell opened the main door but left the screen door hooked. Fontana pulled the screen door open wide enough to slip the machete between the door and the doorframe and popped the hook up and the door opened.

Reverend Caldwell saw the machete and backed away from the door. "I know who you are," he said.

"I hoped you would," said Fontana as he entered. "I've come to deliver a little surprise to you. Do you remember why?"

"I identified you as evil on a First Monday. Nobody believed me but I was right."

"I still don't like being called evil. Do you know what I'm going to do with this machete?"

"Use it on me," said the Reverend.

"That's right, I'm going to cut your head off and then chop you into little pieces. Does that scare you?"

The Reverend didn't answer. Instead, he started to recite as he backed through the house, "The Lord is my shepherd; I shall not want. He maketh me to lie down in green pastures: he leadeth me beside the still waters. He restoreth my soul:

"Stop that or I'll kill you right now."

he leadeth me in the paths of righteousness for his name's sake. Yea, though I walk through the valley of the shadow of death, I will fear no evil: for thou art with me;

"Stop that! You said I'm evil. You better fear me!"

thy rod and thy staff comfort me. Thou preparest a table before me in the presence of mine enemies: thou anointest my head with oil; my cup runneth over."

Fontana screamed at the Reverend, "Damn it you worm stop that preaching. It makes me sick!"

The reverend backed into the doorframe of the little room and fell inside. He used his hands to push himself backwards on the floor while watching Fontana come closer. When his back bumped the desk he reached around for a hand hold and instead felt the cross. He grabbed it and held it tight to his chest.

surely goodness and mercy shall follow me all the days of my life: and I will dwell in the house of the Lord for ever." The Reverend looked up at Fontana but did not utter another word.

Fontana said, "This is payment for what you called me that day," and raised the machete for the fateful blow.

——————

Two hours later Dr. Heart and the County Sheriff with two deputies in tow arrived. They knocked at the door and when no one answered they entered and walked through the house. They found Reverend Caldwell in the little room clutching the cross.

"We tried to call you," said the Sheriff, "but the call wouldn't go through. Fontana's partner Bellheimer said he would try to kill you for calling him evil. I'm just glad we got here in time to warn you."

"I guess he cut the phone line."

"You mean he was here?"

"Yes. He had a machete and said he was going to cut my head off."

"What stopped him?" Asked Heart.

"I don't know. I was reciting the twenty third psalm while I backed through the house. I backed into the doorframe and fell in here. When I tried to reach the bookcase to get up I grabbed the cross instead and pulled it to my chest. He raised the machete. I closed my eyes and the next thing I heard was the screen door slam."

"I'll be damned," said the Sheriff.

"Me, too," said Heart. "And, if you or anyone else tells me someone is evil, I won't laugh, I'll listen."

"You know a couple of years after I called Fontana evil he came again on a First Monday. I saw him across the street from where I was preaching. He was disguised but I knew it was him. He unnerved me. I didn't point him out or anything. I just left. I knew he would try to kill me some day and I was afraid."

"Why didn't you come to see me?" Asked the sheriff.

"He was a prominent doctor, and I had no way of proving the man I saw in disguise was Dr. Rose. And even if I could, what could you have done?

"You're right. I wouldn't have been able to charge him with anything."

"There's something I'm curious about. Why didn't you sense the evil at your door today?" Asked Heart.

"I've been sitting here wondering the same thing. And I think I know why. When Fontana came the second time I failed in my faith, and I failed myself. Today I knew I would die, but my faith was restored. I knew He had a place for me for ever. God showed His ability to confront the Evil. But I am not His instrument to destroy the Evil."

"Do you think you will be able to sense evil again like you did the day you pointed him out?" Asked Heart.

"Yes, I do."

Heart stood watching Reverend Caldwell for a minute then said, "After what happened here today, I do too. I truly do?"

CHAPTER FORTY-THREE

After two months Buford's arm was still in a cast from his shoulder to below the elbow. He and Mary settled back into a routine. It was different from before the Diane Cleary case, but it was beginning to have some semblance of normalcy. He still called her every workday, but not as frequently.

Often, on his day off Vittorino would drive up from Nashville to stay with her. He loved being at the farm and sometimes stayed overnight. Even Agent Connors came by when he was within driving distance and on weekends. They were all concerned about Fontana.

Buford never gave up on Fontana's capture but, like Albert Johnson, he believed it would take a stroke of luck.

One Friday, when Mary was home alone, a strange car came down the lane and drove slowly past the house. A few minutes later it went by in the other direction. It was an older Plymouth or Dodge with a creme colored top and a maroon bottom. She called Buford and he said to keep an eye out for someone walking toward the house. No one came and the car didn't come back.

The next Tuesday morning Buford went in to work early. About 10:30 he called to check on Mary.

"Hello," she said.

"Hi honey, how are things going?" He asked.

"I'm fine, how about you?"

"Things are fine here I'm just working on some paperwork before lunch."

"If you can come home I'll fix you some lunch here."

"That sounds great, I'll see you in a little bit," he said and hung up.

Buford finished his paperwork and left about 10:45. He arrived home about twenty minutes later. Mary was working on lunch when he arrived. Buford spent a few minutes on the back porch with Ed and Bill before she called him in to eat.

"It's ready." She said.

Buford joined her for a ham sandwich and a bowl of homemade vegetable soup. After lunch they sat on the back porch with the dogs for a while then Buford had to leave again.

"Honey, I have to go. I'll see you about 5:30 if nothing happens."

"OK sweetheart, I'll see you then," she said and kissed him goodbye.

Buford left in his patrol car and Mary called Bill and went inside to do some ironing. A little while after Buford left, Mary heard Ed yelp outside. She looked out their bedroom window but couldn't see him in the yard. She looked out the living room window and checked the lock on the door. She tried the phone, but the line was dead. She tried the other bedroom window and didn't see anything unusual. She went to the china closet and got the gun out of a drawer. Next, she called Bill to her side and walked to the kitchen. She looked out the kitchen window but didn't see anything. The main door to the back porch was open but the screen door was shut and hooked.

She called from the doorway, "Here Ed, come on boy. Here Ed, come on boy, come on." The hackles rose on Bill's back, and he began to growl, a low guttural growl. "What's the matter boy. Do you smell something?"

She opened the screen door slightly to look down the length of the porch. Fontana grabbed her wrist and pulled her outside. She raised the gun to shoot but he pushed the barrel aside and the shot missed. He shook the gun from her hand and grabbed her by the throat. Bill bit him on his right side. Mary struggled free and bent to reach the gun on the porch floor. Fontana swung and hit her hard on the right cheekbone. The blow knocked her backwards and she fell off the porch. Dazed, she got up and ran, stumbled and fell to her knees. She got back up and ran, limping and stumbling her way to the barn. At the door she looked back at the porch and saw Bill hanging on Fontana's side, shaking his head and lunging forward. Fontana tried to kick him, but Bill was too close. He lost his balance and fell into a chair. She watched Fontana pull a large knife from a sheath and stab Bill. Bill hung on. Fontana stabbed him again and Bill fell to the porch floor. Fontana staggered off the porch and ran toward her. She closed the barn door and slid the long wooden bolt into place.

At the barn Fontana was stopped at the bolted door. He beat on it and hollered, "You fool. This door won't stop me. I came to kill you, to punish your husband for what he did." He pushed and pulled on the door, rocking it in and out.

On the other side of the door she watched it move in and out, then turned and looked around the barn. She grabbed up a pitchfork, carried it a few steps, threw it down and limped to the ladder. She slowly climbed the ladder to the loft. At the top she crawled over the last step onto the loft floor. She watched the barn door for a few seconds then grabbed the ladder. It was heavy but she managed to stand and pull it up a few feet. She held it tight against the loft edge while she slid her hands down the ladder's 2x4 rails. She pulled it up a few more feet then slid her hands back down the rails. She pulled it up again but this time it was too top-heavy and It slid to her left along the loft edge. She struggled to hold it steady, but its' downward momentum grew and it fell to the floor. She watched the door rock in and out then hid among the loosely stacked bales of hay.

Fontana used all his strength rocking the door until one of the iron supports holding the bolt gave way and it opened. He entered the barn and searched the ground floor. Looking up at the loft he said, "Don't worry dear I know you're up there. I'm coming for you."

He put the ladder back up and started to climb. Mary dragged half a bale of hay to the ladder and when he was about halfway up she pushed it over. It knocked him off the ladder.

His face turned red and the blood vessels on his neck and forehead bulged out. He screamed up at her "You bitch, you'll pay for that," and began climbing again.

She went to the stacked hay and began dragging a full bale to the ladder. He got near the top of the ladder and swung his knife back and forth to keep her away.

They were both near the top of the ladder when they heard, "Fontana, you bastard stop."

Buford ran to the base of the ladder and pointed his revolver in his left hand. Fontana turned around on the ladder and said "This is great. I get to kill you both on the same day," he came down a step then dove at Buford with his knife.

Buford shot twice and stepped out of the way. Fontana landed on the scattered half bale of hay, rolled over and laid still. Buford kicked his side to check for life. Fontana didn't move. Buford holstered his revolver and grabbed one of Fontana's ankles and pulled his body away from the ladder.

"Mary, honey, I shot him. He's dead." said Buford.

Mary came over to the ladder. "He killed Ed, maybe Bill, too."

"I know, can you come down or do you need help?"

"I can make it." She started to come down then yelled, "Watch out."

Buford spun around. Fontana lunged at him with the knife. Buford managed to step out of the way and grab Fontana by the wrist. Both men fell sideways to the barn floor where they struggled for the knife.

"Let it go," said Buford.

"Never," said Fontana and he bit Buford's hand.

They fought, punching and kicking as they rolled back and forth on the barn floor. Buford's one good arm wasn't enough. Fontana got on top and slowly turned the knife toward Buford. He pushed the knife downward, piercing the skin on Buford's chest.

Mary screamed "Stop, stop." Fontana looked up, and Buford managed to push the knife several inches from his chest.

Fontana shouted, "Shut up bitch, you're next." Then to Buford, "I'm going to enjoy her."

Buford's arm strength was waning, he did everything he could to keep the knife away, but Fontana put all his strength into his thrust and slowly the knife again reached Buford's chest.

"Bye bye Deputy, sweet dreams." he said. He pulled the knife up several inches and started the blade back down for the final thrust.

"Burn in Hell," said Buford as the knife approached his chest for the third time.

The roar of a Forty-Five pierced the air. Then came a second shot that seemed louder than the first.

Fontana looked at the source of the sound then collapsed on Buford's chest.

Buford turned his head. There, framed perfectly in the light of the open doorway stood Vittorino Sabatini.

CHAPTER FORTY-FOUR

The world seemed to pause for a long moment in that barn. No one said anything. No one moved. Mary sat at the top of the homemade ladder, tears flowed down her cheeks. Vittorino sat in the doorway, his gun beside him in the dust and loose straw. Finally, Buford managed the strength to push Fontana's body aside and stood up. His chest and stomach were nearly covered in his and Fontana's blood. He looked up at Mary. She looked at him and managed a smile.

"Mary, honey, are you hurt, did he hurt you?"

"I'm okay, he just hurt my wrist. I'll be alright in a minute. It's just that he is so vicious, so evil."

"Can you grip the ladder to come down or do you need help?"

"I'll help her," said Vittorino. He got up and started to the ladder.

"I can make it," she said.

Mary climbed down and the three hugged before they walked to Bill on the porch. He was bleeding but managed to wag his tail. "Stay here, I'm going to radio for help for Bill and report to the Sheriff," said Buford as he walked to the patrol car.

He came back in a few minutes and he and Vittorino took turns holding compresses on Bill's wounds.

Mary went inside and came back with her arms loaded with first aid supplies and a clean shirt for Buford. She poured alcohol and iodine on Buford's chest wound, then bandaged it with gauze and tape. The three of them cleaned Bill's wounds as best they could and continued with the compresses.

Sheriff Scott came with Eddie Evans, Al Wiggins, and Deputies Bean and Bloom. George Harper the local vet came as quickly as he could.

Mary told her story to Sheriff Scott and Eddie Evans who took detailed notes.

Then Buford told his. "I came home to have lunch with Mary and afterwards left for work. I was thinking and riding for a couple of miles when something popped in my mind. The sun had glinted off something shiny not far from home. I had never noticed that before, so I turned around and drove back to see what it was. When I got to the spot, I found brush cut and stacked to hide a creme and maroon Dodge pulled off the road. Mary had told me about someone driving slowly past the house in a car like that a few days ago. I ran back to my patrol car and raced to the house. When I got home I found Ed in the yard and Bill on the back porch. The gun I left for Mary was on the back porch, too. I picked it up and went in the house expecting to find Fontana, but the house was empty. I ran to the barn and saw Fontana near the top of the loft ladder. I hollered at him to stop, and he turned around on the ladder to face me. I ran to the base of the ladder and pointed my pistol at him. That's when he said, 'This is great, I get to kill you both on the same day' and dove at me. I shot at him twice on his way down, unfortunately it was with my off hand. I guess I missed. He laid still a few feet from the ladder. I thought he was dead. The fall alone was a good eight or ten feet. I was worried about Mary, so I called to her, and she came to the ladder. I asked her if she needed help to get down and she said 'no', then shouted 'watch out'. I turned and Fontana came at me with a knife. I grabbed his wrist and we fell sideways. My broken arm wasn't much help during the struggle for the knife. I hung on the best I could, but he got on top and turned it into my chest. Mary screamed 'Stop, stop' and he looked up and cursed her. That scream, and him cursing, stopped his momentum. I pushed the knife up, but he brought it down again and then raised it higher for a hard thrust. I hung onto one wrist, but the knife kept coming, that's when I heard the roar from a forty-five, twice. Vittorino shot him. He saved our lives. Mary came down and we went to check on Bill and Ed. I radioed for Sheriff Scott and George Harper. There's nothing else to tell." He sat down wearily on the porch bench.

Sheriff Scott turned to Vittorino. "How did you happen to come by today?"

"I've been worried Bellheimer's threat that Fontana would seek revenge might be right. So, I've been coming here, when I could, to help in case he tried. I'm just glad I took today off."

"Thank God you're all alive. That Fontana was one vicious S.O.B. I hope we never run into another one like him. Mary that was some struggle you put up and quick thinking about the loft and the hay. In my book you are all three heroes. If you get a chance, write up your statements this evening and I'll send Margie out to get them tomorrow. She'll type them and you can come by and sign them. Buford, take a week or so off to get yourself and Mary calmed down. Vittorino if you would mail me your statement as soon as possible I'd appreciate it," said Scott.

Eddie Evans had taken notes when Mary, Buford and Vittorino gave their stories to Sheriff Scott. He checked several times with Mary and Buford for accuracy then went about making pictures of the crime scene. Doc Wiggins also listened to their stories and then went to check on Fontana. His report reflected Buford's story about Fontana's death except that one of Buford's shots apparently creased Fontana's right hip. He had the body loaded up to take to the county morgue.

Every Deputy Sheriff and State trooper came by that could. They all examined the barn and asked for details about what happened. Buford referred them to Eddie who told their stories several times.

A telephone repairman was summoned and spliced the line Fontana cut.

George Harper sewed Bill's stab wounds and managed to get the bleeding stopped. He loaded him in the back of his station wagon and was preparing to leave. For the rest of his life, he would tell the story of what happened next. Everybody had told him Ed was dead, and he hadn't moved, but for some reason that he never could explain George walked over and checked his jaw for a pulse. He didn't feel anything, then just as he was about to move his hand he felt it. It was very faint, but it was there. He sewed up his wounds and put him in the station wagon next to his brother.

Mary had been watching and asked, "Is there a chance for them?"

"To be honest with you Mary, Bill has a slight chance, but Ed has virtually none."

"If they don't make it, we'll want to bury them here."

"Of course," he said and left.

Finally, after about two hours Sheriff Scott told everyone they had to leave so Buford and Mary could have some privacy.

After everybody left Buford and Vittorino talked.

"I knew he would be making a mistake if he came after you," said Vittorino.

"Thanks to you I finally got a little bit lucky. My luck was you. I didn't know it at the time, but the day I met you was one of the best days of my life. Thank you for our lives."

"I'm just glad I made it in time. Funny, I don't feel happy about shooting Fontana. I'm just glad it's over and he can't hurt or kill anyone anymore. Now I have a decision to make."

"What kind of decision?"

"My father and brother want me to come home."

"That has to be tough, considering the friends you've made and your career."

"Yes, it's very hard. I've been here almost ten years. But before I decide that I feel a strong need to see a Rabbi to help set my life right with God. I blamed Him for not intervening when Fontana and Bellheimer murdered our family. I've been thinking about this for a long time. I believe that Fontana was evil, and God had a plan for his destruction."

"I believe you're right. He certainly was evil. Whatever you decide about staying or going home to Italy, come back to see us. Sheriff Scott has given me some time off."

"Sure. I'll see you later."

"Yeah," said Buford.

They shook hands. Vittorino left for Nashville.

Buford joined Mary on the porch bench. He held her close for a long time. Then said, "How about some catfish?"

"I don't think so, Honey," she said.

They got up and went inside.

THE END, I HOPE YOU ENJOYED IT.

EPILOGUE

Bellheimer received life in prison without the possibility of parole for his role in the Kentucky murders. He avoided extradition to Pennsylvania and New York by confessing his role as an accessory in the murders in those two states. He died in prison in 1970.

Albert Johnson stayed with the U.S. Marshals office in Nashville until retirement in 1975.

Reed and Millie formed a partnership and bought the Hardin Diner. They kept it open for another twenty years.

Special Agent Kennedy was promoted to Deputy Assistant Director of the Southeast Region of the FBI. He visited Buford at work and at the farm when he was in the area.

Agent Robert Connors became a regular visitor to the Hill farm. After Buford and Mary's youngest daughter Sarah graduated from college and moved back to Hardin they started dating and a year or so later were married. They raised two daughters and a son.

Sheriff Scott was elected to two more terms as Rhodes County Sheriff. He then ran for and was elected as a State Representative.

When Scott retired, and Buford refused to run for Sheriff, Matt Williams retired from the State Police and was elected Rhodes County Sheriff.

Diane Cleary spent three weeks in the Shelton Hospital. Her family attorney filed suit against Hardin Mental Asylum, and she was awarded an undisclosed settlement prior to trial. She was also granted lifetime access to Professional Counseling at her residence. She was a patient of Dr. Emery for the next ten years. She married three years after her rescue and raised two boys and a girl. She also became a regular at the Hill Family Farm. Buford and Mary banned anyone from speaking about the Fontana case while Diane was at the farm.

Emma Lee spent two weeks in the Shelton Hospital. Her attorney also filed suit against Hardin Mental Asylum, and she was awarded an undisclosed amount prior to trial. She had been a streetwalker but after her experience with Rose and Bell she decided not to go back to her old trade. Instead, she used some of her settlement money to return to school and became a nurse. She married a doctor, and they raised two sons. They also visited the Hill family farm when they could.

Naomi Shepherd's family attorney filed suit against Hardin Mental Asylum and the family was awarded an undisclosed sum prior to trial.

Vittorino returned to the family farm near Veranza and became an active member in the local synagogue. He was appointed Chief of Police and eventually ran for and was elected Mayor of Veranza. He married a local girl and became the proud father of two daughters. Shortly after his return to Italy he invited several of his American friends to visit. Buford and Mary, Albert and Lori Johnson, and Will and Barbara Scott along with several of Vittorino's friends from Nashville and White Plains visited. Buford and Mary loved Italy and visited several times. So did the Johnsons.

Buford remained a Deputy Sheriff until retirement at age 66. He was encouraged to run for Sheriff by Sheriff Scott when he retired but decided against it. Shortly after the conclusion of the Fontana/Bellheimer case, Special Agent Kennedy convinced him to accept a consulting contract with the FBI, approved by Sheriff Scott. He received a monthly retainer of $150 plus per diem and an Agent's salary when called upon to visit a crime scene or review a case file. He was instrumental in solving several difficult cases. He and Mary stayed in touch with Vittorino and Albert Johnson and the others mentioned above.

Mary bounced back from her battle with Fontana and enjoyed being the hostess for many gatherings of friends and family. For the rest of her life she would say she had four heroes, Ed, Bill, Buford and Vittorino and without any one of them she would have died that fateful day when Fontana attacked her.

When he got the dogs back to his office, George gave them both an I.V. Bill was severely wounded by Fontana. The stab wound to his side caused the loss of a lot of blood and the wound to his back caused temporary paralysis, but he responded fairly quickly. Ed's recovery was much slower. He remained in a coma for over a week before suddenly waking one day. It took another week before he could walk. Within three weeks both dogs were being nursed by Mary at the farm. George refused any payment for his services saying it was an honor to work with the four-legged heroes.

BIBLIOGRAPHY

The following works were consulted and used as references during the writing of this book.

WHAT I WISH MY CHRISTIAN FRIENDS KNEW ABOUT JUDAISM
AUTHOR-ROBERT SCHOEN

JEWISH FAMILY CELEBRATIONS
AUTHOR-ARLENE ROSEN CARDOZO

NEW HISTORY OF WORLD WAR II
by STEPHEN E. AMBROSE
ORIGINAL TEXT BY C.L. SULZBERGER

Made in the USA
Columbia, SC
20 December 2023

29033540R00345